# Floating

### By

## Rohn Federbush

ISBN-13: 978-1496139238
ISBN-10: 1496139232

Book Cover Design and Book Formatting by Rebel Ink Designs

This book is a work of fiction. The characters, events, and places portrayed in this book are products of the author's imagination and are either fictitious or are used fictitiously. Any similarity to real persons, living or dead, is purely coincidental and not intended by the author.

For more information on the author and her works, please visit Rohn's Website at www.RohnFederbush.com.

# Acknowledgements

The late Barbara Becker encouraged my interest in Ann Arbor's history and enabled my access to the Bentley and Clements libraries. To my friends, critique partners, and husband, Paul Federbush, of infinite patience and few demands I am eternally grateful.

# Prologue

*December, 1840*
*Merry Men Pub, County Kerry, Ireland*

Four years of Italian language study refused to penetrate Angela McGovern's brain. With her back to her tutor, she released a ribbon from her hair letting the curly tresses sweep over the page to hide her glances out the window. The gentle hills of the Ring of Kerry blanketed in fresh snow beckoned. Not that she could hear Flicka stomping in her stall, but Angela's own feet tapped impatiently. Blue outlines of the scanty bushes stretched, warning of the day's early decline.

"Repeat the line once more," Master Mitworth instructed.

"No," Angela's rebellious word popped out of her mouth. "I'm not clear how to pronounce dove." She swept up her hair, securing the ribbon while smiling into her teacher's pinched face.

His forehead unfurled. "Doe way, doe way. Doth that make it clearer?"

"Doth is a dusty word for all the doings of Dante." Angela pouted as she endeavored to hold back further words of disdain.

"Dante's Italian soars with the eagles," Master Mitworth rhapsodized. "The English language stuffs the meaning into stones."

Angela patted the pillowed seat beside her. "We've had enough of verse for today, haven't we?"

Master Mitworth availed himself of the comfortable chair before pulling Angela's notebook across the desk to view her translation of the second stanza of the first Canto.

She listened to his low musical voice and felt tempted to touch his chest to feel if the booming base vibrated.

> *...I now sing chants within the second region,*
> *where our human spirits wait until they're purged,*
> *washed and cleansed of sin for the divine heaven."*

Master Mitworth closed the notebook. "You've avoided the harsher phrases and made the stanzas sound almost Irish."

Angela lowered her head, angered by the disparaging hint.

"You're a good but reluctant student, Angela…dear," Master Mitworth nearly whispered the last word.

Ma would have to be told about the softening of Master Mitworth. Classes might have to be continued in the pub where nothing untoward could occur under her mother's watch.

Angela stood, hoping to dismiss the tutor. "Oh and it's getting so late. I'll be needing a romp in the snow with Flicka before I muster down to my duties at the pub."

Master Mitworth seemed glued to his cushion. He shook his head. "I doubt the Earl would approve of your duties."

Now he'd done it. "My father is it?" Angela's hands were on her hips, mimicking her mother's angry stance. Refusing to resemble her mother, Angela clenched her hands behind her back. "Hardly a pinnacle of decorum to set before his illegitimate daughter." Angela was sorry for her harsh temper, immediately.

Master Mitworth appeared ready to weep. "My apologies."

"And mine," Angela stepped behind him and wrapped her arms around the poor man's shoulders. After all, her father paid for Master Mitworth's weekly tutoring and Flicka's upkeep, besides her own. "It's not you I'm that angry with."

"I know…dear." Master Mitworth kissed the back of her hand.

Angela wasn't sure if her wet hand was from his kiss or his tears. "Well we'll have no more mention of my father. Go down, when you're ready, and have a cup of port before you're off."

"I will," he said sniffing into his handkerchief.

She'd been cruel and now couldn't report to Ma without being chastised for her own behavior. Confusing, it was, to be the daughter of an Earl and a saloon keeper. Probably the cleansing water from seven seas would not purge the taints left by the inconstant affection of her parents.

* * *

*December 24, 1840*
*Berkshire, England*


The Halliday residence sparkled across the lawn's snowy glaze of ice. Tethering his woolen scarf under his coat's collar, Michael emerged from the steamy horse barn. He planned to mount the servant stairs to escape into his study before his parents claimed attendance at the Holiday festivities. If luck was on his side, he might be able to re-translate the first stanza of Purgatario. Dante's old Italian sang to him as he curried Splendor's blue-black flanks.

Michael didn't relish Longfellow's stuffy language. The Italian cried out for a furtherance of tone, some depth of emotion missed by the New Englander. At his desk, Michael penned his version:

> *In order to slip among the velvet worries,*
> *my fresh-wizened soul unfurls her wing'ed sails*
> *to quiet the cruel shoals of Hade's dark caves.*

The word 'her' sounded softer than the proper 'his' of either Dante's or Michael's own soul. Michael counted the soft feminine wiles of the visitors waiting for him below among his many worries. His father's entreaties to visit the London clock-work factory in order to learn the family's business caused considerably more anxiety. The life planned by his parents dug a black pit into the dreams Michael harbored.

Dante's Divine Comedy promised to unveil a peaceful way to avoid both. The thought of red sails against a yellow sky eased the tension in his shoulders. A long sigh confirmed the futility of trying to flee. A gentleman didn't break the hearts of his parents, although a man might. Michael kicked his boots off.

He drew a sketch of the mountainous island described as purgatory by Dante. Each path up the mountain symbolized one of the seven deadly sins. Michael added palm trees for the island and extended their shadows into the pictured ocean.

Pride, Michael thought. Pride in his art was probably going to haunt him in the afterlife.

A moment later his father's butler knocked politely on the suite's outer door.

"Come in," Michael called, resigned to the fate of dressing to help entertain the friends gathered below for a holiday supper.

He tried to keep a picture of the richly appointed sailing ship in the forefront of his mind as he maneuvered among the flurry of young women who greeted his descent into the glittering drawing room. Michael met the eyes of 20 jeweled-and-bedecked marriageable ladies:

the innocent, the sultry, the honest, the shy, and the boldly aggressive. A sultan would envy his pick, but Michael didn't want to choose, didn't want the caresses, flattery, affection, houses, or babies that their glances promised. He didn't want to live in London or Berkshire, or England for that matter.

Seeking out his mother's regal stance above the crush reminded him of how a ship's captain might welcome the first glimmer from a lighthouse far above the dark ocean. Would his mother understand his dream of painting alone on some distant island? Perhaps if he promised to come home after a year of freedom, she would convince his father…to let him go.

* * *

*End of April, 1841*
*Merry Men Pub, County Kerry, Ireland*

Scraping as much field muck from her boots as she could on the raised stone outside her mother's pub, Angela bent to unbuckle the smelly clodhoppers. She stepped into the kitchen's back door in her damp socks, leaving her offending boots in the mud room.

Angela stopped in her tracks. "Ma, if I didn't have the odor of rotten potatoes still stuffing my nose, I'd swear that you're using the last of the apples for a pie."

Aunt Elizabeth, fresh from America, swept her up in her arms. "Oh my girl, you're as beautiful as your ma, and twice as strong smelling."

Ma laughed, her cheeks red with the warmth of the kitchen, embarrassment at her daughter's dishevelment, and a few ounces of the best port in the house. "Wash up a bit, Angie. Liz has come to take you to America."

"And you," Angela said wrapping her arms around her teary-eyed mother. "You can come too."

Ma untangled herself, wiping Angela's tears away with her apron. "Now darling, we can't be imposing on Uncle Henry. You know we decided you're old enough to go alone." She poured them all a thimble of port. "I'm where I want to be, among my friends."

"They need her more than ever, Angela," Aunt Elizabeth said quietly.

"I know I should stay too, but I do so want to see America." Angela poured hot water from the kettle into a pan at the sink to wash her face and neck. As she scrubbed the dirt from under her nails, she asked. "When are we scheduled to emmigrate?"

"Is Saturday a good enough day to be starting your new life?" Ma answered. "The trunk is ready, and we'll just add a few things to your suitcase in the morning."

"Tomorrow?" Angela stumbled to the bench at the table to put on her house slippers. "So soon is it?"

The white-washed stone walls of the dear room seemed to telescope away from her. The snowy, eyelet-trimmed curtains, blue checked tablecloth, shining copper kettle at the hearth, and her mother's sheepskin-lined robe on the rocking chair emblazoned permanent memories in her brain.

"We'll need a few days to travel to Liverpool," her aunt explained. Her tone was as sad as a funeral voice, low with no lilts at all.

"I'll be coming that far, darling." Ma wrapped her heavy arms around Angela.

Angela hung onto her apron tie. How would she be able to let go of her life, her ma? "Oh, Ma. I can't leave you. Come with us."

"Now Angie, you're letting yourself get all upset. Starting a family away from this blighted soil is a chance straight from Heaven. You know I've tried to do the best for you. I'll not be having my grandchildren see starvation in the faces of their neighbors."

"Aye that," Angela choked, "but how can I live without seeing your loving face."

Ma kissed Angela's forehead and then spun on her heels. "Liz, talk to the child. My customers have been patient enough for their beers."

Aunt Elizabeth sat down across the table from Angela. "Taste the pie, dear. Antoinette has spent every free moment making it just for you."

Angela stuck her fork in the middle of the pie, then tasted a small bite. "I'm up to the challenge of making my way among your strangers in America." The apple pie was sweeter than usual.

"Your ma was but 14 when she ran away from our father's house." Aunt Elizabeth helped herself to a sizable portion of the pie. "and you're all of 17."

"And fairly well educated for a gal my age." Angela finished her portion and looked longingly at the remaining sections of the aromatic pastry.

Ma hurried back into the warm kitchen to settle down with the sharing of the pie. "I heard you two talking." A bite interrupted her discourse. "Take another piece, Angie. It's made extra sweet for you. When I left home, I didn't have a huge trunk full of money to take along with me, like you do."

"The Earl was already engaged to another woman, when Ma was with child," Angela explained to her aunt.

"As if I wasn't there?" Aunt Elizabeth finished her share of the pie, two huge pieces.

"Did you ever meet the Earl?" Angela hadn't.

"Doesn't matter that you haven't laid eyes on your English father," Ma said. "What matters is that he cared enough to provide a tutor and send money for Flicka's upkeep each year. Come on out to the bar, the boys are waiting for ya."

* * *

Chairs and stools in the 'L' shaped room were filled with town and farm men. The smoke from their pipes failed to hide the odors of farmers' boots and the days' sweat on the millhands. Their loud clamor simmered down a bit when Ma went behind the polished bar, then rose with their orders for refills.

Aunt Elizabeth introduced Angela to Captain Hale. "One of your passengers on the Pannonia, Captain."

"Pleasure," he said, with hardly a bow. His black coat sported more brass than was necessary to button it up against the weather.

"I'm Angela McGovern," Angela said as she stuck out her hand for a shake.

Captain Hale looked at her palm as if she was asking for money, but he finally shook it. "Antoinette's daughter for sure."

"And a beauty," one of the locals added loudly.

"The Pannonia is a fine vessel," Captain Hale tried to change the subject for Angela. "The best of the line, she has twin screw-shaft propellers."

"And contingency sails," Angela said. "I've memorized all their names so no one can tease me about my being ignorant of at least them." She didn't want to consider the length of the voyage, the terror of the bottomless ocean, the perfectly blank page of her future. They were all beyond her ability to fathom.

The customers crowded closer to see if Captain Hale agreed with her naming of the sails.

"Let's hear them," a chap closest to the captain's shoulder demanded.

Angela smiled at her ma, then turned slowly to include everyone in the reciting. "There's the missen, the cross jack, the sky sail or spanker."

"She's a bright one, that beauty." Angela heard her friend's da say.

"The foresail is easy to recall," Angela continued, "And the flying jib appropriate."

Captain Hale turned his back on the bar and explained to the assemblage, "Schooners sport sails in case they need rigging for auxiliary power."

Ma came over and tied Angela's apron around her waist, taking longer than usual. "This will be the last time Angie will be waitin' on you fellows, so give the girl a good send-off to America."

Angela kept her arms around her mother's slight girth, until Ma seemed too close to tears.

"Will you be wanting a refill there?" Angela asked the nearest table of men.

"The boys in America don't stand a chance girlo," the youngest of the codgers chirped as Angela filled his empty glass from a pitcher of beer.

His best mate, the only cousin still kicking in his family, agreed. "Those green eyes of your'n will make Irish magic on any man's heart, young or old."

Father Fitzgerald, the youngest priest in the parish, was sitting between them with his empty glass drumming the table. "High or low born, there's not a man needing a wife who wouldn't be lucky to touch your skirts." He blushed and Angela was pretty sure the redness wasn't because of the fresh beer.

Aunt Elizabeth had enthroned herself next to the father of Angela's friend. "My sister tells me Angela's been helping Colleen in your fields."

Mr. Decker dropped his head. "Replanting the seedling potatoes." He drank down the last of his beer.

Angela refilled the glass wondering if he'd keep hiding the truth of his predicament.

Refreshed, Mr. Decker smiled at her aunt. "Hear you married the bank president."

Aunt Elizabeth laughed. "You bet I did, quick as a wink. He'll be helping Angela find a proper mate."

Angela couldn't hold her tongue. "I'll be finding a hard-working man, not any rich piker."

Hearing her, Ma slapped her rump. "Apologize to your aunt."

Angela kissed her aunt's cheek. "I haven't even met Uncle Henry. I'm sure he's not a bad man. I'm not looking for those swaggering types is all. They expect me to bow and scrape for every coin they put down on Ma's counter."

Mr. Decker buttoned his coat and started to put on his hat.

Angela sat down next to him, sorry that she'd mentioned money. "And will you not be telling me good-bye then?"

Mr. Decker wadded his cap in his lap before kissing her cheek.

Angela sprang up and filled his glass. "Here's to me spreading babies wherever I lay my head."

Ma's hand went to her mouth before she roared with laughter. "Done and legal like you promised."

"I intend to only fall in love with a good and decent man."

The men in the bar, all blithesome fellows, raised their glasses and cheered.

Mr. Decker leaned toward Aunt Elizabeth. "Angela helped dig up the potato skins. They was all filled with that slimy mush."

Angela refilled his glass again, hoping he'd forget the stench of the rotted muck in the fields.

Mr. Decker didn't bend the tale to save his pride. "The girls had to remove all traces of the blight."

The acidic contaminant could make any field barren for next year's crop.

"New seed costs," Mr. Decker drained his glass, "more than any payment I'll get from a crop now." He put on his cap and left.

"Destitute," Aunt Elizabeth said to Angela as she sized up the pub's clientele, who mostly drank on credit or bartered for their beers.

"Ma's not getting rich," Angela whispered. "But it would break her heart to leave all her friends."

Next morning, Angela's mother held the hand mirror as Angela tucked a stray curl under her bonnet. "Mica, mica, parva stella, how I wonder where you'll be."

"Next to your heart, Ma." Angela folded a shawl around the mirror before packing it under a sweater in her smallest suitcase.

"You'll always be safe to shine there, darlin." Ma stepped back to take a better look. "Traveling as a lady, you are."

"What's your opinion, Aunt Elizabeth?" Angela didn't mind hearing compliments from women in the family. You could count on them being just as accommodating with criticisms.

"It's a good thing that I'll be at your very elbow, or you'd be swept away by some handsome man before we get within eyesight of the Pannonia."

* * *

*Berkshire, England*

Early that same afternoon in late April and under the customary duress, Michael Halliday entered his mother's pink parlor to help entertain a fresh bevy of the ladies who dogged Mrs. Halliday's heels for an introduction to him.

"Sit quietly with both feet on the floor," his mother had advised.

Quiet was not a problem, but his feet found it hard to remain still.

His mother was nearly six feet tall with a military carriage. Her elegant stroll among her guests often ended in front of him, where her frown would remind him that tapping one's foot was a show of irritation, definitely improper.

Impatience to be free from the plethora of billowing skirts was more on target. Horses stomped when confinement in the stables became intolerable.

Michael anticipated his escape to the stables at the first opportunity. The wish for freedom triggered the remembered pungent odor of the horses, which seemed to mix with the various perfumes of the ladies surrounding him.

Visions of the stud activities of the horses further warped his social graces. Even the mares' gentle neighings sounded sweeter than any of this feminine, ebullient laughter in the parlor. When he attempted to obey the constraints of manners and verbal censorship, his brain felt bridled. Michael's tongue could barely answer a polite query while he was imprisoned in the elaborate room.

The relative freedom of fenced-in pastures let his father's horses stretch their muscles. Michael's mind took refuge in his plans to emigrate to a lonely American island where the occupation of lighthouse keeper promised room for him to stretch his limbs and breathe. He imagined the winds could buffet him from four directions all at the same time.

No one would force him to sire a passel of children with anyone in this elite group of fortune hunters. The stable's thoroughbred horses didn't share his luxury of choice. Once safe aboard the Pannonia, Michael could dismiss all memories of these attractive, graceful, but false, damsels.

* * *

Later that evening, his short, rotund father stormed around the dinner table, upsetting the maids, who were endeavoring to serve the soup. "A laborer's job? For my only son?"

"Lighthouse keeper," Michael corrected while nervously adjusting his watch. "I don't have time to work here." When his father's back was turned, Michael had the courage to add, "My art demands the freedom of America."

His father roared a curse. The lid on a soup tureen crashed to the table. The youngest addition to the household staff ran from the room, weeping loudly.

Michael turned to his mother for help. "All these women who say they want to marry are only interested in Father's profits from the clockworks and your ten-thousand acres."

"Throwing away his heritage for a lark," was his father's assessment to his mother, whose dark eyes couldn't hide her confusion. Her silent tears quickly followed. "Now look what you've done!" his father bellowed, before returning to the head of the table.

Michael thought his mother should understand. He spoke softly hoping to coax her aid in convincing his father. "The quiet, the solitude of Strawberry Island fits my ideal dream of a place to sketch the endless images hammering in my brain."

His mother looked at him helplessly.

"Lake Superior allows me to circumvent, for a time, the social ambitions of yours and others."

"Let him go," his mother instructed his distraught father. Then she added so quietly Michael strained to hear, "For a year."

# Chapter 1

*May 5th, 1841*
*Aboard the Pannonia out of Liverpool*

Angela McGovern leaned over the ship's rail hoping to keep her mother's green shawl in sight as noisy emigrants jostled each other up the gangplank. Lapping waves against the stone retaining wall below smelled of rank fish.

"There she is, near that red door." At her side on board, Aunt Elizabeth pointed out Angela's mother balancing on top of a wooden crate on the busy dock.

Her mother's hand rose, as if invoking the guardian heavens. The din of the boat's steam engine, shouting sailors in the rigging, and the creaking wooden deck drowned out her mother's exact prayer to the soot-laden sky. Her mother's attention was drawn toward the bow where Captain Hale waved enthusiastically. Ma pointed the tip of her wrap in her daughter's direction. The Captain turned toward them and acknowledged Angela and her aunt with a nod of his head.

Angela remembered their brief conversation at her mother's pub. He fit the category of roaming seamen she'd met in Kerry. Buttoned-up and stiff speaking, they were, as if the winds might blow a tooth out of their iron heads if ever a laugh happened their way.

Losing the familiar spot of green of her mother's shawl in the increasing crush on the shore, Angela followed her aunt toward the Captain's vantage point. A break in the throng of passengers on deck allowed them to approach within earshot of him.

"An unsavory start," Captain Hale gossiped to a tall man standing next to him.

Something deep within Angela turned as she and her aunt retreated toward their port-side cabin. "The saints have mercy! As if setting off to a new world isn't trouble enough."

Once inside their cabin, Aunt Elizabeth untied her bonnet. "Hale's unthinking gossip will limit your possibilities with that stranger. But now, maybe it won't go farther than that young man's ear."

"We might as well get off the ship, while we can." Angela paced the small walking area inside their door. Captain Hale's negative assessment of her mother, her own up-bringing in a common tavern and the Earl's involvement seemed destined to follow them across the ocean. The brave front Angela worked to keep in place since she kissed Ma good-bye slipped as tears threatened.

"Take off your hat, Angela." Aunt Elizabeth blocked her exit. "Captain Hale never meant for you to hear his…"

"…damning remark."

"Don't be swearing the first instant you're under my care now." Aunt Elizabeth clapped her hands. "Or you'll be proving him right as the rain."

"I could conceal the injury." A caught sob in her throat let Angela know that wouldn't be as easy as the saying of it.

"We'll figure out a way to get around the Captain's idle chatter." Aunt Elizabeth opened her trunk. "Keep yourself busy hanging up your wardrobe 'til we do."

"I wanted to watch the lights of Liverpool fade on the horizon."

"Then, don't be hiding out in here." Aunt Elizabeth began to hang up her belongings.

Angela fumbled with the frustrating trunk key. Unpacking might clear her teeming mind. A rush of early homesickness swept over her as she opened the steamer chest. She pressed her familiar blue muslin nightgown to her face, inhaling its freshness. Ma had sown gold birthday-present sovereigns from the Earl into the linings and hems of the rest of Angela's wardrobe. One thousand seven hundred of them made all of Angela's clothes heavier than they needed to be. Each vest, each skirt, even her bonnets held the precious coins, insurance for her bright future in America.

"Ma said at least a thief wouldn't be tempted by a big pile of shiny money."

"My sister is a clever woman, Angela," Aunt Elizabeth smoothed out the bedspread before sitting down. "But Antoinette's heart was always bigger than the brain the Lord put under her flaming hair."

Angela slammed the trunk shut. "I've boxed my way into and out of scrapes. More than one boy at St. Patrick's won a blackened eye for taunts."

"You can't be pounding on the Captain." Her aunt sighed.

"He's no better than those boys calling me, 'dirty petticoats'." Angela also recalled the derogatory tone in "barmaid" some of Ma's customers used when Angela wasn't quick enough with a new pitcher of beer.

"Act as if you haven't been raised among the pigs and cows like most of the citizens of Kerry." Aunt Elizabeth unbuttoned the top button of her dress.

"My friends wouldn't invite me to supper because their dads didn't bring their mothers along to the pub."

"The Merry Men Pub guaranteed a quiet place away from their constant nagging." Aunt Elizabeth reclined against a propped-up pillow. "No harm in that!"

Angry tears felt hot on Angela's face. "Unsavory am I?"

"Lucky is more like it." Her aunt's eyelids started to droop from the long day. "Don't forget to feed your poor horse."

If Angela could get riled up enough, she knew her pride would return. "You makes your luck," she remembered Ma saying. "America needs workers, and a smart gal like you can make short shrift of any job they let you at."

Her aunt's snores excused her from any further encouragement.

The hours flew as Angela carefully unpacked for the two-week voyage. She brushed her fingertips over a neat stack of clothing. Too bad she couldn't keep her thoughts as strictly in line.

Captain Hale's statement was cruel and not the truth at all. The Earl's money was only money, no taint evident, and a few dozen of his sovereigns were well spent for the quick steamship passage to America. Angela determined to go back on deck before her aunt woke.

In the hall Angela steadied her feet as the steamer rolled with another thrust from the propellers. She straightened the collar on her cape. She should have confronted Captain Hale immediately. Who was the tall bloke he spread tales to? She would stomp right up to the buggers and face them off. Irish curses swam in her head. Captain Hale could burn in perdition for all his sanctimonious drivel.

She squared her shoulders. The future in the Old Northwest Territory sounded rosy for young, hard-working women. Unclaimed farmland around the Great Lakes never felt a plow and single fellows were wanting wives. Angela tied her bonnet strings tight and righted her blue woolen cape. No one man was going to ruin her prospects.

She'd see England's lights off yet.

A full moon near the western horizon shimmered over the gentle waves. The ocean air, free of smoke and land smells, revived her. No seagulls ventured this far from land. Only the rumbling engines masked the silence.

The wooden deck was awash with blue twilight. Toward the east Angela could only discern a slim thread of light from the city. She made the sign of the cross and kissed her fingertips in a wave of farewell before heading toward the bow.

She had stayed below longer than she'd planned. Her footsteps thundered on the deck. Angry feet had a right to be noisy and she continued her determined onslaught.

Captain Hale and the taller, slimmer man still stood at the bow. Perhaps they didn't know she'd been offended. Many a time she'd wanted to go back and tell some gossiper at home or even the high and mighty parish priests after Mass exactly what she thought of their cruel words. Ma frequently cautioned her to hold her tongue. Now, on her own for the first time, Angela could tell both of these men what she felt about such callousness.

"Captain Hale!" she called, as forcefully as she could against the head wind.

He turned on his heels in one graceful motion. "Miss McGovern. What can I help you with?"

"You can introduce me to the man you had the audacity to defame me to." Rather too long of a comment. She'd have to shorten her sentences to demand a proper apology.

"Bumble Halliday?" Captain Hale touched the back of the taller man. "I certainly didn't defame anyone."

The tall man with the silly name wobbled around on shaky land legs. He clutched the railing with both hands behind him. "What's this?" he asked.

The moonlight played with the tips of his black curls, casting a dramatic backlight to his height.

"I...I demand an apology." There, she'd said it. "You don't know anything about me, and I won't have you telling falsehoods to perfect strangers."

Captain Hale scratched his short beard. "Well, I'll be damned."

"You will be if I have any say in the matter," Angela boasted.

A strong gust of wind caught the hem of her cape. When she bent down slightly to grab at it, the same wicked breeze lifted her bonnet off her head. Now her best spring hat hung down her back, fastened only by the ties around her neck. Her hair swept across her face, and she pinned it back with one arm as she tried to meet Mr. Halliday's gaze.

"You, sir, have been told that my past is unsavory."

Captain Hale coughed.

Bumble seemed determined to let go of the rail, but a shift of the boat made him clamp his hand back where it was. "I assure you, Miss McGovern, no remarks were made about you."

"The word unsavory wasn't used to describe me?" She wasn't going to excuse them by accepting a polite lie.

Bumble looked at Captain Hale, who pounded his chest and coughed.

"Not that I recall, Miss." Bumble shook his head.

"Well, let me set the record straight." Angela stood on her tiptoes, lifted by the rising wind and her anger. "My mother is a church-going member of St. Thomas parish and belongs to the rosary society."

"I'm sure -- " Captain Hale started.

"Ma kept every sovereign my English father sent for my upkeep." Angela retied an extra tight bow with her hat ribbons. "That's what I'm using to settle in America." Neither of them were going to leave without hearing about her mother. "Ma is an upstanding citizen of Kerry and has kept me in knickers for seventeen years with the profits from her pub."

"Doesn't sound unsavory in the least." Bumble's voice was deep and soothing. "Captain Hale, I think you owe this young woman an apology. She obviously thought you referred to her."

Angela nodded her head. Her cheeks felt hot from embarrassment and anger. Dressing down Captain Hale was harder than she'd imagined.

"You have my deepest apologies." Captain Hale took off his hat and ran his fingers through his white hair. "I assure you, I have never mentioned anything about the town of Kerry or any of its inhabitants."

"Are you saying you never met Ma?"

"No." Captain Hale bowed. "A more lovely woman you couldn't find in all of Ireland."

"Then who was it, you were talking about?" Angela wasn't ready to let them off. Her future in America on the other side of the endless ocean depended on stopping this scandal-mongering.

"Me," Bumble said.

He released his firm grip on the rail and took a step toward her. His legs got tangled up and he landed flat on his back, slipping with the deck's incline toward her feet.

She wanted to take his woolly head on her lap to see if he'd been injured. Instead, she kicked his boot. "Well, see you keep it that way, or I'll send the dead snakes of St. Patrick to drill holes in your dreams."

* * *

Captain Hale helped Michael Halliday to his feet. "There, there, Bumble. Miss McGovern's a sprightly lass."

"Best watch your comments, Captain." Michael grinned. "That Irish sprite intends to hold us both accountable."

Truth was, if he hadn't made such a fool of himself sprawling at her feet, Michael would have kept talking to the blonde angel with those green, almond-shaped eyes. Captain Hale of course referred to the Irish famine as well as Angela's up-bringing in her mother's pub in the exact words Angela heard.

Michael didn't deem her voyage to America in any way unsavory. Famine forced farming tenants, citizens who didn't even have land to sell to flee Ireland. Emigration made perfect sense to Michael especially since Parliament ignored those who demanded help from the potato blight.

When Michael first caught sight of Angela, the artist in him had been seized by the twin colors of her blue wool cloak and the soft blue twilight. After her tirade, when first her cape and then her bonnet behaved with the whims of the wind, he imagined her shock of moonlit hair might lift her off her feet. Like an angel. Nevertheless, time was wasted agonizing over her first impression of him. Saying he was the one who the Captain judged as making an unsavory start, would surely stay in her mind. He'd have to come up with some reason for the Captain to say it.. Perhaps the truth would will out. His body's mayhem with the moving deck already left him with little standing in her eyes. Kicking his boot while he was down. He should feel indignant. Instead he felt mesmerized.

"The child obviously knows how to take care of herself," Captain Hale said. "Taught no doubt by her enterprising mother."

"Her stature reminds me of Taffy, my younger sister." Michael righted his vest before adding, "We lost her to a typhoid epidemic in London last year."

"Sorry," Captain Hale sympathized, taking out his pipe as they resumed their post at the bow. "Shorter women are the sort a giant lunk like you might feel inclined to protect."

"True." Michael added a spark to his pipe. "But my post on Strawberry Island in Lake Superior won't allow that." The pay was enough to keep himself fed without further depleting his father's resources. The wealthy estate would be safe in Berkshire with all the pretty ladies who loved prestige more than they'd ever cared about him.

"How did you land that appointment at the lighthouse?" the Captain inquired.

"Since I was nine, I've read every article in the London Times about New York and the building of the Erie Canal to the Old Northwest Territory around the Great Lakes."

Michael's pipe went out in the wind. After knocking out the unburnt tobacco instead of ashes, he pocketed his pipe. Michael had written to every significant person connected to the canal's construction, saving reams of their answering letters. "I knew exactly who to ask for references."

Captain Hale nodded. Michael remembered the man traveled as far as Lake Superior. "Traveled the Canal more times than I care to count," Captain Hale said. "Lighthouse keepers always complain about what they forget to take with them."

Michael's budget held little constraint. Nevertheless he needed to live within the generous start-up allowance his mother insisted he accept. So he listened carefully to the Captain who would know exactly what to buy, even if he did tend to ramble.

"Before the construction of the Erie Canal," Captain Hale fiddled with lighting his pipe, "shipping goods 30 miles into the interior of the United States from New York cost as much as shipping the same goods all the way to England."

Michael memorized Captain Hale's every word.

"To encourage settlers." Captain Hale added more smoke to the skies. "There are no packet fees on the canal."

"What about the Hudson River and cutter or steamship passages on the Lakes?"

"You need two lists," explained Captain Hale. "One for Detroit supplies and one for New York for items that are harder to locate. If Sault Ste. Marie would have everything available, you would be wise to buy closer to Strawberry Island, but there's no way of knowing what's on hand."

Michael didn't propose to tell Captain Hale about his plans to turn his post on Strawberry Island into the ideal refuge for his art. His stock of paper as well as pen-and-ink supplies were safely packed at the bottom of his trunk, along with three pairs of boots cut large enough for him. The only time Michael didn't feel the barbs people sent his way about his manner of walking, growing into his hands and feet, or being as lanky as a hound puppy, was when his hands turned into instruments of wonder and produced grand ink drawings of his surroundings, of the family's thoroughbred horses or the faces of those he loved.

His happiness depended on pursuing the miracle of creation the Lord had seen fit to bestow. Michael could reproduce the likeness of anything. His mother cherished a picture of Taffy playing with a kitten Michael had sketched from loving memory. Even his father was proud of Michael's work, hanging several sketches of their horses in his den. Until, that is, Michael chose art as a career instead of his father's clockwork factory. Artists were not real men, according to his father. Like most men, even Captain Hale wouldn't be above calling a person unsavory for being an artist.

"I hope my sea legs develop shortly," Michael interrupted Captain Hale's description of the canal boats floating on the aqueducts which bridged deep chasms. The rolling ship's deck was never where Michael's feet found the planks to be.

Nothing new in living up to his knickname, bumbling along in life. Surely he would have the opportunity during the voyage to provide Angela with knowledge of his Christian name. They would be together for nine or ten days of passage, and if she agreed to write to St. Michael's namesake.... The archangel's name fit with Angela's.

The sound of soft bells or coins in her pocket gave her a furtherance into the society of heavenly saints.

"Michael, are you listening to me or mooning about Miss McGovern?" Captain Hale hit the mark.

"I'd better get below." Michael excused himself to avoid further embarrassment, "before I forget half the items you mentioned."

"Good idea," Captain Hale agreed.

* * *

On the way to his cabin, Michael decided to check on his horse, Splendor.

In steerage among the stacks of trunks, crates of food, and caged fowl, Michael's stallion whinnied a worried welcome. "There now." Michael soothed the horse's neck, crooning his usual compliments. "And aren't you the best looking horse in the stable."

"No," a decidedly feminine voice answered.

"Angela." Michael tugged at his forelock mimicking his servants at home.

"My mare, Flicka, is as fine a white horse as any in Ireland." Her blonde curls popped up above the adjoining stall.

"And my black, Splendor, is the finest in England or at least Berkshire." Michael laughed. In the lantern-lit hold, he hadn't noticed Angela's blue cloak hooked to a peg on the stall. "It seems we're destined to be at odds."

"Bumble's an…unusual name." She let him help her on with the blue coat.

Michael could smell the fresh scent of soap in her hair. "Michael is my baptismal name," he explained, "but as you witnessed, Bumble, fits my actions."

"Not at all." she lowered her long lashes.

Michael could accuse any other woman of flirting.

"The archangel suits your height." Angela brushed his arm as she reached to turn the wick of the lantern higher.

Without meaning to, Michael responded by standing higher in the toes of his boots. "There's our common ground."

Angela tilted her head questioningly.

"Your name. We're both, both angels." He stuttered and flushed at the stupid remark.

"Not I." Angela faced him squarely. "As you witnessed."

"The sailors take care to keep the stalls well-padded with hay." Michael searched for further subjects to cover his awkwardness.

"Do horses get sea-sick?" Angela let Flicka nuzzle her hair.

Michael wished for the honor. "My stable manager assured me Splendor would adapt better than I."

"Where are the two of you headed?" she asked.

"Strawberry Island in Lake Superior. I'm a lightkeeper for the lighthouse there." Without provocation he added, "I am an artist." Michael felt his face grow redder. "Please don't inform Captain Hale or he'll think me more unsavory than he already does."

"An artist." Angela said the words with more awe than Michael supposed he deserved. After considering his face, red as it was, she took pity on him. "I understand the thinking of bullies like Captain Hale. Your secret profession is safe with me."

"Thank you," Michael managed to say, bowing slightly.

Angela lingered at her horse's side, her hand quietly rested on the bridge of Flicka's nose. "Why then?" she asked without moving her hand. "Why did the Captain deem your travels to America unsavory, if he doesn't know you're an artist?"

"Because I'm my parents' only heir." Michael felt caught, his soul twisted in discomfort for furthering the lie about which of them Captain Hale tagged as unsavory. The closeness of the quarters allowed him to study Angela's profile for a reaction.

She didn't comment.

"Where is it your aunt and you intend to settle?" Michael couldn't remember her aunt's name. He wished any insincerity in the question wouldn't be noticed. His real intention was to detain Angela to determine why he felt he was swimming in the delicious green pools of her eyes. Had he never looked into green eyes before? Perhaps the ship's motion explained his slight dizziness.

"Aunt Elizabeth's home is in Chicago." Angela blinked.

Michael felt released.

"I plan to buy a farm." Angela patted Flicka's flank. "The Fox River valley near Chicago offers black loam."

Michael regained his equilibrium enough to ask, "May I walk you to your cabin?"

"Of course." Angela blew out the lantern before taking his arm as any lady would, but forgot to replace her bonnet as a farm girl might.

When the sea winds on deck attacked her curls, Angela hastily attempted to replace the thing.

As he tried to help, Michael poked her in the chin with his elbow. "Ow!" Angela cried.

Moon-lit tears glistening in her eyes from the blow. "Sorry, sorry."

She struck him in the chest with her doubled-up fist. It didn't hurt but he acted the stricken warrior for her, falling backwards onto a handy, padded deck chair. He closed his eyes. "You've stopped my heart."

He peeked to watch Angela examine her offending fist.

Then she kicked his boot again. "Faker, that's what you are, Bumble Halliday. I wonder if I should believe any of your blarney."

Michael sprang to his feet as she hurried along the deck to her cabin.

"Not about my heart," he called after her.

Angela didn't turn. She raised her fist as she marched away.

* * *

At six feet four, Michael was unable to stand upright under the low ceiling in his cabin. He smiled at his hunched-over image in the small closet door's mirror. The Captain was right. Why was he wasting plans and time in Angela's direction? She was bound for Illinois, he for Northern Michigan.

Michael lit the hanging lantern and positioned his long legs under the small table, drawing out his pocket diary to add to the list of supplies Captain Hale recommended for a season on the island. Under the Detroit heading, he wrote: two pairs of oars, a buck saw, a hatchet, hammer, chisel, wood-ax and white lye for white wash.

When he pulled out his pipe, he remembered his mother's warning not to smoke in close quarters. To his Detroit list, Michael added smoking tobacco, writing paper, and envelopes. Mail supplies for writing home. Angela might want to write to a friend too, one who lived in a lighthouse.

Angela was a perfect name for the green-eyed angel. She did have beautiful eyes, and when they flashed at him in anger, he imagined they held all the passion a man would want. Not that he would admit to thinking in those terms. She did have morals, that was evident. Michael approved of her not being ashamed of working in her mother's pub. She deserved every ounce of the pride she flaunted. Something to be said for hard work instead of aimlessly turning the pages of a social calendar without accomplishing anything but expense.

Was Angela educated? Her vocabulary certainly indicated her native intelligence. Had her father, an Earl no less, provided tutoring along with the yearly sovereigns she'd mentioned to Captain Hale? Angela's eyes melted for a half-second when Michael sprawled at her feet. He hoped she might bend down to see if he was all right, but she only kicked his boot. Michael could answer her letters in his spare time, if the light was wrong to sketch, or the nights unusually long.

The Lake Superior lighthouse inspector wrote that the Winslow tug brought mail every two weeks in good weather. The Inspector's winter-long correspondence detailed conditions on the island and the expectations of the job. Luck would have it that the Inspector was a distant cousin of the Buffalo mayor with whom Michael had corresponded for 11 years.

He re-dipped his pen and added a padlock against theft. Indians retained fishing and fruit gathering rights on the island. What did the natives assume would happen to their worlds from all the traffic on Lake Superior? Would they welcome his intrusion on their island? Did farmers feel they themselves were the poachers? London newspapers didn't pursue the subject of original ownership, but he'd read about a French philosopher who pontificated any ownership of property was theft.

If improvements were to be made, civilization demanded the wilderness should give way. Michael loved the idea of virgin lands, un-trampled by settlers. Here was another conundrum to ponder once he'd arrived on the island.

Michael continued writing lists long into the night to give details to his dream of a perfect solitary existence. A bedstead, mattress, bedding, pillows.... A clear image of Angela's golden curls gracing a snowy pillow broke his concentration.

Michael struggled to ignore the vision. According to both Captain Hale and the inspector, protecting ships from the dangerous rocks around Strawberry Island would eventually help settle the Old Northwest Territory with enough citizens to gain statehood for

Michigan, Wisconsin, and Illinois. Hardly the "worthless job," as his father deemed it.

Michael was eager to begin his duties of keeping ships free of impending danger. The rocks were said to be razor sharp in Lake Superior, the beaches pebbled waiting for the sands of time. The lake could be the empty crater of an ancient volcano. Jagged cliffs of granite presaged the hazards underwater. In bad weather or at night, a ship's Captain couldn't know how close he was to the rocks along the shore without the warning light from the tower. Michael might have to diligently sound the fog horns. The horn's imagined noise couldn't drown out his father's words of disappointment.

The truth was Michael needed a place to avoid a marriage of social convenience. His parents' dreams of grandchildren were nightmares to him. America would have to count on Angela to fulfill her mother's lifetime of sacrifice and her church's dictates. Angela would marry and produce enough new citizens. Michael would bet hard money on it.

Soon he would no longer be a 20-year-old beggar in his own family. There was more to running a lighthouse than he originally assumed, but he longed for the quiet refuge where no one could disturb him. His fingers itched to sketch Angela's face and the flow of her hair. Her.

# Chapter 2

*Sunday, May 7th, 1841*
*Pannonia on the Atlantic*

"Prayer service will be starting in ten minutes." A voice with Angela's Irish cadence caught Michael's attention. The delicate youth serving as cook's helper, who made the announcement, rousted the lingering breakfast crowd away from the tables.

Michael dropped his uneaten toast into the cold oatmeal before he observed Angela and her aunt at the table farthest from the door. A white-haired, olive-skinned man seemed entranced with Angela's every syllable. Only the syncopation of her words reached Michael's ears. A wave of jealousy heated his face. He felt the hateful emotion the last time when he was just a child, and Taffy, his baby sister, had charmed a smile from his dour father.

But the emotion started in his boots, warming his toes and then flooding his body with sudden passion. None of the ladies at home stimulated the remotest twinge. Now this troublesome farm-girl, this woman, produced a yearning with her voice. His ears wanted all her words to fill a newly opened void. The old man talking to her, no doubt, was experienced enough to compliment her. According to Captain Hale, Angela could see through ploys. Her knowledge of pub traffic should have warned her about that sort.

Michael's boots made a great deal of noise as he tried to scoot his chair back. The chair was bolted to the floor. Neither Angela nor her aunt looked his way. Michael stomped out of the dining room, disgusted with himself. He didn't need her attention. Or did he?

Hooking one leg onto the bottom rung of the ship's rail for support, he concentrated on filling his pipe. Captain Hale would be able to identify the old fellow. Michael intended to be subtle, discuss all twenty-nine passengers and then bring up the older man's description nonchalantly. Michael's stroll around the deck enabled him to survey the Sunday service attendees through the dining room's porthole windows. Now the white-haired man stood between Angela and her aunt.

Angela wore a filmy summer dress with an orange-apricot tint, a shade which closely resembled the color of his sister's favorite rose. A row of pearl buttons started at Angela's modest collar and ended her diminutive waist. The night before he was privy to the rose-scented perfume in her hair. Now this stranger could also enjoy the scent.

On his second circuit of the deck, Michael noticed Angela and the man shared a hymnal. Her embroidered shawl slipped down from the shoulder of her dress to her elbow, brushing the hand of the stranger.

Four strides took Michael to the rail where he contemplated the ocean's endless waves. Peace flooded his heated soul. Here was the Lord's creation as he understood it, appreciated it. Church services seemed like any other social event to him, straining his nerves with the confinement and sameness. He usually dozed off during the sermons. If there was a God, and he hoped there was, then the Lord would know his heart and the thankfulness overwhelming him for life, for the majestic ocean, for the cherished solid earth, for all the gifts of creation.

Turning toward the dining room crowd, Michael noted another passenger also skipped the Sunday ritual. A portly, white uniformed man stopped to look through the same window Michael previously used to watch Angela.

Michael coughed.

"The roast will be ruined if that crew don't hurry up," the man complained.

"Captain Hale has them enthralled with his sermon."

"I've heard it before," the man said dismissedly. "Looks like they could figure out on their own that the fires of hell might be put out by a dip in the sea."

"What's that?" Michael asked, not wanting to agree with the blasphemy.

"Oh, nothing." The portly man tugged on his ill-fitting, white jacket. "Now don't be carrying tales to the captain."

"If you won't tell him I missed the service," Michael held out his hand, "I won't repeat your words."

"Joey Baxter, the cook."

"Halliday, Michael."

"Heard about you." The cook's yellow teeth appeared. "Throwing yourself at that pretty gal's feet."

"Mercy." Michael wanted to swear.

"She is a looker."

"Do you know the name of the man standing next to her?"

"Nope. Gambler, I'm told." He bent to re-assess the two inside. "She'll be making the best of that."

"Be mindful of your words." Michael wanted to stay friendly, but he didn't feel friendly. He felt like throwing the whale of a man back into the ocean where he belonged.

"Heard about that, too," the cook's stomach rumbled before his laughter erupted.

Michael nodded. He couldn't trust himself to say a civil word and headed around the deck again. Anger engulfed his senses. Here he was, just thanking the Lord for his bounty, and then he'd lost all his peacefulness because of a common ruffian. If only he used the same amount of time he spent berating himself for some misbehavior, by advising himself of the correct action before a word or deed, there wouldn't be so much need for repentance.

His past contained similar derision from others. Their station in life didn't restrain their impulse to make jest of him. Something about him seemed to delight cheerful throngs. He knew he was taller than most but not ill-proportioned. Probably the way his arms and legs were loosely attached to his body amused them. Most people appeared stiff to him. Michael purposefully tried to put everyone at ease by relaxing as he walked. Now if he could train himself to join in on the fun, life would be sweet. A vision of Angela's eyes, filled with admiration for him, appeared in his mind.

He could have her if he so desired, but Strawberry Island pulled him in the opposite direction. His family could buy him friends and ladies to court. He did not need to suspend his plans of serenity on the isolated island in order to woo her. Besides she would probably hold out for the highest bidder. Now there was an insulting thought Michael was glad stayed only in his head, to be dismissed as garbage, instead of sharing it with another of God's creatures. If thinking could send him to hell as easily as deeds, he'd been in trouble since the day he was born.

The sea reflected the ribbons of light threading the overhang of clouds. The noon sun broke through the dim heavens on the far horizon. He recalled when he was a small boy showing his mother a similar shaft of sunlight. He'd surprised her by saying with reverence that the column of light was the Lord talking to someone.

If it was the Lord, Michael couldn't hear the words of inspiration, just as he couldn't decipher Angela's tones in the dining room. Nevertheless, this was the last Sunday Michael would miss service. Hope kissed him with surprising cheer.

A final benediction hymn erupted from the dining room.

* * *

After Aunt Elizabeth returned to their cabin, Angela accepted a white-haired gentleman's invitation to promenade around the deck until lunch was laid out. David Leonard seemed affable enough and attended church service. Not like that tall Bumble fellow. The strong odor of Mr. Leonard's cologne was off-putting, but his fingernails were clean. Angela smiled up at him when he opened the door for her. She could always wash him off. Thankfully the sea air freed her nose of the unwanted scent.

"Italian," he answered, when she asked his heritage.

"What are your plans in America?" Master Mitworth, her Italian teacher back home, informed her people who lived too far south were unproductive farmers due to the heat.

"Making more friends." He squeezed her arm for no apparent reason.

"But how will you be making a living?" Angela chided herself for not being more to the point.

"I like to play cards too much to work."

Angela concentrated on the quiet ocean. Play? What an impractical answer. She spotted Bumble Halliday at the railing with his back to them.

"I'd like to learn how to win at cards," Angela announced to draw Michael's attention.

He turned to scowl at them.

Angela stopped next to him. "Bumble Halliday, please meet David Leonard, an Italian card player."

"Michael, Michael Halliday," he said.

"Pleased," Mr. Leonard said, pulling a bit on Angela's arm.

"Do you play cards, Mr. Halliday?" Angela asked to keep the conversation going.

"A vice I am unable to rid myself of, entirely."

Mr. Leonard relaxed at her side. Then he stepped nearly in front of her to address Michael. "Join me for a game, Sir?"

"Not on the Sabbath," Michael replied.

Good answer, Angela thought, smiling until Michaael responded with a gentle grin. This bumbling giant contained the right potential for a valuable friend. She excused herself, letting Mr. Leonard schedule a game for a more suitable day.

If physical grace in a man carried any worth, Mr. Leonard would win in comparison with the ungainly Mr. Halliday. Of course, Michael's youthfulness added charm. The sight of lambs hopping about on all fours on the fields of the Ring of Kerry held a similar quality.

Her solitary walk around the deck brought her back to their side of the ship. Milling passengers, including four nuns and six younger girls, hid her from the gentlemen's view. Angela leaned against an upper deck support to calmly survey the assets of the two men.

Mr. Leonard was a head shorter than Michael, if not more. She noticed for the first time that the heels of Mr. Leonard's boots were unusually thick, adding an inch to his height. He appeared more nervous in front of Michael than in church.

Mr. Leonard constantly pulled at the bottom of his vest as if that would make his craning neck grow. He stepped back half-a-foot to relieve the strain of peering up into Michael's face.

A scurrying child parted them further. Which one of the men would Ma want to father the big family she anticipated for Angela? Being an only child made Angela envious of the fun she imagined other families enjoyed. At least her future children wouldn't spend one day of loneliness; not if she merited any say in the matter.

The child circled the two men, grabbing Mr. Leonard's trouser leg to keep up his momentum before interrupting them again. Mr. Leonard swatted at the child's hand on his trouser, but Michael swept the child up and playfully bumped heads with him before sending the triumphant, laughing boy on his way.

Angela tempered her favorable judgment of Michael with the knowledge that he seemed almost a child himself, giant though his height be.

As she joined them, Mr. Leonard gave her a polite bow, offering his arm in an invitation to continue their stroll. Michael knocked out the contents of his pipe on the ship's railing.

"You're as beautiful as the spring morn, Miss McGovern." Michael's slow, elegant tones satisfied more than the context of the compliment.

"Are we well enough acquainted for you to use my Christian name?"

His eyes were warmer than politeness called for when he pronounced, "Angela."

Her name took on harmonious tones of a quality she'd never heard before -- hymnal her name became in his soft, full-lipped mouth.

"Angela?" Mr. Leonard called as if from a distance, "shall we continue?"

She found the plaintive tone only irritating. She looked back at Michael, who responded with, "We'd best attend to lunch, before my stomach is convinced someone has severed my head from my body."

Angela wanted to hug him to her. Something about him brought out an inordinate amount of affection, as if home resided somewhere near his right shoulder. Instead acting on impulse, Angela offered him her left arm, Mr. Leonard having secured her right.

Michael wrapped his huge paw over her glove. She feared meeting his gaze directly and concentrated on his elegant gloved hand, which sent waves of warmth from its contact all the way to her jumpy insides.

In the dining room, the bar no longer resembled an altar. The open bible and candles were replaced with steaming platters of food. The inviting smell of beef gravy and caramelized onions made Angela's mouth water. The friendly greetings of passengers only parted since prayer service were muted, but here and there a laugh did rise.

Aunt Elizabeth sat at one end of the table farthest from the entrance. Several older ladies seemed headed in her direction, but she raised her hand slightly to Angela and the ladies withdrew to another table.

Aunt Elizabeth warned Angela, that very morning, in their discussions about Captain Hale's story of unsavoriness in Bumble

Halliday's past. "Jilted women often spread false rumors," her aunt had said.

But her Michael, his traits as Bumble long forgotten, would never falsely encourage anyone. This Angela was as sure of as she knew her mother woke up crying that very morning.

After the perfunctory introductions, Mr. Leonard indicated a chair for Angela next to her aunt. Angela realized his gloved hand on her right arm produced no sensation whatsoever.

"Michael," she smiled the mile up to his face, "sit with us."

"Gladly," he said. His eyes held their shared glance steady as he folded himself into the chair next to her.

"Where are you headed?" Mr. Leonard purposefully interrupted their rapport.

"Strawberry Island in Lake Superior." Michael unfolded his napkin. "As lighthouse keeper."

He was sufficiently tall and his dark eyes did shone enough in Angela's direction...beckoning to a danger she couldn't name.

"Angela's lost her tongue," Aunt Elizabeth said, "but she plans to live with me in Chicago."

Michael nodded that he'd heard but began to devour his food.

Satisfied with being near him, Angela wasn't the least bit hungry. She picked at the dry roast beef on her plate.

"Won't you be lonely at the lighthouse?" Aunt Elizabeth asked.

"I sketch," Michael said, turning away from his empty plate.

"Watch out, Angela," Mr. Leonard crowed. "He'll be asking to sketch you next."

Angela swatted Mr. Leonard's shoulder to shut him up, as if he were one of the school ruffians at home. "Michael Halliday's too much of a gentleman to do any such thing."

Michael refolded his napkin. He eyed her untouched plate. "Are you unwell?" he asked.

"No," she said, hoping it wasn't a lie. Her stomach seemed full of him. She handed him her plate. "I haven't tasted it."

Angela noted a slight, "tsk," from her aunt.

He blushed but consumed all the food. When he finished he focused his attention on Angela. "You have extraordinary eyes."

"Here it comes." Mr. Leonard touched her shoulder but she brushed his hand away.

"Is there no one else on the island?" Angela asked.

"Only me," Michael said. "I've never prepared a meal or washed a shirt, but I'm sure I can manage."

"Captain Hale says you're as green as they come." Mr. Leonard laughed.

"I am that." Michael good-naturedly joined in. "The good captain has taught me what to buy and in which port in order to survive."

"For instance?" Angela loved Michael's voice. It was two octaves lower than Mr. Leonard's and seemed to fill the dining hall with its coaxing tones.

"Well I'm only going to buy luxury items in New York." Michael gently touched her apricot shawl which lay on the arm of her chair, then he handed her his pocket diary. "Here's my Detroit list."

Angela read it out loud, solemnly, "One trunk, work shirts, clothespins, shoe blacking, sardines, a pocket knife, a flat iron, coffee pot, a wash tub, wooden pail, soap."

Aunt Elizabeth excused herself. "You two go over the supplies."

Mr. Leonard slapped his hat on his head. "I need a stroll around the deck after this meal."

Ignoring Mr. Leonard's irritation with her, Angela touched Michael's sleeve. "This is fascinating."

Michael frowned.

He thinks I'm flirting. She decided before she got on board the Pannonia not to use any of the ruses she'd seen her mother employ back home. Feminine wiles failed to secure her mother a permanent husband. "I've wondered what a homesteader would be collecting before starting out on the adventure of claiming land."

Angela reached into her reticule and drew out a pencil, flipped to the back page of her prayer book and began writing. "Laundry supplies, canned meats. What else?"

Michael perked up. "A coffee pot, a stove, stove pipes, and a cleaning spider as well as tins of matches."

She could feel him watching her write down: Kitchen utensils including stove.

She looked up at him. "And dinnerware?"

"Two sets," he said. "The lighthouse inspector might call. Although," he paused, "you'll think I'm unsociable, but I'm excited mainly about the time I'll be able to be alone." Michael lowered his voice, "To sketch."

His conspiratorial tone belied the facts. Angela tried to keep in mind that Michael wanted her friendship but not her future. "You've never cooked for yourself?"

"No," he said. "The inspector said that the last tenant left cooking pots, salt and walking flour."

"Weevils." she laughed, crinkling her nose. "You'll need a cook book and a glass crock to keep new flour in."

"Yes," he said as he consulted his pocket diary. "Cinnamon, dried fruit, pepper, a box of nails, salt beef."

"Sugar," she said and watched Michael write it down.

He stopped writing and looked at her as if weighing her worth.

"What?" she said. "What do you want to ask me?"

"I might enjoy receiving mail." He looked away. "The mail packet, the Winslow, comes every two weeks."

"I'd love to receive letters from Strawberry Island." Angela wrote down her aunt's Chicago address in a back page of the prayer book and tore it out to hand to him.

"You'll run out of pages if you do that very many times," Michael said as he slipped the folded note into his diary.

"I don't intend to write every gentleman I meet, thank you."

"Sorry, sorry. No disrespect intended. I'd be more than happy to tell you all about the island." Michael relaxed. "I think even the lighthouse will be fun." He straightened up as if he'd heard someone rebuke him. "I mean, it is serious work to keep the ships safe."

"Certainly is," she said. "Especially when people like me are foolish enough not to know how to swim."

"I can't stay on the island in the winter." His smile made her wish for more. "Perhaps we'll meet when I come to Chicago in November. I will be able to return to my post after the spring thaw."

Angela smiled back, hoping to warm the inner recesses of his handsome heart. "And we have this voyage to become better acquainted." She could feel his spirit back away, even though not a muscle moved. "Do you know anything about the Erie Canal?" she asked innocently.

Hooked again, he began a long description. "That's why I need two lists. Freight up the Hudson costs more than on the Erie Canal. A penny a mile isn't bad."

"No," she said, determined not to push this handsome gent in the direction she'd like him to take. Plenty of time for that.

Then Angela remembered her mother's rules. "Men are the hunters for wives." Her ma asked, "Have you ever seen a rabbit chase a fox?"

"But the rabbit doesn't want to be caught," Angela answered.

"And you'll never be chased if you run after a man," Ma concluded.

Angela believed the rule. Was that how Ma became pregnant with her, before she learned the Earl of Covington had already announced the banns to marry another?

"Let me show you." Michael held his hand out for her prayer book, which she readily gave him. He talked on and on as he drew a tiny map inside the front cover. "The Mohawk River is part of the canal packet passage."

She breathed in deeply, savoring his smell of tobacco and cherries.

"Lake Oneida is near the head of the river, and it's connected by the canal to Lake Erie," Michael didn't seem to notice her fixation with him.

Angela imagined she could smell the fresh ink as he wrote in her prayer book. His voice erased the world. She realized she was missing some information. Had he mentioned the St. Lawrence River and Lake Ontario?

"Lake St. Claire and the Huron, then to the Sault Ste. Marie locks leading to Lake Superior and Lake Michigan."

Suddenly hungry, Angela wished she'd eaten more for lunch. Her stomach churned and the tip of Michael's ear lobe looked sweet enough to nibble. "How do you know so much about the canal?"

"Plenty of news about it in the London Times."

Angela widened her eyes to show she was impressed, but he mistook the look for doubt.

"They're all afraid of the trade America will take from them. Shipments of wheat to England have doubled in the last ten years."

"I think America is like an unplowed field," she said, remembering not to blink so he wouldn't realize she was making eyes at him, "...able to grow any amount of riches with careful tilling."

"It is!" he said, matching her enthusiasm.

The rest of her day passed in a romantic daze promenading with Michael Halliday around the deck. As they came in contact with the other passengers, she tried to memorize their names. The nuns were easy saints' names: Ann Marie, Maurine, Josephine, Sophia, but the six giggling novices were going to be a problem. She could memorize the names, but their similar heights and hair color were going to blur when she tried to figure out if she was talking to Alice, Rosemary, Jean, Susan, Etta or Corinth.

The three families on board were easier. The Farthings were accompanied by four children, one of whom was the scamp who teased Mr. Leonard and Michael. The Thomases proudly showed their baby to every interested passenger.

Another couple seemed bookish, tweeds and soiled collars,...that sort of thing. The captain introduced them as special dignitaries. Angela failed to pay enough attention to their names, although she knew their surname started with a 'D.' The couple was headed for a literary speaking tour in America. The wife seemed right enough, but the husband was definitely green around the gills from seasickness.

"People really ought to pretend they're out riding," she explained to Michael once they shed the crowd. "If you get the feel of the ship, you can ride with it."

Michael stopped in his tracks. "That's it," he said. "I've been trying to hold on to something as I move about, but you do have to ride with the rhythm of the sea. Take in the changes of motion from a gallop to a canter."

"Exactly," she said, taking some pride in his admiration of her. "My father, the Earl of Covington, sent me Flicka, food and all." Michael was still smiling at her, but she couldn't beat back the sadness. She dropped her eyes to admit, "I'll miss Ireland."

He moved forward along the deck as if to avoid her homesickness.

"It's not catching, you know," Angela said as she caught up with him.

"What, what?" he asked. "Oh, the longing for home. My parents didn't approve of my trip." He coughed politely.

Angela tried to stop the thought that he was mouthing a lie, or was just about to. Ma's pub taught her more about the behavior of men than she wanted to know at the moment.

"As I told you," he lied, "That's why the captain referred to my crossing as an unsavory start."

"Did not." The words were out of her mouth before she could stop them. She'd never met her sire, the Earl, and the elocution teacher he provided never curbed her ready tongue, or rid the Irish cadence from her speech.

Michael ignored her comment as he fleshed out his story. "Before my parents married, my mother's family lost their money because a gambling uncle couldn't control himself." He took out his pocket watch and handed it to her.

She didn't pop the lid of the case, so he took it back, opening it before handing it back to her.

"Look at the name on the face plate." He leaned down to examine it with her, almost too close for her to breathe properly, much less read the blurry words.

"Halliday," he said. "My father runs a clock-work factory in London. I was to take over shortly, but I wanted to try my hand at...." He stopped and reclaimed the watch. "Sketching."

"As a lighthouse keeper." Angela couldn't challenge him about any lies right then. She felt his loneliness and his courage was akin to her own. Valuing truth didn't allow her to berate him. Angela knew as surely as she knew her horse's name that Michael was covering up for Captain Hale. Unsavory remained the word attached to her Irish past, not Michael's art or the leaving of his parents. She did take a certain pride in the fact that he thought enough of her to claim the stigma as his own.

Angela kept Michael talking about the canal's construction and what he knew of his island, how he'd answered an advertisement and provided references for the job as lightkeeper. Michael happily read her more lists of supplies that Captain Hale suggested.

They ate the evening's repast with the other passengers while Angela digested Michael's greatest joy came from the sketching he intended to pursue.

Arm-in-arm, Michael and Angela enjoyed their first sunset together. The sky reflected a bright yellow and the ocean played with stripes of pink left over from the sun-tinted clouds.

"I don't make friends easily with women," Michael said, then touched her shawl, as if tempted by its beauty to claim more.

"We are that, Michael Halliday," she said. "And don't let anyone be telling you differently."

"Now who would be telling me differently?" he asked with a twinkle in his eye.

"Who knows," she said lifting her hands above her shoulders, thinking of Captain Hale's epithet and her aunt's warnings.

* * *

That night, Angela's dreams replayed the force of events on her future. Bright clouds over the heaving ocean spawned a crop of cavorting infants. They rolled to the edge of their heavenly bedding and Angela called out in alarm for their safety. One with Michael's shiny black curls fell into the ocean.

Angela woke with Aunt Elizabeth shaking her shoulders. "It's only a nightmare, Angela, darling. We're safe."

# Chapter 3

*Monday, May 8th, 1841*

On the fourth day out of Liverpool, Angela tugged the porthole window all the way open, pushing it flush against the cabin wall. She stole a glimpse of the bright ocean before slipping the privacy curtain tight against the edges of the top and bottom brass rods. The tiny cabin's humid air dissipated quickly with the cool Atlantic breeze.

"What to wear for breakfast?" Aunt Elizabeth misinterpreted Angela's frown.

Angela planned to completely ignore Michael today or he would think she was scheming to penetrate his quiet island dream. She picked out a shimmering white sailor blouse with a blue-ribboned, square-back collar. "Will this do?"

"Your light blue serge skirt will match perfectly." Aunt Elizabeth busied herself with making the beds.

"I am repeating that same nightmare. A baby, looking very much like Mr. Halliday, keeps tumbling into the ocean." Angela braided her long hair. "He falls off a cloud."

"The baby or Mr. Halliday?" Her aunt helped her wrap the braids around the back of Angela's head, pinning stray curls in place.

"The baby," Angela giggled. "I don't believe Mr. Halliday rates a cloud. He didn't even attend church service."

Aunt Elizabeth held up the hand mirror from home. "You're looking almost school-marmish this morning."

Later, when Angela caught a glimpse of her reflection in the dining room mirror, she agreed with her aunt's prim assessment. The same mirror above the bar inspired last Sunday's crowd to positions of perfect posture during the church service.

Mr. Leonard, seated next to Michael, waved Angela and her aunt over to their table. But Michael, after eyeing her over his coffee cup, kept any invitation secret.

Angela shook her head and followed her aunt to a table of older women.

"Let's get acquainted with the rest of our fellow passengers," Aunt Elizabeth said refusing to acknowledge the rebuff.

"Good morning, ladies." Angela stood with her hand on the chair she intended to use. "May we join you?"

The more forbidding of the two only frowned, but the smaller lady laughed nervously and smiled. "Help yourself, dears. We don't have seating assignments here."

"I'm Angela McGovern," she said. "And this is my Aunt Elizabeth Breckenridge from Chicago."

"Mabel Lazarus," the forbidding one said. "This happy child is Winifred Perkins."

The diminutive older woman giggled.

"Call me Winnie," Winifred said. "All my nieces do."

"Winnie." Angela joined them, finally feeling welcomed. "And it is a beautiful morning, isn't it?"

"That it is," Mabel agreed, minding her toast. "What is your uncle's name, dear?" She spread the last bit of jam. "My husband's family lives in Chicago."

"Henry Breckenridge," Aunt Elizabeth answered. "My husband runs the Merchant Exchange Bank."

Winifred, who seemed to giggle every time her mouth opened, asked, "How long has it been since you've seen your husband?" She swept her hand to include the three older women, "People change pretty quickly."

Angela gulped her first sip of coffee. Maybe sitting with the flock of gossip-hungry women wasn't such a good idea. She caught Michael looking at her from his reflection in the large mirror. She had selected her chair to keep an eye on him. Angela smiled heartily at Winifred to pique Michael's interest. He was far enough away not to be able to hear her words, but she wanted him to know she could enjoy herself with people less exciting than he.

"They do," Angela answered. "My aunt left Kerry when she was twenty-three and worked for the bank for about a year in Chicago."

The women waited for Angela to continue.

"Before I married the bank president." Aunt Elizabeth sighed.

"Oh," Winifred crowed as if handed an armful of roses.

"I hadn't seen her for fifteen years." Angela stole a taste of her own porridge.

"Any children?" Mabel asked.

"Unfortunately, no." Aunt Elizabeth said.

Angela seriously considered excusing herself from the table, again. "The Lord hasn't blessed my aunt with any of the wee darlings."

"They're not all darlings," Mabel decreed, passing the remaining piece of bacon to Angela.

Aunt Elizabeth patted Angela's hand. "I'm glad to welcome my niece into Chicago society."

"I plan to work for my uncle." Angela smiled, purposefully not looking at the mirror to see if Michael was paying attention. "But I'm a strong woman and wouldn't mind finding a farming man to marry."

Mabel sniffed. "Farming."

Even Winifred repressed her giggles. "A hard life," she said.

"Bracing," Aunt Elizabeth said. "And the perfect place to raise children."

"Yes." Angela said. "I do love children."

Michael left the breakfast room. She hoped he'd had enough to eat. A big man like that. They should give him extra portions.

Aunt Elizabeth tapped her hand and shook her head no, cocking it toward Mabel.

Angela got the message not to be mooning over some man while under Mabel's watchful eye. Luckily Mabel was busy spooning up the last bite from her egg cup.

"You can raise a large family in the city, just as well as the country," Mabel lectured. "Children from the city are more sophisticated and learn how to advance in society."

Not wanting to prolong the disputed subject, Angela said, "There's plenty of truth in that." Which seemed to adequately take the wind out of the harpy's sails.

Aunt Elizabeth and Angela spent a congenial morning strolling around the deck with Winifred and Mabel. Winifred Perkins was joining her mother and father in Detroit. They needed Winnie's nursing care after her brothers married, moved farther west and left their aging parents to look after themselves. Angela liked the woman from the moment she asked to be called Winnie. The lady possessed an overflowing and generous heart.

Angela wouldn't hazard a guess at Winnie's age, but she was surely older than Ma, because soft creases lined her brow and showed how easily she smiled. Winnie acted like a schoolgirl comparing hats with Angela's. The bonnets were nearly matching, Angela's counted three ribbons to Winnie's one.

Of course they met Mr. Leonard and Michael near the bow, chatting with Captain Hale. Angela introduced a suddenly shy and blushing Miss Perkins to them.

The Captain politely informed Angela, "Bumble here, excuse me, Mr. Halliday, requested a time when you could exercise Flicka."

Angela clapped her hands in anticipation of the good news.

"If your aunt approves," Captain Hale frowned. "Directly after dinner when the children are out of harm's way, you're both welcome to walk your horses, if the weather permits."

"Thank you, Captain." Aunt Elizabeth ended any question of her approval. "We were that worried for the horses' health."

Mr. Leonard added with too much effusion, "Isn't it lucky that you two have so much in common?"

Michael struck the correct note of interest without needing to overwhelm the ladies with his presence. "I'd be happy to show off Splendor, if you ladies would like to see him this evening."

"A polite young man," Aunt Elizabeth said to Mrs. Lazarus as the four women resumed their constitutional.

"But I wouldn't trust that white-haired, pretty man," Winnie added. "Mr. Leonard, was it?"

"He does gamble," Angela admitted. "Do you know the game of poker?"

"No," Winnie's dislike of the subject showed in her wrinkled nose and brow.

"I want to learn how he could possibly make a living," Angela said.

Mabel seemed to approve, "It's best to know what to avoid in life."

"Yes, dear," Aunt Elizabeth said. "But you be careful."

"Raised in a pub?" Angela laughed. "I can take care of myself."

"I hope so," Winnie said. "I'm looking forward to seeing the two horses this evening. When I lived outside Bath, I loved to ride each morning."

* * *

*Friday, May 12th, 1841*

One evening, Angela dressed for dinner with the intention of sitting with Michael and Mr. Leonard. Her open throated, green-apple colored dress showed just enough cleavage, if anyone had the urge to be looking. Her blonde hair was arranged to let a few tendrils of curls fall near her ears, with a free cascade of ringlets down her back.

Aunt Elizabeth insisted she take a soft black cashmere shawl to cover herself if the evening cooled.

Angela collected ten sovereigns from the hem of her Sunday dress to gamble with after dinner. Angela planned to sit facing the mirror in case anyone was foolish enough to reveal their cards. She believed in taking every advantage offered.

Dinner was fun, with Mr. Leonard carrying most of the conversation about his successful gambling exploits. Michael was nearly silent but generous with his smiling warmth. When the remains of the meal were cleared, half of the adult dinner guests usually lingered at the tables, engrossed in conversations about their plans in America. The two older ladies Angela had become better acquainted with, Mabel Lazarus and Winifred Perkins, retired.

Mr. Leonard drew out a deck of cards for Michael to shuffle for Angela's first game of poker. Angela watched Mr. Leonard elbow his way to the crowded bar on the excuse of ordering brandies for all of them. He brought back poker chips and a frail older man who Angela was sure offered nothing to the new world except finances.

"Major Compton, this is Mrs. Henry Breckenridge; her niece, Miss Angela McGovern; and my acquaintance, Michael Halliday." Mr. Leonard took his chair opposite Angela, apparently quite pleased with himself.

"Major," Michael said.

"Major," Angela imitated.

"Oh, child," the major oozed, "call me, Billie."

Angela had no intention of addressing a man old enough to be her grandfather with such familiarity.

Aunt Elizabeth smiled warmly at him.

Angela turned to her left, toward Michael, and asked, "Is there a game called five-card-draw?"

He was frowning, so Mr. Leonard answered. "And a better game for your first couldn't be found."

"Are you mimicking my Irish brogue?" Angela didn't mind being teased, but she didn't want Michael to think she was stupid. Angela took a sip of the brandy. Ma served better tasting in her pub back home.

"It's a lyrical way of speaking," Michael said. "Even when you're sitting across the room it draws me to you."

What a lovely thing to be saying to an Irish lass embarrassed by her remaining language accents. Angela savored the brandy and the compliment, wishing she could earnestly thank Michael. She smiled at him instead.

"Do you know anything about the game, ladies?" Major Compton asked.

"I've seen people play it often enough, that's true," Aunt Elizabeth admitted.

"Ma let me play with the silly cards by myself," Angela said. "But she wouldn't let me join her at the tables with the patrons."

"A wise woman," Michael said.

Mr. Leonard distributed the chips. "Major, what table stakes were you considering?"

"Unlimited," he said, dealing each of them five cards.

Michael intervened. "But with these newest converts, let's keep it to fifty sovereigns."

"Ten would be kinder." Aunt Elizabeth said.

"No one has had two farthings to rub together in a Kerry pub," Angela told Michael, "for at least three years."

"The potato blight," Michael agreed with her.

"Ten it is, then," Mr. Leonard said. "Although it will be a quick evening."

Angela took another sip of brandy before she added her chip, as did Aunt Elizabeth and Michael. Mr. Leonard asked for four cards and folded.

Major Compton gave himself three cards and raised the bet by a sovereign. His stony smile never wavered.

Angela copied him, asking for three new cards and adding another marker to the pile.

Michael asked for one card and folded.

The major's face remained placid, but his left eyelid twitched out of balance with his normal blink when he added another chip to the middle of the table.

Aunt Elizabeth folded. "I'll just watch, if you don't mind."

"I call," Angela said, scooting out another chip.

Major Compton showed his pair of fives and Angela displayed her two aces. The pile of ten chips was hers.

She smiled at Michael as the deal fell to her. "This is fun."

"For those who win," Michael said. He put one of his chips out on the table.

Reluctantly, Angela thought as she let her tongue play with another sip of brandy in her mouth. Her throat felt warm. "It's a relaxing drink, brandy is."

The game was already losing its appeal for her. Mr. Leonard winked at her and increased the bid. Major Compton folded. Angela, who held two kings, raised again.

Michael asked for one card and folded, Mr. Leonard raised.

Angela called him by leaning forward to add another chip to the pile, in spite of Michael's raised eyebrows.

Mr. Leonard produced a pair of tens to Angela's duet of kings.

She cooed as she moved five more chips to her side of the table. She wanted to recount them. Did she have eighteen or nineteen and how many of them originally belonged to her? The money was harder to keep track of than the cards.

Michael's big hands ably dealt the next round.

Angela was tempted to see if his palms were as smooth as the sensuous tops of his hands. She wanted to trace the bulging veins with her fingertips to see if she could make an impact on his pulse.

Mr. Leonard folded without betting. "Never draw to an inside straight."

The major opened. Angela rolled a chip to the center of the table then took another sip of the sweet brandy.

Michael added his chip.

She felt when Michael began to tap his foot, the one closest to her. His knee tantalizingly brushed against her skirt like a secret whisper between them. Angela became aware of a warmth spreading from her spine, of all places, and then her toes began to tingle; but she refused to allow herself to move toward Michael. She didn't think he was aware of tapping his boot.

The Major requested one card and folded.

Angela asked Michael, "Two, if you've a mind to." She smiled, trying not to reveal her aberrant thoughts.

Michael moved a counter to the middle, but didn't take any new cards. "I call," he said.

"You show yours first," she said, adding another chip.

Instead Michael folded. "I was trying to bluff."

Angela gathered the cards together, adding hers to the middle of the deck before minding the chips.

"What did you hold?" Mr. Leonard demanded.

"I don't have to be showing you."

Major Compton's coughing fit was stopped by a large gulp of brandy. "David, I thought you told me she was new at this."

Michael began to fill his pipe. "May I?" he asked, before striking a match.

"I quit," Angela said.

Her head wasn't clear enough to count the possibilities of drawing cards to fit any more winning hands. She looked at the bottom of her glass. "This brandy was stronger than Ma's."

"But we have to have a chance to win back our money," Mr. Leonard complained.

"No, we don't." Michael's face seemed frozen under the cloud of smoke. He'd stopped tapping his feet. "We better hand over the money."

"I don't like this way of earning a living," Angela said, as they counted out their losses to her. "Honestly. It's too easy and I feel like a robber."

"You could give it back," Michael said, in the coldest tone she'd ever heard him use.

"No," Angela said, sharing her most innocent smile with him as she licked a taste of brandy from her bottom lip. "That wouldn't be fair."

* * *

Michael Halliday went straight to the pilot house to put a stop to that sort of thing. "Women gambling and drinking with men," he sputtered. "She's probably down there now, sipping her second brandy with that gambler."

"Angela McGovern can handle herself," Captain Hale said. "I'm not man enough to ask her to stay in her cabin. Are you?"

Michael stood mute. Why was he so upset? He felt like a puppet being manipulated by a bit of a girl. When she licked her bottom lip, he felt he would explode. She was wickedly seductive and knew it!

"Unsavory behavior," he nearly shouted.

"Now you've done it!" Angela had followed him. "You're a weaselly, poor loser."

Michael twisted for help from Captain Hale's direction. But the Captain seemed quite amused.

"You're drunk," Michael said. "Your mother would be scandalized."

"I'm not drunk," Angela put her hands on her hips. "But you, sirrah, are no gentleman." She approached Captain Hale for confirmation. "Rubbed his knee against my skirts all evening, he did."

Michael's mother told him not to move his feet when irritated. Now he'd encouraged Angela's attention, and lost her respect.

"Now, now, children," Captain Hale secured the ship's wheel with a leather strap to the bridge wall, while Angela and Michael stewed in their growing anger. He planted himself in front of the exit door before beginning, obviously, his favorite lecture. "You're both bright people. Bright, not right, mind you. First of all, Michael, Angela may partake in any amusement she sees fit to engage in. On my ship I enforce equality between the sexes, among social classes and religions."

Angela's chin went up at least an inch. He was tempted to remind Captain Hale of his incendiary words of 'an unsavory start,' that caused Michael's dilemma in the first place.

"I won all three hands," Angela said, without a bit of shame.

"She's obviously displaying keen observation." Captain Hale dropped in Michael's estimation with each solicitous word. "...self command, good judgment, and knowledge of character."

"Not his," Angela had the brazenness to rudely point at Michael. "Besides, I don't intend to play another hand." She lowered her eyes, as if a demure stance would change his opinion of her.

"And drinking," was all Michael could sputter. "Leonard probably believes other behavior is also acceptable."

"What other behavior?" Angela came right up to him, not an inch away. "Wait just a minute," she said, as he tried to back away.

The wheel house wasn't a very big room, his back was against the wall opposite Captain Hale.

The good captain continued his well-rehearsed speech. "You're both traveling across an ocean to begin a life in a virgin country where the good de Tocqueville believes...,"

Michael saw him draw in a chest-expanding breath to further his oration.

"...that 'Although man has many points of resemblance with the brutes, one trait is peculiar to himself--he improves. The ideal of perfectibility is therefore as old as the world; equality did not give birth to it, but has imparted to it a new character.'"

Angela wasn't listening, and Michael couldn't blame her. She was busy scooting a stack of chart books as close as possible to Michael's feet. The books were long and wide, not easy for her to maneuver.

Michael considered helping her, but he wasn't too sure what she intended.

She piled a final two on top of the four. Incredible strength, Michael thought before she jumped on top of the books...and slammed her fist into his right eye.

"I hope that changes your opinion of me," she said, brushing Captain Hale away from the door.

Captain Hale owned a vicious laugh.

\* \* \*

No angel in Angela, but quite the gal anyway. Michael tried to stretch out on his bunk. He held a cold cloth to his blackening eye. His bare feet were higher than his head, perched as they were on the trunk at the end of the bed.

The sea got rougher as the night dragged on.

Within minutes, rest was out of the question. He heard water sloshing in the hall outside his door. Even though the oval door frame was set six inches above the level of the hall floor, he could see water seep under it when the ship tilted to his side.

He wondered if Angela was awake and frightened.

# Chapter 4

Who gave Michael Halliday the right to judge her actions? Angela listened to her aunt's untroubled snores. Resentment at Michael's arrogance as well as the embarrassment and guilt for her unladylike temper caused Angela to roll from side to side in her narrow bunk. She tried to lose Michael's words in the rising din of the engines. His height she tacked in her imagination to the forward mast. She could as easily forget him as the wind-driven leaves from the beam's lost tree where ground into dust. Michael's eyes were harder to shut out of her mind, black as the night's ocean and just as unfathomable they were.

She gave up any effort to rest after plummeting into the wall of her bunk. The boat was encountering a vicious storm. She tucked her nightgown into the tops of her highest boots and secured her cape. Aunt Elizabeth continued to sleep so Angela placed pillows next to the bulkhead to cushion her.

A great pounding threatened at the cabin's door. Angela swiftly opened it to shush whoever meant to disturb her aunt.

Mr. Leonard, the gambler, hung onto the door frame. "We must secure a life boat."

"I'm not leaving my aunt." The fear in Mr. Leonard's eyes was unreasonable. "Calm down, Mr. Leonard." Angela could smell brandy on his breath. "Has Captain Hale ordered an evacuation?"

"No." Mr. Leonard endeavored to gain some measure of composure. "There aren't enough life boats. He pulled at her shoulder to come with him.

Angela cringed under his fierce hold.

"What's this?" Michael called from his cabin doorway.

Mr. Leonard didn't release his grip. "The storm's increasing."

"Let go," Angela said, meaning to wake her aunt, if he'd let loose.

"Mr. Leonard," Michael's threatening tone affected the man.

Mr. Leonard dropped his arm to his side. "The danger is real," he said close to Angela's face.

Angela knew the cause of Mr. Leonard's red-rimmed eyes was not unshed tears.

Mr. Leonard twisted in the water-logged hallway to address Michael, "She's all yours." He fled then up the short stairway at the end of the hall.

Michael ignored Mr. Leonard's retreat. Instead he seemed to be re-assessing Angela.

"Should I wake my aunt?" Angela didn't want to speak to him, but the fresh disaster might require help with her aunt.

"I'd wait a moment or two," Michael said, changing the focus of his attention to the rising water in the hall. "Don't be frightened."

"Frightened?" Angela was glad he didn't close his door, but she'd be taking no humiliation from the ornery bloke.

Michael started to advance toward her into the hallway, but the sloshing water deterred him. "I meant if, as you have said, you are not able to swim, not to worry. There are enough life boats to keep us safe."

Ready to take umbrage with any word out of his handsome mouth, Angela eyed him with dismay. "And now you're calling me a liar?"

"I was trying not to frighten you." Michael looked into his cabin.

She didn't want him to close the door. "How long should I wait?" Without meaning to, a desperate whine crept into the last word.

The irritating noise from the groaning engines stopped. Angela couldn't believe that was a good indication for their safety. Now she could hear heavy waves hitting the deck above.

"The horses?" she asked. "I know the stalls are well padded, but they might be frightened."

"I'll just get my boots," Michael said, disappearing into his cabin.

Angela's fear rose with each movement of the undulating ship. She'd read about shipwrecks and they never ended happily. What was the sense of praying for healthy, beautiful babies if death loomed over a body before she could even grasp a chance at marriage?

With the engines silenced, the howling of the wind and rain now muffled shouts from the seamen.

"Mr. Halliday," she called, trying to control her trembling voice. "Are you there?"

Michael stepped noisily out into the water filled hallway. "At least I can stand up straight out here."

She laughed. "You are a sight," she said. A sight she didn't mind seeing and that was the honest truth of it. His curly black hair looked as if he'd run his huge hands through it once or twice.

"Couldn't find my boots fast enough." Michael smiled at her. "Quite a shiner you gave me."

"Sorry," she said automatically. "I mean, you did have it coming, you know."

"I am not sure I want to agree with that." Michael touched the swollen eye gingerly. "Hurts too."

"Oh and what a baby you are about it, now." Angela tried to control her smile. "A big brawny man like you must have gotten into plenty of scrapes."

"Never," Michael's tone sounded shocked. "I take it from your fisticuff abilities that you have pounded on men before?"

"Only on the wanton boys at school," Angela said. Pleased she was that she'd socked Michael now. "A virgin to violence then, are ye?"

"Thank God." Michael shifted his feet in the wake of a worst roll of the ship. More shouts, a few curses, and thundering boots above the storm.

"Maybe the sailors are too busy to alert us," Angela wondered if she should be trading useless blarney with this fellow or making sure her aunt was adequately dressed to abandon ship.

"Actually, I think the sea has slackened a bit." Michael looked toward the stairs.

"Don't leave us!" Angela's voice had a mind of its own, securely placing panic in each syllable. "Sorry. I'm a wee bit unnerved by Mr. Leonard's threats of drowning."

The ship did seem to recover easier from riding the storm's surge. At least the sailors stopped their yelling.

"Perfectly sensible to stay alert," Michael smiled at her. "Your hair is the most beautiful I have ever seen."

Vain glory, Angela remembered a Biblical dictate. "And you're the tallest man I've met. The bossiest, too."

"Me?" Michael's laugh warmed her. "I never give directions to anyone."

"Telling me what I can do and not do?"

The ship was righting itself more easily in the slackening storm.

Angela sighed in relief.

Michael advanced the few steps toward her cabin door. "I worry about a less than pristine reputation following you to America." He reached out and placed his hand over hers as she held onto the door frame.

Angela had no intention of moving her hand. Michael's kindness was imparted in his touch, even though his words threatened to raise her ire. She looked up to meet his gaze. Her toes were tingling and her stomach flutters were not, Angela knew, a sign of seasickness. Michael Halliday was the source of everything. Her blood seemed ready to penetrate her skin in order to get closer to him.

The rolling ship brought his massive body within a half inch from the soft wool of her cape. She imagined she could feel his warmth through the garment. Tempted she was to unbutton the clasps and toss her cloak behind her. Angela resisted her own instincts. She wished Michael would at least secure his free hand around her waist, in case she needed to faint, but Michael didn't seem inclined to do so.

"My aunt knows of my virginity." She raised her chin. "I trust her to find me an acceptable husband." Angela realized the raw state of her nerves allowed disclosure of an intimate fact that no woman should be telling. Certainly not to this fraud of a man whose penetrating eyes sought out the very nature of her soul. "Once she introduces me to Chicago society."

Michael failed to comment on her blush of embarrassment. "A rich husband is a normal desire for a young girl."

"Most farmers aren't rich when they start out." Angela reluctantly pulled her hand out from under his. "And I'll not be marrying an old man."

"I'm not that old."

Michael was flirting with her!

"And neither are you a farmer," Angela sallied. "If I'm to be believing you."

Michael's laugh owned a fresh freedom to it, as if he didn't often let it air.

"Angela," Aunt Elizabeth called. "Are you conversing in your nightgown with Mr. Halliday?"

Before a thought emerged, Angela pulled Michael's head down by grabbing onto his unruly curls, then she kissed him lightly on the

lips, while looking deep into his dark eyes. "And kissing him too."
Angela laughed.

"Angela!" her aunt's shout was dutifully shocked.

Angela shut the door on Michael's wink.

* * *

Michael surprised himself when he couldn't resist the urge to kick
at the receding water in the narrow passageway. Unhappy with the
mild splash on the wall, his delight in being kissed by that scamp,
Angela, urged him to further antics. He held himself up by pushing
against the walls in the hall before gleefully jumping, two-footed into
the remaining puddles. Fifteen again, he felt carefree and powerful, all
at the same time. Angela was the youngster here, not he. His life
encountered little happiness since the death of his sister, Taffy.

The walls of the corridor were discolored from the wet spray he
created. His mother would have five conniption fits at the mess he was
making of his clothing not to mention the painted wainscoting.
Michael marveled at the surge of homesickness brought on by
Angela's feminine contact. Michael regained his normal seriousness.

The engines were starting again, and the ship dipped and dived
between the opposing movements of the twin propelling shafts.

Captain Hale could enlighten him about the direction of the storm.
Michael didn't propose to discuss Angela, but he did want to find out
what havoc, if any, David Leonard wreaked besides frightening
Angela into speaking to him, blackened eye and all. Michael smiled at
their bit of fun.

On deck Michael noted the line of pink sunrise between the ocean
and the clouds scattering to the south. The deck was slick from the
salted waves which crashed over the Pannonia's rails during the storm.
Sails were furled to dry the canvas. The normal rumbling of the steam-
driven engine was quieter on deck. The ocean air smelled of hope and
the freshness of the universe.

"A new day," Captain Hale announced.

Michael gingerly withdrew his pipe from his vest pocket, intent
on lighting the obstinate thing. "Mr. Leonard made quite a scene down
below." Using a rolled up page from his notebook, he borrowed the
flame from a still burning lantern to start the tobacco.

Captain Hale watched the vain attempt. "Your tobacco is packed
too tightly."

"Was the man drinking beyond his capacity?" Michael knocked the butt of his pipe against the mast before setting the flame to the loosened tobacco a second time.

"Mr. Leonard?" The captain turned away to give changing orders to his midshipman. "We tied him to his bunk."

"Did you?" Michael was pleased to feel warm, cherry scented tobacco smoke in his nostrils from the confounded pipe.

Captain Hale showed no sign of the nonchalance Michael expected toward Mr. Leonard's inebriation. "Damn fool tried to cut the ropes securing one of the aft life boats."

"Scandalous behavior toward Miss McGovern, too." Michael could feel himself smiling again at his own less than gentlemanly behavior."

"That so?" Captain Hale eyed him closely.

Michael changed his manner to show how inappropriate he deemed Mr. Leonard's behavior. "Frightened the girl nearly to tears."

"Hard to believe Angela would take easily to panic." Captain Hale busied himself with the compass but Michael felt he was under scrutiny.

"Can't swim, you know." Michael stepped back to allow the smoke to travel past the captain.

"You calmed her down then?" Hale persisted.

"Certainly." Michael said, as if his duty to bolster frightened women was more than obvious. "I need to reassure Splendor and Flicka before breakfast."

On the way to steerage Michael knocked his pipe against the ship's rail sending the glowing contents into the waves. He was fully aware he hadn't fooled the captain about his change of attitude toward Angela. Michael may have lied to himself, but Captain Hale discerned the truth.

Kicking his boot against Splendor's stall caused his horse to eye him sleepily. Michael apologized and patted his nose. Could the horse smell the tobacco on his hands? Michael buried his head in the black flowing mane of the contented stallion. Astonishing how often the odor of horse flesh caused him to remember the perfume of women.

Angela McGovern was a cool breeze compared to the hot-house, orchid-delicate young ladies who frequented his mother's parlor.

Michael bet that when she was by herself Angela even whistled when she felt like it.

Musing about Angela's warm hand resting under his on the door frame of her cabin recalled the scent of her rose perfume. He examined his palm, but he could not get rid of the pleasant pressure where their flesh met. Not even smoking his pipe erased the staying power of her touch. He closed his eyes to remember the slight brush of butterfly wings from her kiss. The kiss was the hardest to dispel. Michael pressed a fingertip to his top lip. The ridge to his nose reminded him of his nanny's tale of an angel's fingerprint leaving an indent there to keep the secrets of birth.

Splendor pushed Michael into the half-door of the stall, inviting him to leave.

When Michael slipped the door's bolt into place, his body surged with longing. The boat's personal sway required more concentration on his reactions than would be required on dry land. Perhaps that's all this physical arousal was. The initial excitement of the storm and Angela needing his protection necessitated the heightened awareness. Surely Angela desired all of his attention then, but now his body needed further excuses.

Michael leaned over Flicka's stall to stroke the white horse's neck. Neither horse showed the least concern for the storm's gyrations of their stalls. Somewhere Michael read that horses were more spiritual than humans.

"Safe in God's hands." Both horses witnessed.

Michael could hear Angela's lilting voice singing in his head.

He sat down on a stack of hay in the crowded compartment, leaned his head back, and passed into a short nap.

A dreamscape of young scamps spilling his ink pots and tearing his sketches to shreds made him moan in his sleep. So loudly in fact, that he woke remembering the entire episode of terrorizing children vividly enough to break out into a most unmanly sweat.

"That devilish woman," he swore for his own edification.

Flicka whinnied at Michael's unnecessary loudness.

# Chapter 5

*Saturday, May 13th, 1841*

Late for breakfast, Michael felt kicked in the stomach when he met Angela's aunt coming out of the ship's dining room.

"Sir' rah," Mrs. Breckenridge signaled with her gloved hand for Michael to follow her. "A word, if you don't mind."

No way of escape occurred, so Michael accompanied her away from the smells of hot bread and crisp bacon. His stomach neither agreed with the direction his feet were taking him nor with the dilemma of manners he was about to encounter.

Captain Hale passed them on his way to breakfast.

Mrs. Breckenridge only nodded to the captain's bright, "Hello."

If Michael hadn't been the gentleman he certainly was, he would have knocked the cocksure smile off the captain's face into the ocean along with that infernal pipe of his. The smell of wet leather in Captain Hale's trailing pipe smoke further infuriated Michael.

"Ma'am," he tried to at least take control of the situation with Mrs. Breckenridge.

"You will listen to me, young man." Mrs. Breckenridge's voice contained little of the lilting music Michael enjoyed in Angela's.

"Yes, Ma'am." Michael tugged at his forelock. He knew he was in serious trouble.

"If I hear one more word of complaint from my niece about you," here Angela's aunt faced him, "or any references to my sister's source of income, I'll contact people who will take personal measure of your worth." Mrs. Breckenridge tapped him, not softly, on the top button of his vest.

Michael looked down at his chest. "My deepest apologies." Michael moved back a step. "I admit my behavior with your niece was completely wrong." It never occurred to him that the slight woman could deliver so much force, but the effort not to rub the spot of impact or cough, required substantial will power. "I hope Angela explained that Mr. Leonard tried to force - -"

"What did I just say to you?"

"Not to sully Miss McGovern's reputation."

"Did I not make myself clear to you then?"

"I'll not mention the incident again." Michael checked to see if anyone was within listening range. "My future holds no plans to include affection."

Mrs. Breckenridge's expression lacked both understanding and mollification, so Michael continued in the same vein, "I feel I have falsely encouraged Miss McGovern's friendship, when I know she is…." Words failed him.

"Looking forward to making a proper match?" her aunt offered.

"Exactly." Michael smiled with the small hope arising that the breakfast things might not be cleared by the time he reached the dining hall.

However, Mrs. Breckenridge secured his elbow and marched him past his intended destination. Michael did catch a glimpse of Angela and waved to her behind his back in a desperate invitation for rescue.

* * *

When Angela caught a glimpse of Michael being towed by her aunt, her heart dipped. But apparently he'd noticed her. She rushed to open the door. "Michael, the waiter is nearly ready to clear."

Her aunt scowled. "We're not finished."

"Surely, you wouldn't be denying a big man like Michael his vitals for the day." Angela pulled at Michael's arm.

Aunt Elizabeth didn't seem inclined to release Michael.

Finally, Michael said, "Please join me, Mrs. Breckenridge. We can continue our discussion away from the wind."

"We'll continue our discourse the next time we meet," Aunt Elizabeth headed back toward the cabin area.

Angela sat down at the nearest table, and Michael waved the young cook's helper over.

The four nuns and six novices marched out of the dining room. Sister Sophia, the last in the black-clad train of women, winked at Angela. Angela winked back before realizing how shocking her mother would consider such behavior from a nun, not to mention her own. Sister Sophia was the most cheerful of the brides of Christ. Perhaps the nun recognized and acknowledged the affection emanating from Angela to Michael with her playful wink.

Angela chatted about the mildness of the weather when Mrs. Farthing stopped at their table. The Farthing's oldest scamp, who teased Mr. Leonard and Michael earlier, stole a biscuit from Michael's plate. Michael was too busy ladling a second helping of eggs to notice.

The calming ocean was the subject with Mr. and Mrs. D., as they passed by. Angela could still smell a musty odor in their clothing, as if all the articles were second-hand. She couldn't imagine how a successful author on his way to speak in America wouldn't have money enough to purchase new wardrobes. Their fingernails were as black as those of the sailors and Angela wasn't accepting the use of ink as an excuse. Even the dark color on Mr. D.'s crusted neck surely couldn't be accounted for by the sun's rays. Angela worried that they were in the habit of putting dirty toes into unclean socks every morning. Mr. D. appeared less ill than the previous time Angela talked to him. She could see he appreciated the lessening of rough seas. Nevertheless, a bar of good soap would have saved the day for those downwind of the D's.

It was pleasant to show off her man, even if Michael's manners were swallowed along with his hunger. Michael continued to eat without responding except by nodding his head in agreement to all conversation.

After the dining room sufficiently emptied, Angela ventured, "So I take it Aunt Elizabeth has been filling your ears with threats to your life and limbs."

"Indeed," Michael managed between sips of coffee.

"Now, Michael, don't be angry with my aunt." Angela smoothed the tablecloth in front of her. "Aunt Elizabeth knows your destination."

Michael stopped swallowing

Angela continued, "Your plans to produce a body of work fit for display at a Paris studio while you're ensconced on your island have been discussed."

Michael folded his napkin.

Angela wasn't finished, but the cook's boy seemed ready to hurl them from the room. "Perhaps we should stroll around the deck?"

"Of course," Michael stood and held the door open.

The Thomases passed by with Mr. Thomas holding the cooing baby.

Angela smiled at the happy couple and easily slipped her arm around Michael's.

Michael stopped and looked at her glove. "Angela…."

Handsome he was with his black lashes lowered. Large too. At five-foot-two Angela would have to stand on her tiptoes if the need ever arose to lock her arms around his neck. She could smell the sweet tobacco permeating his clothing. Angela stepped closer without intending to, as if drawn by his very being. Surely this was the man she could give herself to, eventually.

"What is it, Michael?" The poor man, what a scolding her aunt must have given him.

"Your friendship is the first I've managed to have with a woman," Michael's voice nearly broke, "since my sister passed away."

"You're a dear man." Angela placed her white glove gently on his top vest button. "I'm that sorry to hear of your loss."

Michael lurched back as if she'd struck him.

Her gloved hand stayed in mid air, bereft of its claim.

"A walk will do us good." Michael secured her hand in the crook of his elbow. "Your aunt apparently wants me to explain my intentions."

Angela could feel herself closing up inside, guarding herself from any impending danger to her heart. The wind off the immensity of ocean water began to send a chill all the way through her cloak. Michael seemed to sense her discomfort, moved to the rail and kept her in the lee of the wind. Surely a good sign, if one needed to look.

"My father's wealth and my mother's lands in Berkshire have made me a…." Michael ceased their stroll.

Mabel Lazarus and Winifred Perkins went by. Mrs. Lazarus wore enough black cloth to sail a small fishing boat and Miss Perkins sported an equal amount of pink finery. Angela hoped in the age after child rearing that she would have enough sense never to wear pink. Who would be so money hungry to sell a pink-dyed, wool cloak to a woman over forty?

Angela was too distracted to speak to them. She did try a kind smile, but felt its insincerity. "Bless their hearts," she murmured.

Michael hadn't moved. "How shall I politely say this?" He was still bumbling about with his cold discourse.

Angela knew she should be feeling pity for the poor man, but she only realized the rising force within her, of deadly anger. He could stew for a bit in the juice of his own vanity for all she cared. Tears threatened and she denied their access to her face. Her stomach felt like it was bleeding from the effort to control her reactions. Who needed him! Or his father's money or his mother's land? Who did he think he was, presuming she'd have no other but him? She clutched at the nearest rail, but there it was. Either Michael would husband her or none.

"Oh say it, Michael, and be done with it." She turned on him, hoping her anger would subside with the sight of him.

It did.

"Women have considered me a very good prospect for marriage." Michael scanned the ocean as if innocent of any guile.

His dark eyes sparkled from the sun. Angela tried to memorize every curve in his classic face, the high cheek bones, the straight bold nose, those eyelashes. The softness of his full mouth would have to last in memory only. A tear escaped but she brushed it aside, as if a bit of salt spray bothered her.

Angela lowered her forehead and looked up at him, knowing the effect of her purposeful gaze on men in her mother's pub.

"I know that ploy, Angela," Michael rested his hand on her shoulder.

She couldn't escape. She broke the promise to herself never use her mother's devices to tantalize a man. Now pushed in a corner when all was lost, Angela succumbed to the temptation of employing seduction.

"Friends are honest with each other, Michael." Her courage profited from her own words. "You've been flirting with me and I with you, even though we both know you have other plans."

Her anger almost got the better of her good sense, when she watched the relief spread over his face. Even his ungainly body released itself from an unfamiliar stiffness. All was right with Michael's world.

Not so her own.

\* \* \*

Michael did not remove his hand from Angela's shoulder. He looked deep into the green depths of her slanted eyes. Was she about to weep? Surely not.

Out of the corner of his eye, Michael saw David Leonard and Mrs. Breckenridge passing the time of day near the bow of the ship.

For a fleeting second, Michael worried they were cooking up some scheme to rid him of his influence with Angela. Captain Hale was nowhere to be seen. Would poisoning be beneath them? Michael dismissed the idea, but wondered if he should have insisted on disclosing Mr. Leonard's drunken accosting of Angela to her aunt.

Michael sighed at the prospect, breathing in Angela's rose perfume. "My parents have always purchased people to entertain me." What if he hurt this beautiful child, no woman?

He longed to climb up in the rigging away from all these people. Michael looked at his soft hand on Angela's blue cloak. He envied the tough sailors securing the sails over their heads. They would have known how to handle this situation.

In a secretive whisper he confided, "You would be the first person to choose, on her own, to find me acceptable."

"Oh, Michael. Are you trying to make me cry now?" Angela patted the hand he'd kept on her petite shoulder. "I think you must be mistaken about all those people hanging around you." She pushed his arm down and stepped away from him. "Let's take a turn around the deck to the sunny side of the ship."

Most of the other passengers favored the port side in the morning. Michael did notice the lack of wind there, but he preferred the lessened traffic on the starboard side.

Angela didn't seem to mind the crowd. "I bet you missed more than one chap or intelligent gal who valued you for who you are, in spite of the defect of your riches."

Michael couldn't help but laugh. "Honest you are then?"

"And you, making fun of the way I'm speaking, are you?" She faced the ocean, perhaps to breathe in the cool salty air.

But something worried Michael enough to stop his progress around the deck. "Friends don't break each other's hearts."

Without facing him, she said low and serious. "No, there's no minding that."

"What's that?" Michael asked.

"Nothing to worry the handsome head of a fine artist about." She propelled him along their walk.

Back in the wind, Angela motioned for him to bend down to hear her. "I will clear up any lingering misunderstandings my aunt might harbor of your intentions."

Angela sauntered on and Michael stumbled a bit when he hurried to keep up with her

Angela hadn't noticed. "She'll be as right as rain then."

"Thank you," Michael said.

He'd expected an outburst of hurt pride. Instead Angela comforted him.

She stood aside as if to let him pass without her. She unfastened her cloak when they were on the port side, but now she busied herself re-buttoning it.

Michael wanted to slip his hand around her waist under the soft blue wool, but delayed and lost the opportunity. Whoever won the hand of this precious doll better take care of her, or he.... Useless to speculate. He'd lose her once they got to America. Extraordinary she was and his friend. He should be content with that, but the girl intrigued him more than he could say.

# Chapter 6

*Monday, May 15th, 1841*

Angela retreated to her cabin, where she managed to fake seasickness as an excuse against joining the crowd in the dining hall for two meals. By noon the following day, Aunt Elizabeth requested her company for lunch. Angela's hunger actually demanded more compliance than her aunt's entreaties. She determined to muster whatever courage she needed to rejoin society on the Pannonia.

After all, the nunnery was not an option for her. Although she counted marriage outside of the realm of possibilities in her future, perhaps her aunt would find a use for her in Chicago. Nothing really mattered, now that Michael didn't want her for a wife and mother of his children. Somehow she must speak casually with him.

But Michael didn't appear at noon. After eating a considerable amount if the truth be known, Angela again played with her food, but no Michael Halliday entered the dining hall.

Sister Sophia pinched Angela's arm as she started to leave, whispering. "He only ate breakfast at eleven."

Angela's quick tears caused the good sister to sit down. "A lovers' quarrel?"

"He doesn't want a wife," Angela managed between gulps of unvoiced sobs.

Sister Sophia looked stunned. "I can't believe he's a scoundrel."

"No, not at all." Angela corrected. "He's an artist."

That cheered Sister Sophia up considerably. "Artists often marry, in spite of their intentions."

"Do they?" Angela was embarrassed by the illogical burst of hope she felt.

"I'll pray for you both," the good sister said. "Never give up on true love."

Angela hurried to find her aunt to tell her that lunch did her a world of good. Perhaps Michael was out and about on the promenade deck, too.

Captain Hale saluted her as he rushed to the bow.

The ocean was calm, the engines rumbling along, a few of the sails were holding the wind speeding the ship to its destination. America! Nothing was lost. An entire world of the unknown lay before her, a life of bright sun-filled days, of her own special dreams of a healthy numerous brood. Contentment with the balance of nature and satisfaction with the produce and hard work of farm life, all might be the Lord's will for her. Perhaps she'd raise orphans on a farm. Life would create its own answers for her, surely it would.

Perhaps a man greater than Michael would court her. Angela fought back a wave of despair. Only Michael would do, really. Maybe he would work on his art for a year and then decide to start a family.

Angela resolved to do everything within her power to learn how to be the most important person in Michael Halliday's life.

David Leonard bowed and tipped his hat as he walked toward her.

She smiled at him. "I haven't seen you in the dining hall, Mr. Leonard."

"I was too embarrassed to be seen." A slow smile gained momentum on his face. "You are a pleasure for the eyes."

"Michael told me you got yourself into an awful lot of trouble the night of the storm."

"I did," Mr. Leonard couldn't hide his false pride.

"Stealing a life boat," Angela chided him.

"In the middle of the worst storm Captain Hale has ever witnessed."

"While you were drunk."

Mr. Leonard caught his breath.

"My mother owns a pub in County Kerry, Ireland," Angela explained.

Mr. Leonard relaxed. "That explains your disdain of my panic."

"I could tell you were sincere," Angela dropped her eyes to avoid embarrassing the man further.

"Do you mind if I accompany you around the deck?" Mr. Leonard was on his best behavior, for a minute or two. Finally he couldn't restrain himself. "I heard you socked Michael Halliday in the eye, before the storm."

"I did, didn't I," Angela laughed. "I'm less than the perfect catch." As they rounded the port side, Angela's most troubling thought voiced itself, "How do I fail in convincing people I want as many children as I can have?"

Across from the dining hall entrance on the starboard side, Mr. Leonard leaned against a secured pulley as if he were seriously considering Angela's question. "If you want to work a great kindness on a man, never mention your plans for children."

"But that would be deceitful." Angela took off her bonnet to let the sun and wind have their way with her hair.

"Men are prepared to live with women." Here Mr. Leonard rested his small hands by holding onto the front of his low-cut paisley vest. "You shouldn't presume that they are prepared to live with children."

Angela drew her hair over one shoulder to secure it in the strengthening wind. "Why would they be different from women?"

Mr. Leonard laughed and motioned for Major Billie Compton to join them. "We're discussing the differences between men and women."

"I think we have smaller brains," the Major contributed.

"Never enough brain power to deal with the wiles of women, you mean." Mr. Leonard pounded the Major's back.

* * *

Michael's worst nightmare was happening before his eyes. He hadn't seen Angela McGovern for two days at least during which time she obviously chose to turn her attentions to David Leonard. When Major Compton joined the twosome, Michael's discomfort increased.

Soon they'd all be playing cards and drinking again!

Michael stormed up to the group, knocking the leg of a deck chair which then crashed into a second chair adding more racket when they both collapsed.

"Mr. Halliday," Angela said, putting on her bonnet in response to Michael's frown. "I missed you at lunch."

"Lunch?" Michael repeated.

Sisters Sophia and Josephine with the six novices in tow leaned the dismantled deck chairs against the wall before lining up near the dining room.

"Captain Hale told us to watch for land," the youngest said. Michael recalled her name was Susan.

Sister Sophia apologized, "Don't let us interrupt your discussions. The girls needed an activity and Captain Hale did say at lunch that we might sight land before nightfall."

"Really?" Angela asked, moving to Michael's side. "Are we really that close?"

Her perfume clouded his mind. Michael felt as if some one let hot air out of his balloon of anger. "Land?" He smiled down at her. "I don't know."

All eyes pointed upward to the sailors in the rigging who were indeed keeping watch of the western horizon.

"Nothing yet," one closest to them called.

Michael offered Angela his arm for their customary, circular and somewhat limited stroll. "Could you assist while I shop in New York for the items I won't be able to find in Detroit?"

Angela nodded. "I'd appreciate your help in finding a steamship up the Hudson."

"I'd be happy to be of service to you and your aunt." Michael felt he was making himself useful for his ship family. "Washington Irving's house, Sunnyside, will be the most famous we'll be able to see from the river."

"The writer?"

Michael felt carefree and happy emotions which possessed him whenever Angela McGovern was near. "I read he built his house in 1833 past Yonkers in Tarrytown." He could feel his grin widen. "In the spirit of romanticism, he's added stepped gables, columned chimney stocks, weather vanes, irregular windows, and to make sure we understood his intentions to evoke the early history of the Dutch colony, he added the date 1656 to the cornerstone."

"A bit of vanity that?"

"Well deserved, I think." Michael searched his memory to keep Angela's beautiful green eyes focused on him. "The Locust Grover Tower can be seen next, then the Vanderbilt Hyde Park mansion."

Michael remembered the next columned mansion would be Edgewater, a wedding gift to Margaret Livingston, from her father. Michael definitely did not want to mention the subject of marriage. It would only worry the conversation. Instead he said, "Perhaps we'll be able to take the same packet through the Erie Canal."

"Is that wise?" Aunt Elizabeth waited for them near the group of nuns.

"Wisdom's name is kindness and friends are always kind," Angela said. "Miss Winifred and Mrs. Lazarus might also take the canal route.

"We'll ask," Michael said. A gentle but sustained happiness was taking hold of him.

Angela addressed her aunt. "Mr. Leonard and the Major are settling in New York."

Thank God, Michael prayed earnestly. He didn't think he would be able to remain a gentleman for long if the two gamblers decided to join the group from the Pannonia.

"I'll make arrangements to acquire the Hudson River steamship passage tickets as well as the canal transportation to Detroit." Michael bowed slightly to Angela and her aunt. "If you'll permit me, that is?"

Mrs. Breckenridge hugged her niece. "I'll go ask the sisters if they want to accompany us from Detroit to Chicago."

"Aunt Elizabeth, you remember Winnie Perkins has to care for her parents in Detroit."

"But didn't Mabel Lazarus say she was joining family in Chicago?" Mrs. Breckenridge asked.

They both turned to Michael as if he knew the plans of the older ladies. He was just about to explain he didn't have knowledge of their destinations, when the look-out above made the call.

"Land, Ho!"

Angela threw herself at him, locking her arms around his neck and kissing him soundly on the mouth.

Without meaning to, Michael returned the kiss and hugged her sweet little body to him. It seemed the only way to keep his heart from leaping out of his chest.

Mrs. Breckenridge pulled on the arm he secured around Angela's waist. "Mr. Halliday, Mr. Halliday, you forget yourself."

"Indeed," he said as he kissed Angela once more with his eyes wide open. "The only person I can think of is Angela McGovern."

\* \* \*

Angela could feel the heat of his passion in his kiss. His eyes devoured her face as if he'd never be able to set eyes on her again. When her aunt pulled at his arm, and he repeated his kiss, she felt she could melt into him, hide behind his waistcoat and never come up for air.

During the seconds when he held her close, he'd whispered in her ear. "You're mine, all mine."

With a great swinging motion he spun her around in the air, then sat her down gently next to her aunt. "A thousand apologies," he bowed to her aunt. "I got carried away in the moment."

"I guess you did," Aunt Elizabeth nearly shouted, as she straightened Angela's cloak.

Angela caught a glimpse of Sister Sophia as she herded the young girls around the corner. Smiling she was, and from ear to ear.

Angela never felt such happiness. Even though Michael Halliday had not proposed, not promised undying love, she knew Michael Halliday would never make love to anyone but her.

* * *

Michael stayed with the other passengers as they crowded the rail waiting for their first glimpse of land.

Angela tried to stand next to him, but her aunt squeezed between them.

So Michael talked over her aunt's bonnet, to a happy-faced Angela.

"Look, a bird!" Angela called out.

Captain Hale joined the group. "Calm down people. We won't see the lights of New York until tomorrow morning."

A sigh of disappointment went up.

"If that soon." Captain Hale pointed to the east where dark clouds seemed to be chasing them. "That storm will be on us by nightfall. I've asked for an early supper to be laid. Hopefully, you'll all be in your cabins making ready for your departure by the time the rain gets here."

"So close," Michael heard Angela say.

"We'll be all right," he said. "It's only rain."

* * *

Michael was correct. The storm passed while they were all at supper. By the time the first guests, Mr. and Mrs. D., were ready to leave the dining room, the rain stopped.

Angela counted heads trying to remember each face on the Pannonia's passenger list. The Thomases' baby boy sat on his father's knee while he happily chewed on the lace at his mother's wrist.

Angela's admitted her attention during the days spent on board centered on Michael. She wished she'd spent more time getting to know her aunt.

Sisters Sophia and Josephine dined with three of the novices at their table: the youngest, Susan. Corinth and Rosemary might have been the other two. Angela never did remember who was who. Alice owned the longest nose, but Jean and Etta could have been twins. The three were first to finish and rose with Sisters Ann Marie and Maurine to be the second group out the door.

Angela patted her jumper's pocket as if Michael was safely tucked in there with her lace handkerchief. Sister Sophia informed her that the cloister on Long Island would be the nuns' new home.

Michael predicted correctly, Angela was giving her aunt's address in Chicago to a growing number of people she didn't want to lose contact with. Sister Sophia insisted on knowing when she and Michael would wed.

The sunset lighting up the western windows with a rosy glow drew Angela away from the table. She excused herself to Winnie Perkins and Mrs. Lazarus. They agreed to designate Michael as their trip organizer.

Winnie blushed, "To be in Mr. Halliday's big and capable hands."

Mrs. Lazarus admitted she, "Never liked haggling with pursers."

Supper was sparse: cold meats, cheese and crackers with the last of the fruit on board. Angela swept by the table of men as if they were all invisible. She lost interest in them with the conquest of Michael's better nature. She certainly didn't want to be accused by her aunt of fanning the flames of Michael's desire.

Captain Hale stopped her at the door. He announced to those still in the room, "I promise a hearty breakfast in the morning to wish you all well in America. The ship's cook will be baking all night if he has to."

The Farthings' oldest let out a whoop. His three sisters tittered as their father half-heartedly scolded the boy.

A cheer went up from the rest of the crowd.

Michael waved to her.

"Could I walk you to your cabin, Miss McGovern?" Captain Hale held the door open for her.

"Certainly," she said, nodding to her aunt who watched her leave.

Captain Hale didn't take her arm as they walked slowly toward the bow. The sunset tinted the bottoms of the scurrying clouds a deep purple. Gulls could be heard when the wind shifted in their direction.

Angela took in a deep breath. "Are you able to smell the land yet, Captain?"

The stiff man positioned himself with his back to the sunset, drawing on his pipe, as he watched her. "I'm afraid my nose has been ruined by tobacco," he said. "But my eyes see everything."

Angela's chin went up. "And are you ready then to tell me what you don't like seeing?"

He held up one hand in defense. "Now, now, none of that. I'm the captain yet, you know. What I mean to be telling you is that Michael Halliday's family might be wealthier than he's let on to you."

"I'm sure it's no concern of mine." Angela advanced toward her cabin, but the captain hadn't finished.

"What shall I be telling your mother, when I see her next?"

Now he'd done it, taken her mother's name in vain, as it were. "Well you might drown before you get there, you know."

"Angela."

"I'm sure I don't know nor care what you tattle to my mother." Angela turned the corner and quickened her step. "She'll be believing my letters not your pompous blarney."

Captain Hale raised his hand as if to strike her, but Michael Halliday caught his wrist.

"Captain," Michael said, lowering the man's arm but not letting go. "It seems you're not able to let a month of Sunday's pass without the need for apology to Miss McGovern."

A look of pain crossed the captain's face from the pressure Michael was exerting, before he said between his teeth and the well-bitten pipe stem. "My deepest apologies, again, Miss McGovern. I've overstepped my bounds. I don't know what it is about you that takes over my good sense and manners."

"Could be her unsullied beauty," Michael said as he escorted Captain Hale away from Angela's side of the ship.

Inside her cabin, Angela sat as if moonstruck on the edge of her bunk until Aunt Elizabeth entered.

"What is it?" she wanted to know. "I saw Mr. Halliday nearly pushing Captain Hale to the bow."

Aunt Elizabeth sat down on the bunk and put her arm around her niece's shoulder.

Angela broke down. "He hates me."

Aunt Elizabeth sprang up and rushed to the door.

"Not Michael." Angela sniffed. "Captain Hale."

"Why on earth?" Aunt Elizabeth sat facing her.

"He doesn't know, he said." Angela continued sobbing. "He says I bring out the worst in him." The sobs ceased abruptly and a smile stretched her wet face. "Michael said it was because of my unsullied beauty."

Aunt Elizabeth bowed her head and crossed herself.

# Chapter 7

*Tuesday, May 16th, 1841*

The day of the landing, Aunt Elizabeth bustled about making sure every possession was safely packed away in either their trunks or the hand luggage. "I'm that happy to be home in America," Aunt Elizabeth said. "You'll see for yourself that it's a thriving place."

"Sure, sure," Angela kidded. "And it wouldn't be that you're closer to Mr. Breckenridge each day that passes?"

"You're not telling me what I myself don't know is more than the truth of it." Her aunt hugged Angela before urging her to go on deck.

Angela anticipated her next meeting with Michael, her champion against Captain Hale. Somewhere in the hidden recesses of her heart was the sure knowledge that Michael himself didn't realize. Michael loved her. Angela straightened her bonnet in the morning breeze. She could wait for Michael Halliday to come around.

The south side docks of Manhattan were 50 times more crowded than Liverpool's. Too varied to differentiate, the unknown land smells contrasted sharply with the fresh ocean breezes of the day before. A cacophony of shouts, squeaking machinery, grinding anchor chains and pulleys as well as the constant harangue of hungry sea gulls assailed Angela's ears. Testifying to the extent of brisk commerce, at least 75 steamships were lined up along the long row of piers unloading cargo and passengers.

The morning sky was gray with smoke. A half-finished steeple rose forlornly among the clutter of low tenement buildings. On the street behind the docks, a strange wooden structure, tall enough to qualify as a lighthouse, was too far ashore to be of any practical use. Angela was glad New York was not her final destination. The dark bustling city intimidated her more than she wanted to admit.

Angela spotted Michael chatting with Peter Mulligan, the chap who hollered when he first sighted land. Angela spied as Michael counted out money into the younger man's hand. "Mrs. Breckenridge has ties to the Merchant Exchange Bank on Broadway." Michael pocketed a sizable remaining amount before saying, "if you could take us there first."

"I could," Peter said as he kept his eye on Michael's bulging pocket. "I'll be needing more for renting a carriage, if all four of the ladies are coming along."

Michael transferred a bit more money before he noticed Angela and her aunt. "We'll meet you after breakfast."

Peter jerked his hand in the direction of the dock. "I'll be waiting for you right there."

"Good chap," Michael dismissed him.

"Won't Captain Hale object to your employing one of his seamen?" Aunt Elizabeth asked.

Michael bowed before answering very quietly, after making sure Peter was well down the gangplank. "Captain Hale will be more than happy to stay in his cabin to make our departure as pleasant as possible." Michael then added in a frigid tone, "or I'll have my father buy the Pannonia and make sure Captain Hale never gets another commission to sail."

Angela appreciated the power of money and the amount of funds such a threat involved. "So I've seen the last of that black crow."

Aunt Elizabeth laughed. "And I suppose you've instructed Captain Hale that our County Kerry is out-of-bounds."

"I have," Michael's slow smile endeared him to Angela.

"Michael," she made sure not to look into his black eyes longer than necessary. "What is that wooden lighthouse doing so far from shore?"

"What's that?" His normal method of switching focus amused her. "The Jefferson Market Watch Tower." Michael extended his arm until it reached her waist.

She meant to move away, but Aunt Elizabeth hadn't noticed and Angela felt glued to the spot, as if being designated a part of Michael's world was all the comfort she needed.

He continued speaking, somehow drawing her a step closer to him with each word. "Most of the buildings in the market are wooden. They have been destroyed more than once by fires. When the fire bell rings now, plenty of volunteers show up to fight the flames."

Angela smiled up at him. She only wanted to be consumed by the fires raging deep within Michael.

"Did you notice the unfinished church spire?" The word 'church' caused Michael to drop his hand from her waist.

"I did." Angela tilted her head, as if she wasn't aware of the absence of his hand. "And I suppose you'll be knowing its name."

Michael smiled that teasing grin of his, but he didn't mock her brogue. "Trinity Church. The name of the architect is Richard Upjohn. He's been working on it since 1839."

"That's what happens when you read every daily newspaper in London," Aunt Elizabeth commented on Michael's knowledgeable conversation.

Angela appreciated Aunt Elizabeth's change of heart toward the man. Not that Michael harbored any intention of becoming part of the family, but her aunt's kindness to him did make the day a bit brighter.

* * *

Michael busily prepared to find passage for the growing list of people seeking his help. He tried to keep a much-faded image of the lighthouse and island in his mind. He knew one thing; his money would buy information to find the perfect steamship for travel up the Hudson to the Mohawk River at Albany. There he would arrange for the Erie Canal packet to Lake St. Clair for Detroit.

Michael was first made aware that Angela was watching his transactions with Peter when her rose perfume wafted his way. He concentrated more than usual on the business at hand trying not to be distracted by her presence.

When she asked him about the fire tower, Michael's hand reacted by claiming her waist before he reckoned with his own impropriety. Michael was content not to apologize because the comfort of the gesture was hard to deny. The nonsense about Trinity Church kept her attention for a minute more. He got a grip on himself a moment before Mrs. Breckenridge joined them. She became immeasurably more friendly since Michael protected Angela from Captain Hale's outburst. Angela's rendition no doubt endeared the aunt to him.

* * *

After breakfast, Peter Mulligan appeared in a driver's uniform with a well-appointed brougham and pair of sleek horses. "I've arranged for your luggage to be stored right here," Peter said, indicating the door of a warehouse not two steps from the gangplank. "The horses are safely stabled. You remember Studs Kettle from the ship?"

Indeed Michael remembered the only man on board who came close to his own height. Studs's shoulders and forearms showed powerful muscles earned as a seaman and stevedore.

"Will you be guarding our trunks?" Michael asked, handing the man a sizable donation.

"Until Pete wants them," Studs padlocked the door, behind which Michael noted a collection of carefully stacked luggage and trunks. Studs then crossed his arms for guard duty.

Once Miss Perkins and Mrs. Lazarus joined them in the carriage, the party proceeded to the busy street called Broadway. They easily found the Merchant Exchange Bank that Mr. Breckenridge recommended.

The president of the bank, a Mr. O'Donnell, was acquainted with Angela's uncle in Chicago from lucrative business dealings, according to Angela's aunt.

"Pleased, I am, to be of service to family or friends of Mr. Breckenridge's." Mr. O'Donnell greeted them.

His office in the middle of the hectic bank floor was paneled in rich mahogany. Wall-to-wall windows on all sides of the spacious enclosure allowed the manager to keep track of the various teller transactions. To Michael, the administrative center resembled a lighthouse lookout with the seas of commerce crashing on all sides.

Michael introduced the group of women. "Traveling under my protection, Mrs. Elizabeth Breckenridge and her niece, Miss Angela McGovern." Michael enjoyed saying Angela's name; the sound of it steadied him. "They intend to travel overland to Chicago from Detroit."

Mr. O'Donnell asked his male secretary, a Mr. Stiles, to join them in order to take notes.

Michael repeated the travelers' names and added, "Miss Winifred Perkins will be settling in Detroit. Mrs. Mabel Lazarus also has family in Chicago. I expect she will travel with Mr. Breckenridge's family, once we deliver them safely to Detroit."

"I have more than enough room for you all to stay a night or two with my family until we can arrange a ship up the Hudson to Albany." Mr. O'Donnell moved toward the door. "Mr. Stiles will give your driver the location of my home."

The banker stopped and tapped Mr. Stiles, who was busy with his notepad, on his stooped shoulder. "Make sure the driver takes Mr. Halliday's carriage through Central Park." Mr. O'Donnell stuck out his chest, as if he'd done them a particularly fine favor. "Our Frederick Olmstead designed the park as a respite from all the business traffic."

"Very kind of you, Sir," Michael was much relieved to have the ladies' accommodations for the evening and perhaps the next so generously looked after. "Our luggage is stored at the dock for transfer to the Hudson steamship."

"Fine, fine," Mr. O'Donnell escorted Mrs. Breckenridge from his office with the other ladies trailing. "My secretary is at your disposal to mail any correspondence to Chicago or England."

Michael offered his arm to Angela.

Mrs. Breckenridge slightly frowned at him.

"We have quite a bit of shopping to do," Michael refused to be intimidated by Mrs. Breckenridge. "Shall I have the driver take you ladies to Mrs. O'Donnell's? Angela and I will hail a rental carriage when we finish. Mr. Stiles, will you supply us with written directions?"

"I wouldn't mind resting on an unmoving bed before dinner," Miss Perkins said, then giggled at the implication.

Mrs. Lazarus harrumphed. "Is Mrs. O'Donnell aware of your invitation?"

"Our house is open to travelers." Mr. O'Donnell seemed to understand Mrs. Lazarus' reluctance to intrude. "My wife loves company. She says entertaining will keep her occupied until we start a family."

Mr. O'Donnell blushed slightly after another harrumph from Mrs. Lazarus.

"I promised to help Michael," Angela explained to her aunt, "if he would manage our steamship passage on the Hudson."

"Mr. Halliday wouldn't dare but take good care of your niece," Mrs. Lazarus said.

"I'm not up to shopping, dear, or I would accompany you." Mrs. Breckenridge kissed Angela's cheek. "Mr. Halliday is certainly able to take care of you."

"After you arrive at my home, give your driver instructions about which pieces of luggage you will need for at least two evenings." Mr. O'Donnell kissed Mrs. Breckenridge's hand.

Peter shut the door of the carriage

Michael offered more funds, but Peter waved the money aside.

"You've paid enough, Mr. Halliday." Peter stalled, not climbing up into the driver's seat. "After I get these ladies settled, might I make a side trip to the Tombs, sir?"

Peter took off his cap.

"Has someone in your family been buried here?" Michael didn't think the chap soft-hearted enough to visit a gravesite.

"The Tombs are a prison." Peter set his foot on the carriage step. "My wife's brother has been there for six months, six more to go." He climbed into the driver's seat, as if assured of permission. "I've brought him letters."

"No harm in that, Peter." Angela had overheard. "The ladies can wait for their luggage until you've taken care of your personal business."

Michael felt he should object, but the only wisdom he could count on was kindness, so he nodded his approval of Angela's suggestion.

* * *

From the Broadway bank, Michael and Angela walked to Fifth Avenue in search of a greatcoat and a fitted suit.

"I also require a hat big enough to stay on my head," Michael said.

"Have you thought of clipping off some of your hair." Angela laughed quietly to herself. "Your head would be half as big."

Michael drew her arm closer to his side. "So you don't like my head of premium curls."

"There's such a lot of them." She turned up her nose at his vanity. "I doubt you could be selling them at a profit."

The streets were crowded with shoppers. Her skirt was brushed more than once in the pack of strangers. Angela stopped to admire a baby in a fine wicker perambulator, but Michael dragged her into a haberdashery.

Inside the store, Angela appreciated the quiet. The city streets were noisier than she realized. In the store, the smells of leather and wool seemed to ration out more than their share of the air. A balcony filled with shoppers ran along the second floor. The smells of furniture polish and perfumes caused her stomach to complain. Dust particles danced in strips of sunlight from the front windows.

As Angela reached for Michael's arm to steady herself, she fainted.

* * *

Michael strong-armed the bevy of descending clerks aside. "She only needs a bit of air."

He carried her to the front door, where an enterprising salesman brought a chair. They propped open the door with the chair and Michael gently placed Angela on the seat. He'd seen women in his mother's parlor faint, usually for dramatic affect. How did Angela differ from the rest of the women who chased him?

"Are you better?" Michael asked.

"Such a fuss you're making of me." Angela pushed him away.

A ruby-faced older man commented. "She's a farm girl. I can tell you that." He lectured to his growing audience. "This city air's no good for man nor beast."

Another clerk brought Angela a cool glass of lemonade. "The manager sends his apologies."

"Michael," Angela whispered. "Take my arm. I'm too embarrassed to continue shopping here."

"Plenty of stores," Michael agreed as they proceeded down the boardwalk. "We'll find a smaller one with the windows open."

Although he enjoyed having Angela close to him, he was torn by the force of his attraction to her. He didn't want to wait much longer for a little peace to compose his rattled brain. Michael calculated his arrival on Strawberry Island. Two days waiting for a steamship, two days up the Hudson, perhaps a day on the Mohawk and three in the canal. In Detroit he'd have to shop for supplies and then find another steamship to take him up to at Sauté Ste. Marie, with a final day to reach the island by mail packet. Three weeks at the shortest.

"I feel as if I've only begun to travel to Chicago," Angela said, nearly reading his mind as she plopped different hats on his head.

Michael sat meekly before a full-length mirror in a small store dedicated entirely to men's chapeaux. Angela danced around his stool in her search for the perfect lighthouse-keeper hat.

"Three more weeks before I get to Strawberry Island," Michael said without thinking about the fact that he would miss Angela.

The next hat Angela placed on his head landed with considerable force. Michael took the jammed hat off, then looked closely at his dresser. Angela wiped a tear off her cheek with a quick gesture of her gloved hand. Michael caught her hand. "Angela," he said, pulling her close to his knees. "I'll miss you."

"Not I you," Angela said. "Not a bit of it." She disengaged her hand. "I'll be too busy twirling around in Aunt Elizabeth's string of marriage-broker parlors."

"Dancing on my grave, is it?" Michael captured her waist and leaned in to steal a kiss. Her lips were damp from her tears. He pressed her onto his lap. "Angela, sweetheart, you know I have to paint."

She straightened, patting his vest as she stepped away. "Yes, I know that." She set her bonnet back to its original position. "You'd be the most miserable man on earth, if you didn't allow yourself to bring your dreams to fruition."

Michael stood and drew her to him again, not kissing her but resting his head on the top of her bonnet. Her perfume challenged his resolve to live alone. The softness of her form, the strength of her spirit all tempted him to forget his talent. How he was going to be able to control himself on the long voyage to Detroit?

* * *

They arrived at the O'Donnell's residence with Michael's shopping completed. The guests were already seated for dinner so neither were allotted time to change.

Angela let the butler keep her hat along with her cape. Determining not to gawk at the grand chandelier or the two-story high spiral staircase, she concentrated on Michael as he gave up his packages.

Michael's confidence in the lavish surroundings helped her carry herself with some dignity as they entered the dining room, with a ceiling higher than the Kerry church roof, and the longest table covered in laced damask that she had ever beheld. Of course Michael was unaware of her discomfort. His home in Berkshire probably could compete with the array of candlesticks, china, and glassware.

Angela took a deep breath as they joined the bright assemblage.

Mr. O'Donnell stood as they entered. "Miss McGovern, come sit beside your aunt." He motioned for her to join his end of the table. "Mr. Halliday, my wife and daughter, Teresa, will keep you entertained."

Michael nodded to Mr. O'Donnell's beautiful, black-haired daughter as he secured his seat.

The young woman's shoulders were bare of any covering. Thin gold strands graced her neck and Angela marked the diamonds dangling from the lady's ears.

Angela wished with all her heart for the lost chance to change from her afternoon dress into something equally seductive. Ah, jealousy, she recognized the unusual feeling. It was not a kind thought, so she buried the hatred in memories of Michael's flirting shenanigans on the shopping trip.

As the soup course was cleared, Mr. O'Donnell called to Michael's end of the table. "I found a ship for you. She's called the 'North America.' She has a sister ship the 'South America' which is thirty feet longer. The North America is the faster of the two. She ships out first thing in the morning."

Angela was surprised to note that Michael stopped eating.

"You must excuse me then." Michael rose, somewhat reluctantly from his plate of roast duck. "I need to have our driver transfer the luggage and arrange for the horses."

"Sit, sit," Mrs. O'Donnell said. "We've already attended to that. The ladies will be ready to leave at six in the morning."

"That will get you there in plenty of time," Mr. O'Donnell explained to Angela.

Angela recognized the happiness on her aunt's face. She tried to match the smiles on Winnie and Mabel Lazarus's faces too, but she'd wanted the trip to take as long as possible. A day of delay meant more time with Michael. Would there be enough time to convince him of her worth as his future wife?

Observing Mr. O'Donnell's attractive daughter chat with Michael reminded Angela that danger lurked in alluring competition for Michael even in America.

* * *

*Wednesday, May 17th, 1841*

The enclosed side-paddle wheel of the North America steamer sported freshly painted patriotic American colors of red, white, and blue. Although the promenade deck was necessarily a shorter stroll, Angela's cabin was more spacious than on the Pannonia.

Flicka and Splendor were stabled in bigger stalls too, with more than adequate fresh air and bedding. Everything seemed more spacious in America. Even the sky stretched higher into the realms of heaven.

Did Michael's cabin provide enough head room for him to stand? She remembered his complaint on the Pannonia the night he had rebuffed David Leonard's drunken advances. Traveling the ocean washed away some of Michael's worries and defenses against an intimate friendship, she prayed.

Angela pulled open the sliding glass windows to let the fresh river breezes clear out her city-weary lungs. Angela breathed in deeply. "I wish I owned a singing voice, like Ma's," she remarked to her aunt.

Aunt Elizabeth laughed. "The family used to tell Antoinette the only reason she went to Mass was to show off her voice."

They quietly looked at each other, each remembering their closest relative was alone back in Ireland.

"Now, your ma is happy, Angela." Aunt Elizabeth blew her nose. "Let's not be getting weepy on such a beautiful spring morn."

Angela hugged her. "Have I let you know how much I appreciate your letting me escape from that sad place?"

"More than enough," Aunt Elizabeth kissed her cheek. "We can unpack what we need later. No sense to moping about in here when I could be showing you the most beautiful river in the world."

Angela followed her out of the cabin. "In the world is it? Now whose Irish blarney is showing?"

The first small leaves of spring feathered the trees up the steep slopes of the Hudson River. Among blossoming shrubs and orchards, Angela pointed out weather vanes to her aunt.

The straight tall form of Michael was outlined in pink blossoms. Was it her imagination or had he somehow gotten over his bumbling way of walking? Of course the gentle river current probably accounted for the improvement from his tipsy days of contending with the ocean tossed Pannonia; but some other force held his shoulders in a firmer grip, as if a skyhook was attached to the back of his neck. Whatever the cause, Michael Halliday gained in her estimation on a daily basis.

"Here you are," Michael called to them. "I thought I might need to pound on your door to insist you not miss Sunnyside."

"Michael," Angela asked. "Could it be you're still growing?"

Aunt Elizabeth chided her, "Angela what a personal question you're asking the man!"

Michael laughed that great full laugh of his as if the sun needed brightening. "Not an inch; but I do feel taller when I have no one to compare myself to."

Angela stood on her tiptoes and swiftly kissed his cheek.

"That will humble any man down to his real size," he said.

Aunt Elizabeth regarded them with a less than friendly stance. Her elbows extended as she placed her fists on her hips. "Is this the kind of behavior I'm expected to sanction all the way to Detroit?"

"We are friends, Aunt," Angela stood her ground next to Michael.

"I am to blame." Michael moved toward her aunt.

"If you're going to encourage my niece's affection, knowing full well that you have no intention of marrying the girl," Aunt Elizabeth stepped back as if unduly affected by Michael's charm. "I expect you to allow nothing of a romantic nature to occur."

"Aunt Elizabeth," Angela interrupted. "I refuse to let you insult Michael."

"Should I be scolding you?" Her aunt turned on her.

Angela burst into tears. "Why can't I be friendly to the only man I will ever love?"

"Angela, go to our cabin!" Aunt Elizabeth stomped her foot. "The Earl of Covington, your father, used the same charming tactics to get your mother in a family way."

Michael bowed and withdrew without a word.

"Oh, Aunt." Angela faced a sharp, bleak cliff of the river and her aunt's face. "How could you be that cruel? Michael's been the soul of discretion." In her heart she did know all that kissing on the shopping trip was not entirely her idea. "I'll try to control myself."

"I'm sorry, Angela," her aunt said. "I'll apologize to Michael." She rang her hands. "I try to do what I know is expected; but I've never cautioned a daughter of my own. I couldn't bear it when your mother's heart was broken, and I don't want to see you suffer needlessly."

Angela hugged her aunt. "I'm sorry, too. Michael draws me to him; but I certainly know he has other plans."

"That's what you need to keep in mind, dear." Aunt Elizabeth turned in the direction of Michael's departure. "I'll clear up any misunderstanding right now, if you promise not to declare your affection again, until he asks for your hand."

Angela promised and then guiltily gazed at her aunt as she rounded the corner of the promenade. What malarkey she was selling to her dear aunt. There was no way she intended to leave Michael any chance of not recognizing any and all of her charms while she yet breathed or he was within her bailiwick. Walking on the devil's side she was. She hoped she would somehow be immune to the errors her mother made when love overwhelmed her better senses.

* * *

Michael re-affirmed his honorable intentions to Mrs. Breckenridge. "I should have asked your permission to write to Angela." He looked into her eyes and gave his most innocent smile to accompany the words. He felt like a child lying to his parent. "She's already given me her address while we were onboard the Pannonia. I'll return it to you with a great deal of regret, but I don't want to lose any of the trust that you placed in me."

"Let's forget about my bad manners," Mrs. Breckenridge said, taking Michael's arm and heading him back in Angela's direction.

"There she is," Michael called to Angela. "Have we missed Sunnyside?"

Angela stepped close to her aunt before pointing to the wisteria-clad house across from them. "Michael says Mr. Irving chiseled the year 1696 on a corner stone to secure the house a place in the Dutch colony history books." Angela proudly announced.

"Folly of all kinds," Mrs. Breckenridge commented. "Mr. Breckenridge provided me with a sensible brownstone facing Lake Michigan, the deed is in my name free and clear of all debt." As if somewhat taken aback by her own bragging, she added quietly, "The winds off the lake still surprise me." Then she laughed her good Irish laugh. "Lost more than one bonnet, I have."

"1656," Michael corrected. "And I believe it's forged in wrought iron. Have you heard of Rip Van Winkle?"

Angela shaded her eyes to clearly see Sunnyside. "The Earl of Covington apparently couldn't stand the idea of having a stupid daughter. Besides my horse, my tutor checked on my schooling once a month with a trunk of books. I know the name of Knickenbocker and learned most of what I know about Columbus from Washington Irving."

"The house is called a literary phenomenon," Michael explained to Mrs. Breckenridge.

How was it possible that Angela's attraction increased exponentially? A bonnet he didn't know she owned revealed bits of white straw beneath a collection of yellow fabric roses. The ridiculous hat hung from her hands by its lace-trimmed ribbons. Her day dress matched. His attention was drawn to the snowy latticed bodice of her billowing, sleeved blouse which was layered with a yellow short-sleeved jacket. Angela's small size didn't require her to dress primly. Instead the bright colors of her striped skirt seemed to add an inch or two to her height. Michael suspected her footwear added substantial inches to the heels.

"You are dressed in the day's best colors," Michael nodded respectfully to Mrs. Breckenridge, as if to include her in his summary.

Mrs. Breckenridge smacked his back with her parasol. "What other homes will we see?"

"I'm afraid I don't recall." Michael bowed to Miss Perkins and Mrs. Lazarus as they became members of the group. "But the Locust Grove Tower is one of the sights farther up the river."

Angela seemed to vie for his attention. "When will we see Hyde Park?"

"I'm not sure we'll be able to see it from the river," Michael said.

"The Vanderbilt Mansion is across the river from the Tower," Mrs. Lazarus added. "Perhaps all these leaves will make us miss it."

"Have you been there?" Angela asked.

"Of course, not." Mrs. Lazarus said. "I've only read about it in the gossip columns."

"What about Olana," Michael asked, trying to contain his excitement.

"No," Mrs. Lazarus said, "but I hear the artist, Church I think his name is, traveled to Jerusalem and used Moorish influences to decorate the rooms."

* * *

Not until the next day did Angela find any reason to rue her decision to never love anyone but Michael Halliday.

By late afternoon they passed the Tower and the position of Hyde Park, although not even a chimney was sighted from the river. But on the east side of the Hudson, a grand columned mansion presented itself at the top of a wide slanting lawn.

"Oh," Angela clapped her hands. "And who built this one?"

Michael's wide shoulders towered above all of the ladies' spring bonnets.

"Mr. Livingston, one of the original buyers of the land from the natives." Michael appeared uninterested in the lavish estate.

"Very old money," Mrs. Lazarus added. "He built it for his daughter, Margaret." At this point in her conversation she bent over to quietly add to Angela's aunt. "For a wedding present."

Miss Perkins added her giggling opinion, "Either he was happy to be rid of her or recognized that her husband would never be able to provide such a palace."

"Perhaps she was inordinately loved by her father." Michael said, sadly. "My father would build such a place for my sister, if she were alive."

Mrs. Lazarus spoke again, "But then, Mr. Halliday, you have the wherewithal to purchase a lavish home for your bride." At this she looked in Angela's direction and smiled.

Michael took her aunt's arm, leaving Angela standing with the other women as he proceeded to accompany his aunt away from the group.

Angela blushed at the perceived insult.

Winnie Perkins had the effrontery to pat her arm. "There, there, dear. Men are especially difficult to convert to marriage."

However, as the trip continued and the other passengers traded sight-seeing for an evening's rest, Angela was surprised to find Michael standing close behind her. She first sensed his presence, then his breath in her hair as he kissed the top of her head.

"Angela," Michael grasped her shoulders, turning her to face him. He raised her chin to kiss her lips.

All was forgiven. Every inch of her knew him as if his hands sculpted her body's framework, where each part reacted with warmth from her toes to the roots of her hair. Still she couldn't let him get away with hurting her feelings in front of others.

"Did you mean to embarrass me?"

Michael tried on his innocent face.

Angela wasn't giving in that easy to her charmer. "When you walked away with my aunt at the first mention of the word marriage?"

"Dreadfully sorry." Michael drew her to him with his arms securely around her shoulders. "Didn't want to give the ladies the wrong impression of my intentions."

"Yes," Angela struggled slightly in his embrace. "Are you convinced marriage will never take place in your life?"

"Of course not." Michael let her go, after a quick kiss and nibble of her bottom lip.

She stood unanchored when he let her go. Nevertheless she comforted herself with the idea that she was gaining ground.

The beginning of the lights of Albany could be seen to the left of them.

"If the ladies were present," Michael placed her gloved hand on his chest. "I would declare that Alexander Hamilton married Elizabeth Schuyler in that mansion on that hill to the right in 1780."

"A likely promise," Angela felt lightheaded near him. "With no soul in sight."

"Our Maker knows our hearts," Michael said, pulling off her short glove and tenderly kissing her fingertips.

"The Lord keep me safe from the likes of you," Angela laughed then drew her hand away before running off to her lonely bed.

\* \* \*

Michael was not unaffected by Angela's words of censure. The lass was a nobler person than he. Trifling with her affections would never do.

He tried to summon up Strawberry Island in his head with its grand lighthouse and steep jagged rocks. The loneliness of the night didn't allow the dream to shine in rosy colors as in the past. So Michael concentrated on the number of art supplies stashed in the bottom of his trunk. The Erie Canal would be even quieter than the river. He'd be able to remain steadier. Mrs. Breckenridge might even permit him to sketch her niece. That would allow all the time he needed to catch her essence forever. Portable she would become on a bit of paper all the way to his island, for a keepsake in his ideal world of solitude.

Michael retired to a fitful sleep. All was not well in the world of dreams.

# Chapter 8

*Wednesday, May 24th, 1841*

Angela's morning view brought tears to her eyes. On the north end of the thriving town of Albany, where the side-paddle steamer docked at the Erie Canal's entrance to the Mohawk River, a slight fog kept the greens of the trees and lawns misty and detached as if Ireland had transported itself across the ocean.

Ma could be calling her name shortly, "Angie girl, come in now from gazing o'er the fields." The comfy utterance would have ended with, "The bar needs its tending."

Instead Aunt Elizabeth touched Angela's glove as it gripped the rail of the 'North America' freshly arrived up the Hudson. "Albany reminds me of the Ring of Kerry, too."

"It's all that green on the soggy hills," Angela turned away from the sight. "Will I always miss Ma this much?"

"If you didn't, Angela, we'd be thinking something was wrong with your heart." Aunt Elizabeth straightened the hem of the short coat Angela was wearing.

"Where's the master of our fate?" Aunt Elizabeth surveyed the wide dock that the ship was tethered to.

"If not our fate," Angela laughed, "at least the next step of our trip?"

Michael Halliday appeared right behind them.

Angela worried that he might have heard their slightly mocking tones. Big as he was, Michael walked as softly as a cat.

"You always materialize without a sound," Aunt Elizabeth commented.

"My mother," Michael said, as if that explained everything; to stop their continuing stares, he added, "She was strict about clod-hopping, as she called it."

Angela's memory of her muddy field boots brought heat to her cheeks. "Clod-hoppers have their place."

"I'm off to reserve a hotel for us and a livery for the horses." Michael tipped the new cap Angela picked out for him in New York. He bounded down the gangplank to catch a hansom to Main Street.

Angela secured her aunt's arm in hers. "He could have asked me to accompany him."

"You two are together enough as it is." Aunt Elizabeth stopped to get a better look at Angela. "I worry about you both."

"I'm going to be all right, Aunt," Angela said, hardly believing it herself. "I know most artists' don't include a wife in their plans. I'm certainly not going to let Mr. Halliday take advantage of me. The Lord gave me the good sense to learn from, at least, my dear ma's mistakes."

"Oh, I hope that's the truth of it," Aunt Elizabeth said. "My sister tried to hold out, but the Earl, your father, was so attractive. They say in Kerry that the English Earl of Covington could charm the bluebells off the flower stems and leave them all happy to wave after him, bare of any buds."

"Well, he's still a friend to Ma, as far as my upbringing goes."

"He is," Aunt Elizabeth said. "But Angela, you know, your mother could have been happier raising more than one child, as well as having a man of her own about the house."

Angela nodded. "I'm only hoping I can at least raise some kind of a family." She looked off into the distant horizon over the rooftops of Albany. "Maybe orphans will need a farm to grow up on."

"Orphans?"

"Well, I won't be marrying anyone but Michael Halliday and that's a fact as sure as your bonnet." Angela kissed her aunt's cheek.

Aunt Elizabeth swiftly untied her bonnet strings and threw the pretty thing into the Mohawk River where it bobbed about for a minute before slipping under the dock.

"What have you done, now?" Angela clapped her hands.

"I hope I've given you reason to re-examine your decisions, Angela McGovern!" With that her aunt stomped off, probably to secure another bonnet from her trunk.

Angela sat down on the nearest deck chair. What would she do without Michael? She didn't want to think about it. The Erie Canal trip was days long and there would be tonight in a hotel. Surely there was time for Michael to see the qualities in her that would make a good mother for his children, a partner for his future, a wife.

The Lord wouldn't give her this much affection for the man if it wasn't right. Surely. The thought of her ma's good heart left her doubting her own convictions.

"Lord, have compassion on us all," Angela prayed, doubling up her fists rather than folding her hands in submission.

* * *

Michael tripped as he tried to hop out of the cab to vault an inappropriately placed puddle. He held onto a handy hitching post and saved his knees from contact, but his shoes and the back of his cuffs were less than perfect.

"Which way is the hotel?" he asked the driver who was struggling to keep his grin from breaking into laughter.

"To the right, four doors down."

Michael paid the fare but refused to add a tip. "Enjoy the rest of the day," he said instead.

The storefronts were freshly painted. The Montgomery Hall Hotel's brick façade and tented entrance left no doubt that the eloquent interior would satisfy the four ladies under his charge. Michael enjoyed caring for all the details of their transport. He'd memorized the number of trunks and crates each traveled with because his duties included making sure all were safely aboard the North America for their trip up the Hudson. In a way, he wished their scenic trip up the Hudson River hadn't concluded. Angela was within reach. Not that she wouldn't be on the packet through the Erie Canal, but each mile closer to Detroit meant their time together was drawing to a close.

His plans of sketching on Strawberry Island were still secure, but he didn't dwell as much on the solitariness of the job as lighthouse keeper. Michael constantly drew his thoughts away from the lonely aspect of the job to concentrate on the artistic side of the equation. Like right now he was thinking about the line of curl escaping behind Angela's sunhat. He'd appreciated the soft golden lock on the back collar of her yellow jacket.

Michael was more than content to be kept busy arranging the comings and goings of the four women and two horses. The chores helped keep his mind away from uncharted feminine territory.

"We will, no doubt, need a dray wagon," he told the Montgomery desk clerk, "Each lady has luggage enough to fill a small room."

Michael wasn't exaggerating. Mrs. Lazarus was the worst offender, if numbers counted. Fifteen wooden cartons of books and an additional ten of unwieldy size contained cherished paintings collected from her deceased mother's estate. Michael wished she'd possessed the foresight to sell them in London, but apparently the sentimental value required their being transported to her home in Chicago. Mrs. Lazarus traveled with ready letters of credit to pay for the extra tonnage, but Michael found three trunks of clothing for such an elderly woman beyond his ability to fathom. After all Angela, in all her finery, traveled with one trunk and a small portmanteau.

Angela knew how to handle everything. Michael was sure she could have managed the trip entirely alone, without either his help or her aunt's chaperon. He guiltily fixated on the idea of Angela without her aunt in the hotel. She might need a warm glass of milk at night which only he could deliver at such a late hour. She would be wearing….

"Mr. Halliday, Mr. Halliday, which do you prefer?"

Michael was jarred back to awareness in order to pick out available rooms for the ladies. Gentleman that he was, he took the first-floor room and let the ladies have two suites on the third floor. Each suite included a sunny sitting room with windows facing the river. Bedrooms on each side of the smaller main rooms were endowed with individual lavatories.

"Will you secure us passage on the Canal?" Michael asked.

"Mr. Halliday, I would suggest that you take the ladies with you to pick out a canal packet. They vary in size and accommodations. Ladies appear to complain most about improper ventilation at meal times. If that is of any use to you?" The clerk backed away, happy with his generous tip.

Michael then toured the room he reasoned Angela might pick. The coverlet and curtains were snowy white with strips of bright green flounces. He entered the bath and rubbed his hand inside the copper bathing tub, just to make sure it was clean enough for her. His brain's games were not fooling the rest of his members. Michael fled down the winding stairway of the hotel to make luncheon arrangements for the group. Work yet needed to be done, happily for his sanity's sake.

* * *

"Oh, I'm so pleased with my room, Mr. Halliday," Winnie Perkins giggled into her luncheon napkin.

"Quite adequate." Mrs. Lazarus said as she ladled most of the corn-relish onto her plate.

"Are you staying in a different hotel," Aunt Elizabeth asked, in less than a gratifying tone.

"What? No." Michael straightened his tie, a habit he only exhibited in front of Angela's aunt.

"Is there a laundry?" Angela asked to alleviate his discomfort.

"Yes, Yes." Michael smiled, easing his shoulders back against his chair. "If you ask at the desk they will arrange a maid to follow you to your room and return all the items by morning."

"Splendid," Aunt Elizabeth said. "And, Michael, I want you to know I appreciate your efforts to make our journey a pleasant one."

"Happy to be of service." Michael beamed at her aunt and then turned his merry eyes on Angela.

"Would you all," here he carefully included the group, "care to walk along the canal. The desk clerk thinks my skills insufficient to the task of picking the most comfortable canal packet for our trip."

"What fun!" Winnie Perkins clapped her hands.

Mrs. Lazarus preferred to nap.

Aunt Elizabeth considered the options for a moment or two, then asked, "Winnie, may I impose on you to chaperon these two friends. I'm sure after this heavy meal a nap on a bed unmoved by any water: ocean, river, or canal would be best for my aging bones."

"Happy to," Winnie blushed and giggled.

* * *

Angela ran up the flight of stairs to get their parasols. She chose the green room but couldn't know that Michael manhandled her bathing tub.

On her quick descent down the steps Aunt Elizabeth halted her. "Caution now, Angela. Don't forget the paths that angels fear to tread."

"Not I, Aunt." Angela quickly added a prayer to the Virgin Mary to keep herself safe from the ploys of Michael Halliday.

Michael gave one arm to Winnie and one to Angela as they toured the dockyard. Each boat was represented as far superior to any other. Individual captains and proprietors gave tours of their remarkably different packets. All promised immediate departure until they learned the group would be staying overnight in Albany.

Angela used her olfactory senses in her decision process. Cleanliness furnished an absence of smells while perfumed candles or lingering overtures from bleach convinced Angela that all was not as immaculate as she and the other ladies would desire.

One enterprising cook left a steaming teapot full of cinnamon sticks to mask the musty odor of unwashed linens and the damp resulting from freshly patched leaks in the boat. Michael told her there was no fear of drowning since the canals were only waist high in most places. Nevertheless, Angela passed on to the next boat.

In one packet Angela lifted up a pillow only to set a collect of small bugs scurrying for cover. On several of the floating fleet her first step inside their large cabins provided all the information she needed. Smoke and remnants of food smells let her know sleep would be impossible amidst the pungent rubble from previous passengers.

Eventually, the 'Tennessee' canal packet was engaged for passage with Captain Petree, who promised not to let more than the five of them on board. The newly outfitted boat was almost as wide as the canal. Two huge dray horses were harnessed in tandem for the job of dragging the boat along the canal. Splendor and Flicka could be tethered behind the work horses for safe passage down the canal.

Captain Petree told them he hoped to travel with as many as 30 passengers during the heightened summer business. The narrow three tiers of suspended-shelf bunks could be supplemented by folding cots when the table legs were removed and the table flattened.

Angela worried about the cleanliness of the table with all that traffic. Even now with only five people on board, she asked about the privacy of the sleeping spaces. Michael re-assured her. They would stack all of Mrs. Lazarus' freight as a partial wall in front of the one bunk he would be happy to use in the aft section. The four ladies would be quite comfortable in the forward part of the big cabin.

Slanting-inward windows, not as large as those on the Hudson steamer, did slide open easily. "Of course we could keep the door open to the deck." Angela considered her solution the best way to handle the effluvia of evening chamber pots.

After the cook on board was given directions for Mrs. Lazarus' love of fresh fish by Winnie Perkins, she explained for the couple. "I do so try to limit the grievances Mabel has to endure on the trip. The days are much more pleasant without constant negative details."

"I'm sure that's true," Angela said, uncomfortably aware of the irritated tones in Mrs. Lazarus's complaints when all was not perfect.

Michael asked for tea to be brought to the small table area in the open boarding section of the boat.

To provide a bit of shade for the older lady, Angela placed her parasol and Winnie's along the easily reached roof line. "Please, Winnie, sit under here." Angela removed her own hat and added, "I miss being out in the fields with the warmth of the sun un-mixing my brains."

After tea and peach cobbler, Winnie nodded off.

"Forgetting her duties," Michael whispered close to Angela's sensitive ear.

Angela placed her finger on his mouth not to wake Winnie, but the shock of the inviting softness of his upper lip caused her to give him a quick kiss.

Michael responded by placing his huge arm in her lap. He didn't take her hand or caress her knee. He just let the weight of his arm unnerve her.

"Please, Michael," she said without moving away from the delicious feelings her body was enjoying, "Tell me what our trip will be like on the canal."

He moved closer arranging the arm which had lain in her lap to support Angela's back against the boat. "Hawthorne first wrote glowing articles about the canal being built by 'an enchanter, who waved his magic wand from the Hudson to Lake Erie and united them by a watery highway.' Hawthorne's views of the artificial river changed after he'd taken an unpleasant trip."

"What did he say then?" Angela asked, not minding Winnie's soft snores.

"He complained about the trees damaged by draining of the swamps. I suspect we'll see the broken trees. They're supposed to be a ghostly white in the dark."

Winnie awoke fully cognizant of the fact that she failed as chaperone. "Oh, please, let's return to the hotel." Seemingly embarrassed to imply anything untoward happened, she added, "I do usually need a nap in the afternoon."

Michael continued his comments of Hawthorne's view, "Hawthorne called the canal works along with the railroads, 'the encroachments of civilized man.'"

"But how else could enough farmers settle all these lands?" Angela waved her arm to the west. "America seems to have no end to the available land for farming."

"The Pacific Ocean ends the country," Michael said, then added sadly. "Most good things come to an end."

"Not our friendship, Michael Halliday," Angela stated boldly enough for Winnie Perkins to frown. "Or ours, Winnie Perkins."

Winnie didn't giggle. She pressed Angela's hand to her lips. "As long as I'm alive."

* * *

Michael refused to recite any more of the negative comments he read about the Erie Canal passage. Hopefully limiting the number of passengers would alleviate most of the problems.

He kept secret descriptions of the sudden thumps at night when the craft came too close to the sides of the canals or when boats rammed each other during the dark hours. He would have to caution the ladies about not standing in the open area, less they be injured by the low farmers' bridges spanning the fields. He especially would have to be careful because of his height, even seated.

***

*Thursday, May 25th, 1841*

The next day as they ate their first meal riding the Erie Canal, Michael believed the raw sight of all the space her crates demanded inside the communal cabin may have caused Mrs. Lazarus to give them details of her plans. "Ann Arbor is a lovely town, one day west of Detroit by train."

Mrs. Lazarus possessed impeccable manners which included vying successfully for her share of any amount of food served. Michael found he was often left to finish off the bread Angela made sure he was offered, if he wanted his stomach not to complain before their next repast.

"The Ladies' Library has freshly been established," Mrs. Lazarus continued. "The women are planning to have an architect propose a building on the main thoroughfare. Huron, I believe the street is called, after the river."

Winnie folded her napkin and then her hands in her lap. Michael wondered why she insisted on only wearing pink tones, but lacked the courage to inquire. She was a dove of a woman, cheerful yet quiet. She would make the perfect nurse for her parents.

Why she stayed in Europe when the rest of the family emigrated to Detroit remained a mystery. Michael wasn't above imagining she waited behind for a gentleman's spoiling attentions. She didn't wear the black required in society, like Mrs. Lazarus. Angela seemed very fond of the older woman but took a mothering role in the relationship. Winnie Perkins reminded him of a child, too. She deported herself as if she had suddenly awoken from Rip Van Winkle's dream without knowing how to behave in adult society.

Mrs. Lazarus tapped the table to regain Michael's attention. "My husband's clothing business in Chicago requires my attention. Two of the trunks contain samples of Paris gowns I intend to have copied for the American market."

"Did your mother paint?" Angela asked Mrs. Lazarus, while somehow keeping eye contact only with Michael.

No wonder Angela's aunt worried about the two of them.

"She did, but my father was the collector," Mrs. Lazarus amended. "My home in Chicago is bursting with paintings. Every wall in every room is covered from ceiling to chair height with an eclectic array of styles." She finished off the only remaining dessert portion before adding. "The book shelves are equally over stocked." As if to make sure everyone was listening, Mrs. Lazarus kept silent for an inordinate amount of time; she then pronounced, with a great sweep of her arm which nearly toppled the wine decanter, "I'm leaving all of my family's estate in Ann Arbor."

Then she inclined toward Angela's aunt, "My husband doesn't need to know how much my parents were worth. Men are so competitive, you know."

Mrs. Breckenridge's eyes were appreciatively wide at the generosity of their traveling companion. "You're incredibly philanthropic."

Mrs. Lazarus then spoke quietly to Miss Perkins. "If your parents no longer require your services in Detroit, in the future…" Here she was careful to pat Winnie Perkins' hand. "The job of curator is a lucrative position for a collection of this size. I'd be willing to pay you a generous wage."

Miss Perkins dissolved into tears. It took the entire company a considerable amount of time to attend to her with glasses of water, handkerchiefs, comforting pats and hand-holding, before Winnie answered. "I'd be more than happy to take the position, if…no, when my duty to my parents has been relieved."

"Settled," Mrs. Lazarus stated. "The collection will stay in storage in Ann Arbor until you're able to be employed."

Winnie and Angela embraced in happiness.

"And Angela," Mrs. Lazarus regained the center of attention. "I did bring mother's watercolor paints and paper supplies along, in case any passengers wanted to spend travel time pursuing art."

Winnie still clasped Angela's hands. "Oh let's try," she said. "We can play with them and see what happens."

Angela gave Michael a questioning look.

"I think that's a great idea," he said. "The boat is steady enough to allow painting."

"We should all give it a go," Angela pulled at her aunt's skirt. "Don't you agree, Aunt Elizabeth."

"No harm in that," Angela's aunt smiled her gratitude to Mrs. Lazarus.

Michael promised himself never to condemn another human being as harshly as he had Mrs. Lazarus. He'd judged her as a hoarding miser when in fact she was the soul of generosity. It was a good thing there was a God to keep above the fallibility of human opinions.

\* \* \*

Angela and the group aboard the 'Tennessee' viewed the Rexford aqueduct with due respect.

"These are reminiscent of the ruins of the Roman aqueducts I visited in Italy," Mrs. Lazarus said.

"It's a marvel, men could think up such a clever way to ford the river at cross purposes with the canal," was Aunt Elizabeth's evaluation.

"Indeed," Michael said. "But you've seen these before?"

"Yes and there's more to see," Aunt Elizabeth slipped her arm around Angela's waist. "By half the more impressive than these."

"You mean double, aunt."

"No more than that, Angela," Her aunt seemed carried away with previous memories. "You've only seen this and the small locks we've passed. Up ahead there's more than one sight to make you glad you've come this way."

"Indeed," Mrs. Lazarus said. "She's not exaggerating in the least."

"Not that an Irish lass would ever use her powers of blarney," Michael tried to make a joke but the ladies didn't respond.

The evening was its own adventure. The unfamiliar noises of scraping the sides of the canal, the sounds of animals moving along the shore and the Captain's horn calling the lock keepers to help with their passage combined to deny Angela more than a few minutes rest at a time.

One noise Angela looked forward to she never heard. She expected to be kept awake by the snores of Michael Halliday. Either he didn't make noises in his sleep, he didn't sleep at all, or the crates of Mrs. Lazarus' belongings kept the noises at bay. Her curiosity about his reclining, vulnerable body added to her restlessness during the night.

* * *

*Friday, May 26th, 1841*

At breakfast, Angela and her companions appreciated the Little Falls aqueduct linking nature and civilization. The magnificent cliffs to the west reflected rose hues from the sunrise. The granite stones of the canal shone in competition with nature's heights. Sloping hills east of the river were sprinkled with rows of neat brick homes on each side of a winding road which led into the surrounding dark forest. Even the brilliant falls under the bridge sent up a sparkling pink spray.

"I've never seen the like." Angela clapped her hands.

Mrs. Lazarus remarked, "It's enough of God's glory to keep a person from eating."

Angela noted that wasn't the case, but even Aunt Elizabeth seemed to think today's view better than her previous experience. "There's nothing like it, Angela. It's a miracle God and man have made to bless your journey in the new world."

Michael stood spellbound by the beauty.

"Do you need your sketchbooks?" Angela asked.

"We'll be gone by the time I fish them out." A tear slid down his cheek. Angela empathized, knowing the glories of form and color would affect his sensitive nature. "Architecture has triumphed over sublime nature." Michael shook himself, then glanced in Angela's direction. "Within the reach of my senses is all the beauty a man should expect in one lifetime."

"Mercy!" Winnie had overheard. "Mrs. Breckenridge, our Englishman has caught the blarney bug."

"Oh, I'm serious, Miss Perkins," Michael said, taking Angela's hand in his. "Mrs. Breckenridge, since I've missed the opportunity to sketch the aqueduct and these cliffs, may I have your permission to sketch your niece?"

Angela did not waste the opportunity to stay affixed in Michael's attention to turn around for her aunt's expression.

Instead she heard Aunt Elizabeth's reverent reply. "Of course. I can see no harm in that."

* * *

Michael couldn't seem to stop ordering her about once the sketching began an hour later. Angela hadn't considered the idea before. Was he shy about displaying his talents.

"You must not speak for a while, Angela." Michael placed a cup of tea within her reach. "Try to give me plenty of warning when you need to move."

Mrs. Lazarus and Aunt Elizabeth stopped their conversation as if they, too, were under Michael's dictate.

Winnie used Mrs. Lazarus' watercolors for hurried likenesses of Splendor, Flicka, and the dray horses as they pulled the packet along the shore.

Angela held up her hand. "Michael, tell us about your family."

Aunt Elizabeth happily pursued the subject. "How long has your family lived in Berkshire?"

Michael's piercing eyes didn't waiver as he flourished his pen. "My father's name is new to Berkshire society. I think he met my mother in London. He runs a very lucrative clockwork factory there. Actually I'm supposed to be under his apprenticeship to take over the business."

Angela felt she might float away with happiness. She'd worn her best white gown, the one intended for her coming-out party in Chicago. Aunt Elizabeth decided the weather permitted wearing the elegant dress for Michael.

When she styled and pinned Angela's curls up and away from her neck, her aunt speculated on the future. "I feel as if I'm outfitting you for your wedding."

Angela held the thought as she swept up the short step to the deck outside. Michael's first view of her was obstructed by Captain Petree's bulky frame. Michael was forced to step to the side to get a better look. Then Angela saw Michael's expression of high approval. No matter how his sketch turned out, his view of her would stay in his mind for as long as he lived. No bride could want for more, she told herself.

"Your mother?" Mrs. Lazarus primed the pump for more information from Michael.

"The Cromwell family owned land in Berkshire for as long as the town's been incorporated," Michael said. "Ten-thousand acres. My uncle gambled, and the Cromwells would have lost the land if father hadn't bailed them out from the debts."

"That much?" Winnie asked. She busily wound and unwound a strip of pink satin ribbon.

"Did you ever own a kitten?" Angela couldn't help asking.

"Oh, yes," Winnie said. "But I couldn't bring it. Father hates cats."

With that, Angela's happiness disappeared. She felt sad for Winnie's cat, sad for the people Winnie left behind, sad for her mother who couldn't see her in all this finery, sad at the fact that Michael needed not to marry her. Tears slid down her cheeks. She hoped Michael might not see them and refused to wipe them away.

"Angela," Michael said, putting his pen down. "What has happened?"

"Oh, nothing!" she lied, but she couldn't sit still any longer. She hurried into the cabin and slammed the door on them all.

Aunt Elizabeth was the first to enter tentatively.

"I'm sorry," Angela said. "I'll just wipe my face. Tell Michael I'll be out in a minute.

"You needn't sit under his scrutiny," Aunt Elizabeth said. "None of us want to witness unhappiness in the making."

"I'm happy," Angela said. "Winnie's cat ruined my mood."

"Sure, and there's not another thing to bother either one of us." Her aunt shook her head.

Angela ignored her and picked up her skirts to re-enter the world of sunshine and mirth. "Michael, don't be capping that ink pot. I was feeling sorry for Winnie's cat and Ma." Angela resumed her seat and looked into his eyes.

Sadder they were, the eyes of Michael, the man she loved and couldn't have for as long as he continued to want to be alone to pursue his art.

Mrs. Lazarus intervened, "Michael, now tell us about Strawberry Island."

"In Lake Superior," Michael said to Captain Petree who seemed finally interested in more than his view of Angela.

"My correspondence with the Captain of the mail boat to the island described the lighthouse as sitting on a high bluff over the lake."

"Did you know that Lake Huron is twenty-five feet above Lake Superior?" Captain Petree asked.

"They will have to make locks at Sauté Ste. Marie, eventually," Mrs. Lazarus said.

"Now they have to carry all the tonnage around the falls," Michael said, engrossed in his appraisal of Angela and his sketch pad.

Angela relaxed, resplendent in her ball gown, happy to be the center of Michael's attention while his voice comforted her beyond his words. He was, after all, sketching her so he would have her likeness on his island sabbatical. People needed time alone to sort out and explore their feelings without input from the people who love them and might influence decisions.

'Michael,' she whispered in her brain to her admirer, 'Michael, I belong to you. Now and forever.'

\* \* \*

Before the light failed after dinner, Michael made four sketches of Angela McGovern. He slipped the best under the last sheet of his sketch book and presented one to Mrs. Lazarus and one to Winnie Perkins.

"I know good art," Mrs. Lazarus said. "And this is good. Angela, your friend is very talented."

"Thank you, ma'am," Michael said. "I value your opinion."

"And yours," Michael bowed as he presented Angela with her copy. "I hope, Mrs. Breckenridge, that I'll be allowed to keep sketching."

Michael contemplated the frown line start between her eyes. "The boat moves so slowly in the canal, and I need the experience," he pleaded.

Angela's aunt smiled. "If Angela doesn't mind sitting still for the entire trip."

"I'm lazy enough to let people wait on me." Angela joined in on the fun. "Thank you, Michael. I'll always treasure your view of me…on the Erie Canal."

Winnie tried to collect her watercolor depictions of horses, but Aunt Elizabeth held them up for everyone's inspection. "You've captured their spirits," she said.

"Winnie, you didn't tell us you were so accomplished." Michael kissed the brow of Miss Perkins.

"My friend in Bath painted in oils." Miss Perkins surveyed her hands. "He let me clean his brushes, and I sat behind him as he drew his models."

"You were a model student," Mrs. Lazarus said. "She's quite talented."

"I want you each to keep one of your horses," Winnie said.

"I'll treasure it," Angela said.

Michael carefully packed his away. "I've never received such a beautiful gift," he said, truly touched at the splendid rendering of his stallion.

Michael was surprised that they reached Syracuse by nightfall. "Captain Petree, I thought we changed boats for Oneida Lake."

"A year ago the trip would have been longer," the captain stated. "I do need to let the cook buy more supplies, so the packet won't be moving for a few hours."

"Could we stroll about for a while?" Winnie asked.

"Go to it," Captain Petree said. "I'll be here to watch your belongings."

"Shall we?" Mrs. Lazarus asked Mrs. Breckenridge.

Angela's aunt shook her head no. "You and Winnie go ahead. I'll just help my niece pack this dress away."

"Michael, wait for us, please?" Angela asked.

"I've no one else to please," Michael said as he put away his precious ink.

* * *

*Saturday, May 27th, 1841*

The evening after they passed the breath-taking sights at Lockport, where the deep canal trench on the route to Buffalo had employed thousands upon thousands of men working for 37 different construction companies, Michael couldn't sleep. He couldn't tell if the guilt of deciding not to work for his father's factory was causing him to toss and turn in the shadow of the stupendous efforts of myriad others, or if focusing on Angela's constant image determined his fate. No sleep was to be had for the night.

The perfumes of the ladies were hard to endure, stuck as he was in the bunk farthest from the windows and doorway. Michael put on his long smoking robe and tiptoed through the dark sleeping area of the women, determined to fill his lungs with pipe smoke outside to clear his mind.

He carefully opened the outer door, closing it softly behind him, before he was hit on the back of his head by a farmer's low bridge. Michael lurched forward with one hand on his stricken skull. As he fell face down with only one hand to cushion himself, Michael landed on someone.

Angela let out a scream worthy of an actress stabbed for a death scene on stage.

Michael couldn't move. Not that he wanted to, but Angela was heartily struggling beneath him. With his free hand, the one not clamped on his bleeding head, he tried to hold her mouth closed as he whispered loudly. "Angela, Angela, it's only me."

Apparently it was too late to quiet a row. Mrs. Breckenridge stormed out of the cabin, claimed the nearest object and slammed what felt like a chair against Michael's back.

Michael pretended to black out, still bleeding, still atop Angela's soft body.

"I've killed him," Mrs. Breckenridge shouted.

Captain Petree and the older ladies pushed and tugged Michael's body off Angela, who was moaning seductively into his ear, in Michael's opinion.

"Michael, Michael, don't die."

His brains were not scrambled. Of course, it was less than gentlemanly to let everyone fuss about but Michael decided Angela's hands pressing on his bare chest, patting his cheek, and her lips kissing his brow with her un-corseted breasts beneath him clearly warranted his inaction.

Captain Petree put the foolishness to an end. He propped Michael up in a chair and threw a bucket of cold water at him. That certainly scattered the bawling ladies. The cook patched his noggin, and Mrs. Breckenridge brought out a huge blanket to cover his upper body's nakedness.

Angela handed him a cup of tea with a broad wink. "Michael, this will cure whatever damage the farmer's bridge might have caused."

"Walking about among ladies with only a robe on," Mrs. Lazarus tsked then retired inside the cabin.

"If you're sure you are going to live," Winnie giggled before she too headed back to her bed.

Mrs. Breckenridge didn't move from her chair across from the repentant victim.

# Chapter 9

*Sunday, June 2nd, 1841*

Michael made an entry in his pocket diary, "Sunday, June 2: We reached Buffalo at sunset." Would he always remember the note as the sunset of his innocence. The change his thoughts, his body, and his soul experienced occurred the day he banged the back of his head on the farmer's canal bridge a mile south of Lockport, when his body had been permanently imprinted with Angela's form.

Michael recalled a saying of his father's Yiddish-speaking friend, "Breaking one commandment will lead to breaking them all."

Setting aside the dictate to honor his parents in order to follow his artistic skills with pen and ink, which Michael judged as his first breach of the commandments, he progressed on his path away from God wantonly entertaining indecent cravings for a woman three years younger.

Angela Marie Agnes McGovern was at the mercy of a corrupt brute. He couldn't keep his thoughts from lifting her skirts, unbuttoning her blouses, and forcing his rude hands wherever he had a mind to. Not that Michael accomplished any actions rehearsed in his incessant cravings, but Michael knew his heart was not pure. His only fear was that his sketches might reveal the sinful direction of his mind.

Angela appeared unaware of the effect of her presence. Her friendliness mocked the state of his soul. She looked at him with clear, happy eyes; touched his sleeve as if to encourage his attention, which never wavered; and closed the distance between them at every opportunity.

Her aunt was of no help in the matter.

Michael spoke to her in private when Angela left them alone for a moment. "I'm afraid I will lose control with Angela."

"Again?" Mrs. Breckenridge mocked.

"Please ma'am." Michael tried to take her hand, but she brushed him aside as Angela once brushed off the advances of David Leonard. "I need your help," he persisted.

"You shall not have it, sirrah." Mrs. Breckenridge was adamant. "I will not extend friendship to a man who intends to break the heart of my niece."

She stiffened her back as she moved away from him. "I watched over her mother when a man very much like you couldn't control himself." Mrs. Breckenridge continued her tirade, facing away from Michael, "Take a different ship on Lake Erie. Your services are no longer needed by myself or my niece."

But Michael couldn't do that. He needed to be near Angela for as long as possible.

"Please chaperone us at dinner." He humbled himself to plead. "Mayor Jenkins has invited us for this evening at the mansion. He's been instrumental in securing my position on Lake Superior, and I must accept his invitation. I've asked to bring you all."

Angela overheard the last statements to her aunt. "Oh, Aunt, let's go. Wouldn't Uncle Henry want you to?"

Mrs. Breckenridge stared at Angela then Michael, then Angela. "Yes dear," she smiled at her niece. "Henry would want me to go."

* * *

Angela understood her aunt's reluctance. Michael's behavior was becoming somewhat sinister, if she knew anything about men.

When Michael introduced her to Mayor Jenkins later that evening, the mayor politely complimented her, "Your Irish eyes exactly match the green of your gown."

Michael stood for too long a moment, staring at her for no good reason except passion. He'd already seen the lime green dress she'd worn to gamble with David Leonard and Major Compton. Perhaps he was reliving his disapproval of her behavior on the Pannonia.

Angela introduced her aunt, since Michael seemed content to wallow in his silence, "Mrs. Breckenridge, Mayor Jenkins. My aunt's husband runs the Merchant Exchange Bank in Chicago."

The Mayor was equally hospitable to both Mrs. Lazarus and Winnie.

The home was twice as lavish as the banker's in New York. Embossed leather appeared to line the foyer walls. A half-circle of Doric shaped mahogany columns led them into a circular room, where the mosaic flourishes on the floor of sea monsters and ships depicted all points of the compass. Brightness rained on them from a massive crystal chandelier suspended from a domed ceiling, complete with clouds and a hint of rainbow.

The passed through a massive state dining room with armored sentries from ancient times to a more intimate room where the table was set with blue, gold-rimmed china and crystal. Footmen in blue-and-maize stood behind each chair to assist with the ritual of dinner.

Mrs. Lazarus raved all through dinner about the sophisticated menu of roast pheasant, rabbit, and pork.

Angela ate a slice of the pig, but she didn't relish looking at the poor eyes of the creature with an apple stuffed in its mouth. Ma would have said gluttony didn't need to belittle the dumb beast.

Michael consumed an inordinate amount of wine at dinner. She hoped he slowed down after the men retired for cigars and brandy behind closed doors.

Mrs. Jenkins was a rotund woman whose glistening brownish-pink skin somewhat resembled the bloated pig's on its golden tray. Mrs. Lazarus and even Aunt Elizabeth were very cordial to Mrs. Jenkins. Winnie seemed to find her a bit distasteful.

When Mrs. Jenkins invited them stay the evening, Winnie spoke first. "We couldn't," she said.

Angela filled in to avoid any perceived rudeness, "The hour is well past the point any decent porter would leave his family to transport our luggage out here."

Aunt Elizabeth couldn't help but chide her, even though Angela knew her aunt didn't plan to stay at the Jenkins' mansion. "Angela! Thank you for your kind invitation, Mrs. Jenkins. Buffalo's mansion is the finest mayoral home I've seen. I'm afraid Chicago's seems old-fashioned and even primitive compared to yours. We, however, must decline. The schooner Maria Antoinette is awaiting our dawn departure for Detroit."

"Captain Fox has a great shock of red hair," Mrs. Lazarus flung her arms out rocking the base of a marble figurine of an embarrassing naked couple. "And beard."

Angela assumed Mrs. Lazarus' uncharacteristic outburst the result of unbridled use of spirits.

Mrs. Jenkins rang for the butler.

Michael appeared a second later to help them with their jackets and to climb up into the rented carriage.

Aunt Elizabeth held back when he offered his assistance. "I'll just make sure your best manners have not been compromised by all that expensive liquor, Mr. Halliday."

True, Michael's hands had lingered when he touched Angela, on her elbow to lift her to the carriage's step, on her shoulder after holding her coat, that sort of thing. Nothing to worry Aunt Elizabeth as far as Angela could tell.

However, Angela did know she was winning the battle to gain Michael as a lover, and with her resolve already broken to only love a man who would marry her, she found it difficult to resist his advances. Before she knew she loved Michael, there was never a question in her mind that her mother chose the wrong path when she was intimate with the earl. Now her harsh assessment of Ma's behavior nagged Angela with self-doubts about her own abilities to wear down Michael's defenses against consideration of marriage. There was never a lost moment Michael didn't take advantage, as far as being close to her or at least within sight.

\* \* \*

*Monday, June 3rd, 1841*

The wind on Lake Erie was not favorable for an early departure. Michael, who usually stormed about at any delay in their travel, lounged all day on the deck of the Maria Antoinette.

"When were you supposed to start your job as lighthouse keeper," Aunt Elizabeth asked in a short-tempered way.

"The first of June," Michael answered. "They understand delay in these matters."

Angela tried to mediate the harshness between the two of them. "I'm sure Aunt would like to hear the details of the house you'll be living in."

"Who cares," Aunt Elizabeth seemed to relish her stance of righteousness.

Michael, however, refused to acknowledge her aunt's rudeness. "I'm told the small brick house faces east. It has a dormered slate roof. The lighthouse faces west on a high cliff while the house is somewhat near the shore and jetty. A row boat is provided for fishing."

Here Michael gave a bright, carefree smile to Angela. "I don't know how to fish."

"What a baby you are," Angela took a step closer.

Aunt Elizabeth's frown was so potent, Angela returned to her previous position.

Michael slid his hand along the rail in her direction, but didn't move his big body. "I hope your aunt allows you to help me shop for those supplies we listed when we were on the Pannonia."

He didn't deign to speak to Aunt Elizabeth, and Angela was left to assess the effect of his words.

In the face of her aunt's disapproval, Angela was surprised at her own courage in answering. "New York posed no problems for my aunt, and I'm sure she has no reason to change her opinion that you will be sure to take care of me."

At this point, Angela turned her back to her aunt, unable to continue to countermand Aunt Elizabeth's obvious censure. Angela tipped her face up to Michael, taking the forbidden step closer and even letting him hold her hand. "Remember when I nearly fainted in the haberdashery."

"I carried you to a chair in the doorway."

"What caused you to faint?" Aunt Elizabeth was quickly at her elbow.

"The air, Aunt." Angela found it difficult to let go of the sight of Michael to acknowledge her aunt's question.

"One of the customers insisted to the people passing along the street that Angela was a farm girl." Michael stepped away from the rail, moving directly in front of Aunt Elizabeth.

Her aunt would have had to knock him down to move.

"He said city air was bad for her." Michael loomed over them.

"For man or beast," Angela said, then blushed at the thought that Michael curiously threatened them, as if a large bear meant to devour them both.

Aunt Elizabeth leaned away from him against the rail of the ship.

Michael didn't desist in spite of her aunt's obvious discomfiture. "I have to say goodbye to Angela in Detroit."

Angela could tell his body was shaking. She took his arm and pulled him from her aunt. "Let me see your pocket diary, Michael."

Michael ignored Aunt Elizabeth, who fled to her cabin.

Michael's hands shook as he handed Angela his diary.

Angela tried to tease him. "Are you afraid I'll find a note or two about me?"

"I will never compromise you, Angela." A tear forced its way to his cheek.

She brushed the tear from his face and pulled him down for a long kiss. "You love me, Michael Halliday," she said, braver than she felt. "And someday in the not too distant future," here she stepped back and pulled on her jacket. "I expect you to propose."

He laughed! But he caught her by the waist as she started to flee. "I'm sure you're right. If ever there was a wife in my future, she would be you."

With that he kissed her soundly, then roughly, then sweetly before letting her escape to her aunt.

Angela wasn't sure she wanted to be loved without marriage; instead she intended to rattle the man's body and brain enough to make marriage a necessity. Not that she wanted to trap him with an unwanted child. She did, however, realize she was using all of her feminine ploys to keep him in a continual state of arousal.

The amazing thing was, getting Michael excited, was becoming a habitual, unthinking mode of behavior. Perhaps, his resolve to live alone on an island was lessening, Angela hoped.

* * *

*Tuesday, June 4th, 1841*

The Marie Antoinette hadn't set sail until four o'clock on Monday afternoon, due to the unfavorable direction of the winds. The weather became increasingly formidable. Michael took note of the waves from the severe southwestern gale whipping across the deck. Unexpectedly this late in the spring, ice and snow slashed at the rigging.

Captain Fox's hat blew away and his shock of red hair was quickly filled with trapped snow. A cabin boy brought him a fisherman's oilcloth hat. The bottom section of the waterproof hat protected his beard as well.

Michael joined the ladies below, to apprise them of the conditions.

Mrs. Lazarus paced the aisle between their miniscule cabins. "Is the Captain safe?"

"He is," Michael answered taken aback by the passionate interest of the woman in their Captain. She was at least sixty years old.

The cabins were so small Angela didn't share one with her aunt.

Michael stood in front of the two doors, unable to decide on which to knock. Behind the door, which clearly he should inform out of duty and politeness, an unpleasant face would afflict his good intentions. Behind the second door, which clearly he should not bother, a face wreathed in loving smiles would greet him.

"Mrs. Lazarus," Michael called to the older woman. "Would you please inform Miss Perkins and Mrs. Breckenridge that we have encountered a dangerous storm?"

With his duty thus relieved, Michael tapped gently on Angela's door. There was no answer and he feared she had taken refuge with her aunt.

When she opened the door finally, Angela's face met his expectations, but she slid her hand into his coat front and pulled him into her room.

Michael couldn't tell if the storm sounds were infiltrating his brain or if his heart was beating loud enough to hear. The light in her cabin was almost entirely provided by the swinging lantern in the hall. The shifting effect heightened his nerves. Her perfume swept through him, opposing any prudence on his part.

"Does the storm delay us?" Angela whispered the words close to his ear, then let her lips tantalize his cheek and hot breath.

Striving to control his worst nature, Michael marveled at her power to sway the clashing drives of his body's awareness and his determination to be a perfect friend. "Angela," he said, trying to be stern but lacking the motivation. "I wanted you to know the storm is strong upon us."

Angela let go of him. "Worse than on the Pannonia?"

"No, no." Michael managed, stepping as far away from her as possible, without reopening the door to leave. "The shallow seas of Lake Erie push the water to great heights. Somewhat as if you were to rock the Montgomery Hall copper bathing tub."

"When did you see that?" Angela gripped the buttoned collar of her blouse.

Michael felt his face redden with his attempt at innocence, "When the clerk asked me to pick out a suite for you...and the other ladies."

"Mine was the only copper tub." Angela stared at him suspiciously.

"Your curtains were trimmed in green and being Irish...," Michael stopped. After all, his indiscretion was already revealed.

"I loved the bath," Angela said, letting go of her shirt collar and moving closer.

He could see her sweet body move beneath her clothes. "Angela," he pressed her to his wet coat.

She pushed him. "Take off your coat."

He was about to comply, when he realized he could not. "I'm afraid," he said her name in a crazed tone he didn't recognize, "Angela."

Cautioned by his passion, she let go of his lapel.

Michael opened the door behind him. "I love you too much," he said.

A mighty ground swell of the earth below the seething lake bed forced the ship to roll. Angela was catapulted from her cabin onto Michael as he stood in the hall.

Mrs. Lazarus emerged from Mrs. Breckenridge's cabin. The door remained open into the hall. Mrs. Breckenridge caught the doorway not to be thrown on top of Mrs. Lazarus, but she saw what was going on with Michael and Angela.

"Angela?" was all she cautioned.

"Right." Angela said as she disengaged herself from Michael's arms and retreated to her door.

Above they heard Captain Fox's yell and a great ripping noise.

"I'll find out," Michael managed as he slipped by Mrs. Lazarus, careful to keep his back to the arrows of umbrage emanating from Mrs. Breckenridge.

The storm had carried away the jib boom from the forward section of sails. Captain Fox gave orders to anchor about three miles off the town of Erie. Michael let Mrs. Lazarus inform the other ladies of the facts.

That night the wind changed, and the Captain raised the anchor to quit the harbor and make for the calmer seas in the middle of the lake.

\* \* \*

*Wednesday, June 5th, 1841*

Little headway was made the next day. They were all too seasick to eat much and spent most of the time in their cabins. At sunset Captain Fox anchored near the mouth of Sandusky Bay. He informed Michael it was too dangerous to cross the sand bar in the night. The charted underwater obstacles might have changed formation by the turbulent gyrations of the storm.

During the continued delays, Michael reviewed the exact developments in his plans to live alone on Strawberry Island. How would he muster the courage to let go of Angela? How soon would it take for a beautiful woman like Angela to attract someone serious enough to propose marriage?

Not long, Michael warned himself. Time was running out.

# Chapter 10

*Sunday, June 9th, 1841*

Proud at feeling like a seasoned traveler from Liverpool, Michael greeted Michigan's bright blue sky. He'd spent eleven days crossing the Atlantic and 24 more on waterways to reach Detroit. The Marie Antoinette limped north up the Detroit River. The storm in Lake Erie damaged the schooner's rudder to such an extent two tugboats were called into service to get her safely, if not somewhat noisily, docked. Thirty-four other steamboats vied for dock space.

Michael's warring emotions strove for dominance. Unhappiness should be his lot in life. After all, he was saying goodbye to a woman who loved him, but a certain joyfulness in fleeing the conflict prevailed. His peaceful plans of a hermit's life in Lake Superior would shortly be realized, and his lustful, possessiveness of Angela which left him sleepless at night and agitated by day would be resolved.

Dante's first Canto erupted into Michael's awareness.

*Let dead poetry rise once more accompanying in high strains*
*the sweet color gathering,*
*A cloudless horizon, a pure and perfect radiance.*
*From my oppressed soul which dims my sight*
*To my glad eyes reborn in delight*
*The lovely planet whose influence strengthens my love,*
*Causing the world to laugh with us.*

\* \* \*

In her cabin, Angela struggled unsuccessfully with her hair. Today she must be perfect. Brush and comb in hand, Angela knocked on her aunt's door. "Please, Aunt Elizabeth," she begged. "This will be the last day that I'll be spending time with Michael."

Aunt Elizabeth drew her distraught niece into her small cabin. "I've not seen you wearing this blue satin day-dress before."

"I was keeping it to meet Uncle Henry." Angela started a sob.

"None of that now." Her aunt took the brush from her hand. "You'll be leaving great dark circles under those green Irish eyes of yours."

Angela sat up straighter as if to aid in the putting up of her hair.

"Which bonnet?" her aunt asked.

"I hadn't planned to wear one to meet Uncle."

"Would you be wanting to borrow my white eyelet trimmed one?" Aunt Elizabeth fished the starched hat out from its box. "It matches the lace trim on your skirt."

Angela examined the pretty bonnet. "I've read about a novelist whose books traced the rise of lace-curtain-Irish in Boston." Angela remembered the trim on her mother's kitchen curtains. "Is eyelet considered Irish?" She was forced to redouble her efforts not to sob in front of her aunt.

"That bonnet is straight from the finest shop in Chicago." Aunt Elizabeth patted Angela's curls. "American it is, down to its last gather."

Angela smiled up at her aunt, winding her arms around her waist as she had her mother's. "Aunt Elizabeth," Angela kept her head hidden afraid to face any disappointment. "Will you be kind to Michael?" She ventured a look at her aunt's frown. "His heart is breaking, too."

"I hope it is!" Aunt Elizabeth pulled away, then softened her tone. "I'll be the model of politeness."

"I can't ask for more," Angela conceded.

Angela checked her image in the Kerry mirror and blushed to recall her smitten tutor's translations from Dante,

"Unseen by mortals since the first mankind
I saw close by a solitary soul
Adorned was her face with brightness of love,
She looked as if she found the sun."

"Did you know your tutor was in love with ya?" Aunt Elizabeth asked.

"I did, but how do you know?" Angela hoped the matter was settled when the tutor left their last lesson.

"He begged your mother for my address, according to him so's he could keep up with your education." Aunt Elizabeth sniggered. "As if we didn't know what he had in mind."

"Why didn't Ma tell me?"

"Oh, and she didn't want you to be worrying your head about the likes of him." Aunt Elizabeth patted her shoulder.

"I'm thankful for that," Angela said, even though she continued to feel a bit of guilt for the poor man.

Winnie Perkins in her habitual pink and black-garbed Mrs. Lazarus joined Angela and her aunt in the hallway.

"Oh what a pretty blue dress," Winnie clapped her hands.

"Your bonnet is perfect," Mrs. Lazarus kissed Angela's cheek knocking the bonnet somewhat askew.

Aunt Elizabeth adjusted it with a hearty tug. "She's off with Mr. Halliday to attend church and do a bit of shopping."

"Will the shops be open on the Lord's Day?" Winnie asked as she headed up to the deck.

"Depends on the community," Mrs. Lazarus answered. "Detroit has a collection of churches. I doubt you could even persuade the Anglicans, Methodists, Baptists, and Catholics to agree on which day was the Lord's Day."

"The Anglicans are called Episcopalians in America," Aunt Elizabeth corrected.

"Exactly," Mrs. Lazarus said. As if to prove her point further, she waved at the different spires of churches they could see on shore. "St. Paul's, St. Anne's and several I can't recall."

At the ship's rail, Michael heard their chatter and smiled into Angela's eyes. "What a pretty sight. I've known you all for just over a month, but I've grown that fond of the lot of you."

"Enough to tease the Irish," Mrs. Lazarus kidded him.

"Aye that," Michael said in a low tone.

"Michael," Aunt Elizabeth asked, "If you find a decent hotel with a private dining room for the evening, I'll allow you make train reservations for us to Ann Arbor."

Mrs. Lazarus interrupted. "Don't ask at the American Hotel. My husband and I stayed there only once. The clerks are surly. The meals are served on a common table. At least thirty quite-fragrant people fought for the meats, potatoes, gravy and carrots."

"The Steam Boat Hotel is a better choice," Aunt Elizabeth agreed.

"Why aren't you taking a steamer to Chicago?" Winnie asked.

"Well, darling," Mrs. Lazarus said. "We have to stop at Ann Arbor with my collection."

"Why don't you accompany me to my parents'?" Winnie invited them all.

"Could you miss your Sunday obligation, Elizabeth?" Mrs. Lazarus asked.

"I will," Angela's aunt answered. "Michael, and will you be attending St. Paul's?"

"As soon as they let down the gangplank." Michael took Angela's arm. "You'll put the most fashionable church in Detroit to shame."

"Hopefully not," Angela heard her aunt's aside.

* * *

The Gothic edifice of St. Paul's made Michael feel at home. Angela genuflected before moving into the 'strangers' pew' in the back.

The usher informed them that, "Bishop McCoskry will preach."

A lady across the aisle recited her rosary beads. His mother cautioned him that the Episcopal Church in America freely welcomed Catholics and Jews to their communion in contrast to the English Anglicans. He indicated to Angela the well-used page and began reciting the unchanged opening prayer from the Book of Common Prayers aloud, "Almighty God, to you all hearts are open."

He was pleased that Angela joined his voice after the first phrase, "all desires known, and from you no secrets are hid: Cleanse the thoughts of our hearts by the inspiration of your Holy Spirit, that we may perfectly love you, and worthily magnify your holy Name; through Christ our Lord. Amen."

They smiled at each other knowing full well the secret desires of their hearts were known to the Lord.

Unlike the English church bishop in wig and lawn sleeves, the Bishop of Michigan was young and elegant in a black silk robe. His sermon was on the benefits of giving, not only money, but time. Their very existence, personality, and awareness were required for charitable causes.

When the subject of the state's current voting campaign was brought up, Michael extracted his pocket diary. Captain Hale's assistance and his later disgrace occupied Michael's mind too much to listen attentively to the description of the perils of souls involved on both sides of the disputing political factions.

Michael checked his list of supplies to see if he had indeed memorized the needed purchases in Detroit. Too bad he hadn't added Angela McGovern to the list. Not that he would have been hired as a lighthouse keeper with a wife, as far as he cared to know at the time,but that didn't prevent the wish.

Angela seemed too embarrassed to receive the chalice at the communion rail. Her face was bright red after sticking out her tongue for the host. Instead she was handed a bit of bread torn from a loaf in the server's hand. Before the chalice was offered, Michael helped her up from the communion rail by securing her elbow and then escorted her back to their pew

She knelt for a long time after the service.

Michael whispered an earnest prayer for deliverance from his evil designs to take as much advantage of Angela's affection as she would permit. At the same time, he hoped his Irish angel, Angela, would gain the necessary courage and strength for their last day together. His darker nature receded from the imminent domain of Michael's thoughts. Mrs. Breckenridge appropriately sent them to church before they attempted to shop.

In the vestibule, Bishop McCoskry invited them to share coffee and donuts with the rest of the visitors to his parish in the basement of St. Paul's.

"I could see the spires of Detroit from the Canadian side." A Mr. James Logan, an Advocate in Edinburgh, Scotland, was traveling as a tourist in America. "Yesterday I spent quite a while in Lake St. Clair's Anchor Bay before the river was cleared sufficiently of traffic."

"We arrived up the Detroit River from Lake Erie." Michael enjoyed speaking to the affable young Scot, who was of equal height.

In fact Michael found a certain physical reprieve while conversing with men. Musing in the quiet of chewing his third donut, the liberating image of a lighthouse flashed before him. He recognized his version of Strawberry Island. As he swallowed his last bite, Angela's aunt's request re-surfaced. "Would you recommend decent accommodations for three ladies?"

"I will," Mr. Logan said. "I experienced the American Hotel for one night but ended up without supper. The Steam Boat Hotel serves food in the same common way, but at least I enjoy a private room."

"I'll definitely inquire," Michael said. "Could you also recommend a steamboat for a trip toward Mackinaw bound for Lake Superior?"

"Lake Superior has its own steamships," Mr. Logan added more sugar to his coffee cup. "I'm taking a schooner bound for Green Bay that stops at Mackinaw. The 'Thomas Jefferson' leaves tomorrow morning. You can book passage at the Hotel."

"Thank you," Michael smiled, shaking the young man's hand. His dreams were getting closer to becoming reality.

Angela introduced Michael to Anna Jameson, an older red-faced woman with flaming red hair, who monopolized Angela's time.

"Your friend, Angela, and I were remarking on the history of Michigan," the older lady said, while demolishing at least two of the pastries offered.

Michael watched in fascination as the food disappeared amid the non-stop words. "No place in the United States presents such a series of events. Michigan's flag has changed five times. Three sovereignties have claimed Detroit: twice besieged by Indians and once captured in war when the fort was burned to the ground. Detroit's importance as a frontier town and a place of trade increases every day."

Bishop McCoskry brought over Captain Frederick Marryat to be introduced. "Captain Marryat visited St. Paul's four years ago."

Without further ado, Captain Marryat added, "Mrs. Jameson knows me."

"Oh yes," Mrs. Jameson's face deepened its hue. "Your sea stories are well received."

The Captain laughed. "But not my 'tactless and blundering progress through the drawing rooms and backwoods of America.' Do I correctly quote you?"

"Michigan has shown progress in the last four years, wouldn't you say?" Mrs. Jameson tried to regain her composure.

"Railroads have made the mud and impassable state of the roads a thing of the past." Captain Marryat smiled all round, much to Bishop McCoskry's relief.

"We're hoping to find a shop or two open today," Michael interjected as a fresh tray of donuts appeared. Among this civilized group of people, his obsession with Angela was nearly manageable.

"Corner of Woodward and Jefferson," Mrs. Jameson added. "Will you be here long enough for Daniel Webster's talk at the theatre?"

"I'm afraid not," Angela said, bidding good-bye by walking backwards toward the door. "We only have today to purchase all the supplies Mr. Halliday needs."

Mr. Logan stopped them in the hall. "Please join me for tea whenever your shopping excursion is completed. Most of the disagreeable assemblage at the hotel is not accustomed to either urbanity, order, or cleanliness. And," he added, "there is a want of intelligent conversation in the place."

Michael assured him they would avail themselves of the invitation.

* * *

At the Steam Boat Hotel Michael booked his passage on the 'Thomas Jefferson' with extra space for his supplies. Angela tried to concentrate on their day together instead of the morrow's parting.

Only a minimum of rooms were available for a stay at the hotel for Sunday evening. On the second floor, one dormitory was rented for the three ladies. It contained four beds, but no bureaus or chairs, and only one nightstand with bowl and pitcher. The common bath across the hall was clean and large. Showers let water rain on anyone wishing to bathe, but the outhouse in the back of the hotel was unpleasant at best.

Angela refused to waste time looking elsewhere. "Take it, Michael, before someone else does and we're left to roam the streets all night."

Michael rented larger accommodations for himself on the top floor of the hotel with a snug little parlor and a bedroom with a handsome dark closet.

Across the hall from Michael's room, the clerk showed them a private dining room complete with a table, fifteen chairs and a china cupboard.

"A couple by the name of Toulmin, no that wasn't it." The greasy haired clerk scratched his head and then wiped his hand on the back of

- 121 -

his pants. "Any the ways, they sold me this outfit when they went back to Boston 'bout six years ago. Been used by the best of my clientele."

They were left alone to consider renting the hall when the clerk was called down to the front desk.

Angela tentatively opened the doors of the cupboard. It was stocked with the necessary dishes and cutlery. "Michael, look at this."

He pulled out a long drawer in the base of the cabinet. "Linens."

Angela sat down and emptied her reticule onto the table. Two sovereigns clinked together before rolling onto the floor.

Michael retrieved them. "What's this?"

"Payment," Angela smiled up at him. "Did you think we would forget to repay you?"

"No need," Michael said not handing the coins back.

Angela moved to his side. "I haven't forgotten the limited start-up funds that you intend to return to your mother."

"That's true," he said.

She marveled at the inability of men to respond coherently with more than monosyllables when their minds were elsewhere. "What are you concentrating on?"

"Who are you that up from some blind river my prisoned thoughts fled?"

"You translate Dante?" Angela recognized her homecoming in Michael's words. And she was glad she'd memorized, "Who has guided you or what your lantern, finding your way from the deep loneliness that lies forever blind in the darkest night?"

"You," Michael said, gathering her into her arms for a quick kiss. The embrace lasted longer than the kiss.

Angela doubted he would ever place her on her feet again. "Michael," she whispered over and over.

"We must part," Michael managed in a low guttural tone.

Angela recognized his struggle with his passions. Her body raged against the curbs she tried unsuccessfully to impose on her reactions to his closeness.

Michael paced around the dining room. "You know Purgatorio's Italian?"

"I memorized some of my tutor's translations." Angela busied herself setting the table for later that evening. "Let's invite Mr. Logan to have dinner with us."

When all was ready, Michael knelt before her. "Angela, you have my word that I will never touch any woman until we're reunited."

"You're not telling me something I haven't known for quite a while, Michael Halliday." Angela looked at the open door to the hall and stepped back. "If you're on your knees the next time we meet, it's more than touching you should be asking me for."

He rose to bedevil her. "And is it yes then that you'd be saying to a marriage proposal?"

"If some other chap, the more worthy than you asks." Angela flung her arms around his neck and gave him the warmest, most passionate kiss yet bestowed on him. Then she took a deep refreshing breath and finished with, "If another gentleman, not you, Michael Halliday, has given me reason to believe I'm first in his heart and in all his plans, I'd be open to considering such a marriage proposal."

"I don't believe you, Angela McGovern," Michael pursued her around the table. "What do you think of that?"

Angela continued to circle the table just out of reach. "Can the laws of earth be broken then or some new rule adopted in Heaven?"

Michael interrupted the Dante quote with the next line, "That allows you to wander into my sight?"

Angela stepped safely into the hall, where other hotel guests were passing. "I'd say that you were an astute and clever man."

Michael locked the door to the room and they went below hand-in-hand to order dinner for their going away party.

* * *

Angela found she sighed several times on their stroll down Jefferson Avenue to find the shops Michael would need. She tried to stifle the sighs. Their source was a deep sadness that tears wouldn't alleviate. She could fill all the Great Lakes with her salty tears and the awful dread of being without Michael would stay a part of her.

Most of the stores along the wooden walkway were closed as expected, but on the corner of Woodward Avenue, they could see the owner inside stocking his shelves.

After knocking on the front door, Michael pulled out one of Angela's gold sovereigns and pressed it against the glass.

The owner motioned for them to go behind the store to his back door.

"Bribery will open many a door," the large man said, as he pocketed Angela's gold. "May I ask which church you attended this morning?"

"What's that to you?" Angela asked taken aback at her own fierceness.

"St. Paul's," Michael answered as he stepped into the narrow hall between supply boxes in the store's back room.

"Trouble's not good for business. I'm Jed Brighton the owner." He shook hands with Michael and bowed to Angela. "The Episcopals are the least testy of that church bunch. What can I help you find?"

"We need a few supplies for my trip to Lake Superior," Michael drew out his diary.

"He leaves tomorrow morning." Angela wanted to stress their need for exception to the rule of no commerce on the Lord's Day. "He's going to be the lighthouse keeper for Strawberry Island."

"If I don't have what you need," the man as tall as Michael and as wide as his counter top said, "I'll order it and send it up to you."

"Captain Hale," here Michael stared straight at Angela, "on our Atlantic crossing on the Pannonia, persuaded me that I shouldn't count on back orders."

"He did, did he?" Mr. Brighton was not happy with that bit of information.

Angela didn't like the man, pocketing her money and giving nothing for it but access to his smelly shop.

"Two pairs of oars," Michael started his recitation.

"Get them at the Soo," Mr. Brighton said, then added in a sarcastic tone, "Unless you want me to back order them for you."

"A buck saw and hatchet?" Michael tried again.

"Take me a minute," Mr. Brighton said, heading for the back room's supplies.

Michael followed him. "And a hammer, chisel, wood-ax, and white wash."

Angela found Michael's favorite tobacco, some writing paper and envelopes he might need. She placed them on the counter before remembering the padlock he read to her from his list. Was that only a month ago, when they'd first chatted?

She lifted her skirts away from a dusty corner of the shop and found an assortment of padlocks. "Michael," she called. "You'll need to pick out your own padlock."

Michael re-emerged from the back, laden down with tools "I need a bedstead, a mattress, bedding, and pillows." At the word 'pillows,' Michael tugged on a curl at the back of Angela's neck that must have escaped from her bonnet.

"The padlocks are in that corner," Angela said pointing with one hand and tucking away her errant curl with the other.

Michael placed one of the padlocks on the counter, smiling at Angela when he noticed the tobacco and writing supplies. "Will you be able to crate this for shipment tomorrow morning?"

Mr. Brighton nodded. "I'll call in my boys and we'll work all night if we have to. Which ship is taking you up?"

"The Thomas Jefferson," Michael said, adding, "I've paid for steerage room for these supplies. It leaves at sunrise."

"You'll need a trunk." Angela would miss his clipped way of calling his brain to attention.

"Work shirts, clothespins, shoe blacking, sardines, a pocket knife, flat iron, coffee pot, a wash tub, wooden pail, and soap." Michael smiled as if proud of his memory.

She could best that. "A stove, stove pipes, elbows, and a cleaning spider as well as tins of matches and dinnerware."

"For two," Michael added, tipping his head in appreciation of her recall abilities. "A cook book and a glass crock."

Mr. Brighton was kept busy writing down his list. "Don't have a flat iron but I imagine the Soo might have one."

Angela laughed, "Or you can stay wrinkled."

"Cinnamon, dried fruit, pepper, a box of nails, salt beef," Michael's beloved voice lulled Angela into a near doze.

"Sugar," she recalled. Then she remembered to specifically mention children. "A few orphans."

Both men glanced at her.

"I think your wife is telling you she wants babies," the fat man leered in her direction.

"We're not...," Michael stopped when he saw the man's expression. "planning any, immediately."

But Michael didn't meet her eye.

"Why not?" she again astounded herself by asking in an angry tone, maybe to get his attention.

Mr. Brighton retreated to the back room supposedly to find the supplies.

Angela crept up to Michael who was sorting through the items on the counter.

Suddenly as if he remembered a vital bit of news, he swung around clipping her shoulder with his elbow and sending her crashing against a low open tub of pickles. Her new dress was totally soaked.

She bounded up from the disaster, drunk with rage. "You bumbling idiot! Look what you've done now." Tears threatened to interrupt her tirade. She clamped her hand on the nearest round object and threw it at the man she adored.

Tomato juice splattered against his right cheek bone. The shock of it didn't let him move. Angela had plenty of time to hurl five more missiles, one at that fat Mr. Brighton when he came out of the back, before Michael hauled her out into the street.

"Orphans," she repeated for no earthly reason.

He stood in front of Angela, dripping with tomato juice. The hem of eyelet on her dress was dirty and dripping with vinegar from the vat of pickles.

He laughed as he had a tendency to do at the least expected times. Michael didn't hate her. She hadn't ruined their last few moments alone.

Out of relief, Angela joined in on the laughter. "Michael, call us a cab. We better get back to the hotel so I can change, before my aunt sees the mischief we've been up to."

\* \* \*

Angela assembled a load of laundry for the maid, before dressing conservatively for dinner. She chose a white lace blouse and hunted for her black skirt. In lieu of the black, Angela selected a navy blue skirt.

The room was a shambles, as if her aunt and Mrs. Lazarus hurriedly dressed after meeting with Winnie's parents. Angela held a suspicion that they went searching for Michael and her to spy on them or to at least make sure they were properly chaperoned.

After Angela inquired at the desk about the facilities for laundering, Mrs. Lazarus, Aunt Elizabeth and a much-altered Winnie

Perkins arrived in the lobby. Instantly, Angela divined the cause. Winnie wore black. Clearly she was in mourning. "Winnie," Angela approached her. "I'm so sorry for your loss."

Winnie seemed dazed. "Both of them. Gone."

Mrs. Lazarus guided her charge up the stairs to their room.

In their room, Aunt Elizabeth sat down on a couch against the far wall. "The house was still draped in black when we arrived," she said in almost a whisper. "We rushed Winnie back here and I gave her your black skirt. Mrs. Lazarus's blouse was too big, but my black jacket hid the imperfections." Her aunt stopped to catch her breath.

"When is the funeral," Angela asked stroking her aunt's cold hand.

"Last week! We called on the neighbors after we'd dressed Winnie properly." Aunt Elizabeth untied the black ribbons of her bonnet. "I stripped off all the white and black plaid." She held the bonnet up for Angela's inspection. "You can see the basting threads I missed."

"I'm sure the neighbors didn't notice." Angela gave her aunt her handkerchief. "Did the brothers attend the funeral?"

"Just long enough to sell the house." Aunt Elizabeth said with considerable distaste. "They completely ignored their own sister's rights."

"Mercy," Angela said. "What would Winnie have done if you two hadn't been there?"

"Hopefully, she would have been taken in by a neighbor of her parents or the church." Aunt Elizabeth's eyes enlarged with the horror. "Detroit has a poor house, one of the men whispered to me." Her aunt sat taller. "I informed the chap, no gentleman he, that Winnie Perkins possessed friends who loved her and would care for her."

"Thank the Lord for Mrs. Lazarus," Angela said sincerely.

"Indeed," her aunt bowed her head. "It's as if the Lord knew we would have to show compassion for our Winnie."

"How did Winnie take the shock of it?" Angela asked.

"I best dress for dinner," her aunt said trying to rise from the couch but giving into the softness instead.

"You're dressed fine for dinner," Angela said. "Tell me about Winnie."

Aunt Elizabeth folded her hands. "She's quite strange about it, I suppose. She hadn't seen her parents for 20 years and wasn't looking forward to caring for them. I guess I'm trying to say she was quite relieved."

"With her new job as caretaker of Mrs. Lazarus' estate in Ann Arbor, she won't have to worry about charity from her thieving brothers."

"Yes," her aunt admitted. "She has that rock to stand on."

* * *

Michael was quite astounded by the news of Winnie Perkins' tragedy, especially after meeting her ebullient smile as she entered the dining room.

"I never wear black," Winnie giggled.

Mrs. Lazarus whispered the explanation. "I've given Winnie some of my laudanum to help her through the meal."

Mr. Logan arrived and Michael stalled him in the hall long enough to report on the lay of the land. "Please excuse our Winnie. It's been quite a shock and with the drug…."

"It's important that she's able to take nourishment," Mr. Logan said. "We needn't mention her ordeal, but I would like to meet with Mrs. Lazarus to remedy the injustice from Miss Perkins' brothers."

"Of course," Michael agreed.

Even without the tragedy, dinner would have been a sad affair. The sight of Angela McGovern's lovely face and her very soul would be denied in the morning.

"I'm walking you to your ship in the morning, Michael." Angela told him when he passed her the platter of grilled rabbit.

"Did you find all the supplies you were hoping to purchase?" Mr. Logan thankfully changed the subject.

"Except for a set of spare oars for the boat," Michael said.

"And a flat iron to make a bachelor presentable," Angela winked at Michael.

Michael was surprised at the older ladies not giving him the cold shoulder. It was as if their afternoon visit with death gave them a fresh appreciation for the glories of affection Angela and he felt for each other.

"Michael, remember Captain Fox?" Mrs. Lazarus waved her empty wine glass at him.

"Yes," Michael said giving a knowing look at young Mr. Logan as he refilled Mrs. Lazarus glass.

"I quite fell in love with the man." Mrs. Lazarus put her arm around Winnie. "He's promised to write."

"Oh," Winnie crowed in her usual way. "Isn't that a blessing? We have known more than one romance on this trip." Here she purposefully pointed to Angela and Michael, as if Mr. Logan was not cognizant of the facts.

Michael marked that Angela held her aunt's hand. Neither woman was smiling, and their suffering affected him.

"Mrs. Breckenridge has allowed me to court her daughter," Michael smiled at Winnie. "Even though she knows I'll be out of sight for nearly a year."

"But not out of our hearts," Michael was surprised to hear Angela's aunt say.

# Chapter 11

*Monday, June 10th, 1841*

Michael walked arm in arm with Angela on the boardwalks from Detroit's Steam Boat Hotel to the Thomas Jefferson's dock. An endless line of carriages and dray wagons passed them, heading toward the river and the bustling docks.

The morning sun contained a bit of warmth, but Angela hadn't unfurled her parasol. Perhaps she didn't want the frilly thing to interfere with their synchronized need to be as close as possible, physically. She wore a middy blouse. The wide trim on the square collar, her skirt, and one ribbon holding back the curls from her cherub face all matched the azure hues of the sky.

"The first time I saw you," Michael said, as he removed his jacket, "your cloak harmonized with the Atlantic's twilight. Today your colors are as fresh as the morning."

"You know, Michael, if we'd been together longer, you might have won prizes in Ireland for your gift of blarney." Angela's smile held a bit of sadness. "Catching it is, like madness. Are you sure you shouldn't be buying palettes of paint to go along with your pen and ink supplies?"

Michael had considered the option. "I mostly see the forms and the spaces not encompassed by the shapes I'm drawing. I know I often refer to colors, but the line of your chin, the slight upturn of your nose, the impish slant of your eyes, the divine shape of your body." Michael shut his mouth in order to close down his body's reactions.

Angela moved a step sideways as if to allow a hint of breeze passing between them to cool both their thoughts. "I wish Ma could hear your loving words."

"I wish I knew your ma," Michael said. "I wish I'd traveled every lane and field of your childhood. Seen every sunrise and sunset from your vantage point."

Angela shook her head at the useless wish. "I'm that glad that I didn't barge into your mother's pink parlor. I'd be pushing aside those fainting dragons of silk who drove you to distraction."

"We would have kept ourselves occupied with the horses." Michael breathed in the rose scent of her sparkling golden hair. "We both love to ride."

"Aye," Angela said. "How is it that our different backgrounds led us to this juncture? Now you're off to quiet lawns and endless sky, and I'm destined for tea rooms and yards of silk."

"You'll get no answers from me," Michael said. "I know I have to return to my parents, after this year's sabbatical. You aren't inclined to return to your mother's land, are you?"

"Too sad a land," she said.

Michael memorized how the sun caught highlights in her curls when she shook her head. 'no.'

"Even my journey into the homes of respectable people in Chicago will be temporary." Angela recited the facts they both wanted to ignore. "I'll eventually find a way to buy a small farm to till and then fill with little ones."

"Perhaps by the time I see my parents," Michael bent down to kiss her ear. "They'll become reconciled to the fact that I don't want to run a clock factory."

"After you've been growing your own food on Strawberry Island," Angela reached up to tug on his ear. "You might come to love being outside for the entire day to watch the animals grow and tend the hay."

Silence fell as they chewed on their futures without each other.

"I'll send you back to the hotel in a hansom," Michael drew Angela closer to his side, "but I wanted to be with you for as long as I could."

"Since Winnie arrived like a stricken black bird at the hotel," Angela rubbed his arm that linked them, "I've been terrified this will not be a temporary goodbye."

"Winnie's parents were quite elderly." Michael stopped, but didn't release her arm. "And as you can clearly see I'm as healthy as a man can be." Michael let himself deserve a quick kiss on his cheek. "Nothing can keep me from finding you in Chicago."

Her precious green eyes concentrated on his chest, his forehead, and his mouth.

"I pray the Lord keeps you safe," Angela whispered.

Michael felt her warm blessing take effect.

"You have to put away these superstitious fears, Angela." Michael tapped the top of her head. "My future wife must not be so easily suggestible. All the whims and wiles of the world won't change my determination to marry you."

Angela batted her hand at his vest. "Is it blarney you'll be wanting me to remember about you for the rest of my life?"

"For at least a year," Michael picked her up, spun her in a complete circle and sat her back down in her tracks. "What can happen?"

"Influenza?"

"I've survived influenza."

"A shipwreck?"

"Unlikely." Michael gently herded Angela closer to the docks. "The chances of God overlooking recent opportunities to do away with me by drowning convince me He plans keep me busy on solid ground."

"I hope to keep you in my plans, for all the ever I can control." Angela's seriousness was not in question.

"Even if you hear I've drowned."

"Yes," Michael could see Angela's grin starting.

"Even if you hear the lighthouse has fallen over and clunked me on the head."

"Serve you right, Michael Halliday, for bumbling about and knocking it over." Angela sighed instead of laughing. "Your head's thick enough to sustain life even if a lighthouse fell on you."

"That doesn't sound like a compliment."

"Wasn't meant to."

Michael thought he saw a tear glistening and quickened his steps toward the departure point.

The flags on the side-paddle steamer were flying high in the bright sunshine. The smoke from the ship's lone stack as well as the billowing trails of black from the other 20 or so steamships blew away from the city. Smaller crafts farther away from shore were unfurling their salt-bleached sails to catch the wind.

"If and when you return to Chicago," Angela kept up with Michael's long strides. "you can help me care for the orphans on my farm."

"Orphans?"

"Well, I can't be waiting for you to start my life."

Michael recognized the determined lift of his lover's chin.

"I plan to buy a farm near a river, the Fox, I think Aunt called it." Angela continued, "I'll let the local priest know when I'm ready to care for children and leave the rest to the Lord."

Michael guided Angela safely across the busy thoroughfare in front of the dock. "You want children more than husband?"

"Of course not!" Angela stomped her foot.

They were interrupted by Mr. Logan and the writer, Captain Marryat. "Lovely dinner last night," Mr. Logan tipped his hat. "See you on board."

Captain Marryat pointed behind them. "Mrs. Jameson's entourage is arriving."

A sophisticated looking young man and younger lady, whose vertical feathered bonnet competed in height with the gentleman's silk top-hat, accompanied Mrs. Jameson as well as a portly man.

Michael tipped his cap and wished he had not removed his coat in the heat.

"Oh," Mrs. Jameson called to them. "Let me introduce you to General Schwartz and his family; Governor Mason's sister, Miss Emily Mason, and her friend John Sprague, an attorney like yourself, Mr. Logan."

"Advocate," Mr. Logan corrected. "From Scotland."

"Are you acquaintances of our elegant writing friend?" Miss Mason held out her hand to be kissed by Michael.

Michael complied after disengaging himself from Angela's arm. "Are you traveling with Mrs. Jameson to Chicago?"

"No, no," Miss Mason blushed quite freely. "We missed spending any time with Mrs. Jameson while she was in Detroit, so we wanted to give her a grand send off."

Angela stepped forward, "I'm Angela McGovern. My aunt and friends are traveling to Chicago."

"Not by sea?" Captain Marryat asked, too solicitously for Michael's good opinion.

Then Michael remembered he'd failed to make train reservations for Angela's aunt and Mrs. Lazarus for Ann Arbor.

"Angela," he said, dropping his coat. "I failed to secure your tickets."

She picked up his coat. "It's all right, Dear."

Michael discerned that Angela made sure Miss Mason noted and acknowledged the endearment she used, before continuing, "Aunt Elizabeth thought to change the reservation to include Miss Perkins and we discovered your oversight."

Angela turned toward Miss Mason again. "A new spur has been completed from Kalamazoo which takes us to Grand Rapids. From there will take a ferry to Milwaukee."

"You may arrive before Mrs. Jameson," Miss Mason said. "And you?"

"Michael Halliday," he answered her implied question, purposefully ignoring Angela's whispered 'Bumble.' "I'll be transferring to another ship at the Soo."

"He's a lightkeeper in Lake Superior," Angela offered without being asked.

Miss Mason dismissed them with a nod of her head.

But Mr. Logan rushed back toward the group. "Mr. Sprague, is it?"

"Yes?" the gentleman removed his top-hat.

They all stared as Mr. Logan opened his wallet. "A Miss Winnie Perkins has been defrauded by her brothers in a recent probate sale of her parent's home."

"Step-brothers," Mr. Sprague said. "Put away your money. I'm the State's attorney in this matter. Mrs. Lazarus has already visited our office and we intend to indict the scoundrels."

"Well done," Angela clapped her hands.

"Indeed," Michael said, drawing Angela a step away from the milling crowd. "The groom who moved Splendor from the livery to his stall on board swears my stallion thought Flicka ought to follow him."

"Winnie almost convinces me to leave Flicka in Ann Arbor with her," Angela said sadly, then tried to brighten the conversation with, "until I find a farm."

"May I kiss my intended?" Michael asked.

"You may."

Michael forgot about leaving, forgot the sounds of the paddle wheel in motion, forgot himself as he enfolded Angela into his arms. Her sweet smell, the softness of her lips, the strong hold of her dear hands on his neck, the willowy structure of her youthful body, nailed him to the dock.

Angela broke his embrace at the parting signal from a great bell that swung out from the ship.

"Time's gone." Angela's beautiful green eyes filled with unshed tears.

"Until we meet in a year." Michael was the last person to bound up the gangplank. "I'll write," he called back to Angela.

\* \* \*

"That's taking a chance," Captain Marryat commented. "Beautiful girl like that."

"Have your bans been announced?" Mr. Logan's politeness cautioned the same opinion.

"Not yet," Michael admitted over the rumblings of his empty stomach and desperately beating heart.

Mrs. Jameson came to Michael's rescue. "I've never witnessed such raw affection from a woman, in all the days I've walked this earth. She'll wait."

Michael did hope Angela would decline the offers from other suitors and wait for him to marry her. Now he faced solitude. Once a source of joy and happiness, the dream of his ideal artistic existence resonated with feelings akin to dread. The island would be a living hell without the sight of Angela.

\* \* \*

Angela was all right, but she couldn't seem to make her feet leave the dock. She kept an eye on the Thomas Jefferson until the last trail of smoke was completely lost, and still she couldn't move away from the spot where Michael kissed her for the last time. She prayed for God's will to be done, again and again, but her body refused to turn away from the deep, beckoning river.

A slight breeze swept away the last of Michael's warmth from her lips. Her unopened parasol dropped from leaden arms. The smell of fish and fuel failed to daunt Angela's determination not to return to a world without Michael. She took one step toward the edge of the dock, and a strong hand on her shoulder drew her back.

No one was near, but Angela knew the source. The Lord's will didn't include ending her pain by drowning.

She ran toward the carriage Michael arranged for her return trip to the hotel. Inside the hansom, Angela shook. She'd come close to throwing away her life.

* * *

Michael's trip through Lake St. Clair and the Huron River passed in a blur of regret. If he had the chance to make every decision over again, he honestly would not have changed one thing. There was no one to blame for his unhappiness. He looked at his shaking hands and cursed their ability to transcribe life to paper. Now his heart was being ripped out of his chest. Better he should cut off both hands than cause Angela similar grief.

"Forgive me," he pleaded with his Maker. "Your gifts of beauty tear me in opposite directions."

"Poet?" Captain Marryat intruded. "I thought you were an artist."

"Lighthouse keeper," Michael mumbled, hoping to escape the cynic's discourse.

"Peaceful times on an island." Captain Marryat concentrated on their progress north through the channel to Lake Huron.

Michael needed that moment to shake himself free of the self-pity overwhelming his good sense and manners. "What destination awaits you?"

"Niagara."

"Thomas Jefferson wrote to potential settlers in England and France extolling the beauty of the Falls." Michael breathed easier. Non-emotional subjects relieved his suffering. "However, Jefferson never managed to see them in person."

"Much like myself," Captain Marryat kept his face toward the widening expanse of Lake Huron. "I recommend marrying immediately, but have avoided the risky business to date."

"Unwanted subject at this point." Michael resisted an urge to smash his fist into the back of Captain Marryat's head to share the pain of his own head and heart.

"Sorry," Captain Marryat apologized, leaving Michael to his misery.

Finally, Michael's pain lessened enough for his stomach to inform him lunch had passed without respite. The darkening sky of leaden gray encouraged him to consult his father's watch. Did his mother miss him as much as he missed Angela. More than a month passed and he hadn't thought of his parents other than the minutes taken to describe them to Angela.

He promised himself to write a long letter, describing all of Angela's virtues as soon as he'd seen to partaking of some repast. Perhaps his mother's family, the Cromwells, knew of the Earl of Covington's generosity to his Irish offspring. Just as Angela shared she was happily free of showing up for lessons with her tutor, Michael was happy to be liberated from the obligations of his mother's scheming shows of hospitality to illegible young women.

The Thomas Jefferson's dining hall was not as large as the Pannonia's but twice as ornate. Stained-glass windows served as part of the domed ceiling. Snowy linen tablecloths and matched dinnerware promised and elegant meal. Modest pressed-glass lanterns swayed above each of the three tables. The Captain sat with a group of ministers at one table and part of the crew occupied a second.

Michael joined the already seated group of travelers he'd recently met at the third table.

Mrs. Jameson removed a manuscript from his chair. "Captain Marryat has just been critiquing my novel."

"Soup is about to be served," Captain Marryat said. "We hope."

The Captain's face rendered a grimace which might have been an honest attempt at a welcoming smile.

"Write that young woman a formal engagement letter." Mr. Logan proceeded to admonish him during the soup course. "Your emotions will thank you for it."

Michael noted the critic turned novelist, Mrs. Jameson, offered no advice.

To show them his good humor, he inquired. "Madame, you're the expert. What is the best course of action?"

"Forget your plans." Mrs. Jameson used her knife to poke dispiritedly at a burnt veal chop on her plate. "As soon as the boat docks, book a return passage."

"Aye," Mr. Logan said. "Or continue on with us to Chicago."

"I've promised to serve as a lighthouse keeper for a year," Michael said. Their opinions disheartened him. "Do you think Angela would want me to resign?"

All three nodded their heads to the affirmative.

"If you have any doubt the damsel will be able to wait for you," Captain Marryat amended.

"Ask her to reply back to your invitation to marry as quickly as possible." Mr. Logan waved his hand as if the issue was settled.

Mrs. Jameson said not a word, but her manner showed a bit of displeasure.

"At the present time, I'm not at liberty to pursue Angela," Michael explained. "A lighthouse keeper's job won't support the flock of children Angela plans to bring into the new world."

With that bit of information for the rest of them to chew on, Michael gave into his immediate need to eat. There would be plenty of time to think on Strawberry Island.

* * *

*Tuesday, June 11th, 1841*

Angela didn't find relief in the noisy train ride to Ann Arbor. At least the racket from the engine and rattling wheels kept her aunt's conversation with Mrs. Lazarus and Winnie Perkins to a minimum. The ladies were not able to expound on all the details of Angela's recent injury.

But her mind refused to let Angela enjoy any such reprieve. Instead she relived every moment spent with Michael.

He wasn't the first tall young man she'd ever laid eyes on. Kerry grew lots of bonny lads. But from the moment Michael touched her hand, as she held onto the doorway of her cabin during the Pannonia's encounter with an Atlantic storm, Angela knew she wanted Michael's friendship.

Their first kiss, after Peter Mulligan sighted landfall of the coast of New York, let Angela realize her passions included more than just friendship.

Michael's collapse onto her reclining body on the canal's packet boat, after he'd been knocked over by the farmer's bridge, made it evident Michael wanted more than friendship, too. But Michael obviously didn't want an immediate wife, just one in abeyance. He didn't care how she sustained life while he played at being an artist.

Shame about disloyalty and her growing anger led Angela to excuse herself from the seat next to her aunt. "A breath of air," she said, heading for the walkway between cars.

Angela needed a place to scream, a place to pound on unrelenting metal to vent her growing resentment toward her blameless, bumbling life mate.

* * *

Mrs. Lazarus insisted they had time for tea before boarding the stage to Kalamazoo. Aunt Elizabeth struggled before agreeing. "I miss my husband more than I can understand."

Winnie spoke up. "My parents' death has unnerved you."

"Please," Mrs. Lazarus wheedled. "I've decided to stay a few weeks in Ann Arbor to get Winnie set up properly."

"We haven't had time to talk on that noisy conveyance." Winnie pointed to the empty tracks.

"Let's savor our leave taking," Angela said. Much to her embarrassment, all three women turned their sympathetic attention on her.

"The train station has a tea room," Mrs. Lazarus said.

The public room designated for refreshment other than spirits didn't block out the late afternoon rowdiness of the bar patrons in the adjoining room. Rays from the declining sun filtered through blue and yellow panes of the back windows. The table had no cloth and an indefinite stickiness covered its surface.

Angela raised her cup a moment longer than was customary to breathe in the refreshing scent of mint in her tea. She hoped the cup's inside was as clean as its pretty rose painted outside appeared to be. At least the teapot, sugar and creamer matched her cup.

Concentrating on the details of Aunt Elizabeth yellow tea set with its violet flowers, and Mrs. Lazarus' square pot and cup with matching gold trim, and Winnie's pink painted pot of hot chocolate kept Angela's thoughts away from the sticky part of her brain that longed for an image of Michael. Not only an image. Angela wanted the real man to be sitting with them. He'd be trying to keep his feet quiet, asking for permission to light his pipe after failing at the sport, and all and all causing considerable damage to her nerves and heart. Angela appreciated the threesome's reluctance to bring up Michael Halliday.

"This way you'll have time to introduce Winnie to your friends," Aunt Elizabeth said, "before you return to Chicago."

"Actually, I think I'll purchase a home on Division Street to make sure Winnie can entertain properly before I return to Chicago society."

Winnie clapped her hands. "Really?"

"Certainly," Mrs. Lazarus said. "The Ladies Library needs a place to meet until their new building is constructed."

"In Paris, the Ladies' Library had accommodations," Winnie stopped and traded staring first at Aunt Elizabeth and then Angela.

"I'm sure Angela is old enough to know." Mrs. Lazarus folded a rather thin restaurant napkin. "Husbands often take pleasure in beating out their troubles with the world on their wives."

"And the other way around, in Kerry." Angela poured more cream into her cup.

Winnie's eyes were growing bigger than the saucers. "Well, in Paris, the wives who need a vacation from their duties at home stay in the library's hotel."

"Ann Arbor is no different from the rest of the world." Mrs. Lazarus smiled at Winnie. "If you want to invite the women who need refuge to stay with you, no one will fault you."

"Mrs. Lazarus, could I impose on you to let Winnie keep Flicka for me." Angela held out her hand to Winnie. "Until I settle on a farm in Illinois?"

"Of course, dear." Mrs. Lazarus kept her attention on Winnie's face.

"I'd love to keep her," Winnie said, "while you find a good place."

Angela knew she would miss the horse, but Michael took up so much room in her affections that she feared she wouldn't be able to give Flicka the attention she needed. "I know Flicka will be well cared for."

Winnie was all smiles and finished her pot of chocolate.

"Women make better friends than men," Angela said. "Don't they, Aunt?"

"Not always," Aunt Elizabeth said, wistfully.

"Sad, she is," Angela explained, "being away from Uncle Henry for such a long time."

"Is it a premonition?" Winnie asked.

"No," Aunt Elizabeth said. "I always think I know what the Lord has in store for me, but the fact is, His will for the edification of my soul is always way ahead of my own."

"Your trust in a benevolent God is commendable," Mrs. Lazarus said. "Now we best get you ready to board the stage to Kalamazoo."

Angela prayed the Lord would keep all of the ladies happy, joyous and free. Sooner or later Michael would surely arrange a reunion with her. "God willing," Angela said out loud, startling her aunt.

# Chapter 12

*Stage to Chelsea*

Angela and her aunt were the only passengers in the rocking stage coach heading west at a speedy clip. The ride over rutted narrow roads, which caused constant bouncing about on thin cushions was exhausting.

"Does the driver intend to catch the sunset?" Angela complained of the speed but preferred the quieter stage to the smoke-belching train.

Outside the small windows of the sturdy conveyance, coral-rose tints painted the sky. Early June vegetation in the fields and the leaves in the orchards deepened their hues of green. Angela rolled the canvas rain-shield at the top of the window up as tightly as she could and filled her lungs with the sweet air of the wild strawberry fields.

"I wonder if Michael sees the same sky." Angela asked herself more than her pensive aunt.

Maybe Michael would enjoy the same view next year. Of course his travels by way of Lake Michigan to Chicago would eliminate the possibility. Sad it was for him to miss the scene.

Angela consoled herself with the knowledge that Flicka was happier in the patch of lawn behind the Ann Arbor livery than the horse would have been choking in the dust behind the stage. Winnie's affection for the white mare was evident after Winnie produced the stunning watercolors of the horses. Did Michael reconcile himself to losing their friendship by peering at his sketches of her? One of the reasons Angela allowed Winnie to keep Flicka, temporarily, was because Winnie's world contained no one to love, no one to touch. Angela's fresh love for Michael didn't qualify as a memory. Were Winnie's memories of some lost love fading? Angela's were not.

The ends of her fingers ached to touch Michael. The sight of him lingered outside her field of vision: tall, confident, and waiting for her. His base tones floated in the rumble of the stage, "Come home, come home." Angela swallowed more tears as she pressed the back of her kid glove to her lips remembering the warmth of his kiss and embrace.

\* \* \*

When they arrived in Chelsea, the white houses reflected waning pink tones from the sunset. At this, the first stop for the stage coach trip, Aunt Elizabeth inquired and found a suitable boarding house one block behind the stable. They entrusted their heavy trunks along with a nominal fee, to the stable owner, who explained that he usually rented cots for his male customers in the open attic above the horses.

"Mrs. Pierce serves a decent breakfast," the man said. "We pull out at six in the morning."

A red-headed boy and his small mixed collie were sent from the stable to alert Mrs. Pierce of their arrival.

She stood at the doorway of her neat bungalow with a white apron wrapped around her stout arms. "Now it's a pot of tea you'll be having. I've made up a plate of roast-chicken sandwiches. Jess here is heating up water for your bath upstairs. In the morning I'll get you rolled-out and well-fed in time to catch your stage."

Mrs. Pierce took Angela's travel bag in one hand and Aunt Elizabeth's in the other. "We'll just be settling your belongings a bit later, at least until you taste my raspberry tarts and orange tea." She stopped her welcoming chatter to ask, "Unless you'd be wanting a taste of brandy?"

Angela thought brandy might rouse the melancholy lethargy which seemed to be overwhelming her aunt, but Aunt Elizabeth answered with a forced brightness. "It's a pleasure to be staying with the likes of you."

"Irish, then, are you, too?" Mrs. Pierce laughed. "I married a German farmer thinking I'd be able to feed a brood of young'uns. The Lord held other ideas. Dead the man was before we started more than a chance at parenthood."

"Sorry," Angela said, realizing their hostess couldn't know of her own dreams of farming, or her aunt's fears of losing her husband.

Aunt Elizabeth lapsed into silence.

But Mrs. Pierce recounted enough stories about earlier boarders to cover the awkwardness. At the end of her repertoire, when Angela remembered the bath water was probably boiling, Mrs. Pierce asked: "What parts of America are ya headed for?"

"Chicago," Angela answered for her aunt. "My uncle is a banker there. Aunt Elizabeth came to Ireland to accompany me back to America."

"And you're loving it already. I can always tell a settler from a tourist." Mrs. Pierce took off her apron, but replenished their cups and kept their plates filled.

"The strawberry fields were beautiful."

"Aye they are that." Mrs. Pierce sat in a straight parlor chair at the side of the horsehair couch Angela and her aunt shared.

The parlor was well appointed. Framed paintings of the Sacred Heart of Jesus and one of the Blessed Virgin faced each other from opposite walls. Dark green brocade curtains filtered most of the light and matched the wall coverings. The mantel and fireplace appeared to be black marble. The furnishings and accoutrements surprised Angela. The simple lines of the clap-board cottage were out of tune with the resplendent room.

Angela's curiosity won out over her good manners. "Where did you find such an elegant mantel?"

"You noticed, did you?" Mrs. Pierce nearly clapped her hands. "There's not been a guest in this house who hasn't asked the same thing."

The landlady poured them more tea from the pot decorated with gold trim.

"My husband's older brother brought all this with him. He was to be setting up a priest house for a new parish in Kalamazoo. This is as far as his old body traveled, before the good Lord took him home." Mrs. Pierce broke out into a gleeful laugh, "And you know you can't take it with you." She added more seriously, "Not my taste at all, but my husband said the least we could do for his brother's memory was to put his belongings all to use. Reminds me of a funeral parlor."

The landlady didn't attend to Aunt Elizabeth, who turned a pale shade and clutched her throat.

"The stage will be taking you through Trist." Mrs. Pierce lit a colorful, glass-shaded oil lamp on the center table as evening approached. "It's a pretty town with a little creek running right through the middle. The little burg is only a stone's throw from Seymour Road. The big men downtown are spreading rumors that a rail line from Ann Arbor is going to be laid right through Trist."

"Is Kalamazoo very far?" Aunt Elizabeth asked.

"No, no." Mrs. Pierce rubbed her chin.

The lamp light brought out a rash of white short hairs along Mrs. Pierce's cheeks, chin, and upper lip.

"I've not been that far west, but I hear it's a day's ride." Mrs. Pierce picked up their plates. "I'll just be putting these dishes in the kitchen. Be right back to take you up to your rooms."

"Are you feeling ill, Aunt?" Angela asked as soon as Mrs. Pierce left the room.

"I'm not sick," Aunt Elizabeth answered, "but my mind is running away from me, chasing every imaginable fear."

"Do you think a sip of brandy will relieve you?"

"A little peace and quiet, to pray away my worries will do as well," Aunt Elizabeth smiled and then hugged Angela. "Ask the Virgin to keep Henry safe."

"I'll be doing just that," Angela promised, knowing her list would include more than Uncle Henry to watch over. There was Ma back home, and Michael free from the perils of sea travel.

* * *

*Wednesday, June 12th, 1841*

On the way to Trist, Seymour Road twisted its path though a considerable forest. Did the steep down-hill grade of the landscape discourage planners from routing a train through the town? The few flat areas broke into inevitable wet marshes where flocks of long-legged cranes stepped warily among the last winter's wild grasses. At other points, the road wound between sizable, deep lakes.

Near one lake the road rose up a considerable hill. At the crest, Angela spotted a cleared field with fresh wheat carpeting an acre of rolling hills.

"Aunt, look," Angela demanded. "Creation thought to place another bit of Ireland in America."

"True, it is," Aunt Elizabeth said. "But, those mounds could be hiding an underlay of gravel."

"Well now, Aunt, the earth seems thick and healthy enough to sustain wheat." Angela's head was knitting a yarn for her future. "I wish we could stop so I could taste the soils makeup."

"Nonsense," Aunt Elizabeth said. "You don't know salt from mold."

"Do, and then some," Angela argued, childishly. "My best friend's da taught me. Colleen was that bored with it all, but Mr. Decker liked talking my ears off."

"And where did he have good earth to let you taste, with all his rotten potatoes littering the fields." Aunt Elizabeth seemed to be cheered up by their arguing.

Angela didn't want to bring her down with the answer.

"Thought as much," her aunt dismissed the subject.

Angela lost her temper. "The churchyard."

Aunt Elizabeth went quiet.

"Sorry, Aunt," Angela apologized. "I do know. My tutor brought me one book on animal husbandry with details of the best fields for fodder."

At least, Angela congratulated herself, she hadn't been mean enough to say the word "graveyard." For there was no denying the fact her aunt didn't think Uncle Henry would meet them when they reached Chicago.

"Why else did you think I'd be wanting to buy a farm?" Angela asked.

Aunt Elizabeth waved her hand as if the importance of Angela's knowledge of different tasting soils was lost on her. "Thought you meant to marry a farmer." her aunt smiled a bit wickedly. "One, who couldn't sail away from you."

"Now you've done it." Angela laughed. "Teasing me about that rascal, Michael, is it? And me broken-hearted and trying to cheer you."

"Well," her aunt patted her hand. "We have each other for today. Even if you are my only niece, I'm growing that fond of you."

"And I you," Angela said, holding onto the stage's window frame as she leaned forward and planted an unsteady kiss on her aunt's cheek.

Angela tried to relax in the gyrating stage. She couldn't remove the beautiful rolling field, already planted, from her mind. A barn across from the lake and a house with a porch view of the glistening blue lake arose in her imagination as belonging to her. Smells of fresh plowed earth and animals encouraged her dreamscape. She could almost hear the laughter of children, the chickens' noise, and the baleful call of a calf with Michael striding toward her from the fields for the evening meal.

"Does Illinois have such sights?" Angela asked.

"Near the Fox River there are hills," her aunt remembered. "That's a day's ride west of Chicago. But mostly, Angela, the prairie gives you flat lands where the winds whip away.

"I'll find a place as good as this, or come back," Angela promised herself.

The dark sky at four in the afternoon of the next day threatened rain or worse. Their driver by the name of Ted Koelz stopped at a slight rise before entering the outskirts of Kalamazoo.

"Stretch your l… yourselves, ladies," he said, opening the door and offering his arm.

Poor man couldn't in good manners tell them to stretch their legs. Angela took pity on him. "Aunt wants to rest with the coach stopped," Angela said, as she stepped down from the stage and surveyed the greenish clouds.

"We don't have these monstrous beauties in Ireland. Are they reflecting the green hills?" Then she met Mr. Koelz's eyes.

"They're deadly," he said in a whisper of alarm.

Angela paid more attention. The tops of the clouds seemed to lift their white caps far up into the heavens. The movement of the mass of dark-bottomed clouds coming from the southwest aimed directly at them and the town below.

"Rain?" She asked.

"Hail." He nodded.

Well ice, Angela could handle that. "The change of seasons?" she asked their nervous driver.

"Tornado clouds," he answered.

"Tornado?" Aunt Elizabeth shouted from inside the coach. Angela barely remembered the word. Michael described a water spout they'd seen on the Atlantic. There was no water mass in sight. Aunt Elizabeth pulled Angela's arm, dragging her into the stage. "Drive on," she shouted to the driver, "Try to get us in the lee of the wind."

Mr. Koelz jumped to his seat and drove the horses at full tilt.

Angela watched a twirling white cloud a mile or two from them. Under the darkest part of the storm, a funnel dipped to the earth before vanishing up into the busy sky.

The stage stopped in front of a stone barn.

Ted un-harnessed the horses from their traces before Angela and her aunt descended from the stage.

"They'll be safer on their own." Aunt Elizabeth explained to Angela. "I've seen more than one tornado."

A farmer's wife frantically motioned for them to join her into what appeared to be a root cellar in her kitchen's side yard. "Hurry, hurry."

"Run, Angela!" Her aunt lit out toward the farmhouse.

Angela measured her aunt's fright by her surprising speed. She could hardly keep abreast of her.

The wind increased by the minute.

Aunt Elizabeth's hat sailed away before they could get to the cellar steps. Angela thought to retrieve it, but the hat, ribbons trailing, went straight up into the sky. Trees that lined the nearest field started to bend. The roots of one tree were hauled out by the monstrous storm. The end of the world seemed upon them. Angela's fear prevented her from recalling the words to any prayers.

The roar of the oncoming storm didn't allow introductions in the small enclosure below ground. Three men, five children, the farmer's wife, Ted Koelz, her aunt, and Angela crouched as close to the floor as possible. The children whimpered as they clung to their mother and father.

The doors to their refuge shook, and dust howled through the crevices. At one point half of the door was blown from its hinges. A barn cat, cowering on the first step of the dugout basement, screamed in despair as she was lifted tail first into the air.

Sudden quiet was worse than the roar of the storm.

Angela broke down in tears. "Jesus, Mary and Joseph! Does that happen often in America?"

"There, there," the farmer sympathized. "None of us is hurt and the Lord has His little jokes to play to keep Himself entertained."

Once they summoned the courage to creep out, the damage to the milk house and chicken coups could be assessed. The stone house and barn stood firm; the stage safe.

"A little rebuilding," the farmer said to his wife. "That's all there is."

"Thank the Lord," she said, kissing each child with a fervor they resisted.

Coffee and pieces of the strawberry-rhubarb pies revived the group. The farmer's wife had rescued the pies from the oven before signaling the travelers to follow her to safety. The pastry tasted more than fine to the survivors.

"But next time," her husband warned, "you better let them burn."

"Yes, Dear," she said, winking at the rest of them.

Back on the road with the unharmed team of horses, Angela tried to allay her aunt's fears. "Perhaps this was the disaster you supposed."

"No," Aunt Elizabeth said. "I've not been able to shake the foreboding." She smiled weakly at Angela. "Perhaps the maid has ruined my best tablecloth."

"Or bleached holes in it," Angela added, without much hope of linens being the source of her aunt's anguish.

* * *

*Thursday, June 13, 1841*

The crisp blue sky of Michigan promised calm the next day. They boarded the new Kalamazoo train, whose belching din could surely be heard in the city it was bound for, Grand Rapids. Nevertheless the evenly laid track or early hour lulled Angela's aunt into a fitful slumber. Traveling without the threat of an imminent tornado could be rather pleasant.

The porter, Robert Koelz, discussed the future of his older brother, Ted, who served as their stage coach driver through the storm. "He does not understand. My brother's heels are slipping in the sands of time."

"Won't we always need private conveyances?" Angela enjoyed the company of the dapper old man.

His shoes were shined; his kinky gray hair was styled in a halo of curls. Robert Koelz's moustache occupied the time other men used to fill their pipes in order to gain some privacy of thought.

"Ah." Mr. Koelz pointed at her. "But would the public keep paying for a conveyance that shakes their teeth out of their mouths when they could be riding the train."

Angela laughed and Aunt Elizabeth moaned.

Angela motioned for Mr. Koelz to follow her to the end of the empty car. "My aunt has a premonition that her husband isn't well in Chicago."

"Nonsense," Mr. Koelz said. "Sheer nonsense."

"Do you know Mr. Breckenridge?" Angela asked, hopeful of good news.

"Of course not." Mr. Koelz re-positioned his porter's cap. "If people really experienced premonitions about the future, we'd all be rich."

"Why?" Angela asked. In the past 'why' proved the best weapon in conversation when she couldn't formulate a question to ask about an unfathomable subject.

"Because, you pretty thing, presidents, kings, and financial wizards would pay their entire fortunes for knowledge of the future." He patted his moustache. "And you don't hear of any of them being taken in by such gibberish. Do you?"

"But...." Angela found nothing but faith to refute him.

"No buts." Mr. Koelz wrote on the back of her ticket and handed it to her.

"As it was, it is," Angela read. "What does that mean?"

"That's the trouble with you young people and the likes of my brother." Mr. Koelz rolled the tip of his moustache. "None of you can accept reality. Change who you are; that's the only way to keep ahead of the pack."

\* \* \*

The next mode of travel out of Grand Rapids was river bound. Angela and her silent aunt booked passage down the Grand River on a steamship named the Govenor Mason.

Angela remembered the high-and-mighty sister of the governor who allowed Michael to kiss her hand in Detroit. If the lady had known the amount of wealth under the cap of the lighthouse keeper, she might have been less condescending to them. Angela wasn't unhappy with Miss Mason's lack of education about the matter, but she'd caught a brief glimpse of the sort of woman who gave Michael so much trouble in Berkshire.

Angela's necessity to find a suitable farm included the desire to prove to Michael that she didn't need or want his parents' money. All she wanted was Michael Halliday to share her days, to father her brood, to enjoy the simple life she imagined good and happy people lived; outside, walking the fragrant open fields, tending the woolly flocks, and gratefully gathering the harvest. A Garden of Eden that needed the working but guaranteed happiness, that's all she wanted for Michael and herself. "Please God," Angela prayed out loud.

And her aunt answered with a fervent, "Amen," to silent entreaties for her husband's health.

In Grand Rapids, the Captain of the Governor Mason wouldn't hazard Lake Michigan with his small steamer. "Those winds come screaming up the length of Lake Michigan to drown more than one sailor. Raging fates are too much for me," the captain warned, "and I with the Governor's ship to mind."

"If we meant to make the trip in November," Aunt Elizabeth bickered, "I could see your point, but today is a mild June day."

"Never heard of a June hurricane?" he asked.

Angela hadn't lost the terror instilled by the tornado. "Let him go, Aunt. We'll find a bigger ship."

"Aye. Do that," he dismissed them and then relented, giving them a morsel of help. "The Milwaukee's a sound ship, built in '37 in Scotland. She'll be sailing later today to Chicago."

He pointed to the ship docked next to the Gov. Mason.

From the pier the Milwaukee seemed as large as the Pannonia. The bow rose two stories above them with a pert pilot-house capping the sprightly ship. A bronze eagle stood guard on the tip of the roof over the captain's post. Flags were flying in her bared rigging, but the steam funnel and side-wheel were silent.

"She's big enough for the Atlantic," Angela said.

The captain wasn't buying that. "The Atlantic is a cakewalk compared to the cutting choppy waves of the Great Lakes. I've hired many a swaggering sailor professing to be seaworthy and then had the pleasure of watching them turn as green as the new fellers once they're spilling their guts in a gale." The captain tipped his hat and bade them goodbye. "Sorry for my language ladies."

Angela asked her aunt. "And what was he apologizing for. I didn't hear him swear or mention our limbs or legs?"

"Guts," Aunt Elizabeth directed a stevedore to follow them up the gangplank of the Milwaukee. "Or mentioning seasickness."

"Why is it that we're the nurses who know their bottoms as well as our own from babysitting and caring for them, and they're the ones not able to mention our parts or functions?"

"They like to surround us in a great mystery in order to glamorize their baser needs," her aunt answered.

Angela didn't approve or enjoy the information. "But Aunt, what's a cakewalk?"

"Marabell, my maid at home, told me," her aunt said. "It's a dance where the best performer receives a cake."

"I don't know the steps," Angela said.

"Well, it's not as if I'd be using a servants' dance to entertain my friends."

Angela was surprised at the uppity attitude her aunt assumed. Chicago might be a problem for an Irish girl only wanting to find and buy a good farm.

Aunt Elizabeth's mood changed again as soon as they were in open water. "Did you notice the difference between the Pannonia and the Milwaukee?"

They were promenading along the wooden decks of the stable ship. Bared ropes and sail-wrapped rigging provided a canopy of organized chaos above them. The smoke from the boiler blew north, and the gulls quit their possessive hovering as the ship moved steadily in a southwesterly direction.

"I notice the deck chairs are sturdy benches," Angela said.

Aunt Elizabeth opened the lid of the seat next to them and pulled out two leather cushions. "More comfortable," she said patting the cushion next to her.

"You're feeling much better, aren't you?" Angela happily joined her aunt.

"I am," she said. "I love this boat. I've been a passenger more than once."

"Your honeymoon?"

"Yes," her aunt blushed. "In fact Henry and I sat right here waiting for the shoreline of Illinois to appear."

"How big is this lake?" Angela asked, noticing the round curve of the horizon, which reminded her of the Atlantic's massive distances.

"Bigger than Ireland and twice as cranky." Aunt Elizabeth laughed.

Angela laughed too, in relief. Seeing her aunt unable to shake the burden of her premonition increased the tension of each mile traversed in Michigan. Chicago's destination across the calm waters of Lake Michigan chased her aunt's fears into some hidden recess of her mind.

"Do I need a coming-out party?" Angela asked, thinking of the falseness in Michael's stories of society.

"If you want me to introduce you to anyone as my niece." Aunt Elizabeth bopped the back of Angela's bonnet with a friendly whack.

"I thought the name might imply match-making."

"It does that," Aunt Elizabeth said in a merry tone. "And what's the harm in letting all of the eligible young men in Chicago whet their appetites on an Irish beauty such as yourself."

"Whet their appetites?"

"Well, don't you be letting them bite your neck." Aunt Elizabeth's laugh rang out over the empty sea.

"I've promised Michael I'd be waiting only for him."

"Nonsense," Aunt Elizabeth dismissed. "Wait until you see the whites of his eyeballs or are at least until you're able to count his teeth, before you discourage the attentions of other young men." Looking out to sea, her aunt failed to note Angela's distress. "Perhaps Michael will be toothless by the time he's sketched and inked all the things on the good earth that he deems worthy. We'll have to buy him those wooden teeth I've heard about, if he ever shows up in Chicago."

When Angela didn't answer, her aunt apologized. "Angela, I'm sorry. I feel energized by the smell of home. I've not been gentle with your loss."

"I'm all right, Aunt." Angela lied. "I feel good hearing your laughter."

"But not at your expense, Dear." Aunt Elizabeth drew Angela to her. "Let's walk some more."

Angela headed north and her aunt went south. They stopped and laughed at each other's opposite directions. Angela joined her aunt, but couldn't help wondering what was happening to the north, in Lake Superior. Had Michael reached Strawberry Island yet? Did he miss her as much as she missed him?

When the time came, would she be able to pursue her dream alone like Michael? She would need hired hands, a milkmaid, maybe even a cook when the orphans or children of unwed mothers arrived.

But Angela knew without Michael, all of those people would not be able to fulfill the place her soul required. Her aunt was dear to her, but she'd want to remain in the city boundaries of Chicago. The people they'd met on their journey would stay in Angela's heart. Some would remain correspondents for the rest of her life. Of course, the Lord would be there, always.

"But dear Lord," she prayed, silently. "Let Michael be my refuge day-by-day while I'm destined to serve You on this earth." Angela added, humbled by the desperation of her need, "if it is Your will."

* * *

*Saturday, June 15th, 1841*
*Chicago, Illinois*

The gray day they reached the door of Aunt Elizabeth's home, the maid wept when she answered their knock. "Thank the Lord, you're home," she sobbed.

"Mr. Breckenridge?" Aunt Elizabeth whispered.

"Mighty sick." The black maid's eyes rolled heavenward. "You've not come a moment too soon."

That night a priest, as old and frail as any Angela had ever seen, came to the house to give the last rites.

"Aren't you afraid of the disease?" Angela asked.

"Seen it all," the priest answered. "I've weathered many a storm of influenza, but it must not be my time." As an afterthought he asked, "Is your soul in need of comfort?"

"No," Angela answered, wanting to shout. 'Yes! My man is miles away; my aunt can't speak without weeping. I miss Ma. Why am I here, Lord?' Instead she showed the priest to the door. "Thank you for coming. A blessing on your head."

The priest stopped in his tracks.

Angela thought he'd taken ill. She scooted a chair under him, pushing his shoulder so that he would sit. "Marabell," she called for the maid. "Bring Father a cup of tea."

"I'm all right, girl." The priest said. "I've received perfunctory thanks in these grim duties, but as yet I hadn't received one blessing."

"It's my Irish," Angela felt she should apologize.

"No," he said. "I felt it, a real blessing from the Lord." He looked directly at Angela. "You're missing a young man who's far away." He motioned with his right arm behind him. "North."

"Yes," she said, awed by his knowledge. "I am that. Did Aunt Elizabeth speak of Michael?"

"No," he said, standing to leave and waving off the tea. "I'll pray for you both, Angela. You know you two have the names of angels."

* * *

*Friday, June 21st, 1841*

Angela placed the black wreath of funeral ribbons on the Breckenridge door not a week later. Several neighbors had the same bleak omen on their front doors. The flu swept through the streets of Chicago taking loved and hated both to their eternal homes. At least her aunt had arrived in time to kiss her living husband goodbye. "Faint comfort that," Angela said to the empty hallway.

No funeral would be held with the epidemic raging. During the weeks following her uncle's death, Angela was left to herself. Her aunt worried over the estate and managed her own grief. Uncle Henry owed more debts than Aunt Elizabeth realized.

Angela's wardrobe needed work. After Marabell laundered every last item, Angela surveyed the trip's damage. Her blue woolen cape suffered salt stains on its hem. Angela remembered her courage in defending herself in front of Captain Hale and the last sight of him with his hand raised against her. Where was Michael now? Her defender abandoned her.

She released sovereigns from the cape's hem and stacked them neatly on her bureau. Angela wrote Ma about Uncle Henry and the farm she'd spotted off Seymour Road near Chelsea, Michigan. About the subject of meeting and loving Michael Halliday, Angela referred to, "people I miss after becoming acquainted on the Pannonia.'

Six of Ma's 170 original sovereigns were spent for the Atlantic passage and the Hudson River ticket. Aunt Elizabeth paid for the rest of the trip to Chicago. Angela released each gold coin reverently from the hems of the rest of her skirts and the edges of her bonnets. The poker winnings from the one game aboard the Pannonia more than covered the travel costs. The remaining sovereigns were plenty to buy sizable farm acreage and stock and seed. Better than she could find in all of Ireland, she told herself.

Angela decided her wardrobe would suffice until profits from the farm secured her future. Angela folded and kissed the bright blue ribbon she'd worn when Michael left on the Thomas Jefferson. She missed her gentle giant and prayed he was well.

With Marabell's and her husband, Matt's, help, Angela purchased a carriage of her own. She hired Matt as her faithful driver, when Aunt Elizabeth had no need of him.

Two-day jaunts to the Fox River Valley increased for Angela as the summer wore on. The Hotel Baker in St. Charles served a proper meal, and their stables accommodated the carriage and horses. Matt confided that he didn't mind earning a nickel or two serving an evening as a stable hand.

A farm on McDonald Road west of the town of St. Charles drew Angela back again and again. The short drive leading to the house passed a massive oak that blessed her with its cooling shade. Behind the house, down a slight ravine, a fresh spring-fed creek ran through a narrow pasture.

One prime acre of the 350 acre farm melted Angela's heart. The land stood at a fork in the road leading to the place. The perfect square of flat black fallow land called to her as much as any orphan could.

The abandoned white-washed stone house included a spacious upstairs with four bedrooms. The front entrance was paneled in dark walnut and the two-tiered staircase sported a beveled glass window facing the front yard from its first landing.

The kitchen's wood cooking stove and a basement wood-stoked furnace below the dining room's grate would heat even the upstairs through a cast iron vent in the dining room's ceiling. The large parlor with sliding wood doors was west of the central dining room. And a bedroom at the end of the parlor would serve as a summer bedroom or a library. In winter, Angela planned to pull the sliding doors shut to contain the heat.

Finding the owner was the most difficult part of the transaction. The neighbors related more than one story of farm managers making grievous errors in judgment. By the time Angela secured correspondence with the absentee owner, she heard a story which kept the sovereigns in her bureau undisturbed.

West of the acre winning Angela's heart with its black loam on the far side of the house and barn was a low lying field of peat. The bog caught fire from lightning one night. Angela visited the smoking mess in the daytime, but the neighbors advised her to see the strange thing at night, which she did.

The fiendish red glow under the seemingly moving earth caused by the waves of heat emanating from the fire was as close to Hell as Angela intended to go. She wrote the owner another farmer accepted her offer to buy land. Angela released him to sell his farm to some other unsuspecting buyer.

# Chapter 13

*Earlier: June 10th, 1841*

When Michael left Detroit aboard the side-paddle steamship, the Thomas Jefferson, he knew the extent of his grievous error. The chance Angela might find a sturdy chap looking for an uncommon woman was more than likely to occur. If a farming gentleman needed a wife who loved being outside to inhale the pungent smells of fresh-plowed earth and who just happened to believe in having a big family to love, Angela could be lost to Michael.

He felt sadness close to the grief he'd experienced after his younger sister's death. Despair washed over him as the gentle waves of Lake St. Clair lapped against the side of the rumbling ship. Michael shuddered, realizing he might well end up in the corner of some fashionable English parlor a year hence. A bachelor for life. His failure would be measured by the contaminating atmosphere of his only proficiency - to puff on a pipe.

The problem was Michael's body didn't believe his future with Angela was lost. Every cell reacted to thoughts of her as if she nestled on his lap. The shopping trip in New York, when he drew Angela to him and kissed her dear face, re-emerged in his imagination. His nerves were stretched to their limit. He tried to maintain a certain calm by praying for Angela's happiness. The prayers helped him cling tenaciously to sanity.

He could mesh with Angela's future more easily than he could succumb to his parents' hopes. Farther than the distance of an ocean, England retreated from the realm of possibilities. Instead of a peaceful respite from filial demands, rather than an artist's haven where a sufficiency of unfettered hours promised concentration needed for his art, Strawberry Island conjured a dreadfully lone existence.

Michael rubbed his vest button, the one Angela's aunt pounded when she scolded him for trifling with Angela's affection. The bruise remained, but Michael knew the enemy of his happiness reigned within himself.

Captain Marryat coughed loudly as he approached Michael's stance at the rail.

Michael focused on the ship's progress trying to steady himself for the Captain's cynical conversation.

On some level Marryat seemed to sense Michael's suffering. "My stories of sea disasters contain elements of truth," Captain Marryat began.

"I'm sure they do," Michael said, preparing to disengage his feelings from their favorite fixation, Angela McGovern.

"I watched a schooner trying to reach safety near a lighthouse in Lake Erie, but it ran aground close to the piers." Captain Marryat pulled the brim of his sea cap down, as if to see the mishap the better. "A wave capsized the rescue boat after it had been loaded with helpless passengers."

Wanting to encourage the conversation, Michael offered, "To qualify for the lightkeeper's job, I have to participate in three rescue attempts."

Marryat nodded. "A second rescue boat saved everyone else off the doomed craft."

Story after story of shipwrecks and groundings lightened Michael's black mood by the comparison of his melancholy to actual calamities others suffered. At least Angela still walked the good earth.

After a conversational diet of disasters, Marryat and Michael filled their luncheon plates with roast-beef sandwiches. They managed to walk and swallow at the same time measuring the steamship's decks as it glided up the gently flowing Huron River.

"I can't stop thinking about Angela," Michael admitted.

Marryat slapped his back. "Buck up boy. You'll be busy enough at the lighthouse to keep your mind free of your temporarily lost sweetheart."

"I have lost her," Michael said. "Forever." Part of his sandwich seemed lodged permanently in his constricting throat.

Pointing to the wide expanse of Lake Huron as it came into view at the mouth of the river, Marryat suggested. "Let's wash this lunch down with a pint…to celebrate the grand horizon."

In the bar, disheartened Michael sipped at his glass of port. When had he elected to test his artistic talent on such a secluded island? Lake Huron seemed as huge as the ocean with the watery horizon an endless line. Lake Superior was reportedly even bigger.

Marryat waved to John Logan, the Scottish lawyer, to join them in the bar. "This your first visit to the Great Lakes?"

"It is," John Logan replied. "If one has the means, I think touring the world is the duty of the educated public."

"To enlighten the natives?" Marryat scoffed.

John Logan laughed politely. "More to fill out my repertoire with the young ladies back home."

"Don't mention damsels in front of our suffering swain." Marryat indicated Michael, who lifted his elbows back off the bar.

"Have you any disaster stories?" Michael asked. "Captain Marryat possesses a valuable stock."

"We'll be putting in at Presque Isle for supplies of wood for the boilers." John Logan accepted a glass of port. "I hear there are several wrecked vessels visible near the piers."

The three men kept their eyes on the coastline of Michigan from the port windows of the bar.

Michael considered the possibility that all men, at least these two traveling companions, suffered from wrong life-altering decisions. Perhaps the fates guaranteed suffering once the gates of the Garden of Eden slammed shut.

A near sob escaped, but Michael covered it a coughing fit and a swallow of port. Marryat's pounding on his back provided more comfort. The Captain's hand gripped Michael's upper arm longer than was needed to steady a drinking buddy.

John Logan commented, "I think you can let go of the lad, Marryat. I doubt his religion allows suicide. Besides, the only true love is unrequited love."

"What, what?" Michael said, planting his feet farther apart as if to support continued drinking of the delicious port wine.

Marryat took the conversation into a different direction. "Last year I met Jeremiah Moors, a retired lumberman from Detroit. Plans to build a lighthouse at the harbor. He said there's a handy sawmill at the site."

"I hear Lake Superior has the most storms," Michael said, somewhat embarrassed at his obvious ploy for a contest to divert his thoughts from Angela.

"The most treacherous lake to navigate is Erie," Marryat took off his hat as if to salute the lake.

Michael noted a bald spot as perfectly round as the Berkshire friar's. Angela admired Michael's luxurious curls. After he mentioned the trip to Lake Superior, when she slammed the new hat on his head in the haberdashery, her eyes revealed her frustration with him. Michael stuffed his hands in his coat pockets in order to avoid running his fingers through his hair.

In sympathy for the loss of a good head of hair on Marryat's head, Michael said, "I've heard hidden rocks and dangerous shoals surround Strawberry Island in Lake Superior. They stretch out two miles from the bottom of the cliff."

"Aye," Marryat said, rubbing the crown of his head as if feeling the pity Michael sent his way. "Sand banks and sand bars move about in the storms of Lake Erie."

John Logan poured himself his third glass of port. "Giving due weight for the unknown, I'd cast my vote for the most ominous waters to Lake Superior. The jagged coastlines with their swift currents have earned respect from the fishermen up there. Only a few steamships out of Marquette tried out her seas and came back to tell their tales."

Michael fought to nail his emotions down into the inner recesses of his heart, but he couldn't escape the constant longing for Angela. The pain of missing her could motivate him to deny her, but the hour was too late to stop loving Angela.

"Heard of 30-foot waves," Marryat shook his head. "But Lake Erie has a magnetic reef off the east side of Cockburn Island. Throws off ships' magnetic compasses, and sailors find themselves trapped on the dangerous shoal." He replaced his cap at their rapt attention.

Michael's head was spinning from the wine or the news that he might not have time for his art with all the life-saving he'd have to be doing. Angela's musical voice leapt to his ears in his last unspoken phrase.

The dire state of his broken heart disallowed sleep that night. Escaping the confines of his cabin, Michael sought out Splendor in steerage.

The black horse backed away from his rider. He stomped and snorted making a terrible racket.

"What's the matter, Splendor?" Michael approached quietly. He realized the horse smelled the afternoon's consumption of alcohol. "Do you miss your stall mate, Flicka?"

Michael calmed his horse by speaking softly and moving his hand slowly along the horse's neck. "Don't desert me."

Where Angela was concerned, Michael admitted to being the guilty one. He willingly boarded the ship bound in the opposite direction from her destination.

"I am the culprit," he whispered quietly.

Splendor agreed but allowed himself to be curried.

\* \* \*

*Tuesday, June 11th, 1841*

The simple act of dressing in the morning and leaving his cabin for breakfast called up prodigious amounts of willpower. Michael's feet dragged when he tried to walk the deck, his hands fumbled with the blasted pipe, and his nose decided to catch a cold. The inner weeping took a toll on his youthful energy. At noon he carefully examined his curls to determine if the hair turned white overnight from the extent of his endless travail. He hoped Angela's day had been happier.

\* \* \*

*Wednesday, June 12th, 1841*

The evening of the next day, the Thomas Jefferson reached Forty Mile Point in time for the evening meal to be served. The weather was not as warm, for the month of June, as it was in Michael's lost world of England. What elements of weather were mixing around Angela's world?

Mrs. Jameson dominated the dinner-table conversation. "I don't understand why you didn't bring the lass along with you," she said. "Many a woman has served as lightkeeper when her husband fell ill or worse."

"I thought lightkeepers were expected to be single." A faint light of hope twinkled in Michael's heart. Mica, mica, he recalled Angela quoting her mother's Latin verse of goodbye, parva stella! Miror quae narn sis, ram bella. Twinkle, twinkle, little star; how I wonder where you are.

Mrs. Jameson waved her hand over Michael's plate to gain his attention. "Benajah Wolcott and Rachel have served since 1823 on Marblehead in Ohio."

"I visited near there," John Logan added. "Kelley's Island has exposed glacial formations with native petroglyphs and inscriptions cut into the rocks."

Would Angela consent to join him at the lighthouse? A new bottomless chasm opened for Michael's terrors. She might say no.

"There's another couple I wrote about," Marryat said. "Mrs. Rademuller claims her husband disappeared in 1815. He still haunts the Gibraltar Point Lighthouse in Lake Ontario."

Lines from Dante's Inferno in Angela's voice pierced Michael's darkened soul. "Thy spirit is smitten with cowardice, which often encumbers a man turning him back from honorable enterprise at a mistaken sight, a shying beast."

Mrs. Jameson folded and unfolded her napkin. She licked her lips deciding, no doubt, which dessert would be the healthiest. John Logan polished a not pristine spoon before ladling three scoops of sugar into his tea. Marryat eyed the emptying wine bottle as if a friend's life ebbed before his eyes. The comfort of amplifying the innocent foibles of others diminished the size of Michael's glaring offense.

Michael's body straightened in his chair as he summoned new-found strength in more of Dante's in his beloved Beatrice's words, "Only those things should be feared that have power to do us ill, nothing else."

A fresh hunger inspired Michael to finish the cold greasy vegetables on his plate. Stirred to note the exact moment of transformation, he opened his Berkshire watch. Seven. A lucky number that. The walls of the sumptuously appointed ship's dining room expanded. The reds of the carpet grew more lavish, the greenery in the centerpieces more lush, the sparkle from the oil lanterns waxed eloquently across each shining surface.

Above the chatter of other diners, the comfort of the boilers' rumble reached Michael's ears. All creation hummed in harmony. Unable to remain seated with his potent resolve, Michael rose spilling the continuing quotes from his mind, "Never were men on earth so swift to seek their good and to escape their hurt as I."

Michael excused himself. "I'm taking John Logan's advice," he said. "I have a marriage proposal to compose."

"I never give advice," John Logan protested.

Marryat nodded in approval. "Good show!"

"A finer act couldn't be imagined." Mrs. Jameson stood to shake Michael's hand.

At Mackinac City, Michael disembarked from the Thomas Jefferson after entrusting Mrs. Jameson with his Chicago-bound letter to Angela.

He kissed Mrs. Jameson's plump cheek and shook hands all round. "Thank you for bearing with me while I sorted out the obvious."

# Chapter 14

*June 12th, 1841*

Michael spent a day at Mackinac City to secure passage to the Soo. A steamship piloted by Jerry Cross, the lighthouse inspector for Lake Superior, happened to be docked at the harbor for supplies.

"Portage around the rapids slows us down some," Inspector Cross, a mere wisp of a man, said, "but a year's supply of sperm whale oil can't be found up there. No flower or vegetable seeds either. Got five lighthouses to stock. 300 gallons each per year."

"You portage the steamboat?" Even after seeing first-hand the engineering feats accomplished at the deep trench on the Erie Canal, Michael couldn't imagine the hoists or men needed for such a task.

"Nope," Inspector Cross said. "My lightship's waiting. Other side of St. Mary's River."

Michael planned to pump the man for every morsel of knowledge he possessed about Strawberry Island, just as he had quizzed Captain Hale on the Pannonia. Inspector Cross gave no direct indication he would withhold facts, but his cropped sentences, even his shortened stature, persuaded Michael information would not be offered freely.

Michael lent his back to the business of loading and unloading supplies from the steamship. Portaging and reloading the lightship, the Illinois, used muscles Michael didn't know existed until their sore complaints emerged the next day.

Inspector Cross seemed to appreciate Michael's willingness to share the work load by rewarding him with news of his duties on Strawberry Island. "Efficiency is the key," he said. "Superintendent of Lighthouses, Mr. Thomas Harty, awards a green flag with an "E" on it for the best-run post."

Michael decided not to comment or ask questions. Perhaps the inspector would open up if silence left him unsure of his listener. Michael purposefully surveyed the massive seas of Lake Superior so as not to reveal his stupidity or hunger for enlightenment.

Inspector Cross did continue. "The keeper's logbook lists the passing ships. And the weather every four hours. Night or Day."

Michael fished for his diary, turning it upside down to note down the Inspector's instructions.

That seemed to open the dam of Inspector Cross' directions. "Lantern room scrubbed and brass fixtures polished each day. Strawberry Island's lighthouse tower's made of hand-hewn limestone blocks. Limestone's quarried from Kingston, Ontario. Hexagonal masonry's six feet thick, walls taper up to a height of 70 feet. Because she's setting up on that 40 foot clay bluff her focal point shines horizontally across the lake for a visibility of fifteen miles."

Michael relaxed but kept writing.

Inspector Cross bent over to read what Michael wrote. He pointed his index finger at the word 'Kingston.' "Don't need that," he said.

Michael erased the sentence and kept his pencil poised.

"Each light has its own distinctive flash pattern." Inspector Cross stepped down from the block that let him see over the ship's wheel. He leaned back against the side of the pilot house but kept his eyes on the lake and his hand on the wheel. "I'll take an inventory of the supplies once we land. Take back everything you don't need that I can carry. Lantern used Argand mirrored-image lamps in the past. Haven't retrieved the store of extra wicks for it. Strawberry uses second-order Fresnel lens now. I've brought you fishnet and 20 pounds of soap and two chamois to clean the glass of the lantern. Fresnel lens are arranged in beehive-like patterns of lenses and prisms that surround the light. The lens reflect and refract the light to produce a single, high-intensity beam. The revolving light is driven by a clockwork system. The heavy-weight mechanism that turns the rotating lens has to be rewound by hand every six hours. The lantern sends a warning signal from sunset to sunrise during the navigational season."

"Now, you don't need to write this down," Inspector Cross said, "but my family's been fishermen on Lake Superior for three generations. They first hung a lantern in the trees to guide the family home after dark. Then they built a tower to warn crafts of the location of the shoals around the point so's they could maneuver past in violent storms."

"I haven't participated in any rescues," Michael admitted. "We witnessed one storm on the Atlantic that panicked a few of the passengers, but the lifeboats were not lowered."

"Panic's worse than the storm," Inspector Cross said. His voice faded into recollections.

Michael feared Inspector Cross might even be reconsidering allowing him to take over as lighthouse keeper.

However, Inspector Cross continued, "Many a lightkeeper assists survivors of sunken ships after they arrive in their ship's yawl. There's an anchor on Strawberry Island from a schooner rebuilt at the Soo after disassembling it in St. Marys River and hauling it overland around those dangerous rapids. Sank in winter storms of 1829 or '30. Collided with another ship out of Marquette. No survivors made it to shore. There's a signal hoist to raise weather flags for passing vessels. Can't see them in the dark."

Michael couldn't restrain himself, "A fog-horn."

"Getting to it," Inspector Cross said, pointing to a partially submerged wreck off White Fish Point. "Hadn't seen that one before. This is the graveyard of Superior. My friend Ishmael Hill's a veteran of the 1812 War. Works at Sodus Bay in New York. Anyways, Ishmael always says to mark the wrecks. Enough of 'em pile up, they make a lighthouse out of them."

Michael ventured a smile.

"Yep," Inspector Cross said, deadpan. "That's about it."

Michael flipped a page in his diary and Inspector Cross took up where he left off in his instructions.

"The foghorn gave the last keeper fits. Reverberated through the tower and the house. You'll see. We finally built a boiler house past the kitchen. It's steam powered. Still makes a hellava racket."

"My father runs a clockworks factory in London," Michael offered.

"Good," Inspector Cross said. "Don't have to convince you about the need to rewind the rotating lens mechanism. Keep alert to the port side now. These tall rock faces have outcrops and holes that create natural arches."

"Pretty as a picture," Michael said, wishing he was brave enough to tell Inspector Cross he'd chosen to be a lightkeeper in order to have time for his art. The free time allowed for sketching seemed a lot less than he imagined would be afforded while living on a solitary island.

"Those outcroppings reach out to ships underwater," Inspector Cross said.

Michael waited for more news of his island, Strawberry Island, but the Inspector retreated into his private thoughts.

A half-an-hour, Michael closed his diary.

"Sorry," Inspector Cross said. "My mind wanders when I think of some of the victims I've hauled aboard."

"Must be ghastly," Michael said, softly. Then he asked a question realizing he would be doing the Inspector a service by keeping his mind on less painful subjects. Michael's reflections contained their own harrowing worries. "What's the nearest town to Strawberry Island?"

"Bayfield," Cross answered, before realizing the full scope of the question. "You're part of a group of 22 islands, called the Apostle Islands. Strawberry's the most remote. There's plans underway to build six more lighthouses. Might take a while to finish all of 'em. Yours is the only one manned. Michigan Island, Outer Island, Sand Island, Devil's Island and Chequemegon Point all will sport tall tower lights. With the steamships coming more and more out of Marquette, Bayfield's getting to be a busy shipping port."

\* \* \*

*Thursday, June 13th, 1841*

They reached Strawberry Island's wooden pier early the next morning. Dark clouds scurried across the lake from the north. Inspector Cross wasn't pleased with the weather's development. He worked fiendishly alongside Michael to off-load the supplies.

"Leave them here," the Inspector said, regressing into his monosyllabic speaking style. "I'll light the lamp. Show you where the weights need to be pulled. Will you be able to figure out the foghorn?"

"Not a problem," Michael said with more surety than he possessed. He tied Splendor to the hitching post out front.

The Inspector unlocked the door of the lighthouse and ushered Michael in. "I'm going to ride out this storm in Bayfield harbor. I'll stop by on the way back to the Soo." After starting the oil lamp at the top of the tower Inspector Cross nearly ran back to the lightship. He called back over his shoulder to Michael, "Can you handle it?"

"Yes, Sir." Michael called after him.

"Don't forget to feed the chickens and get them inside before it rains," the Inspector yelled. "The horse stall is behind the chicken house."

Michael continued his surveillance of the lightship with 'Illinois' painted in large red letters on the rear panel until the boat vanished as it rounded the coast line of the nearest island.

Splendor mildly sniffed his new stall, content with the bucket of oats and hastily strewn hay.

Barrels of whale oil awaited transport to the oil barn. The crated chickens anticipated their release. A crude wooden tramway used to haul the rescue boat from the pier during storms served Michael well. He stowed the oil, let the chickens free in a fenced yard next to their coop, stacked the food on the kitchen table and dumped the cleaning supplies in the boiler house, before dark.

Michael had never made a pot of coffee for himself. First he found a dusty cup and saucer, then the coffee pot. After hauling water and wood into the kitchen as well as tackling and overpowering the kitchen's wood stove, Michael drank a cup of water from a hastily wiped cup. He set a pot of water to boil and flaked off a few chips of soap for eventual dishwater.

He hoped food would revive him after the strenuous chores. Fresh tomatoes and a slice of cheese appeared to be the only makings for supper until he found six tins of sardines in one of the cupboards. He finished off all six, four tomatoes and half of the cheese.

"I'd give my eye tooth for a piece of bread," he said to the empty stove.

In another cupboard he came upon a tin box of crackers. "Not that stale," he said until he came to the moldy one.

Then he remembered the chickens. He didn't know if chickens ate crackers but he went out to the coop anyway to make sure they were inside.

The sky was black and the greenish beam from the tower high above him offered no light for the path. Michael went back inside and lit a lamp near the boiler room's back door. He found the chicken coop with every chicken housed within. He shut the side hatch doors before throwing crackers on the floor. Quite a bit of noise and feathers ensued. Spotting an egg, he thanked the chicken and cradled it carefully back to the kitchen.

Eating an egg wasn't nearly as complicated as making one edible. Michael found a small pan and filled it with water. He let the water boil before he delicately lowered the egg down into the pan with a spoon. Holding the handle with a towel, Michael lifted the pan every so often so the rolling egg wouldn't smash against the sides of the pan. After twenty minutes by the hands on his watch Michael deemed the egg good enough to eat.

"Must be an easier way." He placed the egg in the cupboard for tomorrow's breakfast.

Coffee was an even bigger problem, one he decided to leave until morning.

He unpacked his sea chest far enough to find one blanket which he laid on the feather mattress before sinking into a minute of slumber. Michael bolted upright as soon as sleep overtook him. The weights. He would have to check the weights before he let himself succumb to sleep.

The tower's base was the first-floor room in the cottage between arched doorways on opposite sides leading to the kitchen and the one bedroom. A brass chimney reached all the way to the lantern hung over a narrow rectangular table in the center of the room. Michael could see the weights contained in the shaft through windows placed intermittently along its lengthy trip to the top. Michael pulled the chains at the base of the shaft until the weights could be seen in the top window of the brass casing.

After noting the time, nine o'clock, on his watch, he tumbled into bed, hoping he would wake in time to refill the lamp with oil and rewind the clockwork.

Promptly at 3:00 a.m., Michael jumped off the bed, tripping over his shoes. Holding one mangled foot he hopped into the tower room. He pulled the chains of the clockworks in the dark, before lighting a lamp. A dumbwaiter in one half of the brass chimney carried oil up to the top of the lantern. Michael scurried up the stone steps along the inside of the tower to replenish the lamp's oil.

A door in one of the lantern's side led out to a stone walkway with iron balustrades and two railings encircling the wooden cage. Michael hunched over to get out. He held onto the roof of the domed structure as he walked around the tower. The moon shone on the rough water below. Whatever storm threatened Inspector Cross blew itself apart over the lake, but the water still churned up whitecaps for the moon to lick.

Michael forgot to write down the weather before retiring. He set the lamp on the table under the weights and noted the foul weather at sunset. For the next entry he wrote, "3:00 a.m." Storm passed overhead. Clear sky. Full moon. Rough water."

Michael returned to bed planning to be awake in three hours.

At six o'clock he awoke on schedule with a gigantic hunger. He could have devoured his blanket. Thanking the Lord for his cooked egg, Michael set to peeling the egg shell. Popping the entire egg in his mouth, he promptly spit it across the room. Spoiled and inedible.

After cleaning up the egg, he lit the stove and threw a handful of ground coffee into the coffee pot. At least his cup and saucer were clean this time. In storing his supplies, he found the lard and decided to try frying an egg. The cookbook Angela enticed him to buy provided information on biscuit making but not egg frying. Apparently some things are known from birth for women.

The coffee smelled great, and with a sip of the passable brew, Michael felt encouraged enough to hunt out another egg from the chickens. He let Splendor out of his stall to investigate his island pasture without supervision.

Cracking the egg over bubbling fat spat a large jet of hot grease onto his bare arm. He wiped at it with a towel then lifted the pan from the heat. He jiggled the egg around in the cooling fat, then sat the pan back on the heat. Michael basted the top of the egg by spooning hot lard on the yolk, surprised to see it firm up just fine.

He ate the egg before attempting the biscuits, but attempt them he did. A dollop of honey covered the burnt sections and he was actually proud of his full stomach by nine o'clock. He pulled the weights up in order to be able to rotate the beacon at sunset. Efficiency wasn't as easy as people assumed.

He climbed the tower to check the weather. The tower's many windows provided natural lighting for its 69 steps. He extinguished the lamp and went out to the walkway to see if any ships might be passing. The rocky outcroppings looming underwater at the tip of the island were visible from the tower. The calm weather was holding, and the waves on Lake Superior were settling down. No ships were in view. Splendor was visible near the hitching post apparently waiting for his morning ride. When Inspector Cross returned, what would he think of Michael's erratic logbook?

After feeding the chickens the burnt crumbs and replenishing the kitchen's supply of eggs, Michael walked down to the pier with Splendor following like an oversized loyal hound.

Stone balustrades with stone benches on each side of the path led to the pebble-studded shore. Michael arranged fishnets at the end of the pier without much enthusiasm. Why would any self-respecting fish swim into a net.

A flash of a pink-colored trout brought his mother's parlor to mind. He'd escaped the nets of scheming women only to let the love of his life slip through his fingers.

On the way back to the tower, Michael marveled at the size of the lighthouse. He remembered telling Angela it might fall over on him. She'd told him his head was so hard the tower wouldn't dent it. He saw her point, now. Why hadn't he scooped her up and married her while he had the chance?

"Would Angela like my island?" Michael asked his horse. He flung himself onto Splendor's back and rode the outskirts of his territory.

Was there enough ground for the farm Angela envisioned? Probably not. Angela held big dreams. Would she like the house in the meantime, before they sired too many children to feed with the food staples this bit of an island could provide?

The two-story brick, shuttered cottage with its center tower wasn't too ugly. Five Manitoba maples graced the spot. A wrap-around front porch, with roof bracings matching the red carved supports under the lantern's gallery, ran along the front and side of the house. A red dome covered the lantern at the top of the lighthouse. Dormers rose out of a new slate roof and interrupted the eaves supported by more decorative red braces.

Between the house and the chicken coup a grassless square of land indicated the well plowed garden. Michael dismounted and searched out the vegetable seeds from his supplies. He planted tomatoes, onions, carrots, turnips, potatoes, and beans. Included in the stores were four packets of flower seeds: hollyhocks, morning glories, violets, and primroses. Michael spaced out the seeds along the path leading to the front door, leaving the hollyhocks and morning glory seeds closest to the building.

* * *

*Friday, June 21st, 1841*

At the end of two weeks, Michael's chores became an unnoticed part of his morning routine. He tried to remember Berkshire in the morning, but he only recalled lounging about with cups of coffee and an endless array of books before riding off with Splendor.

The afternoons found Michael at his sketch pad. On rainy days the tower provided sheltered views. On the sunny days he sat on the dock where the lake breezes freed him from annoying mosquitoes and flies. At times he worried he might run out of paper.

When the first shoots broke through the ground in the garden, rabbits ate them all. Hoping for a second crop from lazy seeds, Michael constructed an elaborate fence from fishnets and wire. He found extra mosquito netting in one of the bedrooms on the second floor to cover the entire area.

The next morning he was shocked to find two baby rabbits trapped inside. He picked up the two scoundrels by their ears and tossed them into the kitchen. After repairing his fence, he went inside to determine the fate of the varmints.

Not until dark, after he'd lit the lighthouse lantern and released the mechanism for the rotating gears, did he spy the baby rabbits again. They were cuddled together near a drain that collected condensation from the glass and dome produced by the lamp's heat. Discerning he deemed them, able as they were to find and camp out near a water source.

He cuddled the sleeping furry balls into the crook of his arm and transported them down the 69 steps. Michael shredded left-over bread into a tin plate and sat it on the table in the middle room. Quickly grabbing a sketch pad and pencil, he set to drawing the animals as they ate. The table seemed in sharp contrast to the curves of the rabbits. Later, a sagging upholstered chair near his bedroom stove provided a soft nest the two orphans deserved.

At 3 a.m. Michael woke, as was his wont, to pull the lantern's weights and check the night's weather. Surprised to find himself still dressed, he moved the sketch pad to the living room table before managing the weights. He took the pad up the steps with him to view it in the lighthouse's bright lamp.

Instead of the sagging pillow of the chair, Michael had drawn the hands and lap of Angela to cradle his pets. The paper's worthlessness mocked his need for Angela McGovern. A humbling thought swept his being. He failed Angela because she needed him as much as he needed her.

On the walkway outside the lantern, Michael told the winds heading south to Lake Michigan and Angela's destination in Chicago, "I was so selfish to desert you, Angela. Please Lord have compassion on us all. Bring her back to me, if it is your will"

# Chapter 15

*Sunday, July 1st, 1841*
*Chicago*

Aunt Elizabeth's housekeeper, Marabell, banged the lid of the fruit compote dish. The high-ceilinged dining room echoed from the dented silver sound of aggravation. The sideboard situated behind Angela's back didn't allow Angela a view of the maid's expression. Marabell wasn't prone to unprovoked displays of temper. Her affection for Angela's aunt was evident by every sort of daily kindness. Marabell's circle of acceptable people included Angela precisely because of her relationship to Aunt Elizabeth. Angela knew this temporary gaff of annoyance was a clear message of some recent and astounding frustration.

Angela calmly unfolded her napkin. "Did you want to be telling me what's happened?"

"Your aunt won't let me!" Marabell said triumphantly, sweeping back into the kitchen as if the Queen awaited her return.

The poached egg, bacon, and light-as-air biscuit on Angela's plate didn't replace the longing for the taste of Ma's common porridge. The smell of roses from the center piece which Marabell's husband, Matt, reveled in displaying couldn't completely negate the remembered odor of stale beer wafting into Ma's kitchen from the door to the bar. The feel of silk stockings in Angela's soft slippers let her toes wiggle in the pile of the oriental carpeting under the table. It wasn't as if she wanted to be clunking around Chicago in her rough field cold-hoppers, but she didn't want to forget the heft of them against her ankle and their soft plunge into damp welcoming earth. At least Flicka was comfortably stabled in Michigan, but Angela missed the daily ride on the back of her old friend.

Angela couldn't hear the ornery crows from the Ring of Kerry even when the windows were open. Sea gulls claiming ownership of Lake Michigan's shore lacked the individuality of the Irish crows' complaints. Chicago didn't feel like home, never would.

As usual, Aunt Elizabeth was having breakfast alone in her rooms. Grief caused her take-charge aunt to retreat into a listless, nearly uncommunicative state. The house was run by Marabell. Angela managed the social contacts, or rather the apologies for her aunt's avoidance of old friends.

Angela finished her breakfast, and coffee-in-hand mounted the stairs to speak to her aunt. Thoughts of Michael Halliday preceded each step. Chicago mornings in July were humid and the starch in Angela's fresh morning dress was already defeated by the moist air. She hadn't laid eyes on the most important being in her life since June. If Angela didn't know better, she would have sworn the freshet of tears on her cheek was only the day's dampness. Heartache over the loss of Michael nearly matched her aunt's grief for her husband of ten years. But Michael was alive, and Angela wished the Lord would keep him safe and enjoying life for another day, even if she was miserable without him. A year of sighs would somehow pass. He'd asked her to wait, hadn't he?

Aunt Elizabeth's nightgown was blackened with dye to comply with the required year-long period of mourning. The shades had been drawn since Angela's uncle's death. Ferns near the windows were turning brown. One gray shaded lamp next to the bed was the only light in the stuffy room.

"Good morning, Aunt. Would it be proper to let in a little of the Lord's light to keep these plants from completely expiring?"

"I suppose so," her aunt answered without much enthusiasm.

Angela pushed the heavy drapery away from the windows, tying the sashes securely in place. As she turned toward her aunt, she could see dust particles from the drapes dancing in the intense July sunlight. She turned back to the windows and pushed them all the way open to let the fresh air from Lake Michigan in with the light.

"That's better," Angela said, walking towards the bed. "Marabell didn't burn the bacon this fine morning, but I think she wanted to."

Aunt Elizabeth smiled faintly. "I'm glad you came up instead of running off to bother some poor farmer into selling you his land."

"Are you now?" Angela scooted next to her aunt, pulling a bit of curl behind her aunt's ear.

"Matt tells me you insist on driving the team yourself, once you're out of the city."

"He taught me how to harness them up too." Angela smiled, proud of the accomplishment. "You were right about the flatness of the prairies. The wind off the Lake is no match for the wind out there. At least you know which direction the breeze will be catching your bonnet near the shore. The wind off those flat fields comes at you from all four directions at the same time. The gusts circle around you playing with your petticoats, just to make sure you're paying attention to them. The one farm I found near the Fox River, where the hills embrace a bit of land, was an old peat bog. Set afire, the sight at night was off-putting to a simple Catholic girl like me."

Her aunt wasn't listening intently and that was the truth. Angela tapped her shoulder. "And when will you be getting up for the day?"

"Soon enough." Her aunt frowned. "I've got to be selling the place and moving out...somewhere."

"So Marabell is afraid she won't be needed?"

"I've tried to reassure her, God knows." Aunt Elizabeth twisted the counterpane distractedly.

Angela patted her aunt's hands. "We're a family. And you'll be coming with me when I find a place."

"Mrs. Lazarus wrote inviting us to move to Ann Arbor." Aunt Elizabeth wouldn't look at Angela. "I've been writing to her about my financial woes."

"Did Uncle Henry owe that much?"

"Well, the house is free and clear; but there's nothing to live on. Mrs. Lazarus told me to leave the deed in the hands of an attorney and just move away...to Ann Arbor." Aunt Elizabeth waved her hand despondently. "There's so much work to be done."

"You've got the strongest gal in all of Ireland to help with that." Angela went around to her aunt's side of the bed, removing the breakfast tray, and pulling back the covers. "With a nice cup of tea in your hand, you can reign over every room. I'm at your disposal, Aunt." Angela made a grand curtsey, sweeping her hand in front of her as if she were brandishing a fine feathered hat.

Aunt Elizabeth's laughter rang out and Marabell flounced into the room. "Bout time I heard that laugh!"

"It is that. Angela, go ahead and order about twenty wooden shipping crates, large and small. Matt knows where to buy them. Marabell, open all the drapes and windows; we intend to make a bit of dust."

"Yes, ma'am." Marabell slapped Angela on the back hard enough to make her gasp.

* * *

*Monday, July 15th, 1841*

The day the packing crates arrived they set to work. They tackled the upstairs first, leaving the beds made up in two of the four guest rooms, to show the house in the best light for shoppers of the lake-shore real estate. They packed up the extra bedding and linens in one of the larger crates. Two other bedsteads were dismantled and roped together for shipment to Ann Arbor.

Mr. Breckenridge's clothes were sent to the poor house after Matt was given first chance to glean what he could use. Uncle Henry's mahogany canopied bed and matching chiffonier would be sold with the house. Aunt Elizabeth's and Angela's beds and dressers would be in the last shipments to leave the house. They packed up all their winter clothes, but Angela kept out her blue cape for reasons she couldn't explain.

In the attic, Matt and Marabell filled one medium-size crate with their belongings. The old furniture they'd been using would be left for future servants. Angela promised to buy them a new bed and sitting room furniture once they arrived in Ann Arbor. The loyal couple needed recompense of some sort for all their hard work in helping with the relocation.

In one of the two nurseries on the third floor, Angela came to a halt next to a painted crib. "Aunt," she called. "Could we ship the nursery furniture to Ann Arbor? If I'm to start a home for babies of unmarried girls, I'll be needing all the help I can muster."

Aunt Elizabeth stopped in the doorway. "Take all the clothing too, Angela. If the new buyers can't figure out what the rabbits on the wall were meant for, it'll be their loss."

Angela touched the nose of a floppy-eared rabbit near a painted tree. "You'll have your own babies to play with you soon enough."

'If only,' appeared briefly in Angela's thoughts and was dismissed as useless. Only one man could have her love, and Michael wasn't willing to accept her yet. Angela set to work filling a crate with all the baby clothes her aunt accumulated for expected children that the Lord saw fit not to send. At least Aunt Elizabeth was regaining her spirits with all the packing activities. Angela promised herself that her new infant charges would be the best dressed in Ann Arbor. She'd be sure of that.

Aunt Elizabeth shed a few more tears of grief during the long summer days, especially in Uncle Henry's study. "I don't need all these books. The library already filled a good ten crates. That's after Father Michael took away all he could use for St. Patrick's School."

"Father Michael gave me the name of the pastor of St. Thomas in Ann Arbor," Angela said. "He's written ahead to give me a recommendation…for starting a home, once I get a farm in working order."

"Just sell these big books," Marabell decreed, standing with her feet apart and hands on her ample hips. "The less you have to ship, the better."

"The Ladies Library in Ann Arbor might be able to use them," Angela said, placing the law volumes and financial theory books carefully into the smaller shipping crates.

"There's enough of 'em to fill a big crate," Marabell speculated.

"But no one would be able to lift them out of the house," Angela explained. "We could ship some of these ahead of us, Aunt Elizabeth, then we won't have so much to mind along the way."

"Or unpack," Marabell added.

"Excellent," Aunt Elizabeth said as she poured herself another cup of tea. "This is going quite nicely, isn't it?"

At that point the teacup rattled in its saucer as Aunt Elizabeth quickly sat it down and grabbed her handkerchief. "Sorry. Sorry, I miss Henry so much."

Marabell took away the tea service. At the door she turned to Angela's aunt. "Might be better if you moved around some more. Get the blood to flowing, instead of the tears."

"Good idea." Aunt Elizabeth traded her easy chair for her husband's wooden one behind his desk and started piling the contents of the drawers onto the top of the desk.

Angela continued dusting and packing the books. She could hear the carriages outside and the barking of a dog from a block behind their garden. The breeze brought the smell of roses into the stuffy, warm room. Her bodice was wet with perspiration from her efficient packing method: dust a book, lay it in the crate, grab another, dust away. When she turned to comment on an unusual text about Roman coins, she noticed tears streaming down her aunt's face. "Maybe we should tackle another room. I can pack all that away for you to go through once we're in Ann Arbor."

Aunt Elizabeth wiped her face. "Widows are allowed to weep, Angela. It's sad I'm feeling and it won't hurt me to water my face some."

Fighting the lump in her own throat, Angela said, "I miss Michael so much. I know he's alive but he seems lost to me."

"You're a strong person, Angela. I think you can handle anything."

Angela didn't comment. She accepted Michael's rejection, but she couldn't fully understand why he didn't ask her to marry him. She knew he wanted her physically, felt sure her social standing wasn't a barrier, but she refused to accept that he placed the importance of his art above the value she would be to him.

"He's wrong," she said aloud.

"Michael is." Aunt Elizabeth said. "Stupid, he's not; nor stubborn."

Marabell saved them from further ruminations. "Come out of here now. I've set up your luncheon plates in the garden."

Angela clapped her hands and hugged the solid maid. "What would we do without you?"

"Hope you never have to find out." Marabell pushed Angela away. "You'll need a bath after lunch, before you take Matt down to the post office."

"Truth, she's telling you." Aunt Elizabeth laughed, wrinkling her nose. "I would like to see if Mrs. Lazarus has written again."

After the pleasant lunch and tepid bath, Angela felt heartened enough for the rest of the day. She chose to wear the outfit she'd worn the day Michael bid her farewell. Instead of tying the keepsake ribbon in her hair she picked out a broad-brimmed hat to shade her from the July heat. She wore the middy blouse with a fresh white linen skirt instead of her blue one. If Michael happened to meet her, would he recognize her under the hat?

If I could stop thinking about him for an entire day, Angela thought, I'd be a happier woman. Maybe when the children at the farm demand all of my attention, I'll be able to feel joy singing in my heart again. She wondered if Ma suffered for years after the Earl of Covington deserted her to marry his family's choice for a wife. Angela didn't believe loving a child could completely erase the need for the support and intimacy only a husband could provide.

Angela could cry all day if she wanted to: first for Uncle Henry and Aunt Elizabeth's grief, then for Michael and missing Ma, besides all her friends back in Ireland. No sense raining on my troubles, she decided as she went out the kitchen door to the coach house.

Matt wasn't enamored of the work required to harness the horses up. "Mail can't be that urgent," he grumbled as he offered to help Angela into the carriage."

"I agree," Angela said, "but it cheers Aunt Elizabeth."

"Reason enough," Matt said. "Sorry to sound so lazy."

Angela touched the back of his hand. "Matt, one thing you're not is lazy. It's a torrid day and any movement is an effort none of us enjoy."

"Thank you, ma'am. I hope you find a farm soon, away from this frying pan of a city. Not a tree to be had."

Angela felt fresh moisture already dripping down her back. "Let's ride down nearest the lake to smell the sea." Matt rewarded Angela with a grand smile. But the lake breeze nearly blew Angela's hat into the next county. She wasn't sure the cooling mischief was worth the effort of holding onto her hat with both hands.

The post office gave up three personal letters for the Breckenridge address. Two were from Ma and one was from Mrs. Lazarus in Ann Arbor. None arrived from Michael Halliday. Nevertheless, Angela saved her mother's to share with Aunt Elizabeth. Angela controlled her first impulse to open her letter in the carriage. The wind was so strong; it could have ripped the paper out of her hand.

Aunt Elizabeth called for tea on the shaded porch facing the lake when Angela returned to the house. With a nod to each other across the wicker table they opened Antoinette McGovern's letters from Kerry, Ireland.

Marabell interrupted them. "No sense missing family on an empty stomach."

She'd made scones in spite of the heat and unpacked Aunt Elizabeth's best rose tea set. Matt picked an entire bowl of white roses for the tray.

"You do lovely work," Aunt Elizabeth complimented the maid.

"You told Ma about Michael." Angela surmised from her mother's sympathetic comments. Angela was careful not to let her mother know about her broken heart.

"The Earl bought the bar," they said in unison to each other.

Recently widowed, the Earl of Covington tried to visit his illegitimate daughter. Angela's mother wrote that he insisted Ma should journey to Chicago as soon as she could pack.

"My father hired Colleen's da to run the bar." Angela told her aunt. "Remember you sat next to him?"

"Mr. Decker could accept that kind of help," Aunt Elizabeth said not raising her eyes from her letter. "Marabell," Aunt Elizabeth called loudly even though the maid stood directly behind her. "Oh Angela, she's already left by now."

"Will she come here then?" Angela scanned the rest of her letter. "No. Here it is. She's going to stay overnight in Ann Arbor to look up Mrs. Lazarus and Winnie Perkins."

"Marabell," Aunt Elizabeth said to the flustered maid. "Tea is fine; but we must send Matt to Ann Arbor as soon as possible."

"He can take my carriage," Angela offered. Ma would soon be close enough to touch. Angela could feel her chest heave upward with grateful emotion to the Lord.

Marabell stood there refusing to comprehend the need for Matt to dash off to Ann Arbor. "A boat to Mackinac," she said, "is faster than the stage or those trains."

"My sister is coming from Ireland to Ann Arbor, then here." Aunt Elizabeth wrung her hands. "I don't know. We need Matt here too."

"Hire a laborer," Marabell said. "We'll need Matt enough on the other end. No sense dashing back and forth."

Then Aunt Elizabeth opened Mrs. Lazarus' letter. "Well, niece, you own that farm you wanted on Seymour Road."

Angela started to clap her hands but desisted. "How can that be?"

"I told Mrs. Lazarus where the farm in Michigan was located and to purchase it for you. You'll reimburse her when we arrive. Marabell," Aunt Elizabeth called again. "Mrs. Lazarus says she's received a letter from my sister about her visit."

Marabell stood in the doorway, arms akimbo.

Angela learned quite early that the gesture constituted an unhappy stance.

"Mrs. Lazarus says she'll make Antoinette wait there for us to arrive," her aunt said.

Now Angela did clap. "I wondered how we would know if my mother arrived too early for Matt to stop her from heading to Chicago."

"Good. I likes to keep my man within arms' reach," Marabell said, "not gallivanting off in all directions."

Aunt Elizabeth winked at Angela.

There was joy; Angela felt the emotion come to call at the least expected time. "Thank you, Lord," she prayed out loud. Ma would see the farm, help with the little ones, and help with Angela's grieving heart.

"Yes," Aunt Elizabeth said. "We all needed our Antoinette."

\* \* \*

*Monday, July 30th, 1841*
*Chicago Docks*

Two weeks later at the end of July, Aunt Elizabeth, Angela, and Marabell stood on the Chicago, Illinois docks waving goodbye to Matt and most of Aunt Elizabeth's belongings. A buyer hadn't yet been found for the Breckenridge house, but Aunt Elizabeth gave power-of-attorney to one of her husband's trusted friends.

The three women planned to follow Matt up Lake Michigan on the Thomas Jefferson which was scheduled to arrive in Chicago the next week. Twenty huge crates, ten medium and two-dozen smaller crates were part of the cargo aboard the steamship 'Milwaukee' destined for Muskegon, Michigan under Matt's supervision. Mrs. Lazarus promised to meet the ship, lodge Matt, and ship the Breckenridge furniture and belongings to Ann Arbor.

"Two weeks." Aunt Elizabeth comforted Marabell for a change. "That's no time at all. You'll be cuffing your man's ears for not stepping lively enough before you've even missed Matt."

"Men have a way of disappearing." Marabell blew her nose loudly.

Angela patted Marabell's sturdy shoulder. "You know Matt worships the ground touching your feet. He was wiping tears away so fast, I thought he was going to give himself a black eye."

"That man of mine." Marabell giggled and gave her nose a final blow. "He won't know how to eat without me cooking for him." Angela drove them home in the carriage. The streets were a lot busier than the country roads west of St. Charles, but the team knew Angela's voice and responded well to her reins.

# Chapter 16

*Saturday, August 4th, 1841*

News of the Thomas Jefferson's arrival in Chicago arrived at the Breckenridge household during a surprise afternoon visit from Mrs. Jameson, the lady Angela met briefly at Michael's departure from Detroit.

Marabell announced her arrival with a frown because Mrs. Jameson followed her into the drawing room. Only one sofa and tea table furnished the circular room. Angela was hemming her salt-damaged cape with a strip of blue leather, and Aunt Elizabeth sat next to her idly drawing her needle through an embroidery pattern on a silk handkerchief. Neither of them was dressed to receive visitors.

Mrs. Jameson took no note of their inappropriate morning attire as she flounced down on the couch, causing Angela to hand her cape to Marabell and ask for another chair to be brought in before tea was served.

"I've just arrived on the Thomas Jefferson," Mrs. Jameson announced as if that would explain her extraordinary behavior. "So good of you to receive me, Mrs. Breckenridge. I have an important missive for your niece." Here she proceeded to dump the contents of her quite large handbag onto the tea table.

"We've booked passage on the Thomas Jefferson," Aunt Elizabeth said. "Please excuse our reception, but most of our belongings have been shipped ahead on the Milwaukee."

Marabell returned in record time with a pot of tea and cups. No doubt she didn't want to miss any news. She stood at the doorway unable to put the tray on the table.

Mrs. Jameson swept everything onto the floor, except for one envelope. "I can retrieve all that later. Here's the reason for my call." She held out a letter for Angela. "Michael Halliday," Mrs. Jameson answered as if Angela had asked.

Quite befuddled, Angela sat on the floor instead of the chair Marabell provided. "Oh," was all she could say with Michael's letter secured in her hand.

Marabell pulled her up with one arm under her armpit while shoving a chair under her bottom. "Angela's a bit surprised," Marabell apologized for her.

"Would you like some privacy to open it, dear?" Aunt Elizabeth started to rise.

"No, Aunt, please stay." Angela managed, smoothing the letter on her lap as if a cat needed the stroking.

"You might read it better if you opened it," Mrs. Jameson laughed softly.

"Do you know its contents?" Angela asked.

"I do," Mrs. Jameson laughed quite heartedly at some private joke.

Angela looked at her name scrawled across the entire face of the envelope. "Michael gave my letter to you?"

"Well, Mr. Halliday knew I'd be reaching you before he could."

"Is Michael on his way here?" Angela unthinkingly waded the letter in her fist.

"No, no dear," Mrs. Jameson shook her head. "I see this is a shock. Have you already married? Is that why you all are taking passage on the Thomas Jefferson."

Angela heard her aunt explain the details of their return to Ann Arbor as she gingerly unsealed Michael's letter.

"My dearest Angela," the letter from Michael read, "If you would consent to marry me, I will go to the ends of the earth to be with you. America, Ireland, England, any land you deem as worthy of your existence, I will embrace with all my heart as home. I need to see you every day. I was mistaken to let you out of my sight. As soon as the ship steamed away, I realized my grievous error. Please forgive any pain that I might have caused you and agree to be my life mate. Nothing in this world means as much to me as being close to you, hearing your voice, watching the light of love in your eyes. Please, Angela, I beg you. Promise to marry me and all else will fall into place. Awaiting word from you, your humble servant, Michael Halliday"

"He wants to marry me," Angela sat very still as if moving would change the miracle.

"May I read it?" Aunt Elizabeth asked.

Angela handed her the letter.

Mrs. Jameson was all smiles as she repacked her bag.

Marabell poured tea for them, since they had forgotten the need.

"Now what shall we do?" Aunt Elizabeth asked.

Mrs. Jameson advised them, "Quite simple."

\* \* \*

*Monday, August 6th, 1841*

All four women boarded the Thomas Jefferson steamship. Mrs. Jameson and Aunt Elizabeth were bound for a return horse-shoe trip route up Lake Michigan to Lake Superior, then down Lake Huron to Detroit. Mrs. Jameson decreed traveling the lakes was the best way to spend an unseasonably humid summer.

Aunt Elizabeth was positive Mrs. Lazarus and Winnie Perkins would be able to find one more room in Ann Arbor for a famous romance writer. "You could speak at a meeting of the Ladies Library."

"Half the educated wives in the world deem themselves writers," Mrs. Jameson said. "And I for one welcome the competition. Mrs. Breckenridge, I expect you've written a few lines of poetry."

"Prayers," Aunt Elizabeth said. "I think they might be called prayers of the bereaved."

"The greeting card industry is always looking for new efforts," Mrs. Jameson said with respect. "It's difficult to express our feelings of sympathy, even when we're sitting right next to a person." Here she patted Aunt Elizabeth's hand. "You have certainly dealt courageously with your loss."

"My niece and Marabell insisted." Aunt Elizabeth held out her hand for Angela to grasp.

Marabell and Angela planned to terminate their sea travel after the Sturgeon Bay, Wisconsin, stop. Mrs. Jameson assured them the Pittsburgh and Boston Mining Company finished a railroad spur from Iron Mountain to Copper Harbor. Angela planned to accept Michael's proposal in person, on Strawberry Island.

\* \* \*

*Wednesday, August 8th, 1841*

On the second day at sea the three women were again enthroned on the shaded starboard side of the ship. Marabell was taking a much deserved nap. Mrs. Jameson's relentless inquiries caused Angela to wonder if perhaps Michael Halliday might not be the hero of her next romance. "When I met the young man, I guessed his family had means. He possessed none of the 'lean and hungry look about him' that Shakespeare cautions against."

"His father owns a clockwork factory," Aunt Elizabeth unhesitatingly offered. "And his mother is landed gentry." Here she lifted her attention from her embroidery to Angela's frown. "Although," her aunt whispered the added tidbit, "an uncle gambled the old fortune away."

"Michael plans to pursue his artistic talent," Angela said with a possessive pride she hadn't felt before the proposal.

"All very well," Aunt Elizabeth said. "Until the babies arrive to be fed."

"He can sketch on the farm Mrs. Lazarus bought for me."

Aunt Elizabeth explained, "Mrs. Lazarus temporarily purchased a bit of land Angela picked out. Angela's own father has provided enough funds to purchase her future."

"And who is your father?" Mrs. Jameson seemed to be writing notes behind her determined eyes.

"The Earl of Covington," Aunt Elizabeth disclosed, before adding, "Recently widowed."

"Not recently enough," Mrs. Jameson laughed outrageously.

"Mrs. Jameson," Aunt Elizabeth cautioned. "My sister is above reproach."

"I'm sure," Mrs. Jameson apologized. "I know the likes of men and the powers of attraction after all these years of writing about seduction. There's never anyone to blame for love."

Marabell rushed up to the three women. "Sailor just told me to ask you ladies to go inside. There's a storm coming."

Angela helped Marabell stash the seat cushions into the chest under the deck benches. The ship began to roll with the rising sea. "Where are the clouds?" Angela asked a passenger.

"Off the port side," he answered, rushing hopelessly to chase his bowler hat as it was swept overboard.

She wanted to see the cause of the storm and held onto the cabin wall railing as she proceeded aft. The port deck didn't need to be reached; Angela could see the dark green bank of clouds gaining on the ship. She inched her way back to the cabin entrance.

"Aunt, do they have tornadoes on Lake Michigan?"

Aunt Elizabeth looked up from her embroidery.

"Hurricanes," Mrs. Jameson said. "They're brief but deadly in early August."

They gathered in Mrs. Jameson's cabin since it was the most spacious. Marabell seemed frightened as she tried to push back in her chair, bracing her feet against the nearest wall.

"We'll be all right," Angela said, wanting to believe the words. "With the Lord's help. The clouds aren't rotating, Aunt. They're just a long line of green...coming at us."

Mrs. Jameson laughed. "Now ladies, let's not be panicking ourselves. Shall I read to you from my diary when I last visited Detroit in June?"

"Yes, do." Angela said, sitting between her aunt and Marabell. "We need entertainment."

Would she be swept out of the world when Michael was only a week away from embracing her as his wife? Did the Lord want her to love this artist who failed to see her worth when she was at his side? Oh Michael, Angela prayed, stay safe until I arrive.

And Mrs. Jameson read, "The roads by which I have at length reached this beautiful little city were not certainly the smoothest and the easiest in the world; nor can it be said...as of wisdom, 'that all her ways are ways of pleasantness, and her paths are the paths of peace.' On the contrary...,"

Here Mrs. Jameson was interrupted by a great surge of sea which tipped the Thomas Jefferson to the starboard side at a forty-five degree angle. Aunt Elizabeth clutched her embroidery to her throat, pricking her finger in the process. Marabell was silent but her eyes spoke of the terrors she was fighting.

After the ship righted itself with mighty metal shrieks and groans, Mrs. Jameson retrieved her diary from across the room and continued, "On the contrary, one might have fancied oneself in the road to paradise for that matter. It was difficult, narrow, and foul, and steep enough to have led to the seventh heaven, but in heaven I am not yet."

'Perhaps a bit of song would hearten us,' Angela suggested.

Marabell immediately began, "Rock of ages cleft for me," in a rich melodious voice.

The hymn added to Angela's worries. After what seemed like hours, she was about to leave the cabin to look for lifeboats when the ship calmed its rolling and the grinding noises ceased.

"We've weathered it!" Angela was surprised to be unharmed again when the elements of nature had flung their worst tricks at her.

After their rough crossing, Angela clung to her Aunt before leaving the Thomas Jefferson at the Escanaba dock. "I know you'll be safe. Tell Ma, Michael and I are on our way."

"We'll have a wedding set up for seeing the whites of your eyes," Aunt Elizabeth openly sobbed. "The Lord keep you safe."

\* \* \*

*Friday, August 10th, 1841*

From the train's window, the upper peninsula of Michigan scenery was monotonous but beautiful. Uncut timber along the rail spurs right-of-way rose high above them. The crisp air let them forget August was upon them. Deer and smaller critters roamed along the tracks and the hawks and owls knew no fear. Marabell spotted a black bear, but Angela couldn't confirm the sighting. Angela's anticipation for seeing Michael grew with each mile in his direction.

"Does Mr. Halliday live in one of those rickety wood lighthouses at Sturgeon Bay?" Marabell asked.

"I believe he told me his was made of stone." The ramshackle Sturgeon Bay tower had worried Angela. It didn't look sturdy enough to hold Michael's weight to climb it. The lighthouse across from Sturgeon Bay on St. Martin's appeared similarly disreputable.

"A farm might look mighty good to him, if'n he's been living in those toothpicks."

"Yes, it might." Angela laughed. "The sight of Michael Halliday is all I really care about. I appreciate your coming with me. I know you miss Matt. He's a fine, sturdy chap."

Marabell smiled. "And all mine, he is."

\* \* \*

*Friday, August 17th, 1841*

Once they reached Marquette, Angela found aberrant, negative thoughts were overwhelming her good sense. When a steamer couldn't be found for the last leg of their trip up to Copper Harbor and farther west to the Apostle Islands, she talked Marabell into boarding a sailing schooner.

"We're just as safe as on a steamship. Aren't we Captain Maddox?"

Marabell didn't want to set foot on the boat. "I'm a farm gal, but I believe in boilers. Building up all the steam to turn a propeller makes sense to me. Relying on the changing winds of God seems more risky."

Captain Maddox tried to calm her fears. "Sailors have been banking their sails against the winds a lot longer than those nosey steamers have been churning up the waves. They blow up entire ships as well as those damn whistles. I've seen more than one burn down to the water line with sailors being toasted even as they cling to life by hanging on to the anchor chains."

"Captain Maddox," Angela cautioned. "I doubt Marabell can be put at ease by listening to horror stories about shipwrecks."

"Right you are," he amended, giving Marabell his arm. "Come have a look at your quarters. We've got lots of space in our tourist cabins."

The cabins weren't half bad. Marabell shared a sitting room with Angela's accommodations. The hot water available on the steamships was missing, but the beds were comfortable.

All Angela's fears jumped to her mind as soon as she laid her head down for a nap. "Where would they live? When could he leave the lighthouse with her to start farming on Seymour Road in Michigan? Would he want to start a home for orphans? The plans for taking in unwed mothers wouldn't be possible with a man on the place. Maybe he'd want them to start their own family. A thrill passed through Angela.

There was the making love to be thinking of. Soon enough now she'd be in his hands, at his mercy. Was he as virginal as she was? Probably not. She didn't have the courage to ask him and would have to assume he was as innocent as she. Well they'd be all right. Nothing would go wrong, since children were the only outcome of unions. She trotted out images of blonde and black haired infants, girls and boys, toddlers, before dozing off into a pleasant slumber as the ship rocked back and forth rounding Copper Harbor.

Marabell shook her awake. "We're in trouble now."

"Are we?" Angela recognized the thudding about that storms cause. "Is it night?"

"Might as well be," Marabell's voice was strained with panic.

"Now, now," Angela gripped the side of her cot. "Have they asked for us to go to the life boats?"

Marabell turned the handle of the cabin's door only to be flung back across the cabin when an entire wave engulfed them.

# Chapter 17

The baby rabbits gave the lighthouse a welcome air of habitation. They depended on Michael's care as much as the lamp at the top of the tower needed tending through the long nights. He named the bunnies, Sadie and Madelyn. Quick, agile and eager to play, they constantly entertained him. Any thought of using them to add to his meat supply disappeared after the first night when he let them sleep in the arm chair in his bedroom.

He discovered that the rabbits used the sand bin next to the boiler as their in-house facility. Michael had tossed hot pieces of burnt wood and ashes into the metal bin when he re-stoked the kitchen stove or the boiler fire pan. He constructed a new ash bin just outside the backdoor to ensure the rabbits could safely use theirs. Michael had to trudge past the boiler room door to the outside privy for his own needs. He included emptying and refilling the rabbits sand box to his list of chores.

Michael hoped Inspector Cross would knock before entering the front door on his next visit. Otherwise Michael might get caught carrying on intelligent conversations with his floppy-eared friends.

When Inspector Cross returned after the first storm blew over Strawberry Island, he loaded the Illinois with debris left from the previous tenant. Three of the empty barrels of whale oil were left next to the storage shed.

"Scrub those out with beach sand from the south side of the island," Cross directed. "Leave them tied up so the surf can get rid of the last traces of oil, then take some lye soap and a broom and go at them again."

Michael stood with his head lowered, but nodding agreement.

Seemed a waste of time until Inspector Cross added, "Once you rinse them in the surf of all that soap, they make good lake water carriers."

Michael brightened with the realization. "I could use the tram to get them up to the house."

"The boiler, the chickens, and garden don't need well water. Keep that for drinking, Cross said. "Hauling up well water all day can send a saint into doldrums."

When Inspector Cross saw the unfinished, free-standing globe in the middle of the library, he suggested the project, "Might be worth finishing."

The north light from a half-shuttered window made the room as dim as candlelight. Plans for the globe with detailed maps of each continent's exact transfer dimensions were tacked to the walls of the room. The feet and ball of the sphere were complete. Only the joists and joints necessary to keep the rotating devices together remained to be fitted, glued and nailed into place.

Michael agreed if time weighed too heavily on his hands, he would finish up the work. After all, carving wasn't that much removed from sketching. He inked in the continents in case someone else, who wasn't as deft with a pen, might enjoy whittling around the mountains and oceans. Michael spent very little time in the dark room. Even on rainy days, he preferred to add to his sketches, rather than dull a knife on the ball of wood.

After a ride around the island on Splendor near sunset, Michael checked his watch. Three hours remained before he needed to light the lamp. Splendor's fenced-in enclosure allowed him to run along the entire length of the cottage, tower, and out buildings. Michael liked his horse close to him. All other meaningful life seemed distant.

Due to the placement of the tower's circular steps along the sides of the central open room, Michael could see the sun shining through the lower, south window of the storage room from his vantage point in the library on the north side of the cottage. Sadie was rubbing the bottom of her chin on the storage room's threshold. Madelyn proceeded to mimic the territorial behavior on the library's slightly elevated entrance.

Michael busily combed through the books while Madelyn stood guard in the open doorway. "Madelyn, do you think the prior light-tender left a record of last year's weather?"

The hunt for a weather record was precipitated by one of Michael's sketches which had added a windmill structure to the boiler-room end of the cottage. Michael took a minute in his search for the diary to open both shutters away from the windows.

After messing up his life by letting Angela kiss him good-bye in Detroit, Michael recognized the symbolic nature of a windmill. Cervantes' hero's attempt to conquer the dragons of fate when Don Quixote tried to slay the windmills closely paralleled Michael's chances of winning Angela's hand while he remained stuck in this distant outpost of Lake Superior.

Michael hoped the first light-tender had kept storm records. A note or two about the winds during a bout of fog would convince the lighthouse inspector that a windmill to help run the fog-horn was a viable and worthwhile project.

"We need to find those records," Michael reiterated to Madelyn, who seemed to acknowledge the gravity of the situation.

Michael kept the rabbits indoors. Actually he was afraid they would run away given the chance. He would miss them more than he cared to admit to himself. Sadie had won his heart when she hopped up onto the bed one night and cuddled into the crook of his arm. In the morning he rubbed the top of her nose. Michael thought he heard her sigh.

Madelyn was a little standoffish, preferring to sleep alone on the easy chair rather than risking the hop to Michael's bed. Madelyn's winter coat left her looking spotted, whereas Sadie's coat developed into an even tone of tan due in part to her constant preening. Michael noticed Madelyn never missed an opportunity to follow him about. Either she thought he would give her extra morsels of food or her show of friendship included dogging his every step.

The library's walls were filled with empty book shelves and one set of encyclopedias. The underlined pages were dog-eared, as if the previous keeper had spent most of his time fixated on the wider world outside the bounds of the island. Michael ran his hand along the top of the set of tomes and found a small book wedged in horizontally. The pocket diary, very much like Michael's own, was apparently the lightkeeper's duplicate record of ships passing with a fair amount of weather notations.

The first sketches of the globe as well as lists of supplies were incorporated in the diary. A heart-rending inventory of the visits of the Illinois and Inspector Cross' delivery and non-delivery of mail from the lightkeeper's family was sadly recorded. By the news of his garden's harvest and reports of native visitors picking strawberries,

Michael surmised the man had given up his job out of crushing loneliness.

"Should have kept rabbits," Michael explained to Madelyn.

Her ears twitched, and she stepped into the room. Sadie across the hall thumped her back foot and seemed to hiss.

"Jealousy is not a pretty sentiment," Michael called to her. "I'm coming right down."

Michael took the diary with him. He tried to pick up Madelyn but she wasn't buying any cheap or hurried attention.

"Above such things, is it?" Michael watched her run past Sadie's outpost.

Sadie let him pick her up and Michael nuzzled her against his neck. With a quick intake of breath Michael imagined embracing Angela good-bye on the Detroit dock. Her hair had felt soft against his jaw. He dropped the diary and placed Sadie next to his stool in the storage room. Where was Angela now? Was the sun he saw reaching into the room warming her in Chicago? Had she received his proposal from Anna. Jameson yet?

The energy involved in constructing a windmill might relieve the physical pain and frustration Michael was experiencing. His thoughts abounded with Italian from Dante's Inferno. Previously the Purgatario apt lines compared to his situation. But now,

> ..la sconoscente vita che ii fe sozzi
> ad ogni conoscenza or li fa bruni,

"the undiscerning life that makes us foul, now makes us obscure to all discernment."

However Michael sought to justify the toil involved. To him, a wind device to run the fog horn made some sense. The wind constantly blew. But the problem was that Michael couldn't remember if a wind accompanied fog. He seemed to recall the stillness of the air caused the water particles to stay suspended enough to blind a ship. A wind might cause fog to disappear. Nevertheless, Michael kept his drawings of the windmill. He even chipped out shutter slats for windmill arms each time the woodpile needed replenishing. Michael eventually laid out his plans and first models of the arms of the windmill. His designs were stored in the second-floor empty room on the south side of the tower.

Michael wrote to his mother explaining his serious intention to marry, "…a brave and sprightly Irish immigrant, who unfortunately is living with her aunt in Chicago."

At least he didn't need to weather the storm his father was guaranteed to blow all over Berkshire. His mother would take a certain lady-like pleasure in letting the young women (who courted her for news of Michael) know that her son had chosen another.

Time stood still outside the shores of the island. Anything could be happening, but Michael had to wait for Inspector Cross to alert him. Perhaps the Illinois was bringing an acceptance of his wish for Angela to become his bride. The ship could be steaming toward him right now from the Straits of the Soo.

"Maybe love is on the way," Michael said to Sadie, picking her up into his lap while he re-examined the weather diary.

Later that evening after he dined on dandelion soup and scrambled eggs, Michael found the central room needed no illumination from the lamp he'd left in the kitchen. The green light of the lamp radiated downward within the tower. Michael could make out the pulls for the rotation weights. He wondered how much of his work could be accomplished without a lamp, now that he had become familiar with every corner of the cottage and every rock on the island.

Sadie jumped ahead as he made his way across the large room to his bedroom. "We're saving on lamp oil, Sadie," he said, listening to the echo his voice made in the tower room.

A rush of homesickness caught him by surprise. He'd have to attend to his sketches for more hours on the following day or his isolation wouldn't be worth the agony.

He missed Angela. Nothing smelled as good. He tried smelling the wild flowers and the fresh vegetables but her scent of roses eluded him. Michael longed for the sight of her, as he had mentioned in his proposal letter. Nothing moved the way Angela did. Her purposeful walk didn't dally about with a seductive sway. She was all business, truth and he might honestly have lost her…even after the proposal letter.

Three o'clock arrived without Michael closing his eyes.

* * *

*Sunday, July 15th, 1841*

The morning shift allowed Michael an early view of Inspector Cross' scheduled mail run to Strawberry Island. Michael made sure the rabbits were behind his bedroom door while the inspector made his rounds.

There was no mail from his mother or Angela, but Michael had more than one large envelope to send to each of them. Sketches detailed the layout of the tower and cottage with pictures of the ships as they sailed or steamed by, as well as the charming rabbits antics drawn in cartoon strips. He assured his mother that his drawing of Angela gave no hint of her beauty or charm.

Michael asked, "Inspector Cross, if you'll teach me how to skin a chicken, I'll be glad to cook you dinner. I'm quite ashamed to say, I miss hearing another human's voice."

"Skin a chicken?"

"Fix a chicken, then."

"What have you been eating? Rabbits?"

"Rabbits?" Michael was surprised by the emotional lump in his throat. "I couldn't skin a rabbit. They're too intelligent."

Inspector Cross cocked his head and stared at Michael

"I eat eggs and dandelion soup, vegetables and biscuits," Michael said, proving his sanity which seemed to be in question.

"Have to pluck a chicken."

"The cookbook didn't give details."

"Put that pan there on to boil," Inspector Cross said. "Where's your hatchet?"

"Near the back door," Michael pointed, as he filled his largest pan from the water bucket. He set the pot over the wood stove's main grate and stoked the fire.

Inspector Cross tested the hatchet's blade with a wet finger. "I take it you haven't chopped the head off any of your chickens yet."

"No, Sir," Michael admitted

"Where's your whet stone?"

"I don't know what that is."

"Good Lord, Man. How do you keep your ax sharp?"

"Chopping wood is getting harder."

"Now I know, Timmons had him one. Too heavy to have carried it off." Inspector Cross rummaged around the boiler room. "Have you seen a large gray, sparkling stone in here?"

"Oh yes," Michael smiled. "Madelyn…." Actually the rabbit had surprised him by standing on the stone to watch Michael pour water into the boiler for the fog-horn. "A rock was left near the door, so I rolled it outside and kicked it under the wood step."

"That'll be your sharpener." Inspector Cross had an odd habit of constantly shaking his head in a negative direction. "You'll want to haul her back inside. Keep her dry."

After the ax and hatchet had been sharpened and the pot of boiling water carried to the back step of the boiler room, Inspector Cross grabbed a chicken and pinned its head between two nails on a convenient stump that Michael had noted before.

The nails were closely placed on a stump near the chicken pen. Michael previously worried his mind about the possibilities of roping a chicken and the reasons for tying up a recalcitrant hen, but the nails had remained a mystery until Inspector Cross made speedy use of them. The hatchet fell once and the headless chicken flopped around the rocky side yard for less than a minute.

Inspector Cross dipped the chicken by its feet into the boiling water before stripping off great hunks of feathers. He handed the half-plucked chicken to Michael. "You try."

Michael wrinkled his nose, but dunked the chicken and was surprised by the ease with which the feathers could be pulled free of the chicken's skin. After he had completely bared the bird, Inspector Cross took it back.

"See these black things? You wants to get rid of them. They're called pin feathers and they're not that tasty."

Back in the kitchen, Michael split the chicken in half neatly with his sharpened hatchet and then proceeded to clean out the insides.

"If you wants to bake a chicken, you wash out the guts and stick in biscuits or nuts and apples," Inspector Cross said, licking his lips. "…without cutting the bird in half."

Michael could handle that. The cookbook Angela made sure he bought gave detailed ideas on how to bake, boil, broil, fry, baste and just about how to do anything you liked with a plucked chicken, except take the feathers off.

"My cookbook didn't mention the feathers," Michael explained.

"Some things people know," Inspector Cross said, shaking his head again. "Your coffee is better than average," he said as if to apologize for the slight.

While Michael made fixings to go with the chicken: potatoes, carrots, and biscuits, Inspector Cross entertained him with stories of disasters.

"I figure it's my job to scare the b'Jesus out of you fellers. Keeps you on your toes." Cross helped himself to another cup of coffee as Michael peeled a half dozen potatoes.

"I know you've got more learning than I know to hunt for, but there's some things I'm an expert about." Cross waited until Michael acknowledged he'd heard the boast. "Lake Superior's tricks is one of them. Even though the weather seems to be moving clear of winter, there's a whole world of ice to the north just wait'n to blow a storm or two in our direction. Stay vigilant."

Michael remembered to nod his head at the abrupt stops in the inspector's lecture. Inspector Cross seemed to need affirmation to continue his tales.

"This mighty lake can get riled up in three days of wind and it takes three more days to settle her down. If you start to see the clouds rushing around in daylight and the lake throws up spume so's you're not sure where the sea begins and the land ends, light the lamp and sound the fog-horn for seventy-two hours. Day and night. Longer if the seas keep up."

"I will, Inspector," Michael agreed.

He liked Cross and his ready display of mastery. Michael's ignorance of what he had gotten himself into by securing the job of lightkeeper kept him humble enough and eager to listen.

"The gloom in the middle of a day, even if the wind's not picked up that much is your first clue." Inspector Cross drained another cup of coffee. "I sees my job as a race against the deaths that might happen if I don't train you guys." He bowed his head. "I've counted too many of you maimed and killed doing your best against the wicked tempests."

Michael turned his attention to a bunch of carrots and onions that needed scraping and peeling to go along with the potatoes. He hoped the grace of God would keep him from having to deal with the death of others, or for that matter a serious storm.

"Get that row boat out at least once a week, two days would be better, and row around the island. That'll strengthen your arms for rescuing folks off broken ships."

"How many wrecks have you seen?" Michael asked.

"Too many." Cross lapsed into a long seizure of silence.

Michael delayed in interrupting the inspector's inner travels until the floured chicken parts were nearly burnt in the spattering lard and completely white inside. He set the table for two and ladled the vegetables into a bowl, the chicken onto a large platter, and the biscuits into another bowl before calling the inspector's attention to the meal.

"Sir, have a bite or two of supper."

Cross shook himself and picked up his fork. "I know you can see almost the whole fifteen miles that the light travels, nine on a misty day; but in a storm you'll only be able to see a few thousand yards. Not all the way to the end of the rock shoals under the tower."

"I noted them the first time I walked around the tower's parapet." Michael said as Cross busied himself with food. "They resembled teeth waiting for food."

"They've chewed up a few ships: sail and steamer."

"Before the lighthouse was built."

"Then and after." Cross worked at finishing his share of the biscuits, chicken, and vegetables. "In autumn, the sea gulls will leave when it's time for you to start packing." Cross got up and wiped his greasy fingers on a freshly laundered dish towel. "The lake can scream in a northeast gale in July, if she gets a mind to. I've seen ships pounded into two sections by the surf out here. People clinging to both halves and no hope for any of them to come ashore."

Michael stopped eating. "But I could row out to them."

"The sea will throw your boat all the way to the top of the cliff, if she wants. People can't stay in the icy grip of Superior any month of the year."

"Don't castaways ever reach any of the Apostle Islands?" Michael's hunger vanished.

"Some. After storms you start nailing coffins together from the wrecks." Cross said, pushing his chair under the table. "The bodies will come ashore soon enough. I'll help ya clean up the dishes. Where's the bucket for the pump?"

"Next to the sink bench," Michael pointed.

Cross returned with an overflowing bucket.

Michael took it from him to add to the emptied vegetable pot. "It will take a while to boil. How many people have you saved from the lake?"

""I can tell you, I've seen more die than live," Cross said. "I saw one boat manned with strong sailors row from a wreck last year, but the storm blew it away from the islands. They made the mainland the next afternoon. I've seen boats filled with castaways smashed by the surf.

Michael rather wished he hadn't encouraged the subject.

"Seen a schooner hove to and snag her anchor two miles off shore. Tossing like a cork it was. A crowd of ten jumped into the yawl. They were pulling the oars and bailing like mad men. Then the breakers flipped the boat. People went a flying up before the lake ate them on the spot."

"Would you like to inspect the lamp again?" Michael interjected for his own peace of mind.

"Aye," Cross seemed equally relieved to move away from the dire subjects. "I better shove off."

Michael topped off his hospitality with a cup of brandy for them both. Then he followed Inspector Cross down to the dock.

"Stayed longer than I intended," Cross said. "You're a passable cook, Michael. And I thank ya. 'Spect the light is fine. I'll look at it from off-shore. Sound that fog-horn once I'm out of sight. I'll be interested to know how far I can go before I lose the sound."

Sadie seemed glad to see Michael when he opened his bedroom door. Madelyn marched, rather hopped out, with her twitching nose showing her displeasure at being cooped up without use of the boiler room's sand box.

The lunch dishes were done and no one got hurt, but the boiler took its time getting hot enough to create sufficient steam to turn the fly-wheel. Michael used nearly all of the timber freshly stacked against the side of the house. The week before he discovered bugs in the damp logs nearest the building. He decided a free-standing wood pile would be more efficient. The extended roof of the chicken coop would afford shelter from the rain and provide a wind screen for the chicken yard.

Finally the spin of the safety wheel signaled that the fog-horn mechanism could be released. A slow growl, building to a see-sawing wail emitted from the horn.

Laundry needed attention so Michael drained enough boiling water to fill the gigantic wash tub. Besides the collection of dirty clothes, Michael stripped to make efficient use of the hot water for even the shirt and undergarments he was wearing. After hanging his laundry in the buff on a line from the boiler room to a tree that he planned to cut down to make room for the windmill, Michael decided a warm bath wouldn't kill him.

He made a pot of coffee before refilling the large tub and folded himself into a sitting position, knees up in the deep tub. Michael wasn't that sad to see Cross leave, although he would miss the sound of another human's voice. He felt a load of responsibility he'd never experienced before. The stories of death and disaster and the impermanence of life humbled him.

# Chapter 18

When the door to the boiler room opened, Michael still seated in his bath, expected Cross had returned to complain about the shortness of the fog-horn's reach. Instead a buckskin-clad native and his squaw entered.

Michael apologized. "Sorry. Come in, Sir." He covered his essentials, but continued his welcome. "I'm afraid I can't offer your wife the same hospitality. All my clothes are hanging on the line outside."

Michael picked up the coffee pot. "Perhaps you can give her a cup of coffee while I dress."

The native took the pot and Michael's cup and pushed his bright-eyed wife outside, before pulling the door shut.

Michael turned his back and stepped out of the bath. He'd left a blanket nearby to dry himself and he wrapped it around his waist before heading for his clothes in the bedroom.

"Got tobacco?" The native had followed him through the kitchen and main room without a sound.

"Help yourself," Michael said, pointing back toward the round table. "I'll join you outside in a moment. I don't allow tobacco smoke inside my home."

He closed his bedroom door. The rabbits were huddled together on his chair. Not commenting to them, he pulled on trousers without undergarments along with a starched dress shirt he hadn't worn since Detroit.

Regaining his fully clothed decorum, Michael palmed his pipe and joined his smoking visitor outside. 'I make a mean fried chicken. Would you like to join me for supper?"

"Sounds good. I'm Parish North; my wife's name is Dorothy North."

"My apologies," Michael opened the front door for Mrs. North to enter.

She carried the coffee pot and cup in. "Lollygagging around. When we heard the fog horn, we thought you might be needing our help."

"Sorry to cause you any concern. Inspector Cross came this morning to examine the lighthouse. After lunch, he asked me to try the fog-horn to test its reach out into the lake." Michael's pride served to cover his embarrassment. "Thought I'd make efficient use of the heated water."

Mrs. North eyed him suspiciously.

"The fog-horn is run by a steam boiler," he explained further.

"That luke-warm coffee wasn't half bad. If I accept your apology," Mrs. North swept into the house as if she owned it. "Do you think you could afford another cup?"

"Happily," Michael grinned warmly into the remnants of a beautiful face.

Middle-age blurred a fine chin line and dulled Dorothy's mass of gray locks.

Parish stepped between their shared grin. "We normally bring Timmons a deer and half our strawberries."

"A fourth," Dorothy winked at Michael.

"He was a nervous chap, not tall like you." Parish laughed.

"I just learned how to pluck a chicken." Michael started to go inside with Mrs. North, but Parish stopped him.

"You're not close to your father?"

Michael couldn't keep the shock from showing in his voice. "How, how do you know?"

Mrs. North touched his arm. "Okay if I start the coffee while you men smoke?"

"Yes," Michael said. He hadn't recovered his equilibrium from Parish's probing statement.

"My father taught me how to smoke." Parish produced a series of smoke rings. "Said a man needs a man to show him."

Michael admitted the truth, "You couldn't be more correct. My father wanted me to run his clockworks factory." Michael swept his arm to include the island. "I chose to pursue a career as an artist."

"Only son?" Parish watched Michael pack his pipe loosely. "That's right," he encouraged.

"Yes. My sister died a year ago." Michael shared the match Parish handed him.

"Very sad," Parish said. "Draw in short breaths until the bowl is glowing."

Michael followed the directions. He was pleased to fill his lungs with enough smoke to enjoy the rush. "That is an improvement! Lost the woman I love by coming up here."

"You're starting to speak as New Englander's do, short. Not like a British subject."

"The woman I want is Irish." Michael felt lightheaded from the revelation or the tobacco.

"Mine might as well be," his guest said. "Any chance she'll come round?"

"Here?" Michael coughed. "Oh, you mean change her mind. I wrote my proposal after we parted. I haven't received an answer."

"You're turning a might green," Parish laughed. "We better go in and let you start that chicken dinner."

Mrs. North hadn't begun the coffee, so Michael started a pot with the boiler water, but thought better of it. He filled the pot with coffee, a raw egg, and fresh well water and set it on the stove to boil, before adding, "I'm not sure I'm up to skinning a dear."

"Did that." Parish said. "Smoked and salted. Timmons was beyond fixing decent victuals too. I'll just hang it in the boiler room rafters. Slice off what you need and keep it wrapped in the canvas. You'll have tasty meat all season."

"How can I repay you?"

"Couple chickens will do," Dorothy said as she set the table. "You've got nicer things than old Timmons had. He was an unhappy chap."

"We come here for a vacation every summer." Parish added, "Gets hotter than that stove on the Ohio line."

"Do you live near Ann Arbor?" Michael stopped his preparations for the answer. "Angela McGovern has friends there."

"No," Dorothy answered. "That's a day's ride north. We live in Milan. Run a school in the winter. The kids are all busy on the farms this time of year."

Michael coughed unable to word his guestion politely.

Dorothy laughed. "No, neither one of us is a native." Dorothy laughed at him. "Parish's stepparents were natives, and I find these clothes very practical for the long canoe ride."

"You came all the way up the Huron and across Lake Superior in a canoe?"

Parish turned around from hanging the carcass in the boiler room. "Steam's not the only way to move on the lakes. At least we don't blow up or catch fire."

Michael caught a glance between the two older people that could be nothing else but a passion for each other.

After Michael fed them his fried chicken and fried potatoes, Parish pulled out his pipe again. Michael couldn't repeat his rule about smoking outdoors to his new friend.

"Mind if we tent on the southern side?"

"Of course not. Anything I have is yours." After a long silence Michael coughed nervously again.

"Spit it out youngster," Dorothy chuckled.

"Would you like to see my pet rabbits?'

Parish blew a ring of spoke from his pipe. "Pet rabbits."

"I'd also like your permission to sketch you. Maybe next to your tent in the morning."

"Now see," Dorothy pointed to her husband. "I told you that garden showed tending by a man with a calm heart and busy hands." She piled their dishes in the sink and headed for the main room. "Where are those varmints hiding?"

Michael opened the door to his bedroom but the rabbits didn't hop down from their perch. "They're not usually so shy."

Dorothy stuck her head around the corner to view the twitching noses of the rabbits. "Oh bring them out on the pillow. They'll warm up to us once we settle down."

Michael spent an enjoyable evening asking a thousand questions about the couple's background and how they'd met. They told Michael about the land-treaties for building the Erie Canal under the Monroe administration.

"She'll not find a better looking man in Chicago," Dorothy said, as they wished him a good-night.

After they left to camp on the south side of the island, Michael scanned the blue sky from the tower. He thanked God for the sunset's lingering warmth.

"Keep Angela safe," he earnestly prayed. Of course she was safe in Chicago, away from the unknown hazards of sea travel. "Nevertheless, Lord; keep a loving eye on her."

The next few days were as balmy as Michael could want. Mr. and Mrs. North left with sketches of themselves and two live chickens. When they'd promised to return the following year, Michael assured them he would not be the lightkeeper.

* * *

*Monday, July 30th 1841*

A few lazy mosquitoes tried to harass him when he carried in water, but he flicked them off into eternity. It wasn't as if he'd forgotten the stories Cross told about the power of Lake Superior to squash life as easily as he had demolished the insects.

Of all his chores, Michael found fetching water to be the least satisfying. The tram way helped in the transfer of water to the cottage, but the need for well-water kept Michael engaged in constant activity. If the fires of hell could be quenched, Michael imagined his daily script of water duty qualified him as thoroughly rehearsed.

After spending his morning allotment of time sketching the wonders of growth in his flower and vegetable garden, Michael started toward the cottage for lunch. Behind the chicken coop, the first growth of a field of wheat was greener than the sparse grass of the lawn leading to the dock. Feathery carrot tops, the flat vines of potatoes and beans, and spiked onion greens promised abundance. Two rows of sweet corn stood higher than the cuffs of Michael's pants. Tulips and daffodils south of the row of corn faced away from Lake Superior, toward Angela's spirit.

Michael leaned his drawing book against the weight chimney in the main room. With a hot cup of coffee and a large can of kippers, he returned to the central room to critically assess his rendition of the garden.

There was Angela's hand amongst the flowers, her fingers lifting the head of a daffodil. The trim on her eyelet petticoat danced above the umber lumps of turned earth.

"Angela," Michael said. "Visiting me again are you?"

Remembering the woman he loved, Michael felt happiness and sadness combined. A bitter-sweet joy acknowledged her role in his life. He'd gone off to sketch in isolation, only to find parts of Angela flying from his pens at every opportunity.

Madelyn hopped all the way up to the surface of the table, as if to find what had changed the mood of her keeper. Michael rubbed behind her ears.

As if to express the gain of Michael's affections, Madelyn jumped down and exuberantly chased Sadie around the table's legs. Sadie stopped, sitting up to secure her place near Michael's feet. Madelyn cuddled up next to Sadie and began to groom her sister's ears.

Michael supposed Inspector Cross would exhibit some surprise when he demanded to take his furry pets off the island in September. Michael wondered where he'd be headed then. Everything depended on Angela's answer to his proposal. Even if she agreed to marry him, they would have to decide where they belonged. Would she want to return to her mother in Ireland for the wedding? Would Michael's parents insist on meeting the bride? Perhaps they could speed their return by sailing through Lake Ontario and then down the St. Lawrence.

Michael decided somewhere in the middle of Inspector Cross's list of disasters not to stay a lighthouse tender for more than one season. But what, where, and how could he provide for his wife and children without returning to England and his father's clockwork factory?

Michael sat on the floor to be nearer to his animal family. The two does moved closer to his knees to get equal attention.

"The nice thing about you girls is that you never complain about my bad habits," Michael explained.

They're warmth and soft fur equally endeared them; but he recognized each had a different spirit. Sadie would never hop onto a table. She would think it rude and pushy but Madelyn resisted sharing Michael's bed, as if that was an intimacy she could live without. He wondered if he would ever be able to eat a mammal again.

"Chickens don't have big brains. Right?" It worried him, because he liked the taste of chicken dipped in salty flour and fried to a golden brown.

Madelyn apparently recognized the tone of the question as a challenge and provoked Sadie into a heated chase up and down the tower's stairs.

The drawings of windmill drew Michael up to the second floor room. Traces of Angela couldn't be found in the engineering sketches.

Rather disappointed in the unknowing exclusion of his angel, Michael added a drawing of a rope pulley to the well handle, then wondered how he could pipe the water directly into the boiler and the kitchen sink. First he'd have to build the windmill, then he would decide if power could be used for the fog-horn and the well at the same time.

Sadie chased Madelyn into the room. They both stopped and reared up. Comfortably sitting on their haunches, they twitched both their ears and noses at him.

"Right," Michael said, as if their collective thoughts inspired him. "A transport cage big enough for two of you. I'll have to apologize ahead of time. There won't be room for chasing."

With that the rabbits high-tailed it out of the room to continue their play.

"Angela will love you and probably make you even happier by breeding you with a buck." Michael called after them. He made sure the cage was tall enough for the rabbits' ears to fit into, even if they decided to sit up on their haunches.

The windmill might remain an unfinished dream like the free-standing globe in the north bedroom. Michael checked his watch. Six o'clock, time to light the lamp. On the walkway around the lamp, Michael made sure to scan the northern skies for any hint of cloud activity. He wondered if the wind could blow without clouds, and he should have asked Inspector Cross about the fog. He didn't want to mention his windmill idea until he'd constructed a good share of it. The proportions of the cottage necessitated the balance of a windmill for a truly pleasing composition. And the windmill would provide velocity information besides the direction of the winds. Maybe Cross would be interested in that aspect of the building. Michael doubted he would be able to convince him of its need by mentioning any aesthetic appeal.

Supper could wait for the chores to be finished. A ride around the island on Splendor revived Michael with a sense of ownership as well as the pleasure of controlling his strong stallion.

On the ride, another cautionary idea struck Michael. Instead of collecting the empty sardine cans, he'd pound them into some sort of wind-chime near his bedroom window on the first floor, to alert him of slight changes in the breeze. Angela would never hear his handiwork.

He decided to sketch the wind-chime in case Angela might want to see the bit of fancy sometime in the distant future.

"Not too distant, please, Lord."

Michael thought he heard his mother's familiar reply, "Be careful what you pray for, son."

In a flash of fear, Michael meshed Inspector Cross' storm recitations with his prayer. "Safe, Lord, keep her safe, even if I never lay eyes on her in this lifetime."

He couldn't bear thinking of Angela in any form of danger. And he remembered aboard the Pannonia grabbing Captain Hale's angry arm before he could do harm to Angela.

"She loves life, Lord; keep her within your care."

Madelyn and Sadie greeted him at the bottom of the tower stairs.

"Yes, yes. You're right ladies. I'm a little slow with supper this evening. Worries take time away from duties."

* * *

*Thursday, August 16th, 1841*

Michael extinguished the lighthouse lamp at dawn. The cloudless sky was painted in tints of coral and rose by the hidden sun. He turned toward the icy north remembering the sailor's warning of red skies at sunset. He saw no line of clouds, no sail or steamboats in view and reminded himself that, after all, this was sunrise not the ending of the day.

After inhaling and downing one cup of coffee, he donned an extra sweater and directed his feet toward the chicken coop for fresh eggs. A side trip to the garden gleaned new potatoes and onions. A big savory breakfast gave him the energy he needed for his endless and unthinking chores. Half a pan of biscuits and a second pot of coffee declared his fast broken. He fed Madelyn and Sadie the spoils of the meal. Splendor might settle for being curried instead of a ride.

The mirrors of the Fresnel lamp blinded Michael as he rubbed smoke film from its glass sides. Vinegar and water removed the night's grayness from the tower's windows. His eyes teared from the sharp fumes. The bucket and chamois were soon black from the grime. Michael held his breath when he dumped the dirty water in the outhouse so as not to taint the well water. The well had been situated south of the garden on a slight rise. Going downhill with heavy, brimming buckets of fresh water caused Michael to thank his Maker for blessings each day.

Michael checked the calendar on the door between the boiler-room and the kitchen. Thursday. One Sunday he'd read a chapter in Revelations. As a family man, he intended to make daily readings of the bible a morning ritual, but for now, Sunday would do. A family man? How many of Angela's children would mimic her good looks and how many would resemble him?

"Please, Lord, let us have Your blessing on our union," he prayed, "if it is Your will."

When Michael supplied the chickens with their morning meal, he decided the coop needed cleaning. His mind played with names of the children Angela and he might raise some day. He felled a small tree, shed himself of the sweater, and split enough timber to replenish the wood pile.

Of course, Angela would have her say, but Erie and Hudson could serve for boys' names. Michael hoped Angela would agree to name their first girl Beatrice. The lady that guided Dante to Heaven should be honored for their shared love of the poet. The grandmothers would no doubt have their say. And his father. Michael wondered what the Christian name of the Earl of Covington might be. He didn't like the sound of the name Edward, but David would be fine.

Instead of spending time in the kitchen with his sketch pad and the rabbits, as was he wont to do when he waited for the boiler's flywheel to signal the water was hot, he labored outside. He bundled fresh hay from the wheat field harvest. He stacked the shafts in the rafters of the chicken coop. He winnowed the wheat against the same tree stump Inspector Cross had used to slay chickens. Two burlap sacks of wheat were safely stored, ready to provide feed for the chickens.

The boiler hadn't waited for him. The flywheel was spinning at a terrific rate, and Michael used a towel to release the fog-horn pull. Madelyn, at his boot, had pricked up her ears at the first soft noise, but as the horn gained in sound and repetition, she fled to the shelter of Michael's bedroom.

Michael drew off a barrel of hot water before the fog-horn silenced itself. He scrubbed the small chicken house from top to bottom with a broom and lye soap, and used fresh hay to replenish the nests.

Lunch would have to wait until he'd refilled the barrel and a mate from the lake. He loaded the empty barrels on the tram for their trip down to the dock. Deciding on the ingredients for a well-deserved lunch occupied his thoughts as he dragged the half-filled barrels from the lake and then topped them off with more buckets of lake water. After he secured the barrels to the tram, he straightened, raising his cap to push a damp lock of hair away from his eyes.

A purple line of clouds stretched low along the northern horizon of the lake.

"How long have you been on the rise?" he asked.

To make sure of the speed of the incoming storm, Michael stood his ground and checked his watch. One o'clock. He turned the lifeboat over so it wouldn't be full of water if he needed to row it out to rescue anyone.

Michael rushed through the rest of his outdoor chores, pulling the tram up to the back door of the boiler room, harvesting produce from the garden, penning the chickens inside the coop and hauling wood into the boiler room.

Splendor needed a ride but Michael coaxed the nervous horse into the small shed and rubbed his nose. "After the storm, boy. We'll ride out after the storm."

He refilled the boiler and the lamp oil containers for the light. Usually he polished the chimney after he'd pulled the weights and used the elevator to haul the oil up to the light, but his curiosity about the storm's approach caused him to mount the 60 stairs and fill the light. He checked his watch when he saw that the bank of clouds was a quarter of the way from the horizon to the tower. Two o'clock. Too early to light the lamp.

The fire under the boiler was lit. Red coals from burnt timber winked at him, and the side of the boiler was hot to the touch. He could get her smoking in ten minutes. Michael rolled out two pans of biscuits and boiled every egg on the place. He hacked off a big slap of the smoked deer meat and sliced enough for three meals. Cooking might have to wait for the storm to pass. He concentrated on filling extra lamp oil containers. He hauled two-days-worth of whale oil into the elevator, pulling them to the top of the tower.

When he checked on the rabbits, he found they had taken refuge under the bedroom chair, as close together as they could get.

Michael held his hand an inch above their shaking noses. "Don't be afraid of a little noise, girls. I'm bigger than any old storm."

The rabbits visibly relaxed, but they didn't seem intent on moving from under the chair. The wind chime outside the window obviously frightened them. Removing the noisy thing might take more time than Michael could spend at the moment.

Instead he ran up the tower steps to check on the weather. His watch said three o'clock, and the storm was no longer a distant line of clouds. The purple and black giants of wind rushed over the tower. He lit the lamp and scanned the sea.

Sunlight still shone on a southern island. It dimmed as he watched. Then all was gloom. Michael hadn't made out one ship, but the sea was already heaving from the winds. Whitecaps were tossing their warnings. Michael checked the storm clouds' speed; maybe the squall would cease as quickly as it appeared.

The dock rose and fell in the swelling waves. Suddenly the wood broke apart. The broken pieces washed up onto the shore.

Building coffins, as described by Inspector Cross, came to Michael's mind. He could see the dory was still secured behind the stone benches of the sea wall.

When the rain obscured his view from the tower, he hurried down the steps to release the fog-horn mechanism.

"Thank God," he earnestly prayed.

He had refilled the barrels and wood pile. There was enough water and wood at hand to keep the horn sounding for as long as the storm continued. The tension in his shoulders told him he was ready for his war with the storm.

# Chapter 19

*Friday, August 17th, 1841*

The sailing ship, Florida, tossed about on the mountainous seas in Lake Superior as Angela struggled as she disengaged herself from under her heavy maid. "Are you hurt?" Angela pleaded for a response. "Marabell?"

Marabell didn't move. She'd been knocked unconscious by the force of the gigantic wave. Blood dripped from her ears.

She had held Angela's blue cloak over her arm before trying to wrestle open the cabin door. Angela freed the robe from the faithful maid's grasp. As soon as Angela clasped the robe around her neck, she attempted to get help for her stricken friend.

The uncouth sailors refused or couldn't hear her pleas as they slid across the slanting decks. The roar of the black storm and crashing of the seas over the flimsy sailboat made Angela wish they waited to board the heavier steamboat. Remembering how Marabell called the wooden lighthouses matchboxes, Angela knew she'd wrongly entrusted both their lives to this bit of wood floundering upon the surging, angry waters.

The memory of her school chum, Colleen, laughing about her father's saying, "You cannot drown on the Atlantic, so long as you stay on shore," haunted Angela, now.

Angela's cloak kept the icy Lake Superior waters from taking her breath away as it poured over her. However, the weight of her garment was going to be a problem.

"Where are the lifeboats?" she yelled. Maybe she could drag Marabell out of the cabin by herself. "We can't swim!"

Everyone within her view was busy clinging for their lives to ropes and railings.

The weather was growing colder, dark, and dirty. The wind screamed louder, and Lake Superior grew more turbulent.

"Gone!" Someone yelled close to her ear. "The boats are all gone."

Turning to hear who was speaking was difficult as the bitter wind railed behind her. The hood of her cloak clung to the back of her head, shielding her from blasts of icy wet.

Captain Maddox slung a rope around her waist and the main mast. "This is your safest bet, girlie. The water's too cold to survive in."

Fear gripped Angela's senses as she struggled against the ropes and the captain's expert knots. She bit her tongue and tasted the blood of impotent rage. "Let me go!" Angela screamed. "I have to go below. We need help."

The captain tied her so tightly to the mast she couldn't turn around to argue. Before she could think of a suitable Irish curse, the captain was swept over the railing of his doomed craft as a killer surge of the merciless lake threw him overboard. Angela was humbled at the strength of the surrounding storm. She found her anger departed with Captain Maddox.

Then two hope-filled hands grabbed onto the rope around Angela's waist.

A priest with wild eyes scanned her face. "Are you right with your Maker?"

Angela's terror ceased. The pounding of blood in her ears stopped. She breathed away the hot, mind-numbing fear. "I am," she said to the trembling, brandy-soaked priest.

"And you?" She asked.

Horror changed his complexion to a ghostly pallor. "No." The priest mouthed the word that the storm whipped away. Before he let go of the rope, the priest wrapped the trailing end of it around Angela's arms and then her hips. Next he ripped the large crucifix from his neck and tucked it inside her cape. The back of his hand lingered against the warmth of her blouse.

"Pray for me, always," he said, before letting the wind and water plunge him into the frigid bowels of Lake Superior.

Angela searched the decks for another rescuer. Not one living form could be found. Her courage squared her young shoulders. She would have to face death alone. A crazy question presented itself in the midst of the growing chaos. "Lord, I don't know the priest's name."

She accepted the chilling fact that she might not live long enough to forget the name of the ship. The Florida was breaking apart.

"Marabell, forgive me." She hoped the maid would remain unconscious, not have to struggle against drowning. How could she explain to Matt that she hadn't stayed with his wife? Her chances of being alive to detail their last moments were slipping away.

Angela held her breath for as long as possible when the waves washed over her. The Lord wouldn't want her to give up his gift of life without a fight.

Then Angela heard a fog-horn somewhere in front of her. The Florida was being driven south. Landward. She lifted her head against the mast and could make out a greenish glow from a lighthouse.

Was it Michael's lamp?

The Florida was headed straight for whatever dangers the light and fog-horn cautioned against in the dark storm.

"Oh, Michael," Angela cried. "We'll never be together in life."

More than the horrible death she faced, smashed against shoals or into hidden obstacles in the rock-bound coast, Angela feared Michael might never hear from her lips that she wanted to spend the rest of her life with him.

"Shortened as it is," she yelled in defiance at the wind or at the heaving waters around her.

Angela couldn't see clearly through the atmospheric haze and the spectral mist of the tempest. Then the hull of the boat cracked open from contact with unforgiving hindrances. Furious waves continued to inundate her; but the knots didn't slip.

"Ma," she cried, giving into the terror, "Ma!"

The aft section of the ship began to sag.

Angela was held fast to the floundering, twisting and bumping middle section of the abandoned ship. She'd never be able to explain to her mother why Michael Halliday was the only man she would ever marry. The rolling gentle hills of the land she'd bought with the Earl's money would be farmed by another soul. Angela struggled against the ropes. She wanted to live.

A large fish was swept up by the waves. The rainbow colored fish eyed her as it passed by in the air, freed of its watery home.

Then she recalled the last half of a rosary prayer, "Holy Mary, Mother of God, pray for us sinners now and at this sudden pinnacle of death."

She didn't remember the words quite right, but Angela felt lucky to be given the time to say them at all, tied to this tilting vessel and no doubt about to drown. There was no hope of surviving or riding out the storm.

Then across the tumult of water, Angela saw the clear silhouette of a looming lighthouse far above a gale-whipped shore. The heaving sprays and lowering clouds confused her as to where the water ended and the beach began.

Hurling water seemed to reach the roof of the lighthouse. The tower's light bounced off low hanging clouds and bathed the top beam of the Florida. As if in answer, the main mast, to which Angela was tied, exploded from the ongoing strain.

A great pain wrenched her shoulder. In her fight against the darkness of unconsciousness, Angela succumbed to agony.

* * *

Michael Halliday spent every minute stoking and filling the fog-horn boiler and checking on the lamp in the tower. The assistance of a wind-powered fog-horn would have allowed him to rest between his trips to the tower. A night of fog might not have the muscle necessary to turn the gears, but Lake Superior's wind-lashed storms certainly did. Michael knew Inspector Cross would listen to his plans. During the squally seasons, before the ice froze her solid, the unceasing turbulence of Lake Superior could man the fog horn windmill without the aid of humans. A windmill must be built on Strawberry Island.

Michael hauled up extra buckets of drinking water from the well on return trips from feeding the chickens in their shuttered coop. There were enough logs stacked up for the emergency. Michael was thankful for his own strategic planning because he didn't have the time or the energy to split moré wood. He stacked a week's supply in case the weather didn't break even if the boiler ate thick logs like a child consuming peppermint candies.

Lake Superior had built a mighty storm up, throwing up a vicious tantrum. The rabbits weren't eating.

Michael used a lot of energy running between the lamp, up the 60 steps and then down to the fog-horn's boiler. After he fed the boiler more water from the barrels he'd brought up earlier in the week and thoroughly stoked the fire in the boiler's under-belly, Michael stuffed food down his throat. To keep awake through the long siege, he also drank pot after pot of coffee.

The storm's spume began to obscure Michael's view of the lake from the tower, but he remained vigilant, peering through the gloom. At times he could make out his rescue boat still overturned near the stone wall. He had tied a rope from the yawl to the huge steamboat anchor rusting near the door of the cottage. He imagined using the rope to find the small craft in the dark.

Michael strained his eyes and paced the slippery parapet. A fear he hadn't experienced before gripped his stomach. Here was nature on a rampage. The ice age seemed destined to regain dominance. The middle of August didn't stop the wind from hanging icicles off the railings. The lake was screaming in a classic northeast gale.

Michael squinted against the whipping rain and wind. A torn schooner with a gap between the bow section and the stern, or its ghost, materialized. He couldn't see any survivors of the disaster. Then the broken ship came at him through the rain. Tossed and raked by every wave, the keeled over wooden schooner was gripped by the wind. The struggling, doomed remnants of the craft disappeared, then re-appeared, headed toward the rocks.

The giant hull slammed into the shoals and cracked like an egg. The shipwreck had found the rocks in spite of the lighthouse.

Michael staggered against the glass of the lamp. All his efforts drew disaster to his doorstep instead of guiding ships away from his staunch lookout. He was beaten in his war against the storm. Why had he whimsically given away his birthright to pursue solitude? He had nothing to show for his sacrifice.

He might have lost the only woman he loved by selfishly demanding to spend part of his life sketching the beauty on God's earth. He certainly knew he'd lost his reason for expending energy to keep a lamp lit for ships to see and a horn sounding for their protection.

Michael pounded his fist against the tower's windows. Outside, the hammering, victorious surf waited to chew the ship up for the wild breakers to carry off.

* * *

Instead, a burst of cyclonic energy blew the remains of the Florida, with Angela tied to what was left of the central mast, onto the lawn of the Strawberry Island lighthouse. The hull and keel were smashed to pieces by the convulsing, regurgitating lake.

* * *

Michael witnessed the extraordinary phenomenon. He rushed down the 60 steps and threw on his rain gear. He hurriedly secured another rope to the rusting anchor outside the cottage door before scrambling toward the relics of the ship. He heard no cries for help. Michael didn't expect to find any living thing. The storm beat the ship into fragments. He felt beaten too, as if the storm waged its private war against his very soul and found him selfish, prideful and wanting. Defeat seemed shamefully personal.

Broken bits of deck and mast timbers littered the yard. Ropes tugged at his boots and he lifted his storm lantern to make his way through the muddy, flying debris.

Coffins, he remembered. Inspector Cross instructed him to nail coffins together with the ship's lumber for the bodies that would wash ashore after the sounds of the storm diminished.

Michael's lantern illuminated a bit of blue cloth.

The same twilight color once cloaked Angela when he met her aboard the Pannonia. No time to spend remembering the woman he loved, Michael set to work, searching through the broken timbers on the ground.

The blue cloth drew him back to its location. The huge pole of the central mast held the fluttering cloth.

Michael drew his knife and cut the ropes holding the blanketing material. A human form rolled onto the lawn. Angela's blonde hair fell under the beams of the lantern's light.

"Angela!" Michael screamed a hoarse, broken yell as he dropped to his knees.

* * *

He thought she was the first of the corpses. Michael cradled her in his arms. He kissed the sandy mud from her cold mouth and closed eyelids. He removed a large crucifix from her unmoving fingers. That arm lay in its sleeve the way he'd seen a jockey's in Berkshire after being dragged by a horse. Angela's arm was separated from the collar bone and would have to be pulled back into place.

Michael imagined he could still smell the scent of roses in her hair. He carried her to the cottage and laid her soaked body on his bed.

He couldn't bear to cover her dear face. It comforted him as he shed his coat and blew out the lantern.

Kneeling beside the bed, he prayed for what seemed like hours. No words came, except for the one, "Lord."

He repeated the word over and over because he didn't have anything to ask for. Everything he wanted in life was gone. His Angela was dead. He would rather have her alive forsaking him, but alive!

Finally, Michael remembered one prayer of more substance. "Forgive me," he cried again and again, until his body gave into his exhaustion.

Michael slept on the bed embracing Angela's body.

\* \* \*

*Saturday, August 18th, 1841*

At dawn's resurrection, Michael felt warmth on the hand that cradled Angela's face. Her breath was warming his fingers!

Michael jumped to his feet.

The rabbits screamed as the noise of his heavy boots on the floor brought them awake.

Angela didn't stir.

With great reverence, Michael knelt again next to the bed to thank their maker. "Restore her, oh Lord, if it be your will."

The rabbits followed Michael into the kitchen and then to the boiler room, where he laid the last logs under the hot water tank. He disconnected the fog-horn's apparatus.

Angela needed to be bathed in warm water.

While the water heated, Michael set a new pot of coffee on the stove. He ran at full speed to free the chickens from their coop and Splendor from his stall. He scattered feed in the chicken's muddy enclosure before viewing the wreck in the lighthouse's yard.

How Angela could have survived the destruction seemed miracle enough, but Michael wanted her whole. He wanted to hear that sweet voice of hers.

"Please Lord," Michael was content to pray without ceasing for the rest of his life, if only Angela could come back to him.

Why Angela was on the ship surpassed his over-wrought mind. She was in his bed unable to speak, to move, to hear his voice; that's all that mattered to Michael. Had her aunt Parished? He should scour the ground and coastline of the island for more bodies, but his soul wouldn't let him. They would have to wait for the dead to bury them, if they'd been washed ashore.

"Maybe by this afternoon," he promised reluctantly to re-examine the remains of the ship and rubble-strewn shore.

Then Michael bathed his beloved's body. Not a mark could he find. The ropes that bound her to the mast rubbed her flesh a bright red, but no puncture wounds or bruises let him know the cause of her stillness. The beauty of her nude body awakened shameful, lustful thoughts. He was alive, she inert. He kissed her navel, then her knees, then her forehead.

The prayers went on and on in his mind, filling the black space and blocking out his fears and worries. He was too frightened to hope for any outcome.

Michael laid her unconscious, unclothed body on the plank floor in his bedroom. He sat down beside her left arm, holding the limp arm above the wrist. In order to pull the arm out far enough for it to pop naturally back into place in her shoulder, he needed leverage. He anchored one of his bare feet under her arm pit. Praying earnestly, he pulled as hard as he could with his feet braced against her body. Then he let go of the arm and actually heard it pop back into place.

Angela didn't move.

He brushed and combed out her glorious hair letting it cascade over the clean pillows he placed under her head. Michael dressed Angela in his finest, softest shirt. He pulled the blankets up to her chin, tucking them behind her shoulders.

Madelyn's curiosity got the best of her and she hopped onto the bed for the first time. Sadie followed.

The sun came streaming in the window at the head of the bed, touching off the glowing lights in Angela's hair.

Michael was racked with sobs. He couldn't breath and stumbled out of the room. He opened the door to the yard, breathing deeply of the freshened air.

The smell of flowers awakened by the sun's warmth assailed his nerves. He avoided looking at the trampled lawn and gathered all the flowers he could find. He took off the shirt he'd worn for three hectic days and filled it with the hollyhock and morning glory blooms that clung to the cottage. Venturing down the path to the dock destroyed by the storm, he gathered fallen mud-soaked violets and primroses. When the yard was nude of blossoms, he returned to Angela's bed.

He spent an inordinate amount of time washing and arranging the flowers in their most advantageous light. Michael was tempted to sketch his Angela with the glorious colors surrounding her form, but he couldn't reach for his pencils. A sacrilege against the privacy of his lover's repose prevented him.

Michael changed his clothes to reload his lighthouse duties onto his burdened, grieving back. Lamp oil needed replenishment, the weights demanded to be pulled, water needed hauling from the lake in the emptied barrels. When he was splitting logs for the fog-horn's needs, his mind righted itself toward a calmer vein of sanity. He listed his remaining chores: the eggs to be gathered, the bodies to be searched for, the wreckage in the yard stacked behind the wood pile for later uses, if needed.

He ate the last of the provisions he'd prepared before the storm and with the evening lamp lit and weights pulled, Michael rested his overworked body next to Angela's. He hugged her form for comfort.

Finally, in a fitful sleep he lifted the shirt that covered her belly and rested his head on her soft, warm navel. The world felt right in Michael's dreams with the Lord in his heaven watching out for their common safety.

\* \* \*

*Sunday, August 19th, 1841*

Angela awoke from her long recovery coma to the warmth of Michael's breath on her bared leg. A natural desire fired her blood motivating her arms to lift and seek out the origin. Her fingers played with the curls on Michael's head, before her mind recognized the source of her need.

"Michael?" she asked. "Did you die before you reached your island?" Angela stroked Michael's dear cheek.

Michael roused himself and kissed her face sleepily. "No, dear."

"Angela," he shouted, jumping from the bed then back onto it, crushing her in his arms.

"Do I feel dead?"

"No," she answered not hoping to believe. "We're not dead?"

Tears streamed down Michael's face. "No. Thank a merciful God, we're not dead."

Angela wept too. "Marabell is gone."

Michael kissed her mouth, wrapped her in the coverlet and drew her to his lap as he sat with her in the bedroom's cushioned chair.

"I don't know who that is," Michael said, holding her close to his chest.

"My aunt's maid," Angela said. "She came with me on the Florida." Fresh tears stopped her from speaking.

"Are you hungry, Angela?"

`She shook her head. "I am that thirsty. My arm is sore. Is it broken?."

"Your shoulder was dislocated, but I'd seen how to right the situation. I put it back in place while you were unconscious. At first I didn't know you were even breathing."

"Oh, Michael. How horrible!"

Michael left her in the chair as he went to the bedside table where a glass held water. Two rabbits huddled together on the flower petal strewn bed. The rabbits followed Michael's every move.

"I sent you a letter." Michael drew the blanket closer around her after she accepted the glass.

"That's why I came," Angela sobbed again. "And now I've killed Marabell."

Michael knelt beside her, tipping his head to rest on her shoulder. "I'm so thankful you're alive," he whispered.

Angela was nearly nude under the blanket. "Michael, I don't suppose I arrived here as naked as a mermaid."

He met her eyes and blushed. "I had to bathe you. Mud…." Michael stood up.

Angela forgot just how tall he was.

"I'll go check on your clothes." At the door he stopped. "Are you hungry yet?"

"Oh, I am that." She smiled at her hero. "And Michael, it's not that I'm believing you took liberties with your intended whilst she was dead to the world, but we'll be needing separate beds."

Michael only seemed to hear one word. "Intended?" A great smile illuminated his soul. "Is it yes then?"

"And why else would I be risking life and limb to come to you?" Angela smiled, not forgetting the cost of her maid's life.

"I've missed the sweet sound of your voice since the Thomas Jefferson left Detroit."

Angela struggled to stand but gave it up when her head spun the room in circles. "I'll just wait here for a bit of broth or coffee."

"Right," he said not budging from the door. "I can't bear to leave you. Can I carry you into the kitchen?"

"No you cannot," she said, miffed at the impropriety. "After the broth, if you'll be kind enough to bring me my clothes, I'll dress." Angela smiled at his cowed look. "Then we'll sit in the sunshine and you can show me all those sketches you thought leaving me was worth."

"Done," he laughed.

Angela could hear him run across a wood-floored room, into one of stone or tile before banging cups against a pot, presumably filled with coffee. Broth would have been more wholesome, but she missed the sight of her beloved too. Glad she was to have him hurry back.

# Chapter 20

Temporarily weakened by the disastrous voyage, Angela succumbed to Michael's demand she remain in bed. Under the circumstances, Michael's tenderness endeared him even more to her. However, after two days of listening to Michael cook, clean, and tend to the lamp in the tower, Angela's strength returned enough to welcome sharing duties other than stroking the rabbits.

The next time he visited the bedroom, she began to explain. "Michael."

He instantly knelt near the bed.

"I ought to venture outside more." She loved having him within reach but not the constant smothering. "To heal properly."

He swept her up in his strong arms and carried her outside, down the path to where the dock might have been and placed her on a stone bench. After running back to the cottage for pillows and the ever-present pot of hot coffee and cups, Michael sat on the ground next her.

The bright air held a bit of chill, but the sun warmed her sore shoulder. Repetitive waves shimmered in the roughened wake of the storm. The depth of the huge lake's menacing power caused Angela to reach for Michael's arm.

"Marabell," she said quietly.

Michael remained silent.

"From all the pounding of nails I heard, I thought the dock would be in place by now." She hoped to tease him away from the sad subject of drowned travelers.

"Ten coffins," Michael said without amplifying the subject.

"Is Marabell buried?"

Michael met her gaze. "No. Angela, I would have told you if I'd found Marabell."

He stood up, paced behind her and then resumed his seat next to her, enfolding her in his muscled arms.

"No bodies washed ashore, yet." His voice lowered to almost a whisper above the surf. "Inspector Cross said to use the few days before the bodies come ashore to prepare the coffins from the wreckage."

Michael walked to the shore and stared out over the lake.

Angela wept at the thought of Marabell's watery cabin coffin. How could she ever describe the details to Matt, her poor husband?

Her attention was drawn to the steadying figure of her future husband. The breadth of his back seemed larger than the first time she viewed his form against the night's sky on the Pannonia. Perhaps the brightness surrounding his image increased its mass. The manual labor of surviving on the island surely added bulk to his muscles.

When he returned to the bench, Michael said, "Splendor and I rode around the island earlier."

Angela touched his rigid jaw.

He sucked in his breath as if to prevent a sob. "Instead of warning your ship, all my efforts drew your boat to the island's rocks. I worked like a crazed demon. I ate on the run, terrified to let the lamp or the fog-horn miss a beat."

"No possibility existed for the ship to maneuver in those monstrous seas." Angela pulled herself onto Michael's lap. "What were you supposed to do? Blow back?"

Michael grinned. "The opposite of my goal happened."

"Able to control the elements?" Angela tugged on the brim of his hat. "Is that why you came to this outpost?"

Her teasing hit too close to Michael's heart. Angela was distressed to see a tear alongside his handsome nose.

"My art is as meaningless as my efforts to stave off ships."

"Michael, I love your drawings. What are you thinking?"

"I ought not to pick up a pencil." He searched his calloused hands, then balled them into fists. "Art is all vanity, a sin of ego."

"Playing God again, is it." Angela stroked the raised veins on his strong hands. "And wasn't it the good Lord that gave you the talent you're so willing to toss aside?"

"I love you, Angela." Michael kissed her longer than was necessary. "I will, no doubt, keep sketching. Thank the Lord for saving you."

"Perhaps we could row around the island," Angela worried their intimate talk could lead to closer activities. "I don't want you to think

I'll be looking for floating corpses." She smiled tentatively. "I see your rescue boat survived and your muscles seem up to the job."

Michael deterred moving. "You don't have a hat against the sun."

"Couldn't I borrow yours?" She ruffled his curls. "Your complexion is already as brown as a native's."

Michael replenished her coffee cup from the cooling pot. "After Inspector Cross's last visit, two buckskin clad figures surprised me while I was bathing."

"What tribe did they come from," Angela wanted to know.

"They were both white, but the man, Parish, was raised by natives. I don't know which tribe."

"And the woman?"

"His wife, Dorothy North, was white too."

Angela held onto a gnawing thought for as long as she could. "How old were they?"

"Sixty, I think." Michael grinned as if he knew her jealous thought about another woman seeing Michael's body. "Dorothy told me at her advanced stage of life, she bows at the beauty of roses."

Michael squeezed Angela's left hand. "All flowers dim in the glory of your beauty."

"Blarney?" Angela pulled her hand away. "Is that all your offering me after my arduous trip to be with the likes of you? Can't you be showing me the island paradise you deserted me for?"

Michael whipped into action, turning over the yawl, affixing its single sail, before lifting her on board. He took off his boots and dragged the boat out into deep enough water. His pants were wet past his knees.

"I'll have to get started repairing the dock," Michael smiled his winning grin at her. "Inspector Cross will need to tie up his lightship."

Angela was surprised at the terror rising in her throat. Not one to shy away from riding the same horse she fell off of, Angela gripped the boat's side and tried to calm her racing heart.

Michael noticed. "The wind isn't that good today," he said, starting to turn the skiff toward the beach.

"Weather's fine, Michael Halliday." Angela let go of the side. "You're only embarrassed to find you've engaged yourself to a cowardly woman, is all."

He patted her knee. "Shall I take her out further?"

"Please," Angela tried not to grit her teeth. "I know I'm safe in your hands."

No mishap occurred, and Angela finally relaxed as they reached the southern tip of the island.

"Michigan seems far away," she said, pointing at the shoreline further south.

"I missed you every day since I abandoned you in Detroit."

"Mrs. Jameson seemed quite convinced I'd accept your proposal," Angela goaded.

"I wish I had been." He leaned forward to softly kiss her lips.

"Marabell would have chaperoned me." Angela looked at her hands. "I didn't expect to be alone with you on the island." She tried to shake off her grief and smiled faintly. "It's quite scandalous."

Michael's grin held a bit more mischief than was appropriate.

"Guilty we ought to be," Angela slapped at his knee, "to be sharing each other's merriment.

Michael shrugged. "The Lord's plans are out of our hands." He placed his huge paw in her lap.

Surprised, she was, at the turn her body was taking, imagining Michael beside her in the bed. Angela restrained her mind from the avenue it was pursuing. "Best be minding the sails."

Michael checked to see that all was tip top. The sun glinted in his eyes.

Angela hoped his plans matched her own, of their coming together.

"When do you expect the Inspector?" Angela tried a safe subject.

"Soon," Michael said. "I'll get started on the dock tomorrow."

"I can help." Angela felt she was weaning Michael away from his assessment of her infirm condition as a she would a pup from its mother.

He shook his head, but asked her, "If you think you're strong enough."

"I think we both need to pursue a healthy project." Angela lowered her eyes in embarrassment.

"Love making is very healthy," Michael said with his head turned into the wind, his eyes unreadable.

"Michael," she chided him. Than an inspiring idea filtered through the onslaught of sensations caused by Michael's proximity. "Could the Inspector perform a marriage ceremony?"

"Would that do for your mother?"

"Certainly not!" Angela was shocked that he thought anything but a church wedding could please Ma. "Would your own mother in Berkshire approve of a ship's captain marrying us?"

"I wrote her I was in love with you," Michael moved closer to her, after tying the tiller to its stay.

"Did you?" Angela felt her eyes couldn't move away from his penetrating gaze. "I feel like a rabbit under the shadow of a hawk."

Instantly, Michael moved away, unfurled the sail and turned the boat toward shore.

Angela chatted nervously on the return trip. "Ma is in Ann Arbor. The Earl bought her bar and sent her to America. She'll be waiting with Aunt Elizabeth and Matt. Uncle Henry died from influenza a couple days after we reached Chicago. Aunt Elizabeth sold her house to meet unpaid obligations. You remember Winnie and Mrs. Lazarus settled in Ann Arbor. Mrs. Lazarus bought a farm that I picked out when I went through Michigan. It's close to Ann Arbor," Angela continued to babble, "On a lake."

"Michael," Angela persisted. "What will come of us?"

He didn't answer.

Once they were safely on shore with the sail stored under the overturned boat, Angela asked, "Michael, have I angered you then?"

"Why do you ask?" he said with his back turned away as he picked up the coffee pot and cups. "Could you retrieve the pillows?"

She whacked him hard on his back. "Because you're not looking at me and you've stopped talking to me."

"I'm talking," he said as his long legs drew him toward the cottage.

Angela left the pillows on the stone bench and turned away from the house. She walked down to the rocky shore and picked her way among the boulders to the far side of the island. She needed time to think.

Alone on this island, would she keep pushing him away until he didn't want her anymore? What a way to start an engagement! She missed Ma; even Aunt Elizabeth would be a welcomed ear for her worries. Angela wanted to compare her feelings to theirs when they were being courted, seduced.

She searched the waters as they slapped the shore. If she kept the question hanging long enough, aside her fervent prayers, would an answer come from some far off place, from heaven or the departed saints? The breezes brought no whispers, the fresh smell of the island's grasses no place to rest. The gnarled trees twisted into contorted shapes. The sky alone of brilliant blue gave her peace.

When she returned to the cottage, Angela couldn't find Michael. He'd made up the bed in the bedroom. His pallet on the floor was rolled up behind the upholstered chair. The big bed's covers were straightened. The pillows she'd forgotten on the stone bench were fluffed up and positioned against the headboard.

He'd unlatched the windows at the head of the bed, where a tin wind chime musically caught the day's slight breeze. She could smell the hollyhocks and morning glories that grew under the window outside. One bluish-purple bloom swayed toward her at the open window.

Michael's pet rabbits were hiding.

The central room with its odd middle apparatus to the tower's lamp shone from the descending sunshine. Nearly noon and she was famished. She listened for him, thinking he might be tending to lunch in the kitchen. She heard no sound, no footfall, no dish or pot noises.

Angela passed through the kitchen, then returned to pour herself a cup of freshly brewed coffee before heading for the boiler room. She expected to come across Michael feeding the chickens or gathering eggs. Instead she fed the chickens and gathered a half-dozen eggs in her skirt.

Michael had disappeared.

She put the eggs on to boil and rooted out the morning's leftover biscuits. Angela set the table for the light snack.

In the tower she decided. He was up there shining the windows again. After making the dizzying trip, she failed to discover Michael's whereabouts. She held tightly to the railing and walked slowly around the parapet, searching for any sign of him below.

Finally she spied his bare shoulders behind the chicken coop, hauling lumber from a giant scrambled pile. The ship, she surmised. Michael was salvaging wood from the wreck to rebuild the lost dock.

"Michael," she called to him; but her words went north with the breeze. He didn't hear her.

Forgetting her hunger, she watched him drag timber after timber from the Florida down to the shore for the dock. She'd promised to help, but she enjoyed the warmth of the sun on her sore shoulder. The sight of Michael's muscular back this safe distance from him still conjured reactions from her body. At least up here she wouldn't be acting on them.

Angela didn't believe the priests when they said thoughts were sins. Otherwise the looks she caught Father Fitzgerald making at her petticoat or the mad priest's lingering hand near her breast on board the Florida would cause both servants of God to be spending time in hell. Angela decided to use the brain the Lord gave her to determine what was right and what was wrong among her clashing drives, at least until better counsel arrived.

Denying Michael free access to the body she'd promised to give him for the rest of their lives seemed an evil distortion of their love. Disavowing the pleasures they were supposed to withhold until after the sacrament of marriage resembled coquettish ploys to heighten her value in Michael's eyes.

"Michael," she called down to him, when he was directly below her.

He looked up and waved, a beautiful smile gracing the face she loved with all her heart.

"I made us lunch," she shouted.

He waved again and went up the walk to their cottage.

Angela felt her heart expand in love for her man coming home.

# Chapter 21

When Michael opened the cottage door, the vision of Angela flying down the tower's staircase to his outstretched arms secured a place in his permanent memory. Her unbound curls fanned out, their golden cloud framing her face. His best shirt was gathered at her diminutive waist with a flapping scarlet necktie. Against the backdrop of the tower's light-filled staircase, Angela's limbs, clad in a pair of his long hose, revealed their shapeliness under one eyelet petticoat undamaged by the storm.

Embraced, the Irish sprite overwhelmed his senses with her heavenly, soapy smell. Angela was his, all his. Michael touched her sweet upper lip with the tip of his tongue before devouring her mouth. He favored her sore shoulder, lifting her as easily as a piece of sun-dried driftwood. His body knew one goal as he placed her gently on the bed, but his soul churned.

As he sat on the bed, leaden with conflicting drives, Angela curled up to his back with her arms around his neck. "Michael?"

His name triggered his slack brain. "We can't," he said, quickly wrapping his beauty in the counterpane. Holding Angela close, slowly thawed the pillar of salt Michael felt he resembled. He wondered why the Biblical Lot never touched his wife to evoke a similar response. Michael whispered, "We must wait."

Angela shivered.

He kissed her tenderly, passionately, without hope of immediate consummation.

"Nature beat me when the storm threw your ship at my lighthouse." Michael let himself face the trouble in Angela's eyes. "We must not let nature, our bodies, rule our hearts and souls."

"My heart and soul are yours," she purred the words.

Michael stroked her hair. "And mine yours, but we are part of a larger we. The world demands proof of good character. If we let ourselves be carried away into this untimely act, we may rue the broken rules for the rest of our lives."

Angela pulled away from him, curling herself into a defensive ball.

"I love you." Michael lay beside her cupping his body around hers. "We'll marry in Ann Arbor and then be together forever as man and wife."

He stood and turned his back to his intended, shielding his body from her temptation. He heard a soft moan which battered against his resolve.

"Get out," she said to him, then added a more humane. "We'll wait."

He got as far as the other side of the closed door before he slid down the door and beat his fists against the floor.

The rabbits scurried.

Angela opened the door and slipped onto his lap. She kissed him drew his useless arms around her body. "I understand. I love you for keeping our honor safe."

* * *

Angela fought with her own anger. Why did she insist on loving this hulk? At every quick turn in the road of life, Michael followed the wrong path. Delay and misdirection were her judgments of his ideal goals to pursue his art and redeem the peace of his soul at the expense of their physical happiness.

One of Michael's words softened the blow of rejection. He chose the word 'we' for all the gyrations of his soul. She remained at peace. Lovemaking was part and parcel of affection. The Lord created the urges of union for a reason. Her existence as the illegitimate daughter of the Earl of Covington proved the Lord's will. "Come, let's enjoy a cup of coffee." Angela tugged at her reluctant giant.

He shuffled after her with his head hanging.

"And I'll be having done of your down looks." Angela placed a plate of food before him. "If I'm to be married to the man I love, I'll need to be seeing the brightness of the soul he's professing to shine."

"Angela," Michael tugged at her shirt as she swept by. "You really understand?"

"Humph," Angela swatted his hand away. "You're always thinking you're the only one with thoughts about morality." She joined him, across the table. "Remember the crucifix you found on me?"

Michael's brow wrinkled. He didn't understand the significance of the cross. "I know you're religious."

"The cross was put inside my cloak when I was tied to the mast." Angela looked straight into Michael's eyes to watch the contortions of his soul. "The priest's hand lingered longer against my breast than it ought."

She saw the shock and disgust flit through his awareness.

Then he recovered his higher ground. "We can't judge…."

"And that's exactly what you're doing, Michael Halliday. You're as bad as Captain Hale on the Pannonia when he deemed my emigration to America, an unsavory start." She pointed her finger at his nose and watched his eyes cross. Angela laughed at the silliness of his face. "Oh, Michael, you're such a baby at times. I forgave the black-clad sinner. It's you that's judging."

Michael played with his food. "Don't be angry with me, Angela."

She went slowly to his side of the table, aware of the power of her body to seduce his best intentions. He stopped eating. Angela relented. "Eat, eat." Confident enough she was of his love and passion to let him keep his stumbling blocks to their eventual happiness for a while longer. "You're doing the best you can." She rubbed her chin in the thick curls behind his head, careful not to let her breasts brush against his back. "A wife can't be asking for more."

* * *

Michael's frustration needed physical labor. "Are you strong enough to help me build the dock this afternoon?"

Angela punched his shoulder, harder than was absolutely necessary to prove her vigor. "What would you have me doing?"

"Change into one of my older shirts." Michael escaped through the boiler room. "I'll meet you out by the tram."

A partner in the task, Angela lifted as many boards onto the tram's flat bed as Michael did. Of course, he lifted the heaviest lumber, but the miniature person next to him, he could proudly admit, would never be called a shirker.

The day was fine. The storm's northerly weather seemed to recede with each breeze from the south. August could yet warm Strawberry Island. The exertion caused Michael to pull his shirt out from his waistband, thinking to shed himself of a layer of warmth, but Angela's attention kept the unbuttoned shirt in place.

At the rock-strewn shore, Michael waded into the frigid water. His boots might be ruined but he kept his balance the better. The poles for the ruined dock withstood the onslaught of the storm. Working together, they quickly assembled the main frame for the planks. Michael pounded the thick nails into the wood with the only hammer on the island.

"Are these boards from the old dock?" Angela asked.

"The ship." Michael said, not letting up on his pounding.

"Oh," he heard Angela say, too quiet for him not to stop pounding.

"There was planking left from making the coffins." Michael felt like using the hammer on his head, or his tongue.

Angela sat down on the finished portion of the dock, dangling the tips of her shoes in the surf. She turned her face into the sun's warmth, chilled, no doubt, from the cold water he shared.

Then she jumped up, startling him with her quickness.

"Michael, what's that?"

He dreaded what he might find when he pivoted in the direction Angela pointed. But the object was not a floating corpse. From the relief, Michael's energy surged enough to haul a heavy trunk which was mired and partially covered among the rocks, onto the dock next to Angela.

"My trunk!" Angela exclaimed.

She sat on the trunk and wept bitterly. "Marabell."

"A terrible loss." Michael knelt beside the trunk and enclosed Angela in his arms. "I'm sorry for your pain."

He didn't know how to fix her grief. The dock was easier. Grief created a unique time line of agony. But he knew the hours required for healing needed to be honored. "When we lost my little sister, my father took the longest to recover." Angela clung to him as if afraid of drowning in her emotions. Michael hoped talking would ease her distress.

"If the trunk freed itself from the cabin," Angela's weeping hiccupped into a groan. "Marabell's body is floating in the lake, too."

Michael rocked her in his arms as he might their child some day. "Don't cry little one."

"But I'll have to explain to Matt." The husband, Michael remembered.

"No one on earth is to blame," Michael assured her. "The strength of the storm was beyond our fathoming."

An hour seemed to pass before Angela's tears lessened. Michael didn't mind the comfort he received from the intimacy of her warm body on his lap. If he could love her into happiness away from these passing emotions, he was willing to patiently watch the sun set.

Angela touched his face before swiftly kissing him. "We best be getting back to work, or trouble of another sort will be overtaking us soon enough." She scooted off his lap.

"And what trouble would that be, you're thinking of," he tormented her with his attempt at an Irish brogue.

She cuffed him hard on the shoulder. "Don't be mimicking the voice you love or its silence you'll be hearing in your naughty ears."

"Is the trunk waterproof?" Michael asked as they struggled with the latch. "It's a wonder it didn't go straight to the bottom of the lake with all the sovereigns you carried."

"Aunt Elizabeth took the bulk of them with her." Angela pulled back the lid.

The clothes were bone dry. The scent of Angela's perfume rising from her cache of belongings resumed the war with Michael's resolve. He touched the bareness of her wrist as she hunted among her things.

She faced him, lifting the cloud of her curls behind her shoulder. Michael could tell she recognized the struggle of his passions.

They didn't move.

His hand rested on Angela's upturned palm. Michael imagined he could feel her pulse speed under his touch.

There was no cause for words to pass.

A slight wind from the south passed between them, and their fixations calmed slightly. Then the rabbits, Madelyn and Sadie, scurried against Angela's skirts and between Michael's legs.

"They're loose!" Michael nearly fell off the dock as he tried to catch them.

Neither rabbit appeared ready to the jump into the lake when they reached the end of the unfinished dock. Angela grabbed Sadie and Michael managed to secure Madelyn by the ears.

"I'm sorry, Michael," Angela said stroking Sadie. "Perhaps the latch didn't fall when I came out to join you."

"I made cages for them." Sudden sadness surprised Michael. "When I leave the island, I want to take the rabbits with me." He brightened with fresh memory. "Before you came, I told them you would provide a buck on your farm."

A slight rain began to fall. Michael's busy chores prevented his awareness of the weather. "I'll manage the trunk." The clouds were high, the lake serene. "Are you able to handle both of those varmints?"

Angela nuzzled her chin into the soft fur of the rabbits. "Easier than I can manage the fates and you, Michael Halliday."

* * *

The rain continued throughout the night.

Michael fixed his fried chicken and she made a pie from raisins for dessert. The day's warmth dissipated after the sun went down, so they lit a fire in the fireplace in the bedroom. Angela unpacked her trunk by the light of the oil lamp.

Michael strung a clothesline along one side of the room. After he'd tended to the chickens, Splendor's feed, and minded the lamp and fog-horn boiler for the night, he lay on the bed to watch Angela drape her clothes over the rope. Every time he saw a garment he recognized, they chatted about the memories of places they'd seen together when she wore the clothing.

The blue cloak Angela wore on the Pannonia in which Michael found her still tied to the broken mast eluded their happier recollections. The orange and apricot dress and shawl brought questions about the fortunes David Leonard might experience.

"Gamblers usually end up dead on a bar room floor," Michael said with more disdain than Angela thought appropriate.

"He did say he was averse to hard work," Angela admitted. "Do you think Splendor will remember my friend Flicka when they are together finally on the farm?"

"I'll be interested to see, too." Michael reached his arm out the window over the bed to swing the wind chime. "I think they'll know each other from the smells."

"Did you make that wind chime or did the thing hang there when you arrived?"

"I made it out of sardine cans."

Angela was disappointed to hear the pride in his voice. She was hoping to ask him to move the thing closer to the chickens. As she hung the light green colored evening gown over the clothes line, Michael howled as if injured and held his eye.

"You can stop those shenanigans," she said, striding threateningly toward him, "Or I'll match the deed for your other eye."

"A mighty punch from a mighty beautiful creature." He held out his arms, but she ignored him. "I deserved the blow," he admitted.

"That's right," Angela said, "but I can't be lollygagging around, I've all this work to be doing."

"Where's the blouse with the sailor collar?"

"I shipped it with Matt to Ann Arbor." She had wondered if he would remember the last outfit she wore before they parted. "I didn't shop in Chicago because of Aunt Elizabeth's mourning period."

"We've met a lot of people and made a few friends since leaving home. I did worry some young man would convince you I was worthless to wait for."

"I worried you would forget all about me and return to your father's business."

"He'll be disappointed," Michael said.

Angela hardly slept with the noise from Michael's contented snores seeping into her dreams. Angela took pride in the fact she had convinced Michael into sharing the bed. She told him they possessed the moral fiber and courage necessary to sleep next to each other without making love. Angela in her blue flannel nightgown from Ireland and Michael in his monogrammed night shirt, kissed and intended to hold each other all night.

But once asleep, Michael's thrashed about as if he were trying to swim to some distant shore.

The wind chime erased the only possibility Angela would become accustomed to her lover's snores. The wind was erratic and the noise not pretty.

\* \* \*

*Thursday, August 23rd, 1841*

Hours later Angela awoke from what she thought was a light slumber to the smell of coffee in the house.

Michael sat in the chair next to the bed.

"Are you up for all day?" He offered her a cup of hot brew and a biscuit spread with honey.

"How long have you been out of bed?"

"Six," he said. "The lamp doesn't need to burn oil in the daylight."

"And what's the hour now?" This would be her future, she smiled at the sight of him, her husband soon enough. They'd be planning their days with a cup of coffee for many mornings stretching out into the future.

"Eight." Michael sat his empty cup on the floor. "I finished the dock and started to lay out the windmill I think the fog-horn needs."

"I'd better be dressing if we're to be building a windmill."

He laughed. "I'm only laying out the arms. The inspector would have to approve the building."

At breakfast she asked, "Did you ride Splendor along the shore yet?"

* * *

Michael wished she would talk about the chickens or the wind chime, maybe her aunt anything except the ride around the island. "I need something to wrap the bodies in before I place them in the coffins."

"How many?" Angela clenched her teeth and didn't meet his stare.

"No woman," he said to relieve the worst of her fears. "The priest, I think, and the captain. His papers are falling apart."

"Captain Maddox," she said. "He's the one that tied me to the mast."

"He saved your life."

"But Marabell could have been alive, and saved too." Angela fell silent. He didn't see any tears fall. Finally she rallied as if returning from some private journey. "There's rough cloth under the bed." She pushed her hair away from her face. "Maybe extra sailcloth?"

"I'll look," Michael said. "After I wrap the bodies. I found five. Could you sew the cloth shut?"

"I will," Angela said as she dumped their uneaten breakfast into a pail for the chickens to ponder.

Michael found all five of the bodies on the south end of the island. He predicted the bodies would come ashore on the north, dock side, where the ship slammed into the shoals. Instead the bloated bodies washed onto the lee of the island. With Splendor's help, he dragged the coffins to the south end, because of the stench anticipated before Inspector Cross arrived to take the bodies to their homes. He considered digging graves, but he wasn't sure what the inspector would want.

Angela finished her task of sewing the canvas tight around the bodies. "We need to say prayers for them."

Michael agreed and held his hat in his hand, hoping she knew the appropriate words.

"You don't own a Bible?"

"I do," he said defensively, "but I didn't think to bring it. We could have a proper service when Inspector Cross arrives. I expected after the storm that he would make his rounds among the lighthouses."

"He could have been caught in the storm."

"No," Michael said. "He's wise about these things. He would seek a safe shelter quick enough."

Michael moved to return Splendor to his stall, but Angela was still lost in dire thoughts. Michael nearly walked right over her. He stopped in time. They were a hairsbreadth apart. Angela opened her green eyes wide but didn't step back. Her nostrils flared as she breathed in his very soul. Michael was afraid to touch her, afraid of his own body. Splendor nudged Michael's back as if to encourage his advance into Angela's world.

Michael embraced his willing partner. "I love you, Angela."

In between ravaging kisses, he heard her plead, "I need you, Michael."

# Chapter 22

Michael couldn't rid his face of a satisfied grin as he ran through his morning chores.

The union with his angel, his Angela, soared above any expectations or his fantasies. When he mounted Splendor for his daily exercise in the surf around the island, the horse seemed to catch Michael's delight with life.

"Thank the Lord, we're alive," he said to the sky, his horse, and the sea.

He recalled Angela's soft tresses. Expanding his chest, he breathed in deeply of the warm August air. Angela's delicate touch on his lips lingered. He placed his palm on his mouth. Angela's lips, her smell fixated his attention on the woman he loved.

So much loveliness shared with lasting affection required the blessing of marriage. Inspector Cross could marry the,; and if the good inspector wouldn't, the captain of the fastest ship in Lake Superior, or failing that Lake Huron, could listen to them repeat their vows. A splendid church wedding with the whole town of Ann Arbor invited, and Angela's mother from Ireland, the older ladies from the Pannonia, and any other interested parties would add to the celebration of their love-blessed consummation.

He rued the hours lost. Minutes were wasted on the windmill and his chores. Surely the chickens could wait for their grain.

Michael slapped Splendor's side to hurry home. A flock of shore-scavenging birds flew up before the horse's onslaught. Autumn, Michael remembered. Inspector Cross mentioned the shore birds flocking as the first sign that his stay on the island was close to ending by winter's arrival.

The future away from the hazardous lake on a quiet inland farm with his beloved within in reach seemed a heavenly respite compared to the island's purgatory of loneliness. Solitude enough to sketch required a higher cost than he was willing to pay. He needed his lover as much as she needed him.

The promise of a year's absence made to his mother back in Berkshire surfaced. Would she understand why he couldn't return?

The guarantee of a multitude of grandchildren might even appease his father. Probably not. Michael conceded the future of the clockwork factory would be his father's first concern.

\* \* \*

The rabbits, Sadie and Madelyn, hopped around the bed, demanding Angela's attention.

"Thank you, Lord," she prayed, humbled by the miraculous world she was privileged to survive in.

She ran up the stairs to the lighthouse lamp. Michael obviously finished shining the lamp lenses and the windows in the turret, even restocking the oil.

Angela felt the sun's heat on her face as she stepped out onto the circular balcony.

She searched the green acre of the island for a trace of Michael. The sun continued to beat on her head. Slightly dizzy, Angela leaned back on the glass window and gazed lazily out to sea. The sky was clear to the horizon and the lake lay nearly motionless. She counted the islands, careful to note any movement of boats or ships.

Off to the east a small craft without a sail, churned up a considerable wake. A trail of black smoke identified the steam propulsion. Could this be Inspector Cross's boat? She smoothed down her blouse and thanked her neatness compulsion. The bed was made. The cottage pristinely clean.

She renewed her quest for a glimpse of Michael and spied Splendor's shape near the southern shore, where the bodies were coffined. She re-assessed her attire, hurrying down to change her blue skirt to the more somber black.

\* \* \*

Inspector Cross bowed at the waist as he took Angela's hand. "The Florida, you say?"

"Gone," Michael said. "You were right to tell me I wouldn't be able to differentiate between the sea and the storm clouds. The waves' spray crashed as high as the lamp."

"We broke apart," Angela felt the tears start. "Captain Maddox tied me to the mast before I could get help for my maid, Marabell. She was knocked unconscious in our cabin."

"Sit, sit," Inspector Cross moved Angela to the stone bench. "You'll be fainting in a minute."

"Angela is the only survivor," Michael put his arm around her.

"Michael, I bet you thought a mermaid came ashore." Inspector Cross scrutinized every inch of Angela. "Were you injured, Miss."

Angela rubbed her shoulder, remembering the pain when the mast broke.

"Her shoulder was dislocated," Michael said.

"Raise your arm," Inspector Cross dictated.

Angela did as she was bid.

"I'd seen a jockey's arm reset," Michael explained. "She was still unconscious when I popped it into place."

"The Lord must love you." Inspector Cross marched toward the cottage, expecting them to remain within earshot. "Your gift of beauty shouldn't be sneezed at either."

Angela smiled. "Michael and I are engaged."

Inspector Cross stopped, eyeing Michael with a suspicious assessment.

"No," Angela wanted to set the record straight. "We met on the Atlantic crossing. He wrote me and I was headed here, from Chicago." Marabell's death cramped her stomach. Angela bent over in pain. "…to accept his proposal."

Michael swept her up in his arms. "Are you ill?"

"Get her out of this sun." Inspector Cross stepped aside as he opened the cottage door.

"I'm hungry, is all." Angela pushed against Michael. "You can be setting me down anytime now."

He did so and Angela marched to the kitchen. "You've not eaten a hot breakfast have you, Inspector?"

"No," Inspector Cross said. "I thought I'd have to do with cold biscuits and Michael's good coffee until I could talk him into lopping off the head of another of his chickens."

Michael set the table as Angela whipped up cinnamon hot cakes. "I could make the pancakes," he said. "You might fare better, sitting down for a spell."

"Thank you," Angela said. "I do seem a bit weak this morning."

Michael winked at her as he took over the stove. "Inspector Cross, as captain of your lightship, are you allowed to bless a couple in marriage?"

'I can bless the two of you." Inspector Cross put down his cup of coffee indicating a refill could be welcome. "But if it's legal you want, you will need to wait for a captain on a Lake Huron ship."

Angela folded her hands, thankful for the breakfast Michael sat before her. "We need to have a service for those who perished."

"How many did you find?" Inspector Cross asked Michael.

"Five: the captain, a priest, and three other men."

"Not your maid?" Inspector Cross inquired softly.

Angela's hunger warred with the subject. "No," she said, determining to tackle her plate.

"I don't have a Bible," Michael said. "We didn't know the best thing to do. I made the coffins. Angela sewed the sailcloth after I'd wrapped them up. I did not dig any graves."

"We'll get that done first," Inspector Cross nodded. "Relatives can always come to claim them later. You both managed as well as I would, better probably. The 23rd Psalm is the one to read at a burial service."

The first meal of the day continued in respectful silence.

Sadie and Madelyn hopped into the kitchen.

Inspector Cross pointed at them. "Are these the rabbits you wouldn't eat?"

Michael laughed. "They are."

"He made cages for them to take back with us." Angela said happy to be talking about anything other than the departed. "I bought a farm in Ann Arbor."

"Ann Arbor?" Inspector Cross frowned. "I thought you said Michael's letter reached you in Chicago."

Michael interrupted with a heaping plate of pancakes. "The shore birds are flocking."

"Already?" Inspector Cross concentrated on devouring his breakfast.

Angela tipped her head questioningly at Michael.

"We have to leave," Michael explained. "When will you return for us?" he asked the inspector.

"Better leave now," The inspector continued to eat. "In your unmarried state, I think leaving would be best." He swallowed, looked at their obvious disappointment and added, "Before sunset."

"How will we have time?" Angela asked.

"I'll help with the graves." The inspector rose and went out the back door, trailing dictates. "Cage up those chickens and pack your trunks while we're gone. We'll come back to collect you for the service."

"Michael wanted to show you his plans for a windmill to run the fog-horn boiler," Angela said.

"Man makes plans and God laughs," Inspector Cross quoted.

Michael lingered embracing Angela. "We can't possibly get off this island by tonight."

"Yes, yes, we can, Michael." Angela kissed him and smacked his rump to send him on his way.

\* \* \*

Michael couldn't believe the efficiency Angela showed in packing up the cottage while they were off digging the five graves. She had filled the tram's flat-bed with their trunks. She tied the wooden globe and the stand's legs between the two trunks. Cages of chickens and the two rabbits were stacked on top. Splendor was tied to the dock. A picnic basket sat on the stone bench.

"How did you manage the trunks?" He asked, incredulous of her strength.

"I moved them on when they were empty, silly." Angela kissed him and pointed to the basket. "I hope I made enough fried chicken for supper. Inspector Cross owns a mighty appetite for a little man."

After the brief service, Inspector Cross checked the cottage. "Good job," he said to Angela. You're a lucky man, Michael Halliday. I'll miss knowing you longer."

Michael didn't feel he was allowed to hug the inspector after they shook hands, so he embraced Angela, too long by the way she pushed him away.

"Time enough for that," Inspector Cross said as he led Splendor down the dock to his lightship.

# Chapter 23

*Saturday, August 25th, 1841*
*Aboard the Thomas Jefferson on Lake Huron*

"We'll be wearing this paddle-boat out by the time we've finished gallivanting around these lakes." Angela held fast to Michael's arm.

"My ambitions clouded my senses the last time I was a passenger on the Thomas Jefferson." Michael pulled Angela closer to his side. "I left my parents and I deserted you, thinking art held meaning for my life."

"We can't be blaming ourselves for following dreams." Angela stood on her tiptoes to kiss Michael's rough cheek. "If I didn't insist on saying yes to your proposal in person, Marabell would be alive." They stood together humbled by the havoc wreaked by their actions. "The Lord will forgive us quicker than we can forgive ourselves. Michael, I hope you know there will always be time enough and a quiet room on the farm for you to sketch to your heart's content."

"You're my heart's content." Michael's eyes smoldered.

"We'll be having none of that." Angela laughed. "Until after the captain marries us this afternoon."

"I entertained myself on the island by thinking of our children's names." Michael's smile returned.

"Good Irish saints' names?"

"I was thinking more along the line of Dante's characters," he teased.

"And wasn't Beatrice a saint then?"

"She was," Michael said. "And heaven sent."

"Then that will be the first girl's name, with Antoinette as a middle name."

Michael kissed her, "And the second girl?"

Angela blushed to relate, "Since our first kiss, I've dreamt of babies looking a lot like you, Michael Halliday. Elizabeth Winifred would be my second daughter."

Elizabeth Winifred Halliday," Michael added, "And I hope none of the girls resemble me. Can't you see them tripping over their petticoats?"

"Should we name the first boy Lazarus?" Angela asked.

"No, definitely not. But the third daughter could be named Marabell."

Angela nodded. "What was Inspector Cross's Christian name?"

"Only heaven knows," Michael laughed.

"I thought he was sweet to give us the rooster and hens to remember him with." Angela compared the tree-lined Michigan shore of Lake Huron to the daunting cliffs around Lake Superior. "His rough talk belies his tender nature."

"The man needed to harden his nerves, or he wouldn't be able to carry out all his responsibilities." Michael's smile faded into a frown. "I hope I'm half the man."

"Well, you are twice his size." Angela's laughter blew Michael's doubts into the churning wake of the steamship. But the nagging guilt of his broken word to his parents knotted his brow. "What, Michael Halliday? You'll be telling me your worries or I'll be throwing you overboard." Angela pushed him into the railing.

"My father." He admitted.

"They'll try to stop the marriage?"

"No, no. They know me better than that." Michael caught a long tendril of Angela's hair between his fingers. "He expects me back in London to take over his business."

"Are you worried for his business?"

"No." Michael decided. "I'm more concerned for his approval, for the direction my life is taking."

"When our children resist our ideas for their future." Angela pulled him along the deck. "We'll have to be remembering this day."

\* \* \*

*Saturday, September 1st, 1841*
*Ann Arbor, Michigan*

When the Detroit train arrived in Ann Arbor, the platform was crowded with well-wishers. Ma captured Angela into her arms before her foot stepped onto the wooden walkway from the train.

Michael's momentary aloneness was ended by a pat on his shoulder. "Father," he exclaimed, falling affectionately on the shorter man's shoulders. "You're in America?" Michael drew back, "Where is Mother?"

"Here, of course." Mrs. Halliday folded her parasol and allowed him to embrace her. "You'll ruin my hat and I don't care."

Aunt Elizabeth, Winnie Perkins, and Mrs. Lazarus offered their welcoming embraces.

Michael was the first to draw Angela's attention to the tall stranger standing behind Antoinette McGovern. "Is that Matt?"

"No." Angela wanted time alone with Matt. "Aunt Elizabeth, is Matt with the carriage?"

"He'll be here shortly." Aunt Elizabeth smiled, "I suspect he's a bit nervous to greet Marabell in front of us all."

"Oh, Aunt," Angela drew Michael to her. "Come with me in case he has any questions, Michael."

"What's happened?" Matt crumpled his hat in his hand.

"Angela was the only survivor of a terrible storm on Lake Superior." Michael grasped the other man's shoulder and pivoted him away from the audience. "Your wife drowned at sea."

Matt's shoulder shook in grief. "I knew," he said. "I knew she wouldn't be here."

Ma clasped Angela's waist. "Were you injured?"

"My arm," Angela said. "Michael said it was dislocated and he put it back in place while I was unconscious. I should be with Matt."

"Let your husband talk to him," the stranger said.

Angela stared at him.

"The Earl of Covington," Michael's mother introduced the man, "Let me introduce you to your legitimate daughter."

Ma whispered in Angela's ear, "I married him after he arrived with Mr. and Mrs. Halliday."

"Why did you call Michael my husband?" Angela asked the handsome older man.

"Because, my dear; your young man appeared to be more courageous than I ever thought of being." The Earl held out his hand, and Angela let her father kiss her fingertips.

Michael returned to the group without Matt. "He's taking it well," he assured Angela.

"Well, Michael, this stranger is my father." Angela communicated her surprise.

The Covingtons and the Hallidays appeared to know each other better than either Angela or Michael knew each other's in-laws.

Michael's father explained. "Don't fret so, Michael. I can see from your frown that you're wondering how long you need to entertain us."

"We're starting a new life, too." His mother appeared uncharacteristically energized, almost unladylike.

"Purchased a factory in Elgin, Illinois." Mr. Halliday puffed out his chest. "The Elgin Watch Works has a ready-made flock of customers. The factory is at the end of Main Street."

"They have their own observatory," Mrs. Halliday boasted. "On the highest hill overlooking the Fox River."

"Angela," the Earl drew their attention, "Your mother and I are building a hotel on Huron Street. Our grandchildren should have enough room to visit us."

"We have a reception all planned for you," Mrs. Lazarus got her two cents in.

"Michael, I think you've gotten taller," Winnie Perkins giggled.

Angela whispered to Michael, "Now all we need do is re-acquaint Flicka with Splendor."

"Lovers all," Michael said.


The End

# About Rohn Federbush

Rohn Federbush retired as an administrator from the University of Michigan in 1999. She received a Masters of Arts in Creative Writing in 1995 from Eastern Michigan University, where she studied under Janet Kauffman and Larry Smith. In 1998, Vermont College awarded her a summer conference scholarship to work on her novel under Ellen Lesser and Brett Lott. Frederick Busch of Colgate granted a 1997 summer stipend for her ghost-story collection. Michael Joyce of Vassar encouraged earlier writing at Jackson Community College, Jackson, Michigan in 1981. Rohn has completed fourteen novels, with an additional mystery nearly finished, 120 short stories and 150 poems to date.

You can find Rohn on:
Facebook / Twitter / Goodreads /LinkedIn

And on her website:
www.RohnFederbush.com